Through the Shadows

Other Abingdon Press books by Karen Barnett

Mistaken

The Golden Gate Chronicles
Out of the Ruins
Beyond the Ashes
Through the Shadows

KAREN BARNETT

THROUGH *the* SHADOWS

The Golden Gate Chronicles

Abingdon Press
Nashville

Through the Shadows

Copyright © 2016 by Karen Barnett

All rights reserved.

Macro Editor: Teri Wilhelms

Published in association with the Books & Such Literary Agency.

Library of Congress Cataloging-in-Publication Data

Names: Barnett, Karen, 1969- author.
Title: Through the shadows / Karen Barnett.
Description: First edition. | Nashville : Abingdon Press, [2016] | Series: The Golden Gate chronicles ; book 3
Identifiers: LCCN 2015037196 (print) | LCCN 2015041106 (ebook) | ISBN 9781426781452 (softcover) | ISBN 9781501816321 (e-book)
Subjects: LCSH: Man-woman relationships—Fiction. | San Francisco (Calif.)—History—Fiction. | GSAFD: Christian fiction. | Love stories.
Classification: LCC PS3602.A77584 T48 2016 (print) | LCC PS3602.A77584 (ebook) | DDC 813/.6—dc23
LC record available at http://lccn.loc.gov/2015037196

1 2 3 4 5 6 7 8 9 10 / 21 20 19 18 17 16
Printed in the United States of America

To my two precious kids
You bless my life in unimaginable ways.

Acknowledgments

Thank you to:

- My patient family. Who else could put up with my long days and nights at the computer and my incessant talk about people who don't really exist?
- My talented critique / prayer partners: Tammy Bowers, Heidi Gaul, Patricia Lee, Christina Nelson, and Marilyn Rhoads. "As iron sharpens iron, / so one person sharpens another" (Proverbs 27:17 NIV).
- Rachel Kent, my wonderful agent. Thanks for being my "safety bar" on this crazy publishing roller coaster ride.
- Ramona Richards, Cat Hoort, Teri Wilhelms, Pamela Clements, and everyone at Abingdon Fiction. In this challenging time, I appreciate you taking a chance on me and on this series.
- My musically gifted friend, Amy Nelke, for advising me on the secret inner life of a professional musician.
- To the kind volunteers at the Cameron House for inspiring me with several biographies of Donaldina Cameron and a personalized tour of "920."
- My dear friend, Autumn Zimmerman. Thank you for being my cheerleader and tour guide and for enduring countless questions about San Francisco and the legal world.
- The absolutely remarkable "San Francisco History" Facebook group. Whenever I posted a question, they had the answer. Thank you to Nick Wright, John A. Harris, Carol Tigerman, Mark Reed, and so many others!
- The Christian writing community, especially the "Bookies" of Books & Such Literary, Oregon Christian Writers (OCW), American Christian Fiction Writers (ACFW), and the Mount Hermon Christian Writers Conference.

Amazing grace! How sweet the sound
That saved a wretch like me!
I once was lost, but now am found;
Was blind, but now I see.

'Twas grace that taught my heart to fear,
And grace my fears relieved;
How precious did that grace appear
The hour I first believed!

Through many dangers, toils, and snares
I have already come;
'Tis grace hath brought me safe thus far,
And grace will lead me home.

The Lord has promised good to me,
His Word my hope secures;
He will my Shield and Portion be,
As long as life endures.

When we've been there ten thousand years,
Bright shining as the sun,
We've no less days to sing God's praise
Than when we'd first begun.

John Newton (1779)

1

Sacramento, California
June 1908

Elizabeth King held her fingers against the ivory keys, refusing to stir as the final chord faded and silence descended on the parlor. Were God ever to speak to her, she imagined it would be in the precious instant after a last note died away and before an audience responded. The moment preserved a holy space, as if the breath of divinity hung in the air.

No voice arrived today, but there was no audience either.

She ran her fingertips along the cool surface, the black and white pattern softening as her eyes blurred with tears. God wouldn't converse with the likes of her, anyway.

After three years of intense instruction, every note conjured Tobias's memory—his touch. Elizabeth sprang from the stool and stalked to the window, staring out at the darkening clouds. She couldn't let her mind travel to those memories. Before she knew it, she'd be at his door.

"Turn your back on me, and you're finished. You'll never perform again."

She'd done the right thing. So why did the shame still cling, like a vine curling around her soul?

Her mother swept into the room, a cream-colored apron tied over her flowered dress. "Elizabeth—you aren't dressed yet?"

Elizabeth pulled her gaze from the window. "Dressed?"

"Have you forgotten? Mr. McKinley is joining us for supper. I've been trying to get the attorney to come here from San Francisco for months."

The man's name sent a shiver along Elizabeth's skin, like a discordant note in the middle of a Bach concerto. Of course, she'd forgotten—if she'd remembered, she'd have left earlier. "I promised Lillian I would attend the suffrage meeting with her this evening."

"You attend too many of those silly political gatherings. They've ruined you for polite society."

"Mother, you know I've never cared for 'polite society.' That's your arena."

"Your father spoiled all of you children. I thought you, being the youngest, might turn out all right." Her mother straightened one of the cushions.

A lump formed in Elizabeth's throat. Even though she'd been young when he passed away, her father's determination and generous nature shaped her heart. *"Your talent is a gift from God, Elizabeth. It brings Him glory."* Not anymore.

"Hurry, now. Mr. McKinley will be here soon."

No escape. Perhaps she could make excuses after supper. Elizabeth climbed the stairs to her room and dug through the wardrobe for a suitable dress. She couldn't choose anything too nice for the cantankerous old lawyer.

Her fingers lingered on her favorite silk gown. The navy blue had gleamed under the auditorium's electric lights as she'd curtsied to a large crowd. Elizabeth shoved it back and pulled out a russet skirt and matching vest instead. Her stage days were past. If all she had to look forward to were dull evenings in the company of stodgy attorneys, she might as well dress the part.

Her sister, Ruby, had once described Silas McKinley as being akin to a moray eel, and the image cemented itself in Elizabeth's mind. They hadn't seen him in over a year—not since he divulged that most of her late father's assets had been lost in the fires following the San Francisco earthquake.

With her musical dreams crumbling about her ears and the family in financial crisis, Elizabeth needed a new direction for her life—and fast. Perhaps this evening's suffrage meeting would give her some ideas.

&

The Sacramento streetcar glided to a stop as Charles studied the King family's files. The case appeared straightforward, probably the reason his uncle had chosen it for Charles's first consultation. He set his jaw and leafed through the documents for the hundredth time. He'd almost memorized them on the ferry, but good preparation prevented surprises.

A well-dressed young woman climbed up the steps, her eyes scanning the conveyance.

Only one seat remained open—next to him. Charles's throat tightened. Why couldn't she be an elderly spinster or even a middle-aged mother with children? His law school elocution classes had never touched on the art of conversation with young socialites. These lace-bedecked, sweet-smelling mysteries befuddled him.

Her eyes settled on the seat and she flounced his direction, gripping the rail as the streetcar shifted into motion.

He swallowed, scooting over a few inches to allow ample room for her layers of skirts.

"This rain is incorrigible." She unpinned her enormous hat, and set it on her lap, running slim fingers over the sodden peacock plumes. "They're ruined. I knew it."

Was she speaking to herself or to him? He probably should refrain from pointing out the fact that birds were quite accustomed to rainfall—until you removed their plumage and sewed it to women's hats.

She turned to face him. "I'd hoped the rains would hold off until this evening. I do hate conducting excursions in poor weather."

Charles tucked the documents into his valise and withdrew today's issue of *The San Francisco Call.* "I believe the shower's letting up."

He was rewarded with a dazzling smile. Apparently, he'd said the right thing—for once.

She leaned closer, her gaze drawn to the paper. "Now that's intriguing."

Charles lifted the periodical, the headlines dominated by the San Francisco graft trials. A young woman interested in politics? Could he be so lucky? "Cleaning up the city seems to be one of the district attorney's main goals. It's shameful how much city money has been diverted to lining politicians' pockets, especially considering how many still suffer from the 1906 quake," he offered.

The young woman wrinkled her nose. "No . . ." She jabbed a finger at a small column on the right-hand side. "Governor Gillett's wife is hosting a dinner party for visiting Navy Admirals. I wonder what she'll be serving?"

Charles's stomach sank as he lowered the paper to his lap. "I couldn't hazard a guess."

"I bought this hat because she wears one just like it." She tugged at the plumes. "My father took me to a state dinner last month. Dreadfully boring, but it gave me an opportunity to view the season's new styles." Her lips tipped upward, eyes shining as she pinned the ridiculous item atop her coiled hair.

"Well that's . . . something." He turned to the window, gauging how many more blocks until he reached Mrs. King's home.

"Oh, there's my stop. Nice visiting with you." She bounced up the aisle, leaving a cloud of rose petal fragrance in her wake.

Charles shook his head. She'd taken the streetcar rather than walk four blocks? Understanding the female species might prove beyond his grasp.

Charles stepped off at the next stop, lifting the umbrella over his head to protect his new tailored suit from the drizzle. Uncle Silas had demanded Charles discard the typical Sears, Roebuck & Company sack suits he'd worn through law school. *"An attorney is only as respectable as his appearance suggests."*

He squinted at the house on the corner and checked its address against the scrap of paper he clutched in his damp glove. Eager to get in from the storm, he hurried up the steps and rang the bell.

The door creaked open; a petite young woman stared out at him. "Yes?"

Not again. Charles sucked in a quick breath as her large blue eyes sent his carefully rehearsed greeting into disarray. She appeared far too young to be Dr. King's widow. He glanced at her simple attire, which did little to obscure her trim figure. *A housekeeper, perhaps?* He forced his attention back to her face. "Is this the King residence?"

She didn't release the knob, using the other hand to touch her hair, golden as the hills near his hometown. "Yes. May I help you?"

He cleared his throat, jamming the paper into his pocket. "If you could let your employer know Mr. Charles McKinley from McKinley and McClintock Associates is here to speak with her, I'd be most grateful." He pushed back his black derby hat and offered a hesitant smile.

"My employer?" She narrowed her eyes. "Where is Mr. McKinley? I mean—the *other* Mr. McKinley?"

Charles tugged at his stiff collar. She seemed rather impertinent for a maid. Perhaps her beauty only went so deep. "Silas McKinley is my uncle. He sent me in his stead. Now, if you could—"

"I'll inform my mother you are here." The woman stepped back and swung the door wide. "Please, come in out of the rain."

His stomach dropped. "Your mother?" He lowered the umbrella and shook it before stepping over the threshold. "I thought—I thought you were a member of ..."

"The staff?" She curled her fingers into a fist. "I'm Elizabeth King." She gestured toward a sitting room. "You may wait in here. My mother will be right with you."

He placed the umbrella in the corner stand and followed her to the small room. His uncle would be mortified to hear of Charles's gaffe. What a way to start a meeting. "I beg your pardon, Miss King."

"I'm afraid it's just Mother and me this evening." Miss King's pointed gaze reminded him of a prosecutor during cross-examination. "And every evening. I'm sure your uncle has briefed you on our financial status."

Charles scrambled to recover from his misstep. "Yes. Well. I apologize for my uncle's absence, but he's given me responsibility over your father's estate."

The lady's eyes widened. "You must be joking."

An older woman stepped into the hall. "Is Mr. McKinley here already, Elizabeth?"

"Mother, this is Mr. Charles McKinley. Mr. McKinley's nephew."

Charles dried his hand on his jacket before grasping the widow's outstretched fingers. "It's an honor to meet you, Mrs. King. My uncle speaks highly of your late husband. He told me they were friends."

Mrs. King's eyes lit up. "He has spoken of you with high regard, as well, Mr. McKinley. Top of your class at Oregon Law, I hear."

Charles swallowed, his mouth as dry as blotting paper. *Second.* A moment of integrity had cost him top honors, a fact his uncle ignored at will. "Well—"

"I thought your uncle would be joining us. I hope he's not ill."

"No ma'am. He's quite busy, as you know, and he thought I could take care of any questions regarding Mr. King's trust."

"Dr. King." The daughter corrected him.

"Of course—Dr. King." Charles averted his gaze from her flashing eyes and focused on the young lady's mother. He patted his satchel. "I've been reviewing the papers, and I have some ideas that might be of assistance."

Mrs. King waved a dismissive hand. "First we dine, then we will talk *business.*" Her lips curled as if she found the final word distasteful. "How wonderful to have a young man at the table. It's been some time. I only have the one son, Robert—Dr. Robert King—but he's off and married now, living in San Francisco. Most of my daughters are married, as well. Only Elizabeth remains."

The young woman seemed to deflate at her mother's words, a frown darting across her lovely face. "Not everyone marries these days. It's a new century. It's no longer the disgrace it once was."

Her mother sniffed. "So you say. Those suffrage meetings put outlandish ideas in your head. I never should have allowed them." She turned to Charles. "Are you married, Mr. McKinley?"

"Um, no. I haven't had the pleasure."

Mrs. King clicked her tongue. "A bachelor attorney? You'll need to remedy the problem posthaste if you expect to be respected in the legal profession."

Uncle Silas had said something similar just yesterday. Unfortunately, as today proved, every woman Charles met seemed concerned with little more than dinner parties and peacock feathers. Could he really survive a lifetime with such a companion?

The young lady gestured toward the dining room. "Perhaps we should go in to supper?"

Mrs. King's brows drew together as she scrutinized her daughter. "I'll entertain Mr. McKinley while you dress, my dear."

Elizabeth King's rigid posture seemed lost on her mother. With a huff, she turned on a heel and disappeared up the main staircase.

The tension left the room as if attached to Miss King's backside. Charles exhaled, shaking such thoughts from his mind. How would he survive as a court attorney if one young woman could rattle him so? *Lord, grant me focus.*

Hetty King leaned close, her voice low. "Don't mind my Elizabeth. She's the youngest, and I'm afraid we indulged her whims far too much."

Charles stifled a chuckle. Only a family member could burrow under one's skin with such ease. He should know. His uncle had the same talent.

❧

Elizabeth took another bite of the dry chicken, following it with a quick sip of water to wash down the stringy morsel. Her mother's cooking always left much to be desired.

Mr. McKinley sawed at the meat with his knife. She almost felt sorry for the man. Growing up in one of San Francisco's privileged families, he'd probably never imagined life without a housekeeper and a cook. The fine fabric of his suit suggested he was cut from the same cloth as his uncle.

Even so, the odd contrast between the softness in his brown eyes and the firmness of his jaw drew her gaze. At least he didn't look like Silas McKinley, one mark in his favor.

She'd chosen the blue gown after all—not to impress the pretentious attorney, but rather to deflect any more of Mother's pointed remarks. Elizabeth pushed the cooked carrots around the dish with her fork. Now that she didn't have daily rehearsals to take up her time, she'd be at the mercy of her mother's meddling. If she weren't careful, Mother would see her married off to the first eligible bachelor she could sink her claws into. Elizabeth's gaze returned to the young man sitting across the table. Unfortunately, she wasn't marriage-worthy. Tobias had assured as much.

Mother smiled as she passed Mr. McKinley a basket of rolls. "How long have you lived in San Francisco?"

He accepted the container and added a piece of bread to his plate. "Only a few days, actually. I grew up near Redding, but I attended law school in Oregon. My uncle recently brought me into the firm. This is my first assignment."

"Your first?" Tiny lines formed around her mother's mouth.

Elizabeth twisted the napkin in her lap. "I'd have thought your uncle would show more respect for us than to bring in an inexperienced attorney."

The young man glanced up, one brow cocked. "I believe he meant it as a compliment. Uncle Silas would only commit your situation to a trusted family member."

Mother took a sip from her water glass, recovering her composure in less than a heartbeat. "Silas worked diligently for this family for years, Elizabeth. We shouldn't be questioning his intentions. I'm sure young Mr. McKinley will be a breath of fresh air." She patted his arm. "Youth doesn't always mean ignorance. And it comes with certain benefits." Mother smiled, her pale eyes gleaming as if she'd already convinced herself. "Energy. Drive. Ambition. All of which I expect Charles, here, has in abundance. May I call you Charles?"

"Of course."

Leave it to Mother to side with the enemy.

An eager smile brightened his face. "I've been looking over your files. I have some ideas to help with your new situation."

Situation. The word squeezed around Elizabeth's heart. "Our destitution, you mean?" As soon as the accusation escaped her lips, a prickle crept up her cheeks. She'd never learned her mother's gift for subtle conversation.

"Elizabeth!" Mother's face pinched.

The young man frowned. "I wouldn't go so far as to say that. It's a highly complex matter. I'm afraid you might not understand, Miss King. "

Elizabeth's mouth fell open, his condescending tone snapping her control like an overtightened piano string. "I understand more than you realize, Mr. McKinley. For one thing, I know your uncle assured my father the buildings in which he invested were well-insured—he insisted there was little risk."

"My uncle couldn't have foreseen an earthquake of this—"

"Mr. McKinley also claimed to invest in the same properties, and yet he's still living in one of San Francisco's nicest homes. He doesn't appear to have endured the same level of economic ruin." The words tumbled from her mouth faster than she could collect them.

The man's Adam's apple bobbed. "Um, no. He—"

"And explain this to me. My brother, Robert, visited your uncle's office three times during the last month and Silas McKinley refused to see him. Now he sends you here to Sacramento?" The heat in her chest increased with each subsequent thought. "If he believes a fast-talking, handsome man with a fine suit will somehow woo the ladies and get us to acquiesce, he's sorely mistaken. We're not helpless females, no matter what your uncle may have led you to believe." She stood, tossing the linen napkin onto her plate. "Mother, we shouldn't be wasting our time with him. I, for one, have an engagement this evening."

Her mother rose to her feet. "Mr. McKinley is our guest. I will not have him flown at in such a manner."

The young man jumped up, a glint appearing in his eyes. "I assure you, Miss King, my uncle didn't send me to woo anyone." He paused. "I believe I can help."

"I think we should hear him out." Mother pressed a hand to her heart.

Elizabeth locked her gaze on the attorney. "Are you afraid to conduct business with my brother, or do you think it's too complex for a physician to understand, too?"

He placed both palms on the table and leaned forward, matching her stare. "Are you saying your mother is not competent to manage her affairs without a man present?"

A flush climbed Elizabeth's neck, settling under her lace collar.

He turned toward her mother. "I can present my recommendations here, or we can wait until after the meal. If you'd prefer I make an appointment to speak to your son, I'd be more than happy to do so. I also have another engagement this evening, so it would be preferable to expedite my proposals without further interruptions."

Her mother nodded. "Let's retire to the parlor. Elizabeth, you may join us or not, but you will remain silent. I will not have our guest harangued further."

As they departed, Elizabeth sank back into her seat. She lifted the water glass, but her trembling hand splashed the icy water down the front of her dress, chilling her to the skin. She dabbed a napkin against the damp silk, the image of the young man's wide brown eyes tugging at her heart. He hadn't deserved such venom. Why must she make a mess of everything?

Her forthright manner had cost her much over the years. Add such a weakness to a stained past, and she could forget ever walking down the aisle. Elizabeth closed her eyes. Not that marriage was ever her goal . . . at least, not exactly.

Lord, help me.

2

*E*lizabeth hurried up City Hall's marble steps after her friend. The church bells tolled, echoing down the busy street. "We're going to be late."

The cascading flowers on Lillian's hat jounced as she climbed. "If you'd met me at six like I asked, we'd have had plenty of time. Tell me more about this attorney fellow. Was he handsome?"

"He was insufferable. A pompous, overdressed stuffed shirt—like those Brookstone Academy boys who lived to quote Sophocles and Euripides."

Lillian smiled. "I nearly married one of those boys, remember?"

Elizabeth reached for the ornate brass handle, pulling open the heavy door. "Temporary blindness. You eventually came to your senses."

Her friend cocked a pale eyebrow as she stepped through the doorway. "And hasn't anyone turned your head? You haven't had time for me in months. I'd assumed some special fellow consumed all your attentions."

A wave of heat washed over Elizabeth, and she lifted a hand to her cheek. If anyone—even Lillian—guessed her indiscretion, she'd never survive the gossip and disgrace. This secret was between her and God, assuming she could gather the courage to speak to Him about it. Elizabeth followed her friend through the entrance, careful to keep her skirt out of the way. "I've decided men aren't worth the trouble. Who's speaking tonight?"

A few well-dressed women stood in the marble-lined vestibule, lingering outside the door of the meeting room. The sound of children singing floated out into the hall. Elizabeth stopped in her tracks.

"About that…" Lillian grasped Elizabeth's hand and pulled her toward the assembly hall. "The orator is Miss Donaldina Cameron from San Francisco's Presbyterian Mission Home. I heard her speak in Oakland last June."

"Mission? I thought this was a Stanton Club meeting." Elizabeth's skin crawled. "You didn't tell me this was a church event."

"Miss Cameron works with girls rescued from slavery in Chinatown. Their stories will break your heart. Come on." Lillian gave her a knowing glance. "You can't even walk by a street urchin without sharing your coins."

Elizabeth's feet dragged across the tile floor. She couldn't face a missionary. Not now. But the music—and Lillian's expectations—pulled her forward. Elizabeth smoothed a hand across her skirt, trying to ignore the perspiration dampening her palms. *No one knows.*

Few openings remained in the packed room. Lillian guided her down the side aisle to a couple of empty spots near the front.

Three Chinese girls stood on the platform, their smooth hair shining under the electric lights. Their gentle voices rose and fell to the tune of "Safe in the Arms of Jesus." Elizabeth couldn't resist smiling at the sight of the smallest girl—perhaps only six or seven—her embroidered red tunic making her resemble a bright peony.

Elizabeth sidled past knees and feet, taking care not to tromp on anyone's toes, and tucked into her seat with a sigh. A woman's massive Gibson Girl hairstyle blocked most of Elizabeth's view. Ridiculous. *If she tips her head, she'll fall over.* Her sister Ruby often styled her red curls in such magnificent updos, but Elizabeth preferred to maintain a sleek knot at the back of her head. It seemed silly to spend hours on one's hair when there were so many other things to do.

The girls sang two more hymns, their voices as pure as garden wind chimes. The littlest one stepped forward, a wide smile brightening her round face. After a nod from the woman at the back of the platform, the child folded her hands and began to sing. Elizabeth leaned forward, her fingers twitching as she contemplated an arrangement on the piano.

> I'm but a stranger here, Heaven is
> my home;
> Earth is a desert drear, Heaven is
> my home;
> Danger and sorrow stand, round
> me on every hand;
> Heaven is my fatherland, Heaven is
> my home.

Elizabeth and Lillian joined in the applause as the girls returned to their seats. Elizabeth edged a few inches to the side to get a better view of the tall, thin woman taking the podium, her hair glinting like Mother's best silver.

"No truer words have been sung." A hint of a Scottish brogue colored the woman's words. "Yoke Soo and her twin sister came to our shores at the tender age of four, but within hours the children were on the auction block. Yoke Soo began her life in America as a *Mui Tsai*—servant child."

The poor little dear. Elizabeth studied the people in front of her. Two seats down, she couldn't help but admire a muscular set of shoulders, clad in an elegant suit. The man's light brown hair seemed familiar. When he turned to speak to the woman on his left, Elizabeth's breath caught in her chest. Charles McKinley? She'd assumed the young attorney would be visiting with another client, not attending a public meeting. Would she never be free of the man? Elizabeth shrank down in her seat, no longer caring whether she could see the platform.

The woman at the podium expounded on the girl's heartbreaking story, but the words failed to penetrate Elizabeth's dour mood. The lady ahead of her leaned past her neighbor to whisper to Mr. McKinley. His head turned, the profile unmistakable.

Elizabeth pressed a handkerchief to her eyes. With any luck, she wouldn't be recognized.

Lillian patted her sleeve. "I knew you'd be moved."

Elizabeth ducked as the attorney glanced back. *Perhaps I should leave.* She peered down the long row, but a gauntlet of legs and feet prepared to make trouble for anyone who passed. Elizabeth leaned back against the chair. *Trapped.*

After a few minutes, she relaxed, turning her focus to the missionary's stories. The images of beatings, neglect, and hard work pressed on Elizabeth's lungs. Was she truly speaking of the little child who'd just sung like an angel?

Miss Cameron leaned forward, her eyes scanning the audience. "As tragic as this sounds, Yoke Soo had a more daunting problem ahead. After years of servitude, her master would likely sell her again—this time to a house of ill-repute."

The woman with the enormous hair rose, dabbing her cheeks with a silk handkerchief. Excusing herself, she made her way down the long row of seats and slipped out to the back of the room.

Elizabeth straightened. At last, she could see the stage. She willed Mr. McKinley to remain facing forward.

"A kindly neighbor intervened, rescuing the child and delivering her to the Mission." Miss Cameron's gaze lowered, her voice growing husky. "Her sister was not as fortunate."

Elizabeth swallowed. These girls had suffered more than she, and yet they were innocent of their pain. Could she claim the same for herself? Unlikely.

The missionary's voice rose, echoing through the packed room. "This is why I plead with you, good people of Sacramento, to support the Mission's efforts to remove these girls from the clutches of man's carnal desires. With your help, we can bring these children out of darkness and into the light of Christ's love."

Elizabeth pressed her hands into her lap, squeezing herself into as narrow a space as possible. *Man's carnal desires.* The words clutched at her throat like so many tangled threads.

A woman near the front stood. "The little ones, of course. But what of the older girls? Do you bring the prostitutes in with the young children?"

The crowd murmured, all eyes returning to the podium.

Miss Cameron nodded. "We are all God's children. None have fallen so far as to be unredeemable by His love and sacrifice on the cross."

"What do you do with them once they've been rescued?" The woman persisted in her questions.

"We see to our daughters' needs—spiritual, physical, emotional, and intellectual. Right now one of our biggest needs is for teachers at our school. We want good women such as yourselves to come and work with our girls. Teach them English, sewing, cooking, reading, writing, and music."

"Music? What good is music?"

Miss Cameron lifted a hand and gestured to the girls sitting in the front row. "You heard the children sing. Chains bind the body, but music sets the heart free."

As Miss Cameron continued her speech, tears stung at Elizabeth's eyes. She stared down at her smooth, even nails, remembering the feel of the ivory beneath her fingertips. She'd hardly played in weeks. Not since she'd cast Tobias out of her life. He'd taken her heart. Her music. Would it ever return?

She lifted her head and studied the elegant woman at the lectern. Miss Cameron leaned forward, the energy of her plea flooding through the crowd. Her stories continued, telling the tales of one girl after another.

Elizabeth's chest burned, like she'd swallowed an ember from the stove and it scorched its way through her. Could this make up for what she'd done?

The speaker lifted her hands, gesturing to the audience. "What will you do to help our girls? Will you shake your heads and go back to your comfortable homes? Or will you commit yourself to the Lord's work? He's calling you. How will you answer?"

A ripple coursed through Elizabeth's body as she met the missionary's gaze. *If I do this, God, will You forgive me?*

Charles stretched his back after an hour of sitting on the wooden chair. The crowd filtered out of the room, dozens of conversations buzzing around him. He glanced toward the front where Miss Donaldina Cameron stood surrounded by well-wishers. He'd heard about her work and hoped to have the opportunity to meet her in person. Discovering her engagement in Sacramento the same evening he happened to be in town had been fortuitous, indeed.

He shuffled into the aisle in time to see a young woman in a dark blue dress hurry toward the back of the room. She cast a quick glance over her shoulder, eyes widening as she met his gaze.

Elizabeth King? Had she been so close this entire time? Funny, he should've felt those blue eyes boring holes in his spine. He shook himself and turned the opposite direction. Another encounter with the outspoken young woman would not be high on his list of desirable activities. Charles nodded at two elderly gentlemen as he eased his way toward the front.

Miss Cameron smiled and shook the hand of a portly woman dressed in yellow silk before turning toward Charles.

He cleared his throat. "Miss Cameron, it's an honor to meet you. My name is Charles McKinley, of San Francisco. My law professor, Elmer Davis, speaks highly of your work."

A smile spread across the missionary's face. "Does he now? Did he tell you he volunteered as a legal advisor to the Mission back when I first arrived? I asked so many questions, he'd run when he saw me coming."

Charles chuckled. "Professor Davis did mention you had a keen mind and a great aptitude for law."

The youngest child came up beside Miss Cameron and took her hand.

Miss Cameron pulled the girl close to her side. "One must if they are to succeed in keeping these children safe. It is the law which protects them."

"And in some ways, the laws have created the problem—am I right? Wouldn't you say the Exclusion Act is partially to blame?" Charles smiled as the dark-eyed little girl stared up at him. How many stories—and secrets—those eyes contained.

"Halting immigration has made the situation more difficult. There simply aren't enough brides to go around. But I cannot let these children pay the price of politics."

"Of course. No woman should be forced into such work. Especially ones so young." He forced himself to meet Miss Cameron's steely gaze, as he couldn't bear to look at the little girl again. "But don't you think our efforts should be focused on changing the laws creating the issue, rather than merely treating the symptoms of the problem?"

Miss Cameron laid her hand on the child's shoulder. "We must do both, Mr. McKinley, and I pray men like you will take up the challenge."

Charles's pulse quickened. "I hope to try one day. That issue, among others."

"Then I will be certain to keep an eye on you. You should come visit our Mission Home. I can show you firsthand the work we do."

"I'd be honored. Thank you."

"McKinley..." The missionary tipped her head as she studied him. "Are you related to the late president by chance?"

A smile tugged at the corner of his mouth. How many times had he answered the question during his law studies? "No, I'm afraid not."

Miss Cameron cupped her hand against the girl's hair as the child burrowed against her side. "I should be going. I need to get the girls to bed—we're staying with the minister's family—and then I have business to attend to later this evening."

"Business?" An inkling grew in the back of Charles's mind. "Do you mean a rescue? Here in Sacramento?"

"The problem is not isolated to San Francisco, Mr. McKinley. Whenever I travel, I receive pleas from girls in the local communities. How can I refuse to render aid?" She laid one hand on her hip. "And though some would counsel me to focus on politics, I cannot refuse the call God has placed on my life. Where He leads me, I will go."

Where He leads me... Charles pondered the words as he walked Miss Cameron and her young charge to the back of the room to meet the other girls. Had God placed this burning desire in his heart, as well?

Elizabeth lingered by a potted palm in the outer hall, nibbling at a hangnail. She'd sent Lillian home with another friend in hopes of speaking to the missionary alone. The assembly hall emptied, the shuffle of footsteps falling silent, but still Mr. McKinley monopolized Miss Cameron's attention.

Elizabeth pressed a hand to her trembling midsection. Perhaps she should go home and think about this. *Pray about it, Papa would say.* Her throat tightened. If she waited, she'd lose her nerve. Her father had also encouraged them to live for God and to serve their fellow man. She'd failed on the first part; perhaps she could redeem herself in the second.

The voices grew louder as Miss Cameron and Mr. McKinley approached the doorway. Elizabeth steeled herself, her back as taut as piano wire. She stepped out of the shadows and into their path.

Mr. McKinley's eyes widened. "Miss King—I didn't know you were still here. Did you need something else?"

She forced herself to meet his eyes, however briefly. "I'd like a word with Miss Cameron, if she has a moment." Elizabeth turned to the dignified woman, the missionary's plumed hat making her appear even taller than the young attorney.

The oldest of the Chinese girls took the hands of the two smallest and led them to a nearby bench.

The lawyer gestured to Elizabeth. "Miss Cameron, allow me to present Miss Elizabeth King. She's the daughter of one of my clients. I was…delighted…to encounter her here this evening."

Miss Cameron took Elizabeth's hand and shook it warmly. "A pleasure, Miss King."

"Actually, we've met before." A fluttering took up residence in Elizabeth's stomach. "In San Francisco—last year, at my brother's wedding." Elizabeth spotted confusion in the woman's eyes. "Dr. Robert King and his wife, Abby?"

Miss Cameron's face brightened like a gas lamp turned on high. "Abby and Robert, of course! Abby is a dear friend to the Mission. I'm afraid I was unable to stay long enough to make everyone's acquaintance that day. You're Robert's sister? And Ruby's?"

"Yes." Elizabeth swallowed, her throat as dry as day-old toast. Was she really going to do this here, in front of Silas McKinley's nephew? She reached deep within, drawing from a well of inner strength she'd thought lost months before. "I was quite moved by your words— your stories." She cleared her throat in a vain attempt to steady her voice, "If you were sincere about needing teachers, I'd like to offer my services."

Mr. McKinley's jaw dropped.

A wide smile crossed Miss Cameron's face. "I was in earnest. Our English teacher recently left to marry one of the trustees, and we've been without a sewing or music instructor for far too long. What subject interests you?"

Not music. Elizabeth bit her lip. "I graduated from one of the finest schools in Sacramento, but I do not hold a teaching certificate."

"Our girls don't care about such formalities. What matters is the heart."

"I took high marks in English and composition. And I'm told I sew quite well. My sister Ruby taught me everything I know. She's the truly gifted one."

Miss Cameron touched the lace trimming Elizabeth's sleeve. "Did you make this? It's exquisite."

Elizabeth glanced down at her dress, the blue silk gleaming under the light. "Yes. I make all of my own clothes."

Miss Cameron lowered her satchel to the floor. "What of your family? Would they object to your leaving Sacramento, Miss King? And are you...attached to anyone here?" The missionary glanced between her and Mr. McKinley. "Pardon me for being indiscreet, but I do not wish to hire another teacher only to lose her in a few months."

Mr. McKinley stepped back, as if Miss Cameron's implication caught him off guard.

A sour taste rushed into Elizabeth's mouth. "No. I am not attached." *Most certainly not to this cretin.* "And I am the youngest of seven children. All of my siblings are grown and married with families of their own. My mother is quite busy with charity fundraisers, and I believe she would be relieved to see me otherwise occupied. As you already know, two of my siblings reside in San Francisco, so I am familiar with the city."

"And your father?"

A shade dropped over Elizabeth's heart. "He passed when I was young. But he taught me the importance of doing good and putting others' needs before my own." If only she'd clung to that. She set her jaw. *I'll make you proud yet, Papa.*

Mr. McKinley nodded. "Miss King's father was a well-respected physician. I'm told he often donated his time to help the city's underprivileged."

"It seems he passed a legacy to his children." Miss Cameron's brows rose as she focused on Elizabeth. "Your brother treated one of my girls after she had a mishap with a cable car, even though his hospital refuses Chinese patients." She adjusted her hat, resetting the pearl-topped pin holding it in place. "It appears the Mission may have more reasons to be indebted to the King family in the near future."

Elizabeth's spirits lifted like a leaf swirled on an updraft. "I can come?"

"I'll need to speak to the board, but I don't expect any objections. How soon could you start?"

Elizabeth dug her fingers into the folds of her skirt to keep from clapping her hands like a child. "As soon as you have need of me."

3

*C*harles stepped away, giving Miss Cameron and Miss King privacy to discuss their plans. He'd clearly misjudged the young woman. Here she stood, committing a year of her life to God's service in one of the darkest sections of San Francisco. Did she understand what she was volunteering for? The Presbyterian Mission was no ladies' academy. She'd be teaching prostitutes and maltreated waifs. He shook his head. Likely as not, Miss King would be the one receiving an education.

The women concluded their discussion and walked toward the children. Miss Cameron collected them and departed with hearty farewells to Charles and Miss King.

Charles took a deep breath, the day's obligations weighing on his shoulders like the heavy hay bales he used to heft into his father's barn years ago. A night's sleep before returning to the city would be welcome, indeed. The firm's secretary had made reservations for him at the Heritage Hotel. The sumptuous accommodations would be a nice change.

He glanced at Miss King as she fastened a wool cloak over her slight shoulders. His client shouldn't return home unescorted, especially with those blue eyes shining like an overly excited child. His heart jumped at the sight of her flushed cheeks. "May I see you home?" He offered the crook of his arm with a flourish, praying the gesture displayed the admirable presentation his uncle desired of him.

She pulled the garment close, as if to shield herself from his attention. "My friend has a cab waiting outside."

Charles dropped his elbow, unsettled by the disappointment brewing in his gut. He'd just met the woman, why did he already feel a sense of responsibility toward her?

Miss King adjusted a tiny hat atop her sleek blonde hair. He could almost feel the smooth strands under his fingers. He shook away the thought, burying his hand in his coat pocket.

As he walked her to the door, Charles considered the future she'd chosen—a path that led her straight to the city he now called home. Would he be seeing more of her? He cleared his throat. "I admire your fervor, Miss King, but I hope you haven't allowed your feelings to sweep you into a situation you may regret."

Miss King's brows drew low over her eyes. "What do you know of regret?"

"More than you can imagine." The words slipped from his mouth before he could reel them back. His sister never strayed far from his thoughts. *Remember why you're here.* "There is no need to rush your decision."

"Endless equivocation is more your area of expertise, Mr. McKinley. I assure you, I am quite resolute." Her eyes flashed. "My family's situation has changed, as you well know. I understand this teaching position will not undo our loss of income, but at least it will prevent me from being a further drain on my mother's meager resources."

"I told you, there are ways—"

"More investments?" She sighed. "You expect us to entrust our remaining savings to your untried expertise? After what happened under your uncle's supervision?"

He bit down a retort. She had every reason not to trust him—the numbers in Uncle Silas's reports had left unanswered questions in Charles's mind as well. "I understand." He reached out and touched her arm, a second wave of protectiveness sweeping over him, perhaps a result of Josephine's memory. "I live not far from the Mission. If you should need anything—anything at all—please don't hesitate to contact me."

The expression in her blue eyes softened. "I appreciate your concern. But I can watch over myself. And if anything happens, my brother and sister will be nearby." She moved toward the door.

"Of course." He pressed the derby onto his head and touched the brim, a hollowness opening in his chest. "Sometimes even brothers and sisters aren't enough to keep the world at bay."

She cast a steadfast glance across her shoulder. "Then it's a good thing I can take care of myself."

&

Elizabeth hurried down the sidewalk, regretting the falsehood she'd told Charles McKinley. Something about the man triggered unwelcome flutters in her chest. Gooseflesh spread down her arms as she considered his strong shoulders and easy smile. She'd not even shaken off the sensation of Tobias's touch and now a handsome attorney turned her head? What would become of her? *Lord, help me.*

Let him believe her decision was triggered by her family's economic situation. She couldn't bear for him—or anyone else—to know the truth.

She hustled down the sidewalk, determined to be out of sight before the lawyer noticed no cab awaited her. Elizabeth ducked into a shadowed alley, easing between wooden crates and cans of refuse lining the back doors of businesses. The sun had long disappeared from the evening sky. Pulling the cloak tight about her shoulders, Elizabeth walked as fast as her stiff shoes allowed.

A man stepped out of one of the narrow doorways, light spilling out around his bulky form. "Miss? You lost?"

She jerked back a step. "No. I—I'm just taking a shortcut. I turned down the wrong street." Her throat constricted. Her mother would be furious to discover her here. Only disreputable women skulked around in dark alleys at night. *My reputation is all I have left, and even that's hanging by a shoestring.* Her gaze flitted down the path to the street beyond. Elizabeth gestured with a shaking hand. "My father is waiting out there." Another lie. God must have already given up on her.

The man stepped out of the glare and grinned, displaying a row of crooked teeth. He slapped a hand against the metal can. "You got nothing to worry about from me, Miss. I'm just taking out the trash. You hurry on, though."

Elizabeth bobbed her head, her hat sliding to one side. "Yes, thank you. If you'll excuse me..." She picked up the edge of her skirt and dashed through to the main street. She slowed her pace, quelling the commotion in her heart as she turned toward home.

The attorney's words flooded back into her thoughts. *"I hope you haven't allowed your feelings to sweep you into a situation you may regret."* She folded her arms, gripping her elbows as she walked. Her emotions had led her down every single path she'd ever walked. Why change now?

4

*E*lizabeth fiddled through the stack of silk handkerchiefs. How many would she need? The trunk lid yawned open like a hungry alligator, but she'd yet to add a single garment from the pile strewn across her bed. Last time she'd traveled to San Francisco, she'd packed her nicest things in preparation to attend Robert's wedding. It didn't seem likely she'd need frilly evening gowns or lace-covered day dresses for a teaching position. She dropped the handkerchiefs back in the drawer with a sigh, sending up a swirl of fragrance from her lavender sachet. Elizabeth gathered her simplest skirts. All of the instructors at the ladies' college wore muted browns and grays. Unfortunately, other than her russet walking skirt, everything she owned seemed to be in spring colors.

I might not be suited to teaching. Her mind wandered back to the three girls she'd seen at the oratory. She'd been so busy focusing on Miss Cameron, she hadn't even thought to speak to them. Within a few days, she'd be standing before an entire classroom of Chinese students. What if they didn't like her? Elizabeth held up her pink skirt with its matching floral jacket. She could almost picture the girls laughing silently behind their hands.

She sank onto the bed, the thought weighing upon her shoulders. When she'd picked out the pretty rose jacket, she'd imagined herself playing piano on the big stage of the Orpheum Theater. Her dreams had blossomed into thoughts of touring Europe. She'd spend languid afternoons buying hats and gowns in Parisian boutiques and evenings performing at the finest concert halls.

Teaching sewing to Chinese slave girls? It had never crossed her mind until last night. Was it a call from God, or an impulsive plan of escape?

Her concert dreams had been scattered like so many dandelion seeds to the wind. Elizabeth clenched her fists, her nails pressing against the tender skin of her palms. She opened her hand and studied the long fingers—Tobias called them a divine gift. Her stomach roiled. The very idea of touching a piano brought a sour taste to her mouth.

She needed a new dream.

Elizabeth jumped to her feet and folded the pink skirt together with a more serviceable blue one. Likely as not the girls would appreciate a little color in their teacher's wardrobe. She folded her lace blouse and flowered jacket, adding them to the pile. Striding to the wardrobe, Elizabeth retrieved several shirtwaists and petticoats. It didn't make sense to agonize over every choice. If her wardrobe offended, she'd simply make something new when she arrived. Her first demonstration piece could be a dowdy schoolmarm dress.

A gentle rapping on the door stilled her hands. An ache settled in the back of Elizabeth's throat. If only she could avoid this conversation forever. "Come in, Mother."

The door swung open, but her mother remained frozen on the threshold, eyes dark. "I don't understand why you're doing this, Elizabeth. We've had our differences before, but you've never run off on me." She clutched a folded quilt to her chest, like a child in search of comfort.

"I'm not running away. The Mission needs teachers. Besides, there's nothing for me here."

Mother crossed the room, her quick footsteps silent on the rag rug. "How can you say such nonsense? What will I do without your help at the charity auction? And the library luncheon?"

Elizabeth folded a set of winter stockings. "You don't need my help. I'm hopeless at such things."

Mother sat on the edge of the mattress and pulled the quilt into her lap. "I wish you'd consulted me before you committed yourself to such a ridiculous venture. I've never even heard of this mission. If you wanted to serve a worthy cause, there are plenty right here. Why must all my children hightail it off to San Francisco?"

Elizabeth crouched down to peer into the shadowy recesses of the top drawer. "Ah, there they are." She drew out a pair of white gloves wedged in the rear corner. "Not all of your children—only three of us."

"You shouldn't leave me like this."

Elizabeth stopped midway between her bureau and the trunk. "Like what?"

"Alone." Mother's shoulders rounded.

She hadn't seen Mother like this since Robert—always her favorite—left for medical school, years ago. She never anticipated such a reaction for her own departure. "It's not so far. And it's only for a year." She swung her arm toward the window. "Ethel and Jane both live within a mile. I'm not leaving you alone."

"Your sisters have their own lives."

The muscles in Elizabeth's back coiled. "So do I."

"They have husbands, children. No time for their mother."

The comment stung. "Because I'm not married, my life is not my own?"

"Don't put words in my mouth, Elizabeth." Mother pushed to her feet. "I'm concerned. If you were marrying and moving to the city, I wouldn't worry. But you're going off to some mission—"

"I need a change. I can't stay here. Not while..." Elizabeth threw the handkerchiefs into the trunk, the delicate squares dropping out of their neat folds and fluttering down. *Not while Tobias still occupies every thought.*

Mother drew up to her full height. "I forbid it."

"I'm a grown woman."

"Then act like it. Don't run off the moment things grow difficult."

Elizabeth closed her eyes for a moment, determined to unravel the knot growing in her stomach before she said something she'd regret. "If only you could have heard Miss Cameron's plea, you would understand." She laid a hand on her chest. "I felt God's call, Mother. As clear as I hear your voice right now."

Her mother huffed. "I thought God called you to be a concert pianist. Look how quickly you threw it away—after years of training. Why should this be any different?"

Elizabeth sucked in a defensive breath, blinking back tears. She'd never be able to explain to Mother why the remaining concerts had been canceled. She simply couldn't risk Tobias exposing her secrets to the world—or worse—to her family. "Working at the Mission will focus my heart on others."

"Chinese children."

"God's children."

Her mother fell silent. After a long moment, she scooped up the folded quilt. "So much like your father. You'd think of seven offspring, at least one might take after me." She paced to Elizabeth's side, her face softening. She held out the quilt, one wrinkled hand placed on top. "I want you to have this."

Elizabeth lifted her gaze. "What is it?"

"Your grandmother's quilt. She stitched it for me when I was a hair younger than you, but every bit as headstrong." The hint of a smile softened the lines around her mouth. "Perhaps you do take after me...a little."

Air rushed from Elizabeth's lungs. She threw both arms around her mother, the precious quilt crushed between them.

Charles couldn't help but admire the dawn light glowing against the new buildings lining Market Street. Stepping through the door of the Flood Building, he was careful to wipe the road dust from his shoes.

He hadn't been to the new office yet. The firm had been in temporary quarters since the devastating earthquake and fires. Uncle Silas had raved about this new location—centered in the heart of San Francisco's rallying financial district.

"Need a lift, sir?" A young man in a crimson uniform pulled back the elevator's ornamental iron gate with a flourish.

Charles stepped in, trying not to think about the mechanics needed to make such a device function. He'd ridden in them before, but it always made his stomach queasy. "Thank you. Ninth floor, if it's not too much trouble."

An easy grin crossed the young man's angular face. "No trouble at all." He flipped a switch and inched the crank lever to the right. "Ninth—McKinley and McClintock, right?"

"That's correct."

"I'm still getting acquainted with the names. Only been at this post a few days. Lots to learn."

Charles curled his fingers around the railing. Hopefully, the operator knew how to stop.

"But Mr. McKinley—he's memorable."

"Why is that?" Charles pushed back his hat to get a better look at the attendant.

"He doesn't deign to speak to fellows like me, outside of requesting a floor. But you can tell right off, the fellow's influential. Power oozes from every thread of his jacket. Probably not one to be crossed—if you know what I mean." The operator slowed the car, overshooting the floor by a couple of feet and easing it back down.

"Yes. I believe I do." Charles adjusted his collar as the man unclasped the gate and retracted it. "Thanks for the lift, Mr...."

"Clemmons, sir. Eugene Clemmons. Thanks for asking. It's an honor to be of service." He stuck his hand out.

Charles dried his palm on his jacket before grasping the thin hand. "Um—it's Charles."

"It's a pleasure to make your acquaintance, Mr. Charles." Eugene stepped back inside the elevator. "Have a good day, sir. I'll see you on the way down."

Charles stepped back, contemplating using the stairs from now on rather than explaining his personal connections to the young operator. Would he ever be viewed as a powerful force? It'd take more than a tailored suit to accomplish such a lofty goal.

Hurrying down the hall, he paused at the door, admiring the etching on the frosted glass. *McKinley and McClintock, Attorneys at Law.* He might not be the McKinley to which it referred, but he hoped to earn a place, regardless. Charles took a deep breath and straightened his shoulders as he entered the office.

A clerk lifted his gaze from the stack of papers at his desk and rose to his feet. "May I help you, sir?"

Charles strode forward, determined to leave his quivering nerves outside in the hall. "I'm Charles McKinley. Here to see my—to see Mr. Silas McKinley."

The clerk's chin jerked upward. "You're—you're…" His head bobbed on his skinny neck. "Of course, sir. I'll let him know you're here. Please, have a seat." He gestured to a row of chairs before disappearing into the back.

Charles's mind wandered back over his visit with the King family. Considering his uncle's skill with investments, it seemed odd that he'd allowed their situation to become so dire. Even so, Miss King's abrupt decision struck him as unusual. Hopefully, it came from a deeper conviction and not a knee-jerk reaction to his visit.

The clerk reappeared, his gangly limbs seeming to arrive a moment before the rest of him. "You may enter, Mr. McKinley." His voice tightened upon speaking Charles's last name.

Charles snapped up his bag and jumped to his feet, following the man past stacks of wooden crates.

"I must apologize for the mess. We're still unpacking." He paused at the end of the hall and opened the door, gesturing for Charles to enter. "He'll be right with you."

Uncle Silas clutched a telephone receiver, his fingers knotted around the device as a scowl drew down his face.

A tremor raced through Charles's chest. *Not in a good mood, then.* He let his gaze wander the spacious office. The light from the large window gleamed off the rich wood paneling, so glossy Charles might have shaved by its reflection.

Uncle Silas glanced up, quirking one bushy gray brow. He lifted a hand from the blotter and gestured toward a seat located opposite the desk. Reclining in the high-backed swivel chair, he grunted into the receiver. "Nonsense, Cecil. You're in this position because I deemed it appropriate, don't give me any of this voting foolishness. You answer to me, and I say the business needs to relocate. He can't expect to open a trinket shop on the most prestigious corner in the new financial district." He rolled his eyes. "I don't want to hear excuses. If you can't get it done, I'll find a man who can. In fact, I'm sitting across from a rather likely looking candidate right now."

The words sent a chill through Charles. *A candidate for what?*

Uncle Silas cleared his throat and spun the chair toward the window. "I'm glad to hear it. I don't want to drive past that eyesore, again. Have him out by nightfall."

Charles sank into the seat and laid his palms on the edge of the tall desk, feeling like an undersized grammar school student. An odd combination of cigar smoke and furniture polish accosted his nose. If this were his office, he'd crank open those tall windows, first thing.

His uncle laid the receiver on the cradle and grunted. "Insufferable man. Why don't they realize this is our chance to build this city right from the ground up?"

Charles swallowed. "From the looks of things, San Francisco appears to be recovering nicely."

Uncle Silas pointed a crooked finger his direction. "If you ask me, the earthquake did us a favor. Cleaned house. We could use this opportunity to construct a showpiece of the West. But, no—folks want to put everything exactly where it was." He leaned back in his seat and crossed his arms. "How did it go with the King woman?"

Welcome to the firm. Good to see you. How was the ferry ride? Did his uncle always skip the pleasantries? Charles skidded through his thoughts in an attempt to select the most pertinent information to report. "Mrs. King was quite welcoming. She seemed to understand the situation and be open to solutions."

His uncle smiled, sitting forward. "Good, good. After her son showed up demanding answers, I feared she might be handing the reins over to him."

Charles scooted closer to the desk. "I'm more concerned about the younger Miss King. She seemed put out over their predicament and quite vocal about her concerns."

Uncle Silas flapped his hand. "Inconsequential. She's a minor child."

Charles drew the file from his bag. "I'm sorry to correct you, Uncle, but she's no more a minor than I am. She's twenty years old."

"Twenty? How is that possible? Why, she was only in pigtails…" He squinted, as if searching his memories. "Well, I suppose it's been a few years since I was last there. Same thing happened with you. I visit once and you're a freckled-faced tyke in short pants. Now you sit before me a full-fledged attorney." He ran a hand across his graying hair. "How old are you? Eighteen?"

"Twenty-four."

He grunted, rubbing a hand across his eyes before replacing his spectacles, the chain dangling next to his jaw. "And that makes me an old man."

Charles didn't succeed in hiding his smile, the tension easing from his shoulders. "As I was saying, she's highly agitated, throwing around wild accusations."

His uncle drew back. "What sort of accusations?"

"The news about their financial losses must have been a great shock to the family. Miss King suggested their investments might have been mismanaged."

Uncle Silas banged a hand on the desk like a gavel. "Most of the city took a financial loss. Why should the Kings be any different?" He pushed to his feet, the empty chair rotating slowly on its axis. He strode to the window and stared out over the view. "Leave it to a snip of a girl to claim her losses count for more than ours. Does she realize how many of my own assets incinerated during those three days? I'd invested in the same properties as William King, plus several other buildings. Many crumbled in the first shock, the others brought down by dynamite during the fire. The army thought explosives were the only way to stop the conflagration. My house was one of the last to burn." He huffed, turning away from the view. "And I'm supposed to worry about her finances. Twenty years old—what does she know of loss?"

A shudder passed through Charles. He'd read about the disaster, but hadn't realized how deeply it had impacted his uncle. "It must have been terrifying."

"My life's work went up in smoke. I paid a team of men a mighty sum to haul our records across the Bay to safety. If I hadn't saved the documentation of every client who owed me money, I'd have been destitute—sleeping in one of those pathetic relief shacks, like any other yokel. It was a good day when I saw the last of those ramshackle cabins carted out of Golden Gate Park."

"Father wouldn't have allowed that to happen. You could have lived with us."

"My brother knows I was never intended for ranch life." Uncle Silas turned away from the window with a scowl. "And neither are you."

A prickling sensation climbed Charles's back. How easily his uncle saw through him.

"I always sensed you were destined for greatness. First, we'll establish you here in the firm. Show me how hard you can work, and I'll see you get into politics. A councilman, for starters, perhaps. But I plan to have you in the mayor's office before long."

Mayor McKinley. He could do so much good from the mayor's seat. Charles grabbed the reins on his thoughts, determined not to let his dreams run away with him. "Uncle, I just arrived."

A gleam appeared in Uncle Silas's eye. "Oh, you haven't arrived yet, boy." He turned and gazed out at Market Street. "But you will."

<hr />

Elizabeth gripped her case, a long coat draped over one arm. Ever since the ferry came to rest against the dock, sweat had trickled down her back beneath her tailored jacket. Remembering the bay's chilly fog from her last visit, she'd dressed in extra layers. Now as she lined up with the other passengers to disembark, the sun's rays beat down, cooking her. The boat deck swayed under her feet. She couldn't wait to get somewhere quiet where she could shrug off this jacket and wool vest. Likely as not, that wouldn't be until she arrived at the Mission. Her stomach quivered at the thought, her zeal fading with every measured step.

The porter smiled as he helped her down the gangplank. "Welcome to San Francisco, Miss."

She pulled the case close to her hip, as if it would work as a shield against her fears. Elizabeth followed the stream of passengers heading for the Ferry Building and scanned the crowd for Ruby.

Her sister stepped from the crowd, waving a gloved hand. Her red hair sparkled in the sunlight, lace ribbons trailing from her sage-green hat. "Elizabeth!"

A wash of emotion swept over Elizabeth as she rushed into her sister's arms. "I'm so relieved you are here, Ruby. I'm completely wrung out."

"Of course you are, sweetheart. I felt the same way when I arrived two years ago." She pulled her close. "Oh, how I've missed you!"

Elizabeth laid her cheek on her sister's shoulder, biting her lower lip to keep from bursting into tears like a lost child.

Ruby's husband walked up to join them, a smile on his face. "Sisters reunited. A good sight."

Elizabeth pulled back, keeping her grip on Ruby's hand lest she disappear into the crowd. "Dr. Larkspur—Gerald—it's wonderful to see you again." Elizabeth diverted her gaze from the empty sleeve folded and pinned above his elbow. Ruby had written of the surgery, but it was still difficult to see her brother-in-law with only one arm.

He took her case and leaned down to place a kiss on her cheek. "You should have seen Ruby's face when we received your letter."

A laugh bubbled up in Elizabeth's chest, chasing away the malaise that had crept over her. "I guess this is a little out of character."

A blast of air escaped Ruby's lips. "Not at all. My altruistic sister volunteering at a mission? It's a perfect match, if you ask me. How many lost kittens did you bring home when you were little? Now you're going after lost girls." She wrapped her arm around Elizabeth's waist. "You've grown up while we weren't paying attention."

Elizabeth glanced between her sister and Gerald. "As Mother keeps reminding me, you're all busy with your marriages. I decided it was high time I did something worthwhile, since I'm no closer to finding a husband."

"I met Gerald the day I arrived in San Francisco. Perhaps the man of your dreams awaits you here, somewhere."

An ache cut through Elizabeth's heart. If only she'd followed her sister's example. She'd rather have a one-armed man who loved her fiercely than a two-faced musician concerned only with his own pleasure. "I've put such thoughts out of my mind. At least for now."

They arranged for a porter to deliver her trunk to the automobile, and Gerald led the way to the Ferry Building's front door. "We'd love to have you stay at the house for a few days before you begin work."

The weariness dropped back over her shoulders like a cloak. "I wish I could. I told Miss Cameron I'd arrive today and begin classes tomorrow."

Ruby halted on the steps, her lips pulling into a frown. "She can't expect you to start so soon!"

"They've been short on teachers for months. Everything has been in a transition period since the move. She wants to get the girls on a regular schedule as soon as possible."

"I'm claiming your next free day, then." Her sister sighed, taking Elizabeth's coat over her own arm. "The Mission's new building looks beautiful. Did you know Abby has friends there?"

The mention of her sister-in-law's name brought a fresh smile. Elizabeth had spent a couple of weeks with Abby before she and Robert wed, and they'd become immediate friends. "Yes, I remember seeing Miss Cameron at the wedding."

"Of course. Abby is over the moon about you going to work there. She's always wanted to volunteer, but..." She glanced at Gerald, falling silent as they approached the Larkspurs' automobile, parked at the curb.

He helped the porter wedge the trunk into one of the rear seats and handed him a tip. "Your brother has concerns about the Mission."

Elizabeth jerked her head up. "Concerns?"

"It's nothing." Ruby squeezed her hand.

A light danced in Gerald's eyes as he helped Elizabeth into the car. "When he heard your plans, he looked as if he'd swallowed a toad."

Ruby frowned. "Hush now. You'll frighten her."

He chuckled as he walked her around to the opposite side. "Robert's an opinionated fellow. Elizabeth knows that."

Elizabeth folded her hands in her lap, her mother's objections jumping to mind. "Seems to run in our family."

He gave Ruby a hand up into the driver's seat. "I never said that. But I agree with the overall sentiment."

Ruby touched his cheek. "Which is why you love us all so much, right?"

He patted her leg. "Of course. Robert was my assistant and then my partner for a year before I met either of you lovely ladies. I know all about the King temperament."

Ruby's laugh rang out. She drew a long filmy scarf from her bag and tied it around her hat.

Elizabeth sucked in a breath, Robert's qualms forgotten. "Ruby, are you driving?"

Gerald inserted the crank handle and started the motor, the engine roaring to life. "She's a fine driver. Taught her myself." He strode to the rear of the vehicle and climbed into the passenger compartment.

"I thought I was the modern-thinking suffragist in the family. Here you are driving an automobile while your husband sits with the luggage. I don't believe it." *Unless.* She glanced back at her brother-in-law. "Is it because of your—your arm?"

Ruby smiled. "No, dear one. Gerald still drives, even with one hand. But then I couldn't show off for my baby sister."

Gerald hooked one ankle over the opposite knee. "She's not only a wonderful wife and a talented nurse, she's an excellent chauffeur. I've been feeling a bit tired lately, too. It's probably best she drives on days like this."

Ruby pulled away from the curb and into traffic, guiding the vehicle around a passing delivery wagon.

Elizabeth studied her sister's profile. Her demeanor had shifted with Gerald's last comment. Had his cancer returned? Ruby had taken a huge risk marrying a man with an uncertain future, especially since she'd already lost one husband. Elizabeth wrapped her arms about her midsection. The idea that her sister could lose Gerald was almost too much to bear. Elizabeth wasn't certain if she'd have chosen to marry a man with such health problems. She sighed. Likely as not, she wouldn't marry at all.

5

*C*harles sat at a desk in the corner, oblivious to the people conversing nearby. For all of his uncle's talk about a rising star, Charles still merited little more than the cluttered desk of a junior attorney. He gulped down the last mouthful of coffee, the taste of the tepid brew not even registering as he flipped through the stack of legal briefs. He scratched down notes on a pad. How many questions could he ask before people pinned him as a fraud?

The words swam before his weary eyes. Charles dropped the papers into a stack and pressed the heels of his hands against his brow. He'd thought law school would prepare him for the job, but he'd learned more in the past six hours than during the last term at college. At least he'd only be observing during tomorrow's cases. Perhaps after watching the other attorneys in action, he'd figure out the appropriate dance steps.

Uncle Silas and the other senior partner—Ambrose McClintock— had already gone home for the evening, but most other desks were lit, heads bowed over stacks of papers and books. Charles leaned back in his chair and glanced about. Didn't anyone ever leave? A throbbing ache built behind his temples.

Charles swiveled the wooden chair and gazed at the man seated at an identical desk behind him. The heavy-set young fellow had slumped forward, bracing his forehead against his hands, elbows propped on the desk. With fingers hooded before his eyes, it was impossible to know if he was staring at the stack of paper or dozing.

"Excuse me?" Charles tapped the front of the desk.

The clerk jerked upright, a glazed expression on his face. "Ye-yes?"

Charles choked back a laugh. "I'm sorry. I'm new today, and I was just curious—how late does everyone stay?"

The man glanced around at the other desks. "Well, at least until all the partners leave. And Spencer—he's the senior attorney, next up to be partner. You don't want to be seen leaving before any of them." He wiped a huge hand across his face as if to remove any spittle from his chin. "And you've got to wait for the lead attorney working on your case. After that, it just depends on how much you still have to do. But it's important to look industrious, even if you finished up hours before."

Charles grinned. "Is that what you're doing?"

"I'll never be finished. I'm the most junior man here—well, until you arrived, that is. Name's Henry Thurber. What's yours?" He stuck out his hand.

Charles shook it, the friendly welcome bringing a sense of ease. "Charles. Charles McKinley."

Henry's eyes grew large behind the round spectacles. "You're the golden nephew!"

The serenity vanished like steam from a mirror. "Just because I share a last name with a partner doesn't mean I'm anything special."

"I beg your pardon, but I must disagree." Henry straightened, running a quick hand down his shirt front and adjusting his tie. "That's not what I heard. Talk in the office is your uncle's got you on a quick road to partnership. No wonder everyone's working so late today. They're all waiting for *you* to go home."

"For me? Whatever for?"

"You're the next in line. What are you doing out here with the commoners?"

"This is my desk." Charles studied the room again, noticing the furtive glances in his direction. "Is that unusual?"

Henry's countenance relaxed a hair. He lowered his voice, leaning forward so only Charles could hear. "The old man's got to keep up appearances, I suppose. Can't move you to the private offices too soon. Wouldn't be seemly." He nodded, twirling a fountain pen in one hand. "I'll give you three months before you leave the rest of us here in the sticks." Ink splattered across his paper. "I'm just a clerk, anyhow. No partnership in my future, no matter how much I impress folks."

Charles reclined in his chair, the reality of the situation tightening about his neck like a noose. How would he ever make friends if everyone had him pegged as a privileged creature? "Look, Henry...I don't expect to be shepherded through the lower ranks like a crown prince or something. I aim to work my way up like any other fellow. How can I set everyone at ease?"

The man crumpled the ink-stained paper. "You could try going home, for starters."

"How will leaving help my reputation? Won't it make me appear a laggard?"

Henry chuckled. He scooped up a stack of files and jammed them into a case. "Tell you what. Let's head down to the cafe and get a meal. Folks see you hobnobbing with the clerks, they might give you an easier time of it."

Charles reached for his things. "For tonight, we'll say you're the boss. Let's go."

As he followed Henry down the long row of desks, all eyes trailed them. *A few days and everyone will relax. I hope.*

⁂

Late afternoon shadows wrapped the stocky building, odd bricks jutting out at irregular angles. Elizabeth ran a hand across the rough facade, clasping one of the protruding blocks. She drew a deep breath, willing her knees to stop trembling. This is the opportunity she'd hoped for, after all.

"They're clinker bricks left over from the earthquake." Ruby walked up behind her and slipped an arm around Elizabeth's waist. "All around you in this city, you can see God bringing life from the ashes." She gazed up at the Mission Home. "And He's redeeming these girls from the ruins of their lives as well."

Elizabeth clutched her case against her side. She understood ruined lives.

Her sister smiled. "I'm proud of you, you know that? Miss Cameron and the girls are fortunate to have you."

"I hope I can live up to their expectations." A cool wind swept down the narrow street. She didn't even know what to expect of herself. If she were walking onto a stage, she'd understand how to behave. But stepping into a mission? Perhaps teaching was just a different method of performing.

"God knows what He's doing." Ruby gathered her in a half-embrace. "The events of the past few years taught me the importance of trusting in His plans—even when they seem a little off-kilter to our eyes. I know He's brought you here for a reason. I can't wait to see what it is."

Elizabeth managed a nod. She already knew God's purpose—a chance to make up for her mistakes. Why else would He put Miss Cameron in her path the very night she begged Him for direction? Elizabeth straightened her shoulders, strode up the steps, and rang the bell.

Her stomach churned as a few moments passed in silence. She glanced back at her sister.

The lock clicked, the door opening a few scant inches, dark eyes peeping through the crack. "Yes?"

Elizabeth pressed fingernails against her palm for courage. "Miss Elizabeth King—here to see Miss Cameron?"

The door swung wide, revealing a young Chinese woman, her dark hair swept up in a loose bun. A bright smile flooded her face. "Oh, Miss King. Welcome. Please, come in! I'm Kum Yong, Miss Cameron's assistant."

Elizabeth's nerves fluttered back for a landing. She lowered her bag to the step. "My sister and brother-in-law are waiting with my belongings."

Kum Yong hurried outside and greeted Ruby and Gerald. "Mrs. Larkspur, how good to see you again."

Ruby's face lit up as she climbed the cement stairs. "And you, my friend. Abby sends her love. She wishes she could be here."

Elizabeth returned to the automobile as Ruby's husband struggled to lift her small trunk from the rear compartment. "Gerald, let me help, please."

A cockeyed grin crossed his face. "I'm not completely helpless, Elizabeth, but if you want to take one side, I won't object."

"I'm not helpless, either. Let's share the burden, shall we?"

He touched the brim of his hat. "It's what family does, right?"

They maneuvered up the steps, following Ruby and Kum Yong through the narrow entry hall. Their footsteps echoed over the wood floor. A spacious room filled with tables and chairs opened up to the left, a large upright piano tucked in one corner.

Ruby glanced around. "Where is everyone?"

Kum Yong smiled. "At their lessons. All the girls are either studying in their rooms or attending classes. It's a rare moment of quiet. You chose a good time to arrive." She gestured toward a closed door off the entry. "Miss Cameron is meeting with one of the board members now, or she'd be here to welcome you. Perhaps you'd like to see your bedchamber first?"

Elizabeth smoothed her vest. After her long trip, she probably smelled like an organ grinder's monkey. "Yes, I'd love to freshen up before I meet everyone."

"I'll take you up straightaway." Kum Yong glanced at Gerald. "I'm sorry, Dr. Larkspur, but you'll need to wait in the reception area. Men aren't welcomed upstairs, in general." She reached for the trunk. "I can help Miss King."

He released the handle with a grin. "I see I'm not needed here."

Ruby touched his arm. "I'll settle Elizabeth in and be down in a moment."

Elizabeth embraced her brother-in-law. "Thank you so much, Gerald."

He smiled. "I hope we'll see you at the house soon."

The scent of fresh paint stung her eyes as they climbed the steep staircase, the weight of the trunk bumping her knee with each step. Kum Yong led the way to the last room on the right.

Elizabeth set the trunk beside the narrow bed. She straightened and glanced around the sterile chamber. A desk and a small bureau topped with a basin and pitcher took up most of the remaining space.

Kum Yong lifted the window shade, allowing a little light to filter into the room. "We haven't had time to decorate. We've barely moved in ourselves. But the girls are all excited to meet you."

Elizabeth stifled a yawn and leaned against the door frame with a sigh. "I'm just relieved to be still for a moment. I've been rushing from here to there since daybreak."

Ruby squeezed her arm. "You must be weary. I'll leave you to unpack. Besides, Gerald looked a little forlorn being left alone downstairs."

"I'll walk you to the door." Kum Yong stepped into the hall.

After Elizabeth hugged her sister good-bye, she closed the door behind the two women and sank down on the bare mattress. The springs creaked, the sound loud in her ears. She unlatched the trunk and pushed open the lid, the scent of home bringing tears to her eyes. Ridiculous. She'd only been gone a few hours—why did it feel like a lifetime? How would she survive a whole year if her heart ached on arrival? Elizabeth drew out her mother's quilt and pressed it to her chest.

God, how can I be so weak?

The door creaked.

Elizabeth hopped up. Had Kum Yong returned so soon? The door had only opened a crack. Maybe it hadn't latched properly. She placed a hand against it, but met with a slight resistance. Elizabeth put her face to the gap.

A glittering pair of eyes peered back at her. After a quick blink, the tiny girl spun and raced down the hall, her feet thumping across the wooden floor.

"Wait," Elizabeth called, her voice echoing along the corridor. "Don't run off, please."

The child turned, two braids hanging over her shoulders. "I didn't mean to spy."

Elizabeth beckoned her forward. "I don't mind a bit. What's your name?"

The girl approached, her steps measured. "Yoke Soo."

"I'm Miss King. I'm delighted to meet you. I heard you sing in Sacramento." Elizabeth pulled the door all the way open. "Would you like to come in?"

Yoke Soo's eyes widened. "Into your room?"

Elizabeth stepped back and surveyed the tiny chamber. "It's not much to look at yet, but I was just thinking how I might make it more pleasant. Maybe you could help me." Her heart warmed as the child crossed the threshold. Perhaps this wouldn't be so difficult. They were just children, after all. She shook out the quilt and let it fall across the mattress. "How old are you?"

The girl touched the quilt with a trembling hand. "Miss Cameron thinks I'm six, but she's not certain."

Elizabeth frowned. Not certain? She opened the trunk and surveyed the contents. Elizabeth drew out some embroidered handkerchiefs and handed them to the little girl. "Why don't you spread one or two across the top of the bureau?"

Yoke Soo stepped close. "So pretty!" A smile teased at her tiny lips. She unfolded the cloth squares and arranged them on top of the dresser—two matching ones on each side, a different one in the center.

Elizabeth drew out a skirt and laid it across the bed. "Why don't you hand me things, and I'll find a place to put them away?"

The girl dug her hands into the chest and pulled out Elizabeth's blue gown. Her fingers clutched the silk as it cascaded down like a waterfall.

"You like that one?" Elizabeth reached for the dress. "I made it myself. I'll be teaching sewing here. Maybe I can teach you to make pretty things, too."

Yoke Soo ran a finger along the embroidered bodice. "Mai Yoo had a blue silk dress when she came."

Elizabeth knelt at the child's side, trying to read her expression. "What happened to her dress?"

The little girl glanced up, the glossy blue fabric casting a pallor across her skin. "She didn't like us. She went back."

To the brothels? A prickle crept along Elizabeth's back. "I'm sure she must have liked you."

Yoke Soo's lips pressed into a line and she shrugged. "Kum Yong said she missed her pretty things."

"We all like pretty things. You wore a pretty red tunic in Sacramento." Elizabeth eyed the child's simple cotton shirt and loose trousers.

"Lo Mo says beauty comes from within. From Jesus' love shining through us, like a lamp." Yoke Soo's cheeks pinked.

"Yes, well, I'm sure she's correct. Must be why you're so lovely." Elizabeth couldn't resist tweaking the tip of Yoke Soo's nose. Elizabeth shook the wrinkles from the gown and hung it in the small closet.

Yoke Soo beamed and began removing garments from the trunk, admiring each one before handing it to Elizabeth. "You seem nice, for a teacher. I hope you'll stay."

At least she'd won over one pupil. "We'll see if I meet with Miss Cameron's approval."

A sudden flurry of footsteps in the hall drew their attention. Yoke Soo's face paled. A brown shirtwaist dropped from her hands. "Class is over. I should go."

An older girl appeared in the doorway, brows drawn low over her piercing eyes. "Yoke Soo, you shouldn't be here."

Yoke Soo brushed past Elizabeth and hurried to the newcomer's side. "I was just helping our new teacher, Tien Gum."

The girl raised her head, pinning Elizabeth with a hardened gaze. "Teacher won't want your help."

"I beg to differ." Elizabeth spoke up. "Yoke Soo has been quite helpful. In fact, we were just getting to know one another." She stepped forward and clasped the edge of the door. "My name is Elizabeth King. I'm pleased to meet you."

The girl snatched Yoke Soo's hand and pulled her into the hall. "She's not supposed to be upstairs during lesson time." Her chin jutted forward.

Elizabeth sighed. "I see. But please, don't blame Yoke Soo. I asked for her assistance."

She strode away, tugging the younger girl behind her like a toy train.

Yoke Soo glanced back, her shoulders sagging.

Elizabeth waggled her fingers in farewell, earning a faint smile from her new friend. Hopefully, the girl wouldn't get into too much trouble.

Students streamed up and down the hall, their chirping conversations dimming as they spotted the newcomer.

Elizabeth withdrew and closed the door with a gentle click. She should finish her work and dress for her meeting with Miss Cameron.

She lifted the last skirt from the bottom of the trunk—a green silk with pink roses. Her throat tightened remembering Yoke Soo's reaction to the blue gown. Perhaps she'd best save the fancier frocks for times away from the Mission. She'd do her best to fit in, but if—like the child said—beauty was dependent on God's light shining through, Elizabeth still had a lot of work ahead.

⁂

Charles shrugged off his suit jacket, the irresistible scent of roasting meat causing his stomach to growl like a wounded bear. He glanced around the corner cafe, the myriad of raucous conversations a welcome change from the quiet law office. "Not exactly a genteel locale."

"Genteel?" Henry shouted over his shoulder. "San Francisco was founded by gold prospectors. If you want genteel, head east." He ducked through the crowd, securing a table in the back.

Charles hung his coat and hat on the corner of a chair. "I guess I've not seen much outside the financial district."

The man grinned, his round head bobbling on a short neck. "Time for some adventures, my friend." He leaned forward, lowering his voice. "Just keep in mind there are places to avoid, if you want to keep on your uncle's good side."

Charles sat back in his chair, smoothing down his vest. "Like where?"

Henry hitched an eyebrow. "Stay clear of the Barbary Coast and the Chinatown alleys."

"Ah, yes. I've heard of such places." Donaldina Cameron's stories still haunted him.

"The bureaucrats did their best to move Chinatown after the quake, but no such luck."

"Move it? Because of the vice?"

"I'm not sure they cared about those things, but the land down there's worth a fortune. Or it would be, if they could wrest the property from the Chinese."

Charles wrapped his hand around the water glass. "What happened?"

"The land the consulate occupied belonged to the Chinese government. They sent a delegation to the governor, vowing to move all Oriental trade to Seattle if the Celestials—the Chinese immigrants—weren't allowed to return to their property."

"Decisions always come down to the dollar. I imagine the threat got the governor's attention."

"And Mayor Schmitz's, too." Henry smirked. "Of course, he's gone now. Extortion charges don't do much for a political career."

A dark-haired woman appeared to take their order. Charles skimmed the menu, choosing the chicken dinner, the same as his new friend. He took a sip of the steaming coffee. "Was my uncle involved in trying to relocate Chinatown? I overheard him dressing someone down about a trinket shop."

Henry folded both arms across his barrel chest. "Is there anything your uncle isn't involved in? He's fixated on transforming San Francisco into some kind of model city. It's never going to happen, though."

"Why not?"

"It's a jewel of gold in a swine's snout, if you ask me."

Charles choked on his coffee. "A swine's snout?" He mopped a napkin across his chin. "Proverbs, right? 'As a jewel of gold in a swine's snout, so is a fair woman which is without discretion.'"

"Very good." Henry beamed. "You know the Scriptures?"

"A fair amount. But you're comparing the city to a woman with loose morals?"

"No matter how hard the officials try to make us a showpiece, this will always be a gold rush town, complete with crooked streets and crookeder politicians, not to mention countless houses of ill repute."

"There seems to be some housecleaning going on. Maybe we'll see some honest leaders for a change."

"You're an idealist." Henry narrowed his eyes at Charles, as if studying a complex legal brief. "I hope this business doesn't crush it out of you."

The waitress returned, carrying a large platter of food. She spread the bounty before them. Henry asked a quick blessing before the two men dug in.

Charles wiped his mouth with the napkin, casting a glance around at the neighboring tables. If he wasn't mistaken, a few of them were inhabited by other men from the firm. Had the office emptied out after he and Henry departed? "What's on the docket for tomorrow? I'm supposed to observe, but perhaps you can give me a few tips."

The corner of Henry's mouth twisted upward. "You're shadowing Spencer? Figures. Ever since he heard your uncle was bringing you on board, he's tied his bow tie a bit too tight."

"What do you mean?"

"He's spent years trying to impress McKinley and McClintock. You're a threat."

Charles's stomach took a dive. "I never intended to walk in and upset everyone."

"You need to see the situation from Spencer's perspective. He always expects the worst. Next thing you know, he'll be standing on a street corner proclaiming the end of the world."

Charles shook his head. He'd gained an adversary, and he hadn't even met the man. "Where was Spencer today? No one introduced me."

"He was in court all day. He's got a big case with Sanborn Fire Insurance. You'll get a sample tomorrow." Henry wiped grease from his chin. "Not me. I never get out of the office. I'll be shuffling papers until I die, I expect."

Charles pushed the potatoes around his plate. "If I move up as fast as Spencer fears, maybe I'll be needing an assistant."

Henry's eyes brightened. "Now you're talking. I knew I liked you." He squinted across the table. "So, that means you're in charge of the check. Right?"

Charles lifted his coffee cup. "See, I suspected you were clever." He grabbed his fork and began spearing the cooked carrots. "Do you know anything about the King family?"

Henry rubbed his ear. "I met the son—the doctor. He came in a while back, insisting to see Mr. McKinley. Your uncle wouldn't give him the time of day. Something didn't seem quite right. The rest of the morning, Mr. McKinley appeared out of sorts—anxious, even. You spoke with the widow?"

"I did. It's troubling. The numbers in the files don't add up." The niggling doubt burrowed in his thoughts. "I provided her with some options for the future. She accepted the news with dignity, but the daughter..." Charles shook his head. "What a firebrand."

"A pretty one?"

A prickle raced across the back of his neck. "Yes, but not—I mean, she's opinionated. And hotheaded."

"Sounds like fun. The kind to keep a man on his toes."

"Maybe for you." Charles jammed his hand through his hair. "She's moved to San Francisco, so there's a chance she may appear at the office as well."

Henry chewed and swallowed. "Thanks for the warning. Mr. McKinley will be none too pleased."

"I don't relish the thought, myself." The idea of Miss King going toe to toe with his uncle sent a chill down Charles's back. Perhaps he could send a message to the Mission and suggest a second meeting. At a neutral location, preferably. He glanced around the diner. Someplace a little finer than this.

Elizabeth ran a quick hand over her wrinkled skirt, as she followed one of the students down the stairs toward Miss Cameron's office. The girl's slippers made the slightest scuffing sound on the treads, making Elizabeth feel like an elephant trailing a gazelle.

The escort ushered her to the door, vanishing before Elizabeth could offer thanks.

Miss Cameron jumped up from a chair, skirt swishing. "Miss King, I am so delighted you are here. I must apologize for not greeting you upon arrival. You've settled in, I hope?" Her beaming smile warmed the room.

The knot in Elizabeth's stomach uncoiled like a seedling reaching for the sunlight. "Yes, and the room is perfect, thank you."

The missionary laughed. "They're small, I know. I'd hoped when the Mission Board rebuilt 920 they'd provide something homelike, but I'm afraid what they gave us is more like a giant dormitory. But my daughters are grateful to be home again. Two years is a long time to be transient, especially for such a large family."

Elizabeth's heart lifted at Miss Cameron's description of her young charges.

Miss Cameron took Elizabeth's hand and pulled her to a pair of blue mohair seats near the window. "Please, join me for tea. I remember how I felt my first day here. You must be overwhelmed."

Elizabeth sank into the chair. "A little, I'm afraid."

Miss Cameron lifted a white teapot marked with Chinese characters and guided a stream of liquid into two small cups. "I came from a loving home in the countryside and was woefully unprepared for what I faced my first day here." Her Scottish accent colored her words. "Sometimes I think back on that naïve girl and wish I could tell her what grand adventures lay ahead. Much heartache, too, of course. I never imagined my life would turn out this way, but I followed God's leading, and He's taken me places I never anticipated."

Elizabeth wrapped her fingers around the warm cup. "You sound like my sister, Ruby. She speaks often of God's plans and His will."

The light from the window glinted off the silver threads in the woman's hair. "The deeper you involve yourself in His work, the more you're aware of the actions of His hands." She leaned forward, capturing Elizabeth's gaze with her own. "What of you, my dear? Have you seen God's fingerprints in your own life?"

Elizabeth thought over her past. "My father was quite devout, but he passed away when I was young. I've tried hard to live a good life, pleasing to God. I…" A lump formed in her throat. How could she even say such a thing? "I fail often, I'm afraid."

"We all do, child. It's a good thing He loves us, regardless." She stood and retrieved a large, black ledger from the desk. "Each of His children is precious to Him, whether or not we make wise choices." She returned to her seat and placed both hands on the leather cover. "Every time a new girl comes to 920, I record her story in this book— as many details as I know, anyhow. The tales can break one's heart, as I'm sure they do our Heavenly Father's." She ran her fingers around the book's worn edge. "But their old lives are behind them. When one of our daughters embraces Christ's sacrifice, she becomes a new creation. Scripture tells us the old is gone, the new is come. Whether she comes as an innocent babe or from the most sordid brothel, from a privileged home or from the darkest opium den—each girl is made new through Christ."

Elizabeth brushed a loose strand of hair away from her face. A clean slate sounded too good to be true.

Miss Cameron held out the book. "You might care to read up on your students' histories. You'll understand them better if you know from whence they came."

The tome felt heavy in her hand as if the weight of the past could pull her to the floor. "When do I begin teaching?"

"In the morning, if you're ready."

Elizabeth's heart clambered toward her throat. "I can be."

Miss Cameron smiled. "I believe you're going to be a wonderful addition, Elizabeth." She paused. "May I call you Elizabeth? In front of the girls I'll maintain formality, but I prefer to be on a first-name basis otherwise."

"Of course. And I should call you—"

"Donaldina. I think we'll be fine friends, and I can't wait to see you in action. Now, are you hungry? I believe supper is about ready."

Elizabeth nodded, hoping her churning stomach would allow a few swallows of food. She stood and followed Donaldina to the large dining room.

A flurry of conversations hushed as they entered, every face turning to study the newcomer. Elizabeth ran a quick hand over her shirtwaist and straightened her posture. *Hold yourself like a teacher.* She let her gaze wander over the girls, marveling at the wide variety of ages. She longed to know each unique face. At the end of one row, she spotted tiny Yoke Soo, bouncing in her seat. The girl waved. Elizabeth's steps lightened. One down, how many to go?

Donaldina took Elizabeth's arm and guided her to the front of the room, taking her place at a wooden podium.

Elizabeth folded her hands, conscious of the many sets of eyes.

"Good evening, girls." Donaldina nodded to the gathering, as regal as a queen presiding over her subjects.

"Good evening, Lo Mo." The children echoed, a flurry of smiles brightening the room.

Donaldina paused, waiting for them to quiet. "I'm pleased to present our new sewing teacher, Miss Elizabeth King. Miss King comes to us from Sacramento. I know you will make her feel welcome." She waited as the girls' murmuring quieted. "Now, let us pray for our meal, shall we?"

All around the room, heads bowed.

After the prayer, Donaldina led Elizabeth to a small table set off to one side. "Often I join the girls for dinner, but tonight I'd like to get to know you better." She waved Kum Yong over to join them.

The graceful young woman took a seat, nodding to Elizabeth.

Donaldina poured water from a pitcher in the center of the table. "I wanted to speak to both of you about the proceedings tomorrow."

Elizabeth eyed the steaming bowl of thin noodles topped with limp green leaves—spinach? Her last meal seemed like days ago. The food looked unusual, but smelled divine.

Kum Yong held the serving dish out to Elizabeth, directing her words at Donaldina. "We are due in court at nine o'clock."

Taking a small portion, Elizabeth glanced at her tablemates. *Court?*

Donaldina spread a napkin on her lap. "How is Tien Gum? Has she calmed down?"

"I'm afraid not." Kum Yong accepted the platter back and dished up a helping on her plate. "The idea of facing her captors makes her fearful."

"At one time she thought nothing could be more terrifying than *Fahn Quai*." Donaldina shook her head.

Elizabeth took a bite, letting the food linger on her tongue before chewing and swallowing. "What does that mean?"

Kum Yong's nostrils flared. "The distasteful term is what some, outside this house, call Miss Cameron."

Donaldina leaned close and spoke under her breath. "Means 'white devil.' I've earned many names among the Chinese. That's the one they use to frighten their charges into obedience. 'Be good or *Fahn Quai* will get you.'"

"I'd think they'd wish you to come save them." Elizabeth dug at the slippery green vegetables with her fork.

"The stories you're told shape how you view the world. If you heard I stole children away and ate them for breakfast, you might be frightened of me, too."

Kum Yong smiled. "Once they arrive here, they learn the truth—no one is a better friend than Lo Mo." She leaned close to Elizabeth. "Lo Mo is our nickname for Miss Cameron. It means 'old mother.'" She glanced at Donaldina. "Meant in the kindest possible way."

Donaldina touched a napkin to her lips. "You should come along tomorrow, Elizabeth. You can witness some of the challenges they face. We'll return in plenty of time to prepare for class."

"Of course, whatever you think is best." Elizabeth nodded. "What is the case about?"

"We rescued Tien Gum from her captors four weeks ago. I obtained legal custody, thanks to our friends in the court, but her former owners accuse her of stealing. If she is found guilty, they can wrest her from my protection."

Elizabeth's stomach tightened. The dour-faced young woman who had reprimanded Yoke Soo? "She didn't do it, did she?"

"Of course not. It's an age-old trick. If they can get her away from the safety of the Mission Home, she'll vanish into the night and we'll lose track of her."

"Vanish?"

Donaldina sighed. "It's a game of cat and mouse. They'd secret her away—move her up to Oregon or Idaho. I've chased girls as far as Portland. Some we recover, many we do not."

Elizabeth dropped her spoon. "How could a judge let such things happen?"

The missionary blinked twice, as if fighting tears. "I ask the same question every time, Elizabeth. Every single time."

6

*C*harles wrapped an elbow around the cable car's brass rail, his free hand rubbing bleary eyes. He'd spent most of the late night hours memorizing the stack of files from his briefcase. Likely as not, he'd only be expected to observe this morning, but after years in law school, he'd learned not to cut corners. Surprise questions and unannounced examinations were the rule of the day. In order to avoid humiliation, one always overprepared.

The conveyance jerked to a stop, and Charles lost his balance for a moment. Releasing the pole, he hopped to the cobblestones, hurrying across Market Street to the courts' temporary lodgings in the Grant Building. Just a block away from the ruined City Hall and the Hall of Records, what the office building lacked in grandeur, it made up for in functionality.

Charles swiped a hand across his forehead, glaring at the moisture collected on his fingertips. He hadn't been this keyed up since his first day of college. Of course, Henry's unpalatable descriptions of Spencer didn't help.

Charles rehearsed the arguments in his mind. Would Spencer start with the scanty photographic evidence? As he approached the massive doors, one opened. A familiar young woman brushed past him without a glance.

Elizabeth King halted on the curb, her face similar in color to the sidewalk under her feet.

Charles grasped her elbow. "Miss King—are you quite well?" He tugged her back a step. "Why are you here?"

She locked her round eyes on him, her fingers dropping onto his forearm. "Mr. McKinley?"

He nodded. "You look as if you've spied a ghost."

She dropped her hand, the veil of good breeding rushing back over her. "I'm quite well. Thank you for your concern." She glanced up at the Grant Building. Her eyes narrowed. "Is your uncle here, too?"

Charles released her elbow. "No. Not today." Why did he always feel compelled to rush to a woman's rescue, even when he wasn't wanted? "I'm glad to see you made it to San Francisco safely."

"I'm here with Miss Cameron." Her color returned. "I—I just needed a breath of air. You must have business inside. I shouldn't keep you."

"Yes, I'm expected in court—if you're certain you don't need assistance." *She doesn't want your help. Can't you see?*

"I'm fine. You go ahead." She turned her back, as if in dismissal.

His thoughts scattered as he stepped through the doors. Two people in a large city, and they both happen to be at the courts on the same day? He shook his head. His mother always said God moved in mysterious ways.

Charles trained his mind on the matters at hand. The files regarding the Transatlantic Insurance Company contained a massive amount of complex information and detail. Likely as not, the trial would drag on for weeks—months, even. He skirted groups of people, their muted conversations trailing him down the hallway. He'd need to familiarize himself with the opposition if he hoped to be a vital part of the process.

He stepped off the elevator at the fourth floor, checking the clerk's sketched map.

Several well-dressed men stood outside the courtroom, their boisterous conversation carrying down the passage.

Charles stopped short. The man at the judge's side matched Henry's description of Frederick Spencer. The attorney's smile gleamed, almost as if he oiled his teeth in addition to his hair.

The robed judge clasped him on the shoulder. "You just saved us all quite a lengthy headache, Mr. Spencer. I must admit, I'm more than relieved—I'm delighted."

Spencer grasped the third man's hand and pumped it. "Pleasure doing business with you, Robbins. You've made a wise decision that will save your company millions."

Robbins nodded. "Can't say I'm pleased, but I believe you're right. It's a fair arrangement. Just see you abide by it. I want no more claims to cross my desk, you hear?"

Spencer's mouth quirked up on one side. "A deal's a deal. And a profitable one at that."

Robbins and the judge proceeded down the hall together as Spencer shoved a file into his briefcase.

Charles stepped forward. "Mr. Spencer?"

The man's head jerked up, his eyes gray as granite. "Yes?"

Charles thrust his hand out. "Charles McKinley. It's a pleasure."

Spencer's brows lowered. "Oh. McKinley. Yes, your uncle told me to expect you." He shook Charles's hand with a grip that made the younger man's knuckles pop. "Too bad you wasted a trip."

"What do you mean?"

"We arrived at a mutual agreement. Best for all involved."

Charles's skin prickled. "The insurance company settled out of court?"

Spencer chuckled. "I negotiated a package that's...generous. To our clients, to the city." He lifted a hand and rubbed his fingertips against each other as if rubbing two coins together. "And to us, of course. I believe Mr. McKinley—the actual Mr. McKinley—will be pleased." Spencer cocked his head to the side. "Too bad you missed out on the negotiations. You might've learned something. Don't worry, though. I'm sure *Uncle* Silas will come up with some more errands for you to run."

Charles swallowed down a bitter reply. No need to burrow into the muck with the combative attorney. "Any chance the King family's investments were included in this deal?" Even if he hadn't taken part in the case, perhaps he could share the good news. A smile on Miss King's face would be a welcome sight, indeed.

The man's brows rose. "We're talking big accounts here, McKinley, not everyone who lost a few cents in the blaze. Hotels, banks, factories, railroads—those are the players who bring in the money. No one cares about the beggars scraping by, barely able to make ends meet." A fire kindled in Charles's belly. "I'd care to remind you, it's those families on which this city is built."

Spencer's shoulders jerked with a shallow laugh. "I knew you'd be green, McKinley, but I'd no idea you were a fool as well. No worries—a few months working for me and I'll sand off those rough edges." He tucked the attaché under an elbow and strode away, chin high.

Charles's overloaded bag pulled at his arm. He'd wasted yesterday and last night cramming for a case that would never go before a judge. The nature of the business, he understood, but foreknowledge didn't ease the disappointment.

Charles tugged on his watch chain, drawing the timepiece from his vest pocket. The idea of returning to the office and poring over more paperwork made his eyes glaze. Perhaps he could spare a few minutes to watch part of the trial Miss King mentioned. He could use a reminder that some lawyers actually made a positive difference in the world.

℘

Elizabeth willed her stomach to stop rolling as her heels clicked down the long corridor toward the courtroom. She'd read Tien Gum's story in the Mission ledger last night, but hearing it in the girl's own voice—or in Kum Yong's as she translated—tore Elizabeth's heart to shreds. She paused outside the closed door. If she couldn't handle this, how would she endure working with the students day after day?

Elizabeth bounced her fingertips against her leg, fingering the chords of "Amazing Grace." The song never failed to make her father smile, even in the final days of his illness. How quickly the melody returned to her in moments of worry. Elizabeth clenched her fist. Music wouldn't make Tien's pain go away, any more than it had Elizabeth's temptations.

The door opened and Donaldina strode out, Kum Yong and Tien Gum on her heels. The girl clung to Kum Yong, her hiccupping sobs drawing the attention of many of the passersby. Donaldina stroked her arm and gestured for Elizabeth to join them. "Are you all right? I saw you slip out."

"I'm fine. What happened? Is it over?"

"Judge Reinhardt declared a recess. I believe the final decision will be rendered shortly."

Elizabeth pressed a knuckle against her lashes, the sight of Tien Gum's tears causing her own eyes to water. "They must realize she didn't steal the ring. How could anyone hear her testify and think she could be a thief?" She glanced over Donaldina's shoulder, a familiar face catching her attention.

Mr. McKinley strode down the hallway toward her. The warmth in his brown eyes tightened the knot in Elizabeth's throat.

"Miss King, Miss Cameron—I'm sorry to interrupt. My trial was cancelled, and I noticed you were here." He glanced at Tien Gum, his brows drawing together. Mr. McKinley turned to Miss Cameron. "Do you need anything?"

Donaldina cocked her head as she studied the young man. "Mr. McKinley, right? We met in Sacramento."

The attorney nodded, pulling off his derby and pressing it to his chest. "At your service."

Helpful or meddlesome? Elizabeth sighed. At least he was a welcome distraction.

Donaldina straightened her lace cravat. "I appreciate your kindness. Tien Gum is a bit overwrought, but our lawyer, Mr. Allen, assures me he has everything in hand. The decision should be rendered soon, and we'll be able to return to the Mission."

"I'm glad to hear it." He rolled a pocket watch around in his palm. "I was quite moved by your speech, Miss Cameron. I'd like . . . if you ever find yourself in need . . ." his gaze wandered to Elizabeth. "I'd like to assist in your work." He returned his attention to Donaldina. "Do you mind if I come in and observe the proceedings?"

Donaldina touched his arm. "Of course. We'd appreciate your perspective."

The man bobbed his head before disappearing into the courtroom. Elizabeth turned to Donaldina. "Why do you think he's so interested?"

The missionary smiled. "The Lord brings people into our lives as He sees fit. Our paths have crossed with Mr. McKinley's more than once now. Perhaps God is at work in his heart." She tipped her head, her gaze locked on Elizabeth. "But I can't speak as to his plans."

God's plans or Mr. McKinley's?

As Donaldina, Kum Yong, and Tien Gum returned to their chairs in the front, Elizabeth found a seat in the gallery and folded her trembling hands in her lap. What would happen to the young girl if the judge ruled against her? She glanced around the room until she located Mr. McKinley sitting near the front on the opposite side.

The trial began anew, and though Elizabeth tried to focus her thoughts, her eyes kept returning to the Chinese girl. Her former captors sat just across the aisle. How could these men sit there so dignified, knowing what had been done to the young woman in question? And now they had the gall to accuse her of stealing? Had they no hearts?

At long last the judge called the trial to a completion. The room sank into a crushing silence as the man cleared his throat. "I find the defendant, Tien Gum, guilty of theft."

Elizabeth's heart crashed against her ribs. *Guilty.* The word echoed deep within her own soul.

⁂

Charles jammed the pen into his shirt pocket as the folks in the gallery rose to their feet, cries of disbelief ringing through the courtroom.

The judge slammed down his gavel. "I will have order or I will clear the room." A sickening hush fell across the assembly as he continued. "The minor child is remanded into state custody until deportation proceedings can commence."

The defendant's keening sobs carried through the hall. "I not, I not…" She lapsed into Cantonese, the sound tearing at Charles's heart.

Miss Cameron placed a protective arm around the young girl.

Charles sank back in his seat, the impact of the decision causing a familiar clawing at his throat. He closed his eyes for a moment, the memory of his sister's trial etched forever in his mind. A quick glance back at Elizabeth's tearstained face heaped coals on the fire.

The judge shot a bushy-browed glance at the defense table. "The defendant—the minor child, Tien Gum—will be transported to the city jail until further arrangements can be made."

Donaldina Cameron's chin jerked up. "Your honor, she wouldn't be safe. I must insist she remain in my custody. She could serve—"

The bang of Judge Reinhardt's gavel cut off her words. "You are out of order, Miss Cameron. The court has been very tolerant of your outspoken manner in the past, but—"

"You have yet to experience my outspoken manner." The woman's fingers curled into fists.

Charles braced himself on the seat back in front of him. The Mission's attorney needed to intervene.

As if on cue, Miss Cameron's lawyer grasped her elbow, muttering in the woman's ear.

She shook her head, brows pinched low. "I will not." She shoved the man's hand away and turned back to the bench. "If you insist on imprisoning this child, I'm going with her."

The judge rose halfway off his seat, like a vulture hunched over its meal. "That can be arranged."

Miss Cameron pulled the sobbing girl close. "Take her, you take me." She glared at the judge as if daring him to defy her.

Judge Reinhardt sounded the gavel, the crack echoing through the room. "Miss Cameron, you are in contempt."

Miss Cameron's attorney stepped in front of the women, lifting his palms toward the front. "Your honor—"

The judge pointed the mallet at the counselor. "One more word, Mr. Allen, and you'll join them."

Charles bit his lip as the bailiff and guard escorted the two women out of the room. This had gotten out of hand. After the judge dismissed the buzzing courtroom and withdrew, Charles leaped from his seat and pushed past the spectators to reach the defense attorney. "I need to speak with you."

The man heaved a sigh and jammed a hat atop his thinning hair. "No questions, please. I'll have a statement for the press later. Right now, I need a drink."

Charles pushed down the growl climbing his throat. "I'm not a reporter. I'm with McKinley and McClintock." He cast the names out like a fishing line.

The counselor's shoulders sagged. "I'm sorry. It's been a long day." His eyes traveled over Charles's frame. "You new there?"

"What are you planning to do about Miss Cameron? You know they won't allow her to accompany the girl to her cell. You need to get her out of there. Both of them, if possible."

The man shoved his hat back from his forehead. "Look, young man—I don't care who you are. I've had it with the woman. I do everything I can to keep her girls out of trouble. If she wants to simmer down by spending a night in jail, who am I to object?" He jammed his papers into a folder. "In fact, I'm done arguing—both with her and for her."

The young woman who had served as Tien Gum's translator appeared at Mr. Allen's elbow. "I don't understand what's happened. Why are they taking Miss Cameron?"

Charles caught Mr. Allen's arm. "You can't just leave them. This case needs to be appealed, and quickly."

The man shoved the files against Charles's chest. "You do it. I quit."

A breathless Elizabeth appeared at Charles's elbow. "What's Donaldina doing?"

Mr. Allen jerked a thumb toward the judge's chambers. "She challenged this judge one too many times. She can deal with the consequences, but I'm not threatening my career by antagonizing Reinhardt. The ruling's ludicrous. You ask me, someone slipped him a wad of cash. No, strike that—don't ask me. I'm leaving." Hoisting his bag up under his arm, he shoved past Elizabeth and hurried toward the door.

"Wait, you can't just..." She followed him for two steps before turning and surging back to Charles. "What do we do?" Twin spots of pink dotted Elizabeth's cheeks. "We can't let them take Donaldina and Tien Gum!"

A tremor cascaded through his chest. He blew out a long exhale. "You two return to the Mission. I'll speak to the judge." *If he'll see me.* Charles locked his eyes on the young woman who'd sent his life pitching out of control the moment they'd met. "Don't worry. I'll take care of it."

7

Elizabeth followed Kum Yong into the Mission house, fighting the sensation of being on a boat lost at sea, the captain gone overboard. Leaving court without Donaldina had never crossed her mind. What were Donaldina and Tien Gum facing now?

Kum Yong fastened the locks on the main door. "Lo Mo has the heart of a lion. Little frightens her."

"I wish the same were true of me."

"In the meantime, we have classes to teach." Kum Yong lifted her shoulders in a semi-shrug.

Elizabeth's stomach plummeted. "I'd almost forgotten."

Kum Yong hung her wrap on a long row of hooks. "Miss Cameron trusts us to carry on without her. I will teach her English lesson and help you get started in your sewing class."

At least she'd no time to get nervous. Elizabeth checked the time-piece pinned to her vest pocket. "Only thirty minutes?" Her heart jumped.

Her new friend took her arm and walked toward the kitchen. "Let's get some tea and take it to the classroom. You'll do fine."

Elizabeth brushed her fingers through the loosened wisps of hair over her ears. No opportunity to freshen up or change out of her court clothes. She followed behind Kum Yong, smiling and nodding at girls going about their daily tasks.

Mrs. Lee, the cook, poured two steaming cups of tea for them, her round cheeks stretching into a smile.

Elizabeth's mind kept returning to Tien Gum and Donaldina. Thank goodness Mr. McKinley had arrived to take charge. When she'd first met the man, she'd thought him presumptuous and entitled, but perhaps those were required qualities in a good attorney. He'd have a word with the judge, file some sort of paperwork, and have Donaldina back before supper. But what of Tien Gum?

A tug at her skirt brought Elizabeth back to the moment. Yoke Soo's sparkling eyes stared up at her. "Teacher?"

Elizabeth balanced the cup in one hand and crouched down, her skirts crumpling beneath her. She couldn't resist the little one's smile, a warm ray of light on this otherwise trying day. "Yes, Yoke Soo?"

"Where's Lo Mo?"

Kum Yong was already disappearing down the hall to the schoolrooms. Elizabeth took the girl's hand in her own. "Lo Mo will return soon."

"I drew a picture of you in art class." Yoke Soo pressed a folded piece of stationery into Elizabeth's palm. The soft paper retained the warmth of the girl's fingers.

"Thank you." Elizabeth juggled the cup so she could unfold the gift.

Yoke Soo grabbed her wrist, nearly upsetting the hot drink. "Not now. Later."

"I look forward to seeing it." Elizabeth tucked the square into her pocket. "I'd better go find Kum Yong. I'm teaching my first class today."

The little girl nodded and skipped away, joining two other children in the dining room.

Elizabeth kept the hand in her pocket as she rose, the soft note tickling her fingertips. Hurrying to her classroom, she kept her head high, conscious of the many sets of eyes watching. The idea of hiding in her bedroom appealed, but she'd taken the job as teacher, and a teacher she would be.

Even if she had no idea where to begin.

Charles ran a palm over his suit front, sucking in a deep breath for confidence. He knocked, the sound lost in the crowded hallway. Leaning forward, he placed his ear close to the wood and rapped a second time.

The door yanked open. The judge's eyes bulged, almost matching his bald head. "What is it? I have business to take care of."

Doesn't he have a secretary? Charles swallowed. "I was hoping to speak to you—about the case you just finished."

The man's brows lowered menacingly. "*Finished* is the key word in your statement. The case is decided."

"I understand, Your Honor. But I'd like to speak to you, regardless."

The judge stepped back, his black robe hanging open over his gray suit. "Come in—just for a moment."

Charles stepped inside and shut the door behind him, the noise in the hall subsiding. "I apologize for interrupting." He cleared his throat, hoping his voice wouldn't crack. "I'm with McKinley and McClintock."

The judge's eyes narrowed. "Not a McKinley type of case. No money in it. Not the good kind anyway."

"The defendant is a friend."

The man's arms unfolded, and he straightened. "Can't imagine a girl like that has too many friends. Nonpaying ones, that is. I hope you're not implying—"

"Nothing of the sort." Charles tightened his grip on his briefcase. "I've taken interest in the Mission, not the…the girl." A creeping heat climbed his neck. "I don't mean to waste your time, sir, but I'm curious what value there is in locking up the one defender those girls have. Miss Cameron's work—"

"Don't talk to me about the woman." Judge Reinhardt lifted a crooked finger and jabbed it in Charles's direction. "A self-righteous do-gooder. She stirs the pot down there in Chinatown, and every time she does it boils over on the good folk of this city. If she'd let the Chinese deal with their own, we'd all be better off."

"Perhaps you're right. But someone needs to look to the interests of the children. The law is here to protect the helpless."

"You've got no business meddling in this case."

The door flung open, nearly catching Charles in the back.

Miss Cameron pushed inside, her hat dangling over one ear and her dress splattered with mud. She dragged a single guard behind her, clinging to one arm. "I will see the judge, now. This is an outrage!" She swayed, as if every last bit of energy had been spent.

Charles grabbed the chair he'd been leaning upon and thrust it toward the woman.

Miss Cameron gestured to her skirt. "No, thank you. I wouldn't want to soil the furniture." She yanked her elbow from the guard's grasp.

Judge Reinhardt's jaw dropped open. "What in the blazes is going on? Officer, what is the meaning of this?"

The guard's face flamed red. "Judge, they're gone."

"Gone? Who's gone?"

"I was putting the women in the car when two Chinamen jumped me from behind. They took off with the girl."

Miss Cameron huffed. "I tried to chase them down, but this hooligan grabbed me."

"I didn't want both of 'em to get away."

She slammed her palm on the desk. "Tien Gum wasn't escaping. She was abducted!" Miss Cameron turned to the judge. "This man knocked me to the street and stood watching as the highbinders fled with my daughter. I intend to have his badge for this!"

Judge Reinhardt scrubbed a hand across the back of his neck. "That's a serious accusation, Miss. It sounds to me like you're part of a foiled escape plan."

Miss Cameron's nostrils flared, a vein twitching at the side of her forehead. This woman was going to erupt like Vesuvius if he didn't step in.

Charles took a step forward. "Judge, I noticed a reporter from the *Chronicle* in the gallery during the trial, and he appeared quite moved by the girl's story. He was lingering in the hall as I made my way in here. I believe he'd like a few words with Miss Cameron before the guard escorts her to jail." He let his gaze settle on Miss Cameron's soiled dress. "Perhaps a photograph."

"No." The judge pushed up from his seat, straightening his robes. "Miss Cameron, since the girl is no longer in custody, I see no reason to detain you further." He cleared his throat. "And I'd appreciate it if you would not speak to the press until we ascertain the girl's whereabouts. If she's been abducted, as you put it..." his nose wrinkled at the words. "We wouldn't want to tip our hand to the criminals."

Miss Cameron pressed her lips together and shot a quick glance at Charles before returning her attention to Judge Reinhardt. "Do I have your word you'll pursue the matter? Tien Gum is but sixteen years old and a guest on our shores. She doesn't deserve the life that's been thrust upon her."

The judge glowered. "We'll find her."

༄

Elizabeth pressed the bolt of bleached muslin against her pounding heart and stared at the parquet flooring rather than the three rows of students. Whatever had made her think she could teach sewing?

Kum Yong looped her arm around Elizabeth's waist as she addressed the class. "I know Miss Cameron wanted to be here to introduce you to the newest teacher at 920, but I'm afraid she's been detained. Miss Elizabeth King is eager to take part in our work, and if you've seen any of her beautiful frocks, you already know she's a gifted seamstress."

Elizabeth ran a hand down the royal blue jacket she'd worn to court. There went her intentions of dressing simply, like every school-teacher she'd known. Buoyed by Kum Yong's words, she lifted her gaze and studied the room's occupants. Twelve students of varying ages sat clustered at six sewing machines. Most of the girls wore stony expressions, their faces holding no hints of the impressions within.

Kum Yong nodded at the class. "I'm confident you will show Miss King all due respect. I can't wait to see the beautiful things you will produce. May you work with eager hands." After another quick squeeze to Elizabeth's arm, Kum Yong departed.

For a sickening moment, the silent room seemed to swallow her. Elizabeth placed the cloth on the front table, bracing her hands against it for balance. "I'm honored to be here with you." She dug in her pocket for the speech she'd written the night before, her fingers settling on the folded paper. "I wish to say a few words." Elizabeth drew out the stationery and opened it. An oblong face, surrounded by pink flowers, stared up at her. *Yoke Soo*. Her carefully penned thoughts must still be sitting atop the bureau. Elizabeth sighed and returned the drawing to her pocket. "I have a confession to make." She glanced around, taking in each face. "I've never taught school before. I hope you will show patience."

Two older students glanced at each other and rolled their eyes. One young girl raised her hand, her quivering palm extended upward. "Teacher, my name is Ah Cheng, and I've never attended school."

The class broke in hesitant giggles.

The knots in Elizabeth's neck uncurled, the laughter coaxing a smile to her lips. "Then we're even." Perhaps this wouldn't be so hard.

She unrolled the fabric, spreading it on the table. "This building smells of new paint and tile, but I've noticed very few curtains. Do any of your rooms have window coverings yet?"

The girls shook their heads, eyes widening.

"I think it's time we fixed the problem. We can learn some basic stitches for practice. When we're finished, you can hang your projects in your rooms. Then, if Miss Cameron approves, we can design some decorative ones for the common areas."

The murmur of excitement lifted Elizabeth's spirits. She lifted several cut pieces of muslin. "These will serve as the lining. We'll start there, so if we make a few mistakes at first, they'll be less noticeable. Have any of you threaded a machine before?"

A few tentative hands went up.

Elizabeth beckoned the four girls forward and distributed spools. "Will you help the other students? Make sure to show them all the steps."

The children nodded, smiling.

The room dissolved into a steady hum of voices as the helpers took over, speaking a mixture of English and Cantonese.

Elizabeth pulled her stool close to the sewing machine, noting her white thread already in place. Someone must have prepared it beforehand. *Isn't that fortuitous?* She placed her feet on the treadle and gave a couple cautious rocks, studying the needle as it rose and fell in quick succession.

Once the conversations settled, she waved the pupils up front. "Come close, where you'll be able to see."

Ah Cheng nestled beside her elbow. The others fanned about in a semicircle behind her.

Elizabeth lifted the fabric pieces, rotating on her stool so everyone could see. "You see how I have this section folded under? We're going to stitch it down, so we have a nice edge and nothing unravels. I've already measured the windows and marked where you should stitch. I'll show you how to do that another time." She slid the material into place. After a quick demonstration on how the needle mechanism functioned, she rocked the treadle with her feet. Several stitches later, the tension on the thread increased, slowing the needle. Elizabeth frowned. Perhaps it hadn't been used in awhile. She reversed the belt wheel and tried a second time.

A hush descended over the room. The girls leaned forward.

Heat gathered under Elizabeth's collar. Some seamstress she turned out to be. If only it were a piano. She jammed her treadle down, working the device like a reluctant pump organ.

The device seized up, the needle yanking free from its clamp. Thread spilled loose, the spool bouncing like a marionette in the hands of an overexcited toddler.

The girls closest to her gasped while a few of the older ones drew back, tittering behind their palms.

Elizabeth's throat clenched as her heart pounded against her ribs. She returned the spool to its place and wrenched the damaged fabric from the pressure foot, a tangled mess of knotted thread dangling from the half-finished seam. "I don't know what happened here." She bit her lip, studying the apparatus. Crouching down she stared at the thread controller. The needle dangled off-kilter from its screw, as if someone had installed it sideways. Why would someone do such a foolish thing?

She straightened and glanced around at the class. Two of the older students smirked.

Could this be a test of her authority? So soon? Elizabeth pushed down the tremors building in her stomach. "Did one of you set up this machine?"

All gazes dropped to the floor, except for one tall girl in the back. The student's dark eyes narrowed as they fixed on Elizabeth, her hard stare sending a quiver through Elizabeth's heart.

Settling both hands on the table, Elizabeth ignored her clammy palms. What could she do? How did one punish a girl who'd already lived through torture? Old Miss Westin at the Sacramento School for Girls would have had a ruler at the ready. Did Elizabeth dare do the same? *You're the instructor now. Act like it.* She straightened, pressing her shoulders back. "What's your name?"

The student's brows shot up. "Qui N'gun... Teacher." Her words were halting and loud, lips quivering.

Ah Cheng tugged Elizabeth's sleeve. "It wasn't her, teacher."

Elizabeth lowered herself a few inches to meet the girl's eyes. "How do you know?"

The little one stretched up on her toes. "Teacher. I did it. I wanted to surprise you." Blotches of pink bloomed on her cheeks. "I thought I knew how."

Elizabeth sucked in her breath. Not a prank. An innocent mistake. "Oh..." Perhaps Miss Westin wasn't the best role model for this group of fragile souls. Elizabeth shook her head. "I'm sorry. Please forgive me." She reached a hand out to Qui N'gun.

The student shook her head and tapped her ear. "I... I..." Her clumsy voice rattled.

Another tug on Elizabeth's skirt drew her attention to her young helper. "She doesn't hear well, teacher. She needs to see your mouth."

Elizabeth sank back on the stool. Less than ten minutes in and she'd already proven her incompetence as a teacher. Perhaps she should pack her trunk now. "I understand." She moistened her dry lips, gazing around at the students. She hadn't even bothered to ask their names. Her father's voice filtered into her memory. *A patient is first and foremost a person. Treat them as such.*

"Let's begin again." Elizabeth stood and dragged her stool away from the machine. "I'd like to get acquainted first. Can each of you say your name and a little bit about yourself? Why don't you tell me what sort of projects you'd like to sew. Dresses? Waists? Handkerchiefs?"

The children glanced around at each other with shy smiles.

As the students returned to their seats, Elizabeth sat back and listened. The girls began chattering—slowly at first, then with greater animation as she prodded with additional questions. Sometimes a student interpreted for another, explaining a word or two. By the end of class, Elizabeth knew each name, plus the Cantonese words for fabric, thread, sewing, and thank you. Even when the foreign words muddled in her ears, the sound of the girls' voices entranced her. Their pitches rose and fell like twittering birds. *Maybe the key to being a teacher is remembering to be a student as well.*

She glanced down at her timepiece with a grimace. The class period had filtered away with no sewing accomplished. And yet, she may have cleared a path for the future. "You have all been very helpful. *M gah.*" Elizabeth wrapped her mouth around the odd words.

The girls giggled.

"No!" Little Ah Cheng clicked her tongue. "*M goi*, teacher, *m goi.*" She bounced in her seat. "And we should be thanking you." She jumped up and pressed herself into Elizabeth's arms. "I'm sorry about your machine. I hope it can be fixed."

"Of course it can. And you were a dear to try to help me. Tomorrow we will start on your new curtains."

The students filed out, and Elizabeth lowered her head to the table for a brief moment. What a day. First the courtroom trial, then the trial of teaching. What more could happen?

A gentle rapping sounded from the door frame.

Elizabeth lifted her gaze.

Kum Yong waited in the doorway. "Good, you're finished. Miss Cameron is back, and the new attorney is at her side."

8

*C*harles escorted Miss Cameron into the Mission's front hall. "I hate to take my leave, but I must return to the office. My uncle expected me hours ago."

"I require one additional moment of your time, Mr. McKinley." Miss Cameron gestured for him to follow, leading the way to a small room off the hall. Unlike Uncle Silas's palatial office, the missionary barely had room for a desk, a few packed shelves, and two chairs by the window.

Charles lingered in the doorway, reaching into his trouser pocket for his watch. If he didn't report back soon, his first official day at the firm might be his last.

She slid open a drawer. "We are in your debt, sir. If you could leave one of your calling cards, I'd like to send your uncle a letter of gratitude." She lifted out a leather-bound book and flipped open the cover.

"I'm sure it's not necessary. Coming to your aid was an honor."

"Nonetheless, it's the least I can do."

Charles withdrew his uncle's card from a vest pocket and laid it in her hand. "I'm new to the firm, so I don't have one of my own yet."

Elizabeth rushed in, sweeping past him like a breath of wind. "Miss Cameron, I'm so relieved." She halted midstep, eyes wide. "Your dress!"

"It's nothing, child. I had a minor altercation with some tong members. They took Tien Gum." Her face pinched into a frown. "My dress can be replaced; she cannot." She lifted a hand toward Charles.

"Mr. McKinley served as my champion before the judge. He frightened the poor man into releasing me."

Elizabeth rewarded him with a wide smile. "We owe you a debt of gratitude, Mr. McKinley." She poured a glass of water and handed the drink to her disheveled employer. "What shall we do about Tien Gum?"

Miss Cameron laid the card on her desk. "After I've changed, we'll make some inquiries around Chinatown."

Charles pushed a hand through his hair. "While those thugs are still on the loose? It's too dangerous."

Elizabeth frowned. "Won't the police take care of it?"

"To the police, she is one Chinese outcast among the masses of unwanted immigrants. They're probably relieved to be rid of her." The missionary pressed a hand against her chest. "We know the truth—she is a precious daughter of the King. A pearl of great price."

Elizabeth folded her arms, a spark rising in her blue eyes. "I will accompany you."

"Don't be—" He cut off the words. *Ridiculous.* Charles's throat tightened at the thought. What were two women against the tongs? "How would you know where to search? I hear Chinatown is a maze of interconnected passages."

Miss Cameron rifled through her notebook. "I have my sources—shopkeepers and businessmen, sympathetic to our cause. Word travels fast in this community. If she is still in San Francisco, they'll know."

"Where else would she be?" Elizabeth's brows drew down.

"They sometimes move girls to other cities to hide them from us. Oakland, Los Angeles, Portland."

Charles's mind raced. He couldn't leave these women to wander Chinatown unescorted. Uncle Silas would understand if he accompanied them. *Or not.* "Perhaps I should come along."

Elizabeth's lips pursed. Obviously, her gratitude had its limits.

Was there no way to redeem himself in Elizabeth's eyes? "I'm involved in this case now. I'd like to see it through."

"It's gallant of you, Mr. McKinley." Miss Cameron smiled. "But I'm quite at home in this community, and we're more likely to get beneficial information without a stranger in tow. I will inform you of what we learn, if anything."

The set of Elizabeth's jaw triggered an odd swirl of emotions in Charles's gut. She looked as if she'd follow the missionary anywhere, regardless of the risk. He cleared his throat. "After what happened today, I'm concerned for your safety."

The older woman tapped the Bible sitting open on her desk. " 'He is my shield, and the horn of my salvation, my high tower, and my refuge, my savior.' Do you feel you could protect us better than our Lord?"

Charles curled his fingers into a fist behind his back. "Of course not."

"Then you may depart in peace."

He blew out a long breath. "Please, don't hesitate to summon me if you need anything."

Miss Cameron inclined her head. "We will. Thank you."

"I'll walk you to the door." Elizabeth brushed past him.

That eager to be rid of me? Charles followed her to the outer hall. When they reached the door, he paused, hat pressed to his chest. "Promise me you'll be careful."

The dim light caught a curious glint in her blue eyes. "Ever since we met, you keep appearing—like a melody trapped in my mind."

He rubbed a hand across the back of his neck. "My mother says, 'A bad penny always turns up.' "

A hint of a smile teased at her lips. "You helped Donaldina today, so I wouldn't call you a bad penny." She shook her head. "I don't know what to make of you."

Charles settled the hat on his head, trying not to focus on the single honey-blonde curl at the nape of her neck. "Considering you accused me of being a swindler a few days ago, I'd call it a distinct improvement."

The dimple in her left cheek deepened as she walked him to the door. "I suppose."

Charles bid her farewell and tromped down the steps to the street, conscious of her presence lingering in the doorway. A few more smiles, a few less scowls. Progress, indeed. If only he didn't need to return to work.

Work. The pocket watch hung heavy from its chain, a reminder of how much time had passed since the morning's cancelled trial. His mood crashed like a judge's gavel.

Uncle Silas would certainly be sporting a scowl.

&

As they entered Chinatown, Elizabeth followed close to Donaldina and Kum Yong's heels, darting glances from beneath her hat's brim. They'd only traveled four blocks from the Mission, but it resembled no place she'd ever experienced. Could this still be San Francisco? Signs littered with foreign characters, store windows sporting unidentifiable goods, groups of Chinese men in their dark clothes and long braided queues—Elizabeth didn't know where to look first. She pulled her gray shawl further over her blue gown, the splash of color making her feel conspicuous among the shoppers.

Donaldina wandered from store to store, a picture of calm as she swung her shopping basket and stopped to point out delicacies in the market stands. She lifted her face and gestured to a nearby cafe. "Mmm. Roast duck. Can you smell it?"

Elizabeth squeezed her gloved fingers, willing away the uneasy sensation in her chest. The scent turned her stomach. How could they discuss food and shopping, knowing Tien Gum remained in harm's way?

A young girl, barely older than Yoke Soo, walked along the edge of the street, a chubby baby strapped to her back. Her eyes widened as they settled on Donaldina and Kum Yong. Turning mid-step, she scampered back the way she'd come.

Elizabeth's mouth went dry. She'd read too many stories from the Mission's ledger to imagine anything but the worst. Another child slave?

Donaldina and Kum Yong approached a corner store, its windows filled with bundles of dried plants and strange packages Elizabeth couldn't identify. Spicy smells drifted through the air as she followed the women inside. She fought the urge to reach for a handkerchief.

A young man bustled around the counter to greet them, a white apron tied around his middle. "Miss Cameron, Kum Yong, so good of you to come. Are you in need of remedies today?" He swung his arm around, gesturing to the wares crowding the tiny shop. "How is your gout? Has the aniseed tea eased the trouble?"

Donaldina bobbed her head in respect. "You are a good friend, George. The tea has been a delight. I've never felt better." She lifted a gloved hand toward Elizabeth. "I'd like you to meet our new teacher, Miss King. I am introducing her to the sights and sounds of Chinatown. Elizabeth, this is George Wu. He knows everything one could know about Chinese medicine and herbs."

Elizabeth mustered a smile. "I'm very honored to meet you, Mr. Wu."

The storekeeper chuckled. "No 'mister,' please. Call me George. Everyone does. My father ran the store until we lost everything in the big quake. I've rebuilt from the ground up, with many modern features. Let me know if there's anything you need."

"Your store appears very…" she glanced around at the towering shelves and the stacked barrels containing mysterious items, "well-stocked." Robert might have a different opinion on some of the young apothecary's pharmaceutical offerings. It would certainly be a fun story to share with him.

Kum Yong stood in the doorway, watching the sidewalk outside.

Donaldina lowered her voice. "George, you must know why we're here."

The man rubbed a hand across his chin. "I heard about Tien Gum. Such a shame." He ducked behind the counter and retrieved a piece of robin's-egg-blue paper and a pencil. Scribbling a quick note, his face grew grim. "These are trying times. It's not wise to challenge the tongs. They grow more violent each passing day."

A tremor passed through Elizabeth's chest. Was this a warning or a veiled threat? She glanced at Donaldina, but the missionary's face betrayed no concern.

Donaldina lifted a bottle from the counter. "You carry orange bitters now? I'm much in need of some. A few of the little ones have been complaining of sour stomachs."

He cocked an eyebrow, adding a few more scratches to the note. "Yes, but I can recommend something better." The shopkeeper reached under the counter and pulled out a red paper box. "I think you'll find this to be more effective. I've been saving it for you."

She took the box and peeked under the lid. A smile creased her face. "You always know best." She reached into her reticule, retrieved a few coins, and pressed them into his hand. She lowered her voice. "Thank you."

The shopkeeper darted a glance around the store before offering a quick nod. "Always a pleasure. If you see no improvement, come back tomorrow. I'll find something else."

Donaldina tipped her head, the striped feathers on her hat bobbing with the motion. "Tomorrow." She gestured to Elizabeth and Kum Yong and headed for the door.

"Send my girl my love, Miss Cameron."

Donaldina's eyes softened. "Of course." She turned for the door.

His girl? Elizabeth cast one last glance at the shopkeeper. Did Miss Cameron allow men to court the Mission girls? He seemed like a nice enough fellow.

He nodded at Elizabeth, a twinkle in his eye. "Welcome to Chinatown, young miss."

She hurried to join Donaldina and Kum Yong on the sidewalk. "Did you learn anything?"

Donaldina lifted the folded note. "I think so. But let's wait until we return to 920." She tucked it and the red box into her basket. Grasping Elizabeth's arm, she strode down the cobblestone street. "Now, let's find something for supper, shall we? I believe we're low on some basics."

The three women purchased a few items in the shops lining the narrow street, Donaldina pointing out some of the brothels and gambling houses masquerading as legitimate businesses.

Donaldina stopped to barter at one of the corner market stands while Elizabeth and Kum Yong walked ahead. Kum Yong paused at the entrance to a dark alley, turning to Elizabeth. "Can you smell it?"

"Duck, again?" Chinatown proved to be a feast for the senses.

"No, the other." Kum Yong lifted her chin, sniffing the light breeze.

Elizabeth closed her eyes and tried to distinguish the strange combination of odors. "Something sweet?"

Kum Yong inclined her head toward a nearby door topped with red Chinese characters. "Opium."

Elizabeth covered her nose. "And no one does anything about it?"

"The police don't much care." She pointed out a few more doors leading to not-so-secret opium dens. "Not so many now, since the earthquake. But it's still in much demand. Many girls who come to us can't loosen opium's hold. I'm glad I was too young to have dealt with it."

"How old were you when you came to the Mission?" Elizabeth stepped away from the alley.

"Only eight. Not much older than Yoke Soo. I was *Mui Tsai*—child slave. I took care of the mistress's baby and did household chores. At least until I was old enough to be ready for other work." Her nose wrinkled.

Elizabeth's throat tightened as she gazed at the well-spoken young woman. It was difficult to believe she'd ever been a friendless waif. She took Kum Yong's arm. "And now you help others."

Kum Yong smiled, ducking her head so her bangs covered her dark eyes. "I do what I can. I owe Miss Cameron—and the Mission—my life."

Once their baskets were full, the three women walked back up the hill. Several of the youngest children met them at the door, their faces bright with smiles.

"Lo Mo, you're back!" Yoke Soo danced around their legs, catching Elizabeth's free hand and trying to steal a look inside the basket.

Donaldina crouched on the floor, drawing the girl close. "Your friend sends his love."

Yoke Soo clapped her hands, her giggle ringing through the entrance hall. "I wish I could see him."

"Perhaps soon. But he sent something." She drew the red box from her basket.

Elizabeth held her breath—the medicine? Was the child ill?

Yoke Soo popped off the lid and tiny wrapped sweets spilled onto the floor. Her squeal echoed through the hall, bringing other girls running.

"One each. You know the rules." Donaldina stood, a smile smoothing the lines from her face.

A laugh bubbled from deep inside Elizabeth. "Candy? I thought he was sending medicine."

Kum Yong laced her arm around Elizabeth's waist. "We have much to teach you."

Donaldina held up the tightly folded slip of blue paper. "This is the only remedy we need."

&

Charles fidgeted as the lift door opened on the ninth floor. With a quick nod to the operator, Eugene, Charles hurried down the hall, shoving his arms into the suit jacket's sleeves. The coat settled across his sticky back. Jogging to the office had saved a few minutes, but it wasn't likely to make up for being hours later than expected. Charles swallowed hard before turning the knob.

Henry glanced up from his desk, a horrified expression on his face. "Where have you been?" He jumped up and met Charles in the doorway. His voice lowered. "Your uncle is on the warpath. He wanted to introduce you to Ambrose McClintock this afternoon."

Charles's stomach dropped further. "I was detained."

Spencer poked his head and shoulders out from Uncle Silas's office. "The prodigal returns."

Charles fought the urge to creep back into the hallway and make a run for it. Years of law school, wasted in one careless afternoon. He could still practice in another town, right?

Uncle Silas appeared in his doorway. He clenched a rolled-up newspaper in his fist, as if prepared to discipline a wayward pup. "Charles, my office." He disappeared without another word.

Charles's heart leapt and sank, all in one swift motion. "Yes, sir."

Henry held out a hand. "Let me take your hat."

Charles pulled it off, running a hand over the damp strands of hair clinging to his forehead.

"Good luck." Henry clasped his shoulder.

Spencer lifted his chin, not bothering to conceal a snorting half-laugh. "He's going to need it."

Charles focused on not dragging his feet on the long march to his uncle's office. Every head turned, a hush descending over the room. He pulled the door closed behind him, certain the clerks would dissolve into gossip before the latch clicked.

Uncle Silas stood behind the massive desk, his spectacles low on his nose. He folded his wiry arms. "I hope you can explain this. Spencer has been back for hours."

"I ran into Miss King in the courthouse." Seemed wise to lead off with a client's name. "She was observing a case for her employer. I thought it best to accompany her."

His uncle's eyes narrowed. "I don't pay you to chase after young women."

A wave of heat climbed Charles's neck. "No, sir. Of course not. I only meant—she's a client. You placed me in charge of her family's case." He reached for his collar, finding himself in need of a breath of air.

Uncle Silas fell silent for a moment, his mustache twitching. "Why was she in court? Was it related to the estate?"

"No, sir. It involved her employer, the Presbyterian Mission Home. I thought, if she needed legal counsel, it'd be advantageous if one of your representatives was on hand. You wouldn't want her turning elsewhere." *A weak argument at best.*

Uncle Silas coughed, his mouth opening and closing twice in quick succession. He grabbed a glass of water from the desk and took a couple of sips. "No. You're right. We wouldn't."

The hairs on Charles's arms rose. Uncle Silas agreed?

His uncle pulled out the desk chair and sat, the years appearing to drape over his shoulders like a threadbare coat. "Did you learn anything of value?" He flicked his fingers at the seat behind Charles.

Charles brought the chair forward and sat down. *Value?* He quickly explained the Mission's case and the shocking outcome, including Tien Gum's disappearance.

The man's eyes glazed over after a few sentences. He fiddled with a gold watch chain. "Nothing of interest, then."

"A young woman was abducted—you don't find that newsworthy?"

"A Chinese woman. A prostitute." Uncle Silas sat back, the seat creaking. "This sort of business is a waste of the court's time. And yours." His uncle ran a hand over his chin. "We handle cases for prominent clients, not society's castoffs. You need to set your mind to that fact, if you're to remain here."

A sour taste collected in the back of Charles's throat, but he managed a nod.

"I don't want you to soil your hands on such cases. It could endanger your political future."

Charles leaned forward. "Sir, I mean no disrespect, but the reason I desire a future in politics is to help people like Tien Gum."

"Ideals are well and good, Charles, but first you must gain a position of influence. Until then you are powerless. Controversial topics will divide your following and leave you with no hope for election." He stroked his whiskers. "Now, I brought you into this firm on my good graces. Ambrose McClintock had serious reservations about your youth. Please don't prove him right in your first week."

"Yes, sir. I mean, no, sir. I won't." He had years of tuition to repay. He couldn't afford to lose this position.

"Good. Good. And Charles," he locked Charles with a stern gaze, "as the senior partner, it's unseemly for me to be constantly giving you direction. From now on, you'll answer to Mr. Spencer. Do you understand?"

Charles stiffened his back to keep from sinking down in the seat. "Of course."

"Head over to his office, then. I believe he has a few tasks for you."

"Yes, sir." Charles rose. "And thank you for your faith in me, sir."

Uncle Silas leaned across the desk, grasping Charles's palm in a firm handshake. "Don't disappoint me again."

9

*A*s Elizabeth, Donaldina, and Kum Yong hurried through a circle of light cast by a street lamp, Elizabeth lifted the blue paper
and scanned the words. *Sullivan 261. After 9 pm.* Her boot splashed
through a puddle, the cold water seeping in to soak her stockings.
She folded the note and pressed it back into her pocket. "Are you
sure we can trust this man? What if he's working with Tien Gum's
kidnappers?"

Kum Yong cast a glance over her shoulder. "Not every Chinese
man is evil, Elizabeth. Most are quite respectable."

"Of course." Elizabeth chewed on her lip.

Miss Cameron pulled her arms close, as if protecting herself
against the chill of the evening. "There's our escort."

A policeman waited on the corner, his dark uniform blending
with the night. He fiddled with a baton, tapping it against his leg.
"Miss Cameron, I presume?"

"Yes. And you are?"

The man jammed the stick into its loop on his belt. "Officer
Kelley, Ma'am."

"You're new to the Chinatown beat, aren't you?"

The officer ran a quick hand across his nose. "Yes'm. I had an
unfortunate incident with the commissioner. I think I may be here
awhile."

Miss Cameron sighed. "Come along, then. You'll need to follow
my lead."

The officer's eyes widened. "Follow *your* lead?"

"I've done hundreds of these visits, but each one is different. Some run as smooth as silk, others turn loathsome the moment you knock on the door."

The man grunted as he shoved back his round helmet. "The fellows warned me, but I thought they were joshing." He gestured down the narrow street with his stick. "After you, ma'am."

Elizabeth fell in between the two women and the policeman, a trickle of unease edging its way along her spine. This certainly wasn't the innocent teaching post she'd described to her mother. Robert's misgivings replayed through her mind.

Donaldina approached a nondescript door and gestured to Officer Kelley. "Will you do the honors?"

He pounded on the door, the sound echoing through the shadows.

Elizabeth held her breath. She'd heard Kum Yong tell stories of Donaldina using a hatchet to force her way into brothels. Would such be the case tonight?

The door creaked open about four inches, revealing a haggard-faced old woman. She cackled at them in Cantonese. The harsh words bore little resemblance to the pleasant greetings the girls had taught Elizabeth.

Kum Yong answered, her melodic voice firm as she gestured at their official escort.

Officer Kelley held out the warrant.

The woman squinted, unchained the door, and swung it wide. She switched to broken English. "No girls here. Only me."

"We'll see." Donaldina slipped past the stout woman and proceeded to open every door and cabinet she passed. Kum Yong and Elizabeth hurried after her, the sense of urgency deepening as they moved further into the dwelling. Each room stood empty.

Kum Yong returned to the woman. "Where is everyone?"

"I tell you, no one but me." Her pencil-thin eyebrows rose, nearly disappearing into her hairline.

The policeman fidgeted. "Perhaps your informant lied to you."

Elizabeth wandered past the edge of a large table. The silk covering draped to the floor, puddling against the floorboards. Careful not to garner the woman's attention, she lifted a corner of the fabric with her toe. Movement underneath made her heart jump. Dropping to her knees, she pushed the cloth to one side.

Three frightened sets of eyes stared back.

The old woman hissed and darted forward, but Officer Kelley caught her arm, halting her in her tracks. She stamped her foot, yanking against his grip. "Not your girl. My girls. Daughters."

"Then why're you hiding them, eh?" Officer Kelley held her in place. "Now be quiet while the ladies talk to your *daughters*, will you?"

In a few moments, Donaldina and Kum Yong crouched at Elizabeth's side, beckoning to the young women hiding in the shadows. Kum Yong murmured in their native language.

Elizabeth's heart ached as she studied the three young faces peeking out from under the tablecloth. Their fear hung heavy in the air. None resembled the girl they sought. "What do we do? Can we bring them to the home?"

Donaldina sighed. "We cannot take every woman out of Chinatown—not without proof of wrongdoing. We'd be as bad as those who steal girls from us."

Kum Yong's brow furrowed. She edged forward, reaching for one of the girl's hands as she spoke in hushed tones.

The girl's gaze darted around the room, settling on the woman near the door. In a hushed voice, she chattered a few more phrases, gesturing to herself and the others.

"What is she saying?" Elizabeth touched Kum Yong's arm. "Does she know where Tien Gum is? Do they need rescue?"

Kum Yong turned to her, round eyes brimming. "She says Tien was here, but highbinders took her away before we arrived."

The girl pulled the pink silk around her face, like a hood. "Tien Gum say, we go with Lo Mo."

The older woman shrieked, jabbing an elbow into the policeman's gut.

Officer Kelley grunted, clamped an arm about her midsection, and lifted her off her tiny feet. "I've had about enough of you. My head is splitting from you yammering in my ear."

Donaldina nodded. "Tien Gum may be lost, but she's brought us three more daughters."

They crawled out on hands and knees, their faces powdered and lips painted.

Elizabeth's skin crawled. The girls couldn't be more than thirteen. What had she been doing at the same age—paper dolls, piano recitals, household chores? She helped the tallest one as she scuttled into the light of the lantern. "We'll help you."

The girl pulled away from Elizabeth's hands. She cowered close to her two companions and to Kum Yong.

Donaldina touched Elizabeth's back. "It's all right. They cringe from me, too. They don't know who to trust."

Elizabeth glanced down the hall. "Could there be others?"

"Perhaps. But not the one we seek."

"How will we find her?"

Donaldina's gaze flickered to the woman scowling in the doorway. She leaned close to Elizabeth's ear. "Our contact said to come back tomorrow if things didn't improve. I expect he may have other ideas."

Elizabeth thought back over the apothecary's words. She'd assumed he'd been talking about the medicine. Then again, he'd sent no mysterious herbs, only candies.

Until tomorrow, then.

ॐ

Charles lifted the next stack of legal volumes from the shelf and balanced them in the crook of his arm. Spencer had assigned a ridiculous amount of research. Charles's eyelids already grated like sandpaper, but the idea of returning empty-handed curdled his stomach.

The first time he'd cracked a law book, five years ago, the thrill of the crisp pages had filled him with confidence. Enough study and he'd understand how to prevent the type of atrocity that cost his sister her freedom.

He plunked the books down on the desk. Rifling through financial cases struck him as somewhat less intriguing. Charles sat down and pulled the volume close, bending his head over the yellowed pages to read about the 1868 earthquake. The forty-year-old text's references to the "Great Earthquake" coaxed a snort of disbelief. Perhaps every earthquake seemed "great" until the next big one rolled through. He scribbled a few notes, ignoring the knot growing between his shoulder blades.

Charles pushed a hand to his forehead, focusing on the words. The darkness outside the office window and the glare of the desk lamp did little to help his tired eyes. His thoughts wandered back to Elizabeth and her new life. Had she enjoyed her first day teaching? Charles dug his heels against the floorboards and pushed back the chair, stretching his back. Why did his mind keep returning to her? She obviously wanted nothing to do with him.

Henry walked past, depositing a full coffee mug on the desktop. "Here. Looks like you're going to need this."

Charles brushed a wrist across his bleary eyes. "Only five books to go. How long could it take?"

His friend leaned against the neighboring desk. "All night, if your eyes keep sinking shut. What'd you do to earn this abuse from Spencer?"

"Perhaps he's just breaking me in."

"Breaking your back, more like. I've seen him be kinder to first-year clerks." Henry reached for one of the volumes. "Let me give you a hand."

Charles put his hand on the stack. "No. Thank you. I need to prove I can do this. To myself, if not to Spencer."

"It's half past two. You're going to be a wreck tomorrow if you don't get some shut-eye."

"You mean today." Charles swallowed a yawn before it could validate Henry's argument. "I'll get there. But first, I've got some dues to pay." He eyed the heap of books. "A lot of dues."

&

Elizabeth stole into the kitchen before dawn, the black and white tile floor cold beneath her feet. After a few restless hours spent tossing in her bed, a cup of tea might settle her jangled nerves. She couldn't help thinking what might happen to Tien Gum, trapped with her captors. Had they already smuggled her out of the city? Elizabeth rubbed a fist against her eyes, determined not to cry. She wouldn't survive this job if she fell to pieces before the third full day.

Elizabeth filled the kettle from the tap and carried it to the gas stove. She might as well enjoy the few moments of peace before the kitchen staff arrived.

A rapping at the door made her heart freeze mid-beat. *What now?* She crept over to the door, careful to stay out of sight. Elizabeth peeked around the shelves of pots and pans, tightening the belt on her wrapper.

George Wu peered through window grille.

She hurried to unfasten the door. "George, why are you here?"

"Miss King." The shopkeeper bobbed his head twice, glancing behind him before stepping inside. "I heard you were unable to retrieve Tien Gum."

"Yes, that's right. We brought home three girls, but they said she'd been moved shortly before we arrived."

He ran a hand over his long dark shirt. "I'm told she is back at the same house. If you hurry, you'll find her there. But they plan to move her soon. They say she'll be transported to a mining camp in Idaho."

Elizabeth's heart jumped to her throat. "Let me get Miss Cameron."

He touched her wrist. "I cannot stay. Just give her the message. And hurry."

She nodded. "Thank you."

He ducked outside and hurried away.

Elizabeth bolted the door as the kettle hissed. In her rush, she yanked it from the stovetop, splashing scalding water on her arm. With a yelp, she dropped the pot into the sink and grabbed a damp towel from the rack. Pressing it to her forearm, she dashed out of the kitchen and up the stairs.

"Donaldina!" She pounded on the bedroom door.

A rustling from inside met her ears. The door creaked open, Donaldina's eyes wide. "Elizabeth?"

Elizabeth explained the situation, blinking back stinging tears. The angry blisters rising on her wrist seemed the least of their problems.

Donaldina leaned against the door frame. "Wake Kum Yong, and tell her to meet me downstairs."

"What about me?"

"Elizabeth, I don't have time to arrange a police escort, and you've only been on one rescue. I'm not sure it's wise."

Elizabeth drew herself upward, tucking her injured arm behind her back. "Please—I'd like to accompany you. There's safety in numbers, isn't there?"

Donaldina pressed fingertips against her eyes and sighed. "All right. But you will stay close to us, you understand?"

"I will." A surge of energy ran through Elizabeth. "Let's bring Tien Gum home."

10

*C*harles's chair jerked, waking him from a sound sleep. He jolted upright, swiping a hand across his chin.

Spencer drew back his foot, a cocky grin spreading across his clean-shaven face. "Well, if it isn't the next mayor of San Francisco. You're not drooling on my notes, are you?"

Charles reached for his watch. How long had he been asleep? "I...I stayed late."

"Obviously." The senior attorney snorted. "Don't worry, McKinley, your uncle isn't in yet." Spencer yanked the documents from under Charles's elbow. "Let's see if you found anything useful before drifting off." He pressed the papers against his chest, striding down the row of desks toward his pigeonhole office.

Charles battled the urge to lay his head back on the desk. Ten more minutes rest and the idea of wakefulness might become appealing. He struggled to his feet, instead, and staggered off to the washroom. *I'm going to be chewing gum under Spencer's shoe.*

His reflection announced the verdict. Charles's tie hung loose above a coffee-stained shirt, the imprint of a book engraved into his cheek, ink smudges on his eyebrow. With a groan, Charles splashed icy water on his face, the liquid doing little to cleanse away his morose attitude. He should be grateful Spencer woke him before Uncle Silas arrived.

Charles fastened the celluloid collar and buttoned the vest over the discolored spot. Rolling down his sleeves, he jammed the cufflinks into place and sighed. His mother had picked out the baubles with great care, but they appeared simple and sentimental compared to those of the other attorneys. *Chosen with love.*

Plunging his hands back into the water, he ran damp fingers through his hair, scowling at the crimped crease. He leaned toward the glass and checked his teeth. Nothing amiss. Had he eaten since the midday meal yesterday? *Man cannot function on coffee alone.*

A knock at the door chased off his self-pity. "Charles, that you?" Henry's voice wafted from the other side of the frosted window.

With a final glance at his reflection, Charles pulled the door open.

Henry whistled a low tone, shaking his head slowly. "You look like last week's garbage pail. Spencer is crowing to everyone how you slept at your desk. He thinks it's an insult, but as I figure—it makes you look industrious. I think it'll backfire on him."

Charles slumped against the doorframe. "He's right. I've got nothing to show for it but a smelly shirt and a bad attitude."

"Classic case-file hangover. Too many hours at the desk without sustenance. Here, I brought you some breakfast." He held out a brown paper bag.

"You what? How did you know?" Charles straightened.

"I've seen it before." He lowered his voice. "And just between you and me, I've got my own reasons to want Spencer brought down a peg. Assistant—remember?" The man winked and shook the bag. "I stopped at the bakery down the street. Fresh sweet rolls and a hunk of cheese. That should see you through. Oh, and I keep a clean shirt at my desk. Figure you'll need it more than me, today." His nostrils flared. "You smell like a livery stable."

Charles shook his friend's hand, resisting the urge to fall at his feet in gratitude. "I owe you, Henry. Thank you."

The rotund fellow folded his arms. "Introduce me to the lovely heiress you mentioned yesterday, and we'll call it even."

"She's hardly an heiress, and if she meets you, she'll never look my way again." Not that she had, anyway, but no sense in encouraging Henry's interest.

"A fellow can hope." Henry grinned.

Elizabeth dressed by the faint light drifting in the bedroom window, not wanting to waste time with the lamp. Stiff from the cold, her fingers fumbled as she wrapped a scrap of linen around her blistered forearm. Managing to fasten a few buttons on her wrist, the sleeves concealed her foolishness. The last thing Donaldina needed was one more person to worry over.

Kum Yong stuck her head inside. "Are you ready?"

Elizabeth snatched a coat from the hook. "I am."

The pair hurried down the stairs to where Donaldina waited in the front hall, a picture of calm. She fastened a pin through her hat, her mouth a firm line. "Let's go. I don't intend to miss Tien Gum again."

Elizabeth slipped the jacket over her arms with care. "George said they were moving her to Idaho. Would they really take her so far just to escape you?"

"They'd take her to the moon, if they were able." Donaldina stepped out onto the street.

The women hurried to Chinatown with only a scattering of words spoken between them. Elizabeth's heart raced. What awaited Tien Gum in Idaho—a dirty camp reeking with sweaty miners? She brushed away the thought. No need to borrow trouble, as her father used to say.

The neighborhood buzzed with early morning activity. Shopkeepers propped open doors as they prepared for business while crowds of neatly dressed Chinese men made their way down the street, presumably to service jobs elsewhere in the city.

Donaldina stopped around the corner from their destination, turning to Kum Yong and Elizabeth. "Remember, we are without police support on this. George's information should be accurate, but there's always a chance things can go wrong. If we get separated, return home as fast as you can."

Kum Yong nodded, taking Elizabeth's gloved hand. "We will follow as close as your shadow."

The missionary brushed back a strand of silver hair. "The enemy crouches like a roaring lion. Keep prayers on your lips."

Glancing up and down the sidewalk, Elizabeth fiddled with the lace on her sleeve. What did the bystanders think of this tight bevy of women, talking in the street? She forced her shoulders into a more relaxed position, considering Donaldina's advice. *God, protect us. And Tien Gum.*

Donaldina grasped their elbows. "I am thankful for both of you." A smile softened her grim face. "Let's go." Without another word, she ducked around the corner.

Elizabeth caught her breath and hurried after. Kum Yong followed a few steps behind.

The missionary twisted the doorknob, pounding on the wooden panels.

The door swung open, and a boy with huge eyes waved them inside. "Upstairs. Hurry."

Donaldina paused for only a moment at the unexpected welcome. She shot through the doorway, powering up the stairs, skirts flapping.

Elizabeth's throat tightened as she dashed after her new mentor. Hopefully, Donaldina wasn't hurtling into disaster.

Donaldina halted at the top of the stairs. She turned to a door on the right, gesturing for Elizabeth and Kum Yong to take the room opposite.

Fumbling with the brass knob, Elizabeth pushed through a strange door. What kind of foolishness was this? Anything, or *anyone*, could be inside. She gazed around the shadowy room, filled with narrow cots and pallets. A small window stood open, the curtains flapping in the cold morning air.

She stepped over twisted bedclothes scattered on the floor and poked her head outside, the sight of a rickety fire escape confirming her fears. If Tien Gum's captors climbed down to the street, they could be anywhere by now. The ladder appeared undisturbed. Elizabeth ducked back inside. "Would they go up to the roof?"

Kum Yong paused from checking under cots. Her dark eyes widened, nearly filling her pale face. "Yes."

Elizabeth hoisted the window open further and sat on the sill.

"What are you—Elizabeth, no!" Kum Yong rushed over and gripped Elizabeth's elbow. "We need to get Lo Mo."

"Go." Elizabeth's heart pounded in her ears. She couldn't let them take Tien Gum to Idaho. She couldn't.

"Wait for us."

As her friend dashed from the room, Elizabeth swung both shoes out onto the metal structure. It wouldn't hurt to get in position. Her stomach tensed as she gazed down at the street. Was it really only one story? She grabbed the rickety railing and stood to her feet.

Elizabeth tore off her gloves and jammed them in her pocket, preferring a firm grip on the icy steel. She took a tentative step, followed by another. Miss Cameron could only be a moment behind. A cry from above dissolved her restraint. Elizabeth surged upward, digging her soles against the narrow steps. A trickle of sweat ran down her back.

Pushing up onto the roof edge, she took a moment to steady her nerves. She scanned the rooftop, the flat surface dotted with chimneys and pipes.

Two forms huddled in the far corner. A man jumped to his feet and yelled a string of Cantonese words at her.

"Tien Gum?" Elizabeth's voice sounded far away to her ears.

Donaldina clambered over the roof edge, huffing as she swung her skirts into place.

Tien Gum lunged out from behind him, her loose hair doing little to obscure a bleeding lip and blackened eye. "Lo Mo! I'm here."

The man flung an arm in front of her. "She's staying."

Donaldina gestured to the girl. "She's one of my daughters. You've no right to her."

A twisted smile curved his mouth. "You talk of rights? You're nothing but a thief, posing as a Jesus-woman." He grabbed Tien Gum's arm and twisted it behind her. "You come too close, she goes off the side. We'll see how well she flies."

The bruises on Tien Gum's face tore at Elizabeth's heart. Would the man really kill her?

Donaldina raised her hands, white gloves stained with dirt. "Don't be foolish."

"You go back the same way you came." The man leaned close to Tien Gum's cheek. "See your Fahn Quai? She not save you."

Tien Gum's eyes bulged, her ragged breathing evident from a distance.

God, please. Elizabeth's stomach knotted. The highbinder couldn't be allowed to disappear a second time. "You can't leave."

"You going to stop me?"

"She's wanted by the police. They're waiting downstairs to arrest her. And you, presumably." The falsehood caught in her throat.

His eyes widened. He glanced around, as if gauging escape routes. "You lie."

"Perhaps." Elizabeth settled both hands on her hips so he wouldn't see them tremble. "Go downstairs and you'll learn the truth."

"I tell you, I'll throw her down to the street."

Elizabeth swallowed, trying to relax her voice enough to sound confident. "And add murder to the kidnapping charges? You'll hang."

Tien Gum fell to her knees, as if trying to make herself small.

He yanked her up. "You can't—"

The roof access door rattled, freezing his words. The man shoved Tien Gum, sending her stumbling toward Elizabeth. He spun and darted across the roof. With a wild leap, he cleared the gap to the next building, landing on hands and knees.

Elizabeth wrapped her arms around the sobbing child, tears blurring her own eyes.

Kum Yong pushed through the door, followed by the boy from downstairs.

Donaldina joined Elizabeth, placed a trembling hand on Tien Gum's back, and drew them both close. "Elizabeth King, you are a wonder. I don't know whether to reprimand you or pledge my undying gratitude. Perhaps a little of both."

Elizabeth let her head fall forward against the girl's shoulder. *Thank You, Lord.*

Elizabeth's trembling worsened as she followed the others home along Sacramento Street. All this, and she still had a class to teach. She gazed at Tien Gum's back, the young woman's arm looped through Kum Yong's. *It was worth it.*

"I can't wait for breakfast." Donaldina sighed as they climbed the hill to the Mission. "We've earned it today, I think."

Kum Yong slowed her pace. "There's an auto out front, Lo Mo."

"Oh, dear. I hope it isn't the police. I'd like to have a few minutes to get everyone settled before I deal with the authorities."

"Would they take her away, again?" Elizabeth came up beside the missionary. "Hasn't she been through enough?"

Tien Gum pressed into Kum Yong's side. "I want to stay."

Donaldina took her other arm. "I know, dear one. We may need to call that attorney fellow again."

A fresh quiver gripped Elizabeth. Why was her life suddenly entwined with Charles McKinley's?

Spotting the familiar red Ford, Elizabeth's heart jumped. "That's Gerald's car."

As they approached the building, her brother stepped out of the portico.

"Robert!" Elizabeth gasped, lunging forward to greet him. "I'm so glad to see you."

His arms pulled her in for a quick squeeze. "I was alarmed when they informed me you weren't here."

She drew back. "We had a little business to take care of."

"Yes, I heard." His eyes darkened as he tipped his hat to the women following Elizabeth. "Miss Cameron...Kum Yong." He hesitated, his voice dropping to a lower timbre than normal.

Elizabeth leaned against her brother's side, wrapping an arm around his waist. The iron-rod back seemed so unlike him. "Why are you here? I told Abby I'd come for dinner next weekend."

With the sun silhouetting him, it was difficult to tell where his brown hair ended and his chocolate brown derby began. "Abby has been feeling..." His voice softened. "She's been a little blue. I brought her over to visit Ruby and Gerald. Ruby's hoping you'll join them."

Elizabeth drew away, the uncertainty in his tone pricking her heart. "What's wrong? Is she unwell?"

"She's fine. I think she'd rather tell you herself, though. Can you come?"

She pressed a hand against her forehead. "I have a class to teach this afternoon."

"Elizabeth, I'm worried about you. I wish you'd spoken with me before committing yourself here." He settled his fingers on her wrist and squeezed.

A jolt of pain shot up Elizabeth's scalded arm. She inhaled, sharply.

"What's wrong?" Robert released his grip like he'd touched a live wire.

She cradled her wrist. "Nothing. I spilled some hot water."

Donaldina stepped close, her lips pulling downward. "Why didn't you say anything?"

"It's not serious."

Robert's brows scrunched. "Let me see."

Elizabeth sighed. She unbuttoned the sleeve, drawing it up to her elbow. The handkerchief slipped loose, revealing angry red blisters on her inner arm.

The sight drew a unanimous murmur of dismay from her friends.

Robert took her hand and lifted her wrist for better inspection. "It must have hurt like the dickens." He glanced at Donaldina, his head cocked. "You let her go out like this?"

"Robert!" Elizabeth frowned. "I didn't tell anyone."

He tugged her a few steps away. "Ruby said you were teaching, yet I find you traipsing about Chinatown." He lowered his voice, his gaze raking across Tien Gum and Kum Yong. "What were you doing there?"

Elizabeth yanked her wrist free. "We can discuss it later. Now, I have a class to prepare. I'm sorry about Abby. Please give her my regrets."

Donaldina cleared her throat. "Elizabeth, go with your brother. He can see to your burn, and you can spend time with your family. I'll reschedule your class. The girls won't mind."

Elizabeth's stomach dropped. Missing her second day of class? "If you think it best."

"I do. We'll get Tien Gum cleaned up and decide what happens next." Donaldina smiled. "When you return, we will have a conversation about your actions this morning."

Oh, yes. My actions. Elizabeth blew a slow exhale between her lips. Not only was Robert cross with her, she'd disobeyed Donaldina, too. Perhaps a day with Abby and Ruby would be preferable.

Robert offered an arm to Elizabeth as the women went inside. "Do you need anything before we go?"

Elizabeth held her breath until the door closed behind her friends. A lump formed in her throat. "How dare you embarrass me, Robert. I'm not a child to be coddled."

He rubbed his brow. "You are my sister. I have a responsibility to keep you safe, and I know what kind of work they do here. Chinatown is nothing but opium dens and brothels."

Elizabeth folded her arms across her midsection, ignoring her tender wrist. "I attended one rescue and returned to discover my overprotective brother on the front steps." She spun on her heel and headed for the automobile. "I make my own decisions. You know that."

"Unfortunately, I do." Robert reached for the door handle.

A few deep breaths helped chase away her irritation as she took a seat in the automobile. "Now, what's going on with Abby? You must give me a hint."

He waited to answer until he'd cranked the engine and climbed behind the wheel. "We've been married for almost eighteen months."

"Being married to you is such torture?"

Robert rolled his eyes. "We've been praying for a baby."

Elizabeth's spirits spiraled upward. "A baby?" Several of their older siblings already had large families of their own. But her brother? He always seemed so busy with his hospital work. "Why would that make her sad?"

The circles deepened beneath his brown eyes. "It's not happening."

Charles straightened his tie and combed fingers through his hair. With a cup of coffee in his system and the fresh shirt on his back, no one would realize he'd slept at his desk. Now he just needed to prove himself in court and win Spencer's respect. He'd settle for the former.

Across the room, the dark-haired attorney shrugged on his black coat, the silk lapels catching the light.

Charles snatched up his briefcase and hurried over. "Is it time to leave for court?"

Spencer adjusted his vest and checked his timepiece. "Yes, I'll be going in a moment. Why do you ask?"

A stone sank in Charles's gut. "I thought—I assumed I'd accompany you. Isn't that why I took notes all night?"

Spencer cocked a brow. "Is that what you call it? Looked more like you were sleeping at your desk." He patted his pocket. "I've got your summary right here, for what it's worth. I've no need of a wet-behind-the-ears law student getting in the way. I'm not your nursemaid."

Charles cleared his throat, determined to keep his temper in check. "Uncle Silas said you'd be training me." His words sounded whiny, even to his own ears.

Spencer sniffed. "Mr. McKinley said you'd answer to me. Not the other way around." He jammed a black derby on his head. "He's not *Uncle Silas*, here. You'd do well to remember that."

"Then…" Charles hid his fist behind his back, stripping the frustration from his voice. "*Sir*, how can I serve you while you are away?"

"I have another trial tomorrow. The files are in the top drawer. Let's see what you can find. It shouldn't take you all night." A smile played at his mouth. "Maybe just half of it."

Charles sank into his chair as Spencer sauntered out.

Henry walked by, balancing a stack of books. "He's sure got it in for you."

Charles lowered his chin onto his knuckles, elbows propped on the desktop. "I knew I'd have to pay my dues, but I'd hoped to see some court time, too." He blinked gritty eyes. "I'd better get to it, I suppose."

"Charles?" His uncle's voice bellowed from the back offices.

The clerk jumped, juggling the tomes to keep them from dropping to the floor.

Charles twisted in his chair, a sudden chill racing down his back. What had he done now? Jumping from his seat, he hurried to his uncle's doorway.

Uncle Silas clutched the telephone's cone-shaped receiver to his chest. "I was just informed by a rather impertinent caller that she was not ringing for me, but for a Mr. *Charles* McKinley."

"I'm sorry, sir. Would you like me to—"

"Highly irregular." The older man huffed, his face reddening. He jutted the object toward his nephew. "Here, take it."

Charles clutched the receiver, hand trembling. He pressed the device to his ear, leaning over to speak into the mouthpiece. "Um, yes. This is Charles McKinley. May I help you?"

"Oh, thank goodness." A woman's voice sputtered on the line. "This is Donaldina Cameron. You said to telephone if we needed any assistance."

Charles darted a glance up at his uncle, simmering like an over-heated stewpot. "Yes, Miss Cameron. How may I be of assistance?"

"We located Tien Gum and brought her home. No one knows, yet. I abhor the idea of returning her to police custody."

Charles swallowed, turning aside to avoid his uncle's glare. "In the eyes of the court, she's a convicted criminal." He squeezed the bridge of his nose between his thumb and finger. "You cannot harbor a fugitive."

"Couldn't you intervene with the judge? Convince him to grant me temporary custody until the appeal?"

"I'll…" A film of sweat dampened his palm. He adjusted the receiver. His uncle had made it clear he was to have nothing to do with the Mission. "I could make a few telephone calls." He retrieved his watch and flipped open the lid. "Perhaps I can come by later this evening, and we can go over some possibilities."

"Thank you, Charles. God sent you to us for just a time as this. I'm certain of it."

A lump settled in the back of his throat as he returned the receiver to the stand.

Uncle Silas's chair squeaked. "Harboring a fugitive?"

Charles raked a hand through his hair. "Just a mix-up. I'll sort it out."

"I told you not to get mixed up with that woman."

Technically he said not to get mixed up with Elizabeth, but Charles wasn't about to correct him.

"You're not to drag our firm into any shady dealings." Uncle Silas's brow wrinkled.

"Of course not, sir, but I offered assistance. It would reflect poorly on you if I reneged on my word, don't you agree?"

"Hmm. I suppose. But after today, I want you to tell her to look elsewhere." Uncle Silas ran a hand over his silver mustache. "And tell the switchboard clerk not to send me any more calls meant for you."

Charles backed through the door. "Yes, sir. Thank you, sir." He fought the urge to genuflect on his way out.

Perhaps he could use Spencer's office to telephone Judge Reinhardt. The senior attorney was likely to be out all day.

Or at least Charles could hope.

11

Elizabeth brushed the raindrops off her sleeves as she stepped into the front hall of Ruby and Gerald's home. The scent of molasses wafted through the air, like a hint of Christmas come early. "Mmm. Has Ruby been baking?"

Robert helped her slip the coat off her shoulders. "More likely it's the other Mrs. Larkspur—Gerald's mother. I don't think Ruby has to lift a finger in the kitchen."

"Nor would I desire to." Ruby's voice rang out as she hurried toward them from the dining room, arms outstretched. "Elizabeth, I'm so glad you came."

Elizabeth stepped into her sister's embrace, warmth rushing into her chest. "You can thank Robert. I should be teaching today, but he intervened."

Ruby tucked a ginger curl behind her ear, glancing over Elizabeth's shoulder to where their brother stood. "Robert's always been persuasive. He should have been an attorney."

"Please, no." Elizabeth shuddered. "I've had my fill of attorneys lately."

Robert frowned. "What do you mean?"

Elizabeth sighed. "Remember Mr. McKinley? He had the audacity to send his young nephew to meet with Mother regarding our father's estate. Oddly enough, the man also volunteers with the Mission—offering legal assistance. It just seems like every time I turn around, he's near."

Ruby's lip curled. "Old moray eel McKinley? I'd be afraid to set eyes on a relative of his."

"Charles is actually quite attractive." The words rolled off Elizabeth's tongue before she could retrieve them. She swallowed and dropped her gaze to the floor. "Nothing like his uncle."

A lilting tone appeared in her sister's voice. "Oh?"

Robert hung up his hat. "I've left messages with McKinley's office offering to meet him there. I don't know why he felt it necessary to bother Mother all the way in Sacramento."

"Charles McKinley said he was taking over the estate case." Elizabeth glanced down as Ruby's little dog scampered into the room, nails scrabbling over the wood floor. "Otto!" She bent down to scratch the dachshund's ears, a welcome distraction. "Look how gray you've become."

"Yes, Otto's looking quite distinguished." Ruby lifted the dog into her arms.

Her husband's voice carried in from the hall. "And he does nothing but sleep. And bark at guests." Elizabeth's brother-in-law joined them in the front hall, coming up behind Ruby and placing a kiss on her cheek. He aimed a glare at Otto, as if challenging the canine for possession. "Can I invite everyone into the living room, or do you intend to remain here by the door?"

Elizabeth smiled, the warmth of family sweeping over her like a wool coat. "I'm so glad to be here." She folded her arms to prevent herself from throwing them around everyone at once. "I miss this."

Her brother cocked an eyebrow. "You've been in town less than a week. Are you homesick already?"

"Not homesick, exactly." She thought back to Mother and the big empty house in Sacramento. "But, I don't quite know where I fit, yet. Everything's so new."

Ruby slipped an arm around Elizabeth's waist. "Gerald's right, let's go in. It's chilly here by the door." She flicked her fingers at the men. "I know you two were heading in to the hospital. This is a girls' afternoon. Remember?" She lowered Otto to the floor and steered Elizabeth toward the kitchen. "Let's go join Abby and Mae. We'll see Robert and Gerald at supper."

Gerald chuckled, reaching for his hat. "I believe we've been dismissed."

"Looks that way." Robert shook his head. "Elizabeth, don't forget to have Ruby dress that burn for you."

The good smells intensified as Elizabeth stepped into the kitchen, the warmth from the stove a welcome sensation after the chilly raindrops.

Abby placed a pan into the stove and straightened, wiping her hands on her white apron. "Elizabeth, it's such a joy to have you here." A soft smile brightened her freckled face. "Come sit at the table so we can catch up on all your news."

Mae Larkspur, Gerald's mother, draped a white towel over a pan of rolls rising on the counter. "Welcome, Elizabeth." The elderly woman placed a hand against her lower back and stretched. "I know you girls wish to chat. I'm quite weary after our morning's work. I think I'll go upstairs and lie down."

Abby turned to her. "Aunt Mae, you don't need to leave."

"I'll visit with Elizabeth at supper." She glanced at Elizabeth. "I hope you don't think me rude."

"Certainly not." Elizabeth laid her hands on the back of one of the wooden chairs. "Thank you for having me in your home, Mrs. Larkspur."

Mae smiled. "Oh, nonsense. It's Gerald and Ruby's home. I'm grateful to be included, though. Like many, my home was lost in the disaster. But I'm content here—close to my children."

Elizabeth's heart skipped as the woman's tender gaze turned to Ruby. How precious that Mrs. Larkspur thought of Ruby in those terms. Since their father died and all of Elizabeth's siblings had moved out, her family had felt fractured—just Mother and her.

Ruby gestured for Elizabeth to take a seat. "Mae, can I get you anything before you go up? Are you feeling poorly?"

The woman adjusted her gold-rimmed spectacles. "No, child. I'm only tired. The body slows down, you know. I'll be fine after a few winks." Gripping the handrail, she climbed each step with effort.

Abby took a plate of cookies from the counter and set them in the center of the large table next to a pot of tea. With a sigh, she sank into a seat. "I've never baked so many cookies. I'm not sure what's gotten into my great-aunt, lately. She's wanted to do nothing but bake for weeks."

Ruby leaned against one of the tall chairs. "I think she's trying to fatten us up for winter."

A giggle rose in Elizabeth's chest. "Makes you sound like a couple of farm pigs—getting ready for the holiday meal."

"More like broody hens." Abby reached for the teapot and poured the steaming hot liquid into several cups, passing them around. "Except with no chicks to be hatched."

Ruby retrieved a pitcher of cream from the icebox, her silence telling.

Elizabeth's throat tightened. "You and Robert haven't been married that long. You can't expect anything to happen overnight."

Abby's eyes glistened with unshed tears. "It's hardly overnight. Elizabeth, we're going on two years. Every month I hope and I wait—but nothing." She pressed the heel of her hand against her eyes. "I'm being foolish. You've only just arrived, and I'm behaving like a ninny."

"Don't be ridiculous." Elizabeth scooted closer. "That's what sisters are for—right, Ruby?"

Abby's chin trembled. She jumped from her seat and hurried from the room.

Elizabeth's heart jumped. "What—what did I say?"

Ruby pulled out her chair and dropped into it. "Her sister died three years ago—today would have been her birthday."

A flood of remorse cascaded over Elizabeth. "Why didn't Robert tell me?"

"I'm not sure he realizes. Abby tends to be quiet about things like this, even with him. I only know because Mae mentioned it to me this morning."

Elizabeth propped her chin on her hand and studied Ruby's heart-shaped face. "So, she's not sad about babies?"

Her sister's pale eyes locked on her teacup. "Babies, families, life. We have a tendency to plan out our future. We have expectations and dreams for how things will go. But God doesn't always inform us when our plans conflict with His will." Her gaze flickered up to meet Elizabeth's. "He knows best, but it can be a bitter pill to swallow."

Who would understand better than Ruby? A shiver coursed through her. Ruby's first husband had been like a big brother to Elizabeth. "Is there more I should know?" She glanced toward the stairs. "Your mother-in-law?" A thought froze her heart. "Gerald?"

Ruby's gaze flickered. She reached for her tea, the cup rattling against the saucer. "Mae is fine. Gerald? It's day to day, week to week. We knew the risks when we wed. God's been good to us. We've had more time than I anticipated." She brought the cup to her lips, but didn't drink. "So far, there's been no sign of the cancer returning, but his heart was badly damaged by the diphtheria. He has to be careful."

How could her sister be so nonchalant about life and death? Elizabeth wrapped her fingers around the warm drink, willing the heat to penetrate her chilled skin. "I'm surprised you can speak of God's plans after all you've endured." Her voice dropped low, rattling in her chest. The image of Tobias sprang to her mind as though summoned. With him, she'd thought nothing of God's plans, only her own.

Ruby finally took a sip and lowered the tea back to the table. "It's *because* of what I've endured, Elizabeth. I gave up my own will long ago."

Leaning forward, Elizabeth braced herself against the table. "And what about babies for you? Have you given up on those dreams, too?"

A rueful smile graced her sister's face. "Gerald has been too ill. After the diphtheria, the cancer, the surgery..." She shook her head. "Robert thinks the X-ray research may have played a part as well—for them both. In all honesty, I'm just thankful Gerald's alive. To ask for more seems ungrateful."

Abby reappeared in the doorway. "You don't believe that, do you, Ruby? Ungrateful?"

Elizabeth jerked up, turning to face her sister-in-law.

Ruby blew out a long breath. "I only mean, I choose to focus on what God has given me, rather than what He hasn't."

"Or what He's taken away." Abby brushed away a tear. "I suppose you're wise to think in those terms. But doesn't the Bible say something about God being able to do more? 'Abundantly—above all that we ask or think.'"

Elizabeth ran a hand down her sleeve, smoothing it over her sore wrist. "I'm sorry for what I said earlier, Abby. I didn't mean to upset you."

The young woman returned to her seat. "It wasn't you, Elizabeth. I haven't been myself today." She folded her apron in her lap. "It's incomprehensible to me that God wouldn't want Robert and me to have a child. Or Ruby and Gerald, for that matter." She raised her chin. "And I choose to pray boldly. To approach God's throne of grace with confidence, if you will."

Ruby lifted her gaze. "And if He says no?"

"He's denied me before. I'll accept it... in time." The corner of Abby's mouth lifted, a dimple deepening in her cheek. "But not yet." She turned to Elizabeth. "Will you pray, too?"

Elizabeth's palms dampened, and she pressed them against her skirt. She'd been asked to pray twice in one day. Would He even hear a petition from one such as herself? "Of course. I'll try."

"Thank you." Abby folded her hands and laid them on the tablecloth. "And I'm blessed to have such wonderful sisters-in-law. Cecelia would be pleased. Thank you for reminding me how fortunate I am."

"You're a King girl now." Elizabeth laughed, retrieving a cookie from the plate. "We won't let you forget."

Charles ran a finger under his stiff collar, using the opposite hand to press Spencer's telephone receiver against his ear. His knee bounced under the desk, his heel pounding out a jittery rhythm on the floor. Any moment, the surly attorney could walk through the door. Unfortunately, it was either this office or the main clerk's desk, and this was one conversation he didn't want overheard.

A familiar voice sounded in his ear. "Presbyterian Mission, Miss Cameron speaking."

His shoulder muscles loosened a hair. "Miss Cameron, it's Charles McKinley. I've spoken with the judge, and under the circumstances, he's willing to grant you temporary custody until the appeal can be heard."

"Bless you, Mr. McKinley. You're an answer to prayer. Will you be filing the appeal directly?"

"I do have some bad news on that front. I'm afraid I won't be able to represent you, after all."

The line went silent for a long moment. Charles shifted in his seat. "I apologize, but I misjudged my work requirements at the firm. I won't have the time necessary to adequately advise you."

"I understand." Miss Cameron's voice softened until Charles had to press the receiver hard against his ear to make out the words. "I'm disappointed, of course. I thought you had a good understanding of the challenges we face."

A hole opened in Charles's chest. "Perhaps in the future—after I've advanced in my career—I can be of more assistance." How many times would he be forced to choose between his heart and his career? After finishing the conversation, Charles laid down the receiver and flopped back in Spencer's chair. Not only did this opportunity slip away, so did any hope of spending more time with Elizabeth King.

Gazing out at the busy office, he shook his head. Whom could he recommend to take his place at the Mission? The junior attorneys were too busy scrabbling their way up the mountain, and the senior attorneys too arrogant to commit to unpaid hours. Who bothered to defend Chinese prostitutes? *Only fools like me.*

"Charles?" His uncle's faraway voice carried into the office.

Charles leapt to his feet, desperate not to be found in Spencer's space. He stepped through the door in time to intercept his uncle.

"There you are." Uncle Silas shrugged on his suit jacket. "I'm going out. I need you to run an errand."

Spencer's lackey *and* Uncle Silas's errand boy? This was sizing up to be a red-letter day. "What can I do for you, sir?" Charles followed his uncle back into the office as the man retrieved a stack of papers from his desk and shoved them into a folder.

"Take these—they're in regards to the King family. I received another call from the oldest son. Deliver the documents to his home, and answer any questions he might have. Perhaps if we throw the dog a bone, he'll leave me alone for a few weeks." Uncle Silas wiped a silk handkerchief across his nose before jamming it into his coat pocket. "The address is inside."

"Yes, sir." A surge of energy pulsed through Charles's system. "Are there new developments on the case?"

His uncle snorted. "There is no case. The man invested in property. The property's gone. Case closed."

Charles clutched the file to his chest. "But Mr. Spencer brokered a deal yesterday with the insurance adjustors. Surely there is some relief money for the families."

Uncle Silas's brows drew down into a pinched line. "Families? We're not about families, here, Charles. That money is earmarked for our big accounts. The Kings are nobodies. We wouldn't even be handing their finances if William King hadn't been a personal friend."

"If he were a personal friend, I'd think his kin might be the first to benefit, instead of waiting for scraps leftover by the heavy purses of Market Street."

Uncle Silas's eyes narrowed. He lifted a knobby finger. "You're overstepping. Don't question me again or you'll find yourself back wrestling hay bales."

Charles shut his mouth, his fingers tightening on the manila folder. He tried to muster an apology, but his jaw refused to unclench. He only managed a curt nod as his uncle strode out of the office. Leaning against the door frame, Charles closed his eyes for a moment. *What was I thinking coming here? I'll never help anyone.*

&

Elizabeth took the rose between her fingers and bent to sniff the petals, leftover droplets of rainwater dampening her gloves. "Mmm. What do you call this one?"

"Morning Tea." Abby took a pair of shears from her apron pocket and clipped a few spent blossoms. "One of my favorites."

"I can see why. It's lovely."

"My parents have a massive bush climbing up an arbor by the barn. My baby brother loves to play under it." Abby gazed out over the flowered shrubs, as if she could see the flowers in her memory.

"Where do they live?"

"On a fruit orchard near San Jose. They raise peaches and pears, mostly. Some cherries and apples, too." She dropped the blooms into a canvas bag at her feet.

"It sounds like you miss them."

Abby's lips curled into a wry smile. "Does it show? I know Robert's work is here, in San Francisco, but I miss my family. And my trees."

"They must need doctors in San Jose, also."

"Not in research. He's overseeing the X-ray project since Gerald accepted the teaching position at Cooper Medical College."

Elizabeth's hands stilled. "I thought they'd given up the research. Weren't they suspicious the X-rays caused Gerald's..." She paused, her throat closing.

Abby cut some fresh flowers, laying them on a piece of newspaper. "You can say the word—cancer. And yes, they believe so. But Robert is putting in safeguards so no one else will suffer the same fate."

"And he worries for my safety." Elizabeth shook off the dark cloud growing in her mind. "Have you been back to see your family?"

"Not in a while."

Elizabeth strolled along the row, admiring each rose in turn. "Perhaps you should. Maybe it would take your mind off...other things."

"We're busy getting settled in our new house. It might be difficult to get away just now." She brightened. "You should come visit. It's out in the Sunset District, near the ocean."

Elizabeth smiled. "Sounds lovely. Maybe on my next day off."

Ruby came down the steps to join them, the sunlight catching her red hair. "I checked on Mae. She's not sleeping, she's knitting. I think she just wanted to give us some time to visit."

Abby smiled. "We're cutting some roses for the table. I hope you don't mind."

"Why on earth would I mind?" Ruby lifted her hands. "You work on them more than I do. Every time I try my hand at gardening, something dies. People are so much more sensible than plants. I'll stay with nursing, thank you."

Abby tucked another bloom into the bouquet. "And sewing. Don't forget that."

Elizabeth brightened. "I was going to speak to you about that, Ruby. I thought you might like to come to the Mission and help some of the girls with their projects. You're far more talented than me when it comes to dressmaking. They've got some grand ideas of things they want to construct, but some of it might be a bit much for beginners."

"I'd love to. I'm not at the hospital as much these days, since Gerald's been lecturing." Ruby folded her hands in front of her skirt. "And Mae does so much in the kitchen—it leaves me with few responsibilities, really. I prefer being busy."

Abby gathered up the basket. "Perhaps I can come, too. I'm not a seamstress, but I'd love to visit with Kum Yong. It's so nice having them back in the city."

Elizabeth clapped her hands together. "Wonderful! Let me check with Donaldina, and we'll set a date."

Ruby took Elizabeth's arm. "Having you in the city is going to be delightful, little sister. Let's plan lots of outings together for the three of us. Robert and Gerald spend so much time together, I think we need to form our own girl's club. What do you think?"

Abby smiled. "I love it. Where shall we go first? Golden Gate Park?"

"How about Chinatown?" Elizabeth plucked one of the blooms from Abby's basket and twirled it between her fingers. "I went there with Kum Yong and Donaldina this morning. Some of the shops had beautiful displays—silk, jade, fans. We could decorate your new home."

Abby rubbed the back of her neck. "Perhaps. I've only been to Chinatown once or twice." She exchanged a glance with Ruby. "Robert's probably made his concerns clear to you."

Butterfly wings tickled in Elizabeth's stomach. "And how do you feel about it?"

Her sister-in-law frowned. "Kum Yong is a dear friend. We met during the disaster, and she and Donaldina offered me shelter the first night. I would have slept on the street otherwise."

"What's Robert's problem with the Chinese, anyway?"

She lowered her eyes. "I think you should ask him."

An icy tendril coiled around Elizabeth's heart. Her brother wouldn't have gotten involved in any of Chinatown's vices, would he? And yet, she'd never have expected herself to fall so easily into sin. Just because she'd idolized her brother, it didn't make him immune to life's temptations.

Ruby's pale eyes gleamed. "I know. We can visit the Sutro Baths. Indoor swimming pools, can you imagine?"

"We should bring Robert and Gerald for that." Abby cocked a brow. "Your brother told me he doesn't know how to swim, so I've been threatening to take him to the farm and throw him in the pond."

"That I'd like to see." Elizabeth stifled a giggle.

Ruby placed an arm around Elizabeth's shoulders. "If we invite the men, we'll need to bring someone along to keep Elizabeth company. Who was this handsome attorney you spoke of with such affection?"

Elizabeth pushed her sister's arm away. "Don't get any silly ideas." The last thing she needed was to be seen in a bathing costume by a man like Charles McKinley.

12

*C*harles rang the bell a second time. He could hear a dog barking inside, but no one came to answer the door. The sound of women's laughter carried out the slim gap between the tall Victorian homes. Could they be in the yard?

He glanced down at the file folders. He'd rather not schedule a return visit, considering it might infringe on his ability to observe in court. Clutching the briefcase to his chest, he poked his head around the corner, between the houses. "Hello? Can you hear me back there?"

More laughter. And one of the voices sounded like Elizabeth's.

Charles set his jaw and strode down the narrow path. Growing up in ranch country, the idea of having a neighbor less than a few feet away gave him claustrophobia. Hopefully, the Kings didn't have another dog, or he might risk receiving a hole in the seat of his new pants. He called out again, preferring not to startle the family.

The voices went silent as he approached the rear yard.

A woman's face peered around the corner. Her red hair curled under a flowered hat. "Can I assist you?"

"I—I rang the bell." Charles paused, the walls suddenly feeling even closer. "Excuse me, I don't mean to interrupt, but I'm here to see Dr. Robert King."

Her head tilted. "Is it a medical emergency?"

He stopped in his tracks. "No. I'm an attorney. We have business to discuss. Are you Mrs. King?"

One corner of the woman's mouth lifted. "No, I'm Mrs. Larkspur, his sister." She opened the low gate. "Come on through. We're in the garden."

Charles exhaled the breath he'd been holding. He followed her out into a bright oasis of flowers. "This is beautiful."

"Thank you." Mrs. Larkspur gestured to another woman approaching from the center of the rose garden. "My sister-in-law, Mrs. Abby King, is mostly responsible."

Charles nodded to the women. "It's an honor meeting you both. My name is—"

"Let me guess—" A smile spread across Mrs. Larkspur's face. "Mr. Charles McKinley?" She dragged out his first name with a lilt to her voice.

"Um, yes, in fact."

Elizabeth popped out from an arbor in the corner of the yard. "Charles?" She hurried over. "Whatever are you doing here? Is there a problem at the Mission?"

"I—uh—no. I'm here to see your brother."

Elizabeth stopped in front of him, her brow furrowing. "But this isn't Robert's house."

Charles's skin crawled. Elizabeth must think he was following her. "This is the address we have on file."

Mrs. Larkspur laughed. "Robert and Abby lived here until just a few weeks ago." She turned to face Charles. "I'm afraid Robert's at the hospital. Obviously, he wasn't expecting you. I'm sure he wouldn't have forgotten."

"My apologies. I should have telephoned first."

"Nonsense." Mrs. Larkspur took a basket of flowers from Mrs. King. "Come join us. Charles, was it?"

"Yes. No. I mean, yes, it's Charles. No, I don't wish to interrupt you." Charles's collar suddenly felt two sizes too tight. He glanced at Elizabeth, the dimple in her left cheek scattering his thoughts like so many leaves in the wind.

Dr. King's wife lifted her brows, brown eyes sparkling in the sunshine. "Elizabeth was telling us about you earlier. I'm sure my husband will be pleased to hear someone's taken an interest in his father's estate." She pulled off her gardening gloves. "He and Gerald should be returning soon. Why don't you and Elizabeth visit out here in the arbor while you wait?" She gestured to an iron bench half hidden by curling grape vines. "Ruby and I should get supper started."

Elizabeth frowned. "I intended to help you."

Mrs. Larkspur linked arms with Mrs. King. "Stay and keep our guest company. I'm sure Robert won't want to miss him."

Charles pulled the case close to his chest. Spend time in a lovely garden with an equally lovely partner or return to the office? The choice seemed simple. "If Miss King doesn't mind keeping me company, I would be delighted to stay."

&

Elizabeth gritted her teeth as she led the way to the bench in Ruby's back yard. *I make one comment about a man to my sister, and the next thing you know I'm entertaining him in a romantic setting.*

"I had no idea you would be here." Charles's voice trailed behind her as she entered the grape arbor. "I thought you would be teaching today."

"Trying to leave me out of the meeting?" She dropped into the seat, the iron bench cold against her backside.

"Of course not. I didn't mean—"

"I'm only teasing." She interrupted him, amused by the blush creeping across his face. "I encouraged you to meet with Robert, remember?"

He sat with a sigh. "Yes. It's not a conversation I'll soon forget."

Elizabeth tugged her sleeve down to hide the bandage Ruby had placed on her arm. "I was too harsh. I'm sorry. It's no excuse, but I wasn't myself that day."

"I understood. The news must have been difficult to accept."

"I had also endured a crushing blow on a personal front, and you provided a convenient target. I apologize."

"I'm sorry if I added to the disappointment." He leaned forward, his brown eyes entreating. "Since Uncle Silas has made me responsible for the case, I hope I can turn things around for your family."

His earnest gaze warmed Elizabeth's heart. She took the moment to study him. The afternoon sun shone through the grapevines, sending dappled shadows across his broad shoulders. "Forgive me for saying so, but you don't much look like an attorney."

Charles straightened, running a hand down his vest front. "My uncle would be crushed to hear it. He constantly reminds me an attorney is only as respectable as he appears. He picked out the suit himself." He frowned, gazing down at the jacket. "Or he had someone do it for him."

"It's not the suit." Elizabeth scooted back for a better look—and to give herself some much needed space. "I guess you just don't match my expectations."

"What did you expect?"

"A decrepit old man, shoulders curved from spending too much time huddled over books."

Charles chuckled. "I wonder where you acquired such an image?"

She ducked her head. "I apologize. I shouldn't judge people so quickly."

He laid his arm across the back of the bench, his hand dangerously close to her shoulder. "We all do, I imagine. I know I don't fit the mold. My folks were taken aback when I chose the profession."

"What did they think you should do?"

"I grew up working on my father's cattle ranch, near Redding. I'm probably more comfortable on a horse than in a courtroom."

Elizabeth laughed, a fluttery sensation rising in her stomach. The man surprised her at every turn. "Then why did you choose the law? I can't imagine anything more contradictory."

A cloud passed in front of his eyes, and he glanced away. "It's a long story."

More mystery? He knew how to intrigue a girl. "I'm sorry. I didn't mean to pry."

"My older sister was hurt by someone she trusted." His gaze faltered. He rose from the bench and took several steps away, turning his back. "The courts failed her."

Elizabeth wrapped her hands around her knees, the man's honesty peeling back another layer of resistance. "I'd think such an experience would drive you away from the legal profession, not toward it."

"I thought I could prevent it happening to another. I'd never be able to do that as a rancher." Charles pulled off his derby and ran a hand through his brown hair. "Unfortunately, law school taught me it's not so simple. The laws themselves need to be changed, but to be honest, most politicians don't care much about these types of issues."

"That is why women need the vote." Elizabeth raised her chin. "How else can we work toward protecting women and children?"

Flashing a grin, Charles replaced his hat and sat down beside her. "I believe you're right, and with my uncle's assistance, I might be in a position to make a real difference in a few years. He wants to help me break into local politics."

Elizabeth's heart lifted. "That's wonderful." She might need to revise her opinion of Silas McKinley—putting the needs of his nephew above his own ambitions.

Charles rubbed his square jaw. "The only problem is, I'm fairly beholden to him. His good opinion of me is critical if I'm to succeed."

She brushed fingers against his arm. "Obviously he has a good opinion of you, or he wouldn't be grooming you for success." Elizabeth swallowed. She drew her hand away as memories of Tobias darkened her thoughts.

He lowered his gaze. "And that's why I had to tell Miss Cameron I was wrong to offer my support to the Mission."

Elizabeth's blood chilled. "Wrong? How could it be wrong?"

"I need to focus my efforts on the cases at McKinley and McClintock." Charles folded his hands.

"But Donaldina needs you. You saw what happened to Tien Gum—someone needs to speak for the girls." She clenched her fists, crushing the fabric of her skirt. "You just said you wanted to help women and children."

"And I do. But I won't be able to if I'm drawn into scandal."

Her throat tightened. "Scandal? You'd be a hero."

He shook his head. "Most people wouldn't see it that way. Defending Chinese prostitutes? You must see how the press could misconstrue my intentions."

Elizabeth pushed to her feet, heat rushing to her face. "In other words, I was right about you all along." Her throat squeezed until she could barely force the words through her windpipe. "You might look like a handsome cowboy, but you've the twisted heart of an attorney."

"No, Elizabeth..." He stood and caught both of her hands. "I have to think of my future. Of where could I do the most good."

She yanked them away, jerking back a few steps to put a cushion of space between her and the two-faced man. "Go ahead—sacrifice the Chinese girls. Who cares about them, anyway? What really matters is to see yourself in a plush office with so-called *clean* hands." Elizabeth choked back a surge of emotions. Were all men so self-absorbed? "Don't do this, Charles. If you turn your back, you'll be no better than your uncle and all the other hypocrites and shysters who created the problem in the first place."

He stood silent, mouth open, fingers clutching his vest front.

The sound of the back door slamming broke Elizabeth from her frozen stupor. She spun and headed for the house, eager to put the man as far behind her as she could. Perhaps it was good Ruby had forced them together, if only to prove their incompatibility.

Charles emerged from the arbor, his brow crumpled. "Elizabeth, wait."

Robert stood on the back steps, a puzzled frown on his face. "There you are, Elizabeth. Abby said she'd like you to invite Mr. McKinley to supper."

She brushed past her brother, surging up the steps. "Never."

&

Charles stopped at the edge of the lawn, his chest aching as Elizabeth marched into the house.

The man who'd spoken to her a moment before turned and shot Charles a quizzical look. "Dare I ask what you said to my sister?"

Charles's stomach plummeted. Her brother. Of course. "A simple misunderstanding."

The fellow huffed. "I'm sure." He strode down the steps and extended a hand toward Charles. "I'm Robert King. I assume you're Mr. McKinley?"

"Yes. It's a pleasure to meet you." Charles returned the doctor's handshake.

Dr. King folded his arms. "I've been trying to meet with Silas McKinley for months. My wife tells me you're his nephew?"

"Yes, sir." Charles swallowed, forcing himself back into a business state of mind. Elizabeth's accusations hung like prison chains about his neck. Was he just like his uncle? "I've taken over the case. I hope I'll meet with your approval."

"We'll see." He glanced back to the door. "It doesn't look like you've gained Elizabeth's. Were you speaking of our father's case?"

"No. It was a more personal matter."

The doctor's brows pulled low over his dark eyes. "Personal business—with my sister?"

A cold sweat washed over Charles. Would every meeting with a King family member begin badly? He glanced at the back door. *And end badly?* "Regarding the Chinese Mission. I'd been advising Miss King's employer on some legal matters—that's all."

The grooves on the man's forehead deepened. "Not you, too."

"Not anymore, no."

Dr. King waved his hand in dismissal. "It doesn't matter. Let's get to the issue at hand, shall we?"

Charles nodded. "I brought some papers for you to sign. And I can update you on the status of your father's estate."

"No, not that issue—I meant supper." He chuckled. "My wife and older sister insist you stay and dine with us. You must have made a favorable impression on them, at least."

Charles swallowed. Another uncomfortable family meal with Elizabeth? He'd barely recovered from the last one. "Your sister would just as soon see me on my way."

The doctor clapped him on the shoulder. "I'll make sure the medical cabinet is locked, so she's not tempted to add arsenic to your soup." He smiled. "Elizabeth will come around. She's got a temper, but she cools off quickly. As her brother, I've been on the receiving end more times than you can count. We'll put you two at opposite ends of the table, just in case."

Charles drew in a deep breath, the tension in his chest making it difficult. "If you insist."

"Abby and Ruby insist. I'm along for the ride." He nodded. "Afterward, we can retire to the study to discuss the case. I hope you have good news. I could use some today." He turned and strode toward the house.

Good news. This evening would not end well. That much was certain.

13

Elizabeth stared out Ruby's kitchen window, fingers tightening on the sill. Her brother had his hand on Charles's shoulder and they were heading for the house. "No, no, no..."

"What's the matter, honey?" Ruby swept into the room, an apron tied over her green gown. "Is Charles staying to supper? I told Robert to invite him."

Elizabeth rounded on her sister. "Why? Why would you do that?"

She stopped short, lips drawing down. "I thought you would approve. You lit up like a sunrise when you mentioned his name, earlier."

"Before I knew he was a hypocritical snake like his uncle." Elizabeth blinked to clear her eyes. She barely knew the man—he hadn't earned the right to evoke tears. "I won't sit across a table from him."

Ruby took her hand. "It appears you won't have a choice. I'm sorry, Elizabeth. He seemed like such a nice young fellow." She smiled. "Definitely a nice-looking one. You'd hardly know he was a McKinley."

"But he is." Elizabeth gritted her teeth as the back door rattled. "Perhaps I should have Gerald drive me back to the Mission."

As if hearing his name, Gerald trotted down the back steps just as the back door opened.

Ruby smiled at the three men as they paraded into the kitchen. "Are you joining us then, Mr. McKinley? How wonderful. Gerald's mother is setting the table. I asked her to add a place for you."

Elizabeth frowned. *Wonderful.*

Charles nodded. "I'm honored by the invitation, Mrs. Larkspur. But I wanted to be certain it's all right with Miss King." His eyes darted her way, his head hung low like a guilty pup.

"Why wouldn't it be?" Gerald shook the attorney's hand.

Elizabeth pushed down her sour attitude. "Mr. McKinley, you are quite welcome to join us. As long as you can handle three King siblings at one table."

Charles glanced around, as if overwhelmed by the number of people crushed into the small kitchen. "Thank you. I'm new to the city. I haven't had much opportunity to make friends. I'd be pleased to join you."

"And for such a challenge, the man will need sustenance." Gerald's mother poked her head into the kitchen. "Why don't you boys show Mr. McKinley into the dining room?"

As the kitchen emptied of menfolk, Elizabeth leaned against a counter with a sigh.

"I hope you'll forgive me, Elizabeth." Ruby whispered. "I put the cart before the horse, I'm afraid. I wanted your visit here to be pleasurable. I thought having another young man at dinner might liven things up."

Elizabeth pressed cool palms against her cheeks. "I'm sure it will. But perhaps not in the way you'd hoped."

&

The scent of the home-cooked meal drifted through the house, heavy and luxurious in the evening air. Charles's stomach grumbled in response. He hung his hat on the coat rack in the front entry, rolling his shoulders to ease the growing tension. Hopefully he'd be able to taste the good food before the evening soured. Likely as not, Elizabeth would glower at him from across the table, and Dr. King would demand an explanation of their father's accounts. He'd barely met Dr. and Mrs. Larkspur, but Charles was certain he'd find a way to offend them as well, by the meal's conclusion. Why had he agreed to this?

Dr. Larkspur poked his head out into the entry. "Are you ready?" *As ready as I'll ever be.* "Yes, sir. And thank you for inviting me."

"Ruby and I are pleased to have you. Usually it's just the three of us, including my mother. We love having guests. After the great earthquake, we had so many people living here we had to eat in shifts."

"It must have been a challenging time." Charles glanced around. The Larkspurs' comfortable decor reminded him of home.

Dr. Larkspur rubbed his chin. "In a way, I miss it. My young nephew running underfoot, my cousins and friends gathered near. When I built this house, I pictured it filled with family." A shadow seemed to pass in front of his eyes as his hand dropped to caress his right arm. The limb ended abruptly near the elbow.

Did he lose it in the disaster? "I was in Oregon when the quake happened, but I've heard many accounts."

The doctor shook his head. "Stories never seem to do those days justice, but God found ways to bless us in the midst of the chaos. It brought Robert and Abby together, in a way. Afterward, Ruby came to render aid to the refugees. That's how we met." He shrugged. "He turns mourning into joy, brings rejoicing from sorrow."

After Charles's discussion with Elizabeth, thoughts of his sister still hovered close. If only she could have discovered such joy. "Perhaps now everything has settled, you and Mrs. Larkspur can enjoy the big family of your dreams."

A faint smile touched the man's lips, not matching the hollow-ness in his eyes. "Perhaps." He stepped back and gestured to the dining room. "Come on in."

Time to face the judge and jury. Charles followed his host into the dining room, seven chairs arranged around a long table.

Mrs. Mae Larkspur bustled around, adding dishes and serving spoons. Her small form reminded him of his grandmother—her mind always focused on the needs of others. "I think we'll sit you here, Mr. McKinley, next to Elizabeth."

Elizabeth's brother turned from where he'd been stoking the fire-place. "Perhaps he should sit next to me—we can discuss the estate while we eat."

"Robert—" the older woman straightened with a huff. "Business at the table? Really? A recipe for indigestion."

Dr. Larkspur chuckled. "You know better than to argue with my mother, Robert."

Charles backed a step, placing the wall behind him. The idea of sitting near Elizabeth might have appealed earlier in the day, but now it sounded like a dangerous undertaking. "I'm at your mercy, Mrs. Larkspur. Wherever you think best." *Like maybe at the neighbor's house.*

The gray-haired matron patted the high back of the nearest seat. "Here. Elizabeth will be to your right and Robert to your left." She lifted a silvery brow at young Dr. King as if entreating the younger man to remember her admonishment.

Nothing like being seated between the two with the most potential for hostility. Dr. Larkspur's wife might also be a King sibling, but she seemed far more welcoming.

Dr. King hurried to assist his wife with a large platter. The young woman smiled, her brown hair and freckles somehow fitting her quiet demeanor. She'd barely said two words since he arrived.

Elizabeth followed, her eyes narrowing as she spotted him at the table.

"Let's all sit, shall we?" Dr. Larkspur motioned everyone in. "Mr. McKinley, you'll find we're not very formal around here. I'm sure you're accustomed to fine manners and fancy parties, but we're fairly simple folk."

Charles drew back Elizabeth's chair before claiming his own. "I grew up on a ranch, Doctor. Trust me when I say this is elegant enough for me."

Dr. King raised a brow. "A ranch? I thought you were Silas McKinley's nephew. The man's practically a legend around here."

"My uncle is a self-made man. He and my father are brothers, but two more different men you'll rarely encounter."

"I never would have guessed." Dr. King shook his head. "Be careful, you'll damage his well-crafted reputation."

"Honesty has always been my failing."

The elder Mrs. Larkspur nodded. "And a good trait for an attorney."

"Albeit an unusual one." Dr. King raised a brow.

Dr. Larkspur cleared his throat. "Shall I ask the blessing? This food isn't going to eat itself."

Charles bowed his head, his mind too busy to concentrate on Dr. Larkspur's prayer. The plates began passing after the blessing, and the conversations began anew.

Elizabeth remained silent, taking small portions from each dish and handing it along to him.

He'd obviously put a damper on her visit. Perhaps he could do something to redeem himself. He waited for a lull in the conversation and glanced over at her brother. "I'm sure you must be proud of the work Elizabeth is doing at the Mission. Very few women would take on such a cause."

"Elizabeth always has a cause or campaign of some sort." Dr. King unfolded his napkin.

"My sister has a big heart." Ruby tucked a loose curl behind her ear. "We couldn't be more pleased. And we're delighted to have her in San Francisco."

Dr. King's quiet wife brightened. "Elizabeth, I'd love to hear more about what you're doing."

Elizabeth pushed food about her plate, but Charles had yet to see her take a bite. "I've only taught one class so far, but the girls seemed to enjoy it."

"I found you returning from Chinatown." Her brother took a sip from his water glass. "You said something about a rescue."

Elizabeth shifted in her chair. "Yes. It wasn't anything, really. One of the students was being...detained. We went to retrieve her."

"Detained?" Charles swallowed his bite. She was being far too modest. "Members of a Chinese tong abducted one of the students from under the nose of two prison guards. From what Miss Cameron told me, Elizabeth stormed a rooftop and demanded the girl's freedom."

Eyes widened around the table and forks stilled. Ruby turned to her sister. "Is that true?"

Elizabeth's cheeks reddened. "He's exaggerating. But, yes. I accompanied Miss Cameron on the rescue, and we succeeded in recovering Tien Gum."

Robert laid down his fork. "Elizabeth, I don't like you putting yourself in such danger. What if these men had been armed?"

She shrugged. "I couldn't let them take her. Word was they were going to move her to Idaho in an attempt to escape our reach. I shudder to think what sort of life she'd have there."

Charles took a bite of the roast, the tender meat practically melting in his mouth. Elizabeth King's courage impressed him. In one week, she'd gone from socialite to crusader. No wonder she'd reacted poorly when he explained his reasons for not helping the Mission. She could stand up to kidnappers and brothel owners, but he couldn't contradict his own uncle?

Elizabeth straightened in her chair, as if warming to her subject. "These girls are subjected to unimaginable horrors at the hands of men. And they never asked for this life. Most were brought to our shores under false pretenses—promised jobs or marriages to successful merchants. They took the risk to help their families back home. Instead, they ended up as slaves to men's baser desires." Her gaze flickered between her brother and Charles.

She counts me in the same camp. Charles's stomach fell.

Robert held up a hand. "Perhaps this is a discussion better held until we can speak in private."

Her nostrils flared. "Don't dismiss me like a child. You say you want me safe, and yet you care nothing for the safety of those girls."

The doctor scowled. "They are not my sisters."

Mrs. King touched her husband's arm. "And their brothers are not here to protect them." She glanced up at Elizabeth. "We are proud of you, and you know the Mission is dear to my heart. But please, do be careful. We love you."

Elizabeth fell silent, her gaze settling on her plate.

Charles studied Elizabeth, as if seeing her for the first time. The young woman had grit, as his father would say. Determination, compassion, and beauty all in one package. He never thought such a thing possible.

Unfortunately, she despised him.

Elizabeth lifted a stack of dishes from the table, the hum of conversations blurring into a peaceful lull around her. Gerald's mother had succeeded in redirecting the conversation by offering pie, and it seemed everyone around the table breathed a sigh of relief. Everyone but Elizabeth.

How dare Charles McKinley horn in on her evening with her family? Why wasn't he off at some dinner party with his uncle and a room filled with sparkling politicians and their well-mannered wives? He'd made it clear he'd have nothing more to do with the Mission Home. Her father's estate was clearly bankrupt. What reason did he have to stay?

She glanced down the table to where he sat conversing with Gerald over a cup of coffee. A smile danced around the young man's face, as if he felt more at home here than she did. She paused, her gaze sliding along his strong jaw and muscled arms. She pulled the stacked china close and headed for the kitchen. It took more than a handsome face to turn her head. She'd already endured the consequences of such folly.

Ruby met her at the drain board. "I'll take those. I think Robert is getting ready to invite Mr. McKinley into the parlor to discuss Father's accounts. Do you want to join them? Or should I drive you home to the Mission?"

Home . . . Mission. For a few brief moments, she'd forgotten what awaited her at the end of the day. She needed to prepare for tomorrow's class. She hadn't even stopped to wonder how Tien Gum fared after her harrowing experience.

"What's the matter?" Ruby's lips turned down. "You look as though you've lost your best friend."

"No, nothing like that." Elizabeth put her arm around her sister's waist and laid her head on her shoulder. "I've just enjoyed spending time with you and Abby today. Part of me doesn't want to leave."

Ruby squeezed her close. "You didn't seem to be enjoying yourself at dinner. I hate to see you quarrel with Robert."

"I know." Elizabeth bit her lip. "I shouldn't let him irk me so. He still treats me as though I'm the little girl he left at home when he moved away."

"He's concerned. We all are." Ruby's pale blue eyes shimmered. "But I understand how much this means to you." She set the plates in the soapy water. "And whether or not you approve, I think Mr. McKinley—Charles—is quite taken with you."

"What? No, you're mistaken." Elizabeth's throat grew tight. "I think…" she glanced back at the door to make sure the man wasn't lurking nearby. "I think he feels responsible for me. Father's estate was his first assignment." The words sounded hollow. Why was Charles constantly turning up? A shiver ran down her back. He couldn't be smitten with her. She'd been rude at their first meeting, and cold to him, really, since then. And then today…her stomach dropped. Once again, her temper had ruled the day.

No matter. She'd already failed one relationship. The last thing she needed was another. And if Charles was concerned for his reputation—as he'd suggested today—she'd clearly be the wrong choice.

Robert poked his head into the kitchen. "Do either of you wish to join us?"

Ruby shook her head. "You can fill me in later. I want to tackle these dishes before Mae gets ahold of them. She's done so much today, she must be exhausted."

Elizabeth let go of her sister's waist. "Should I stay and help?"

"No, you go on ahead. When you're done, one of us will drive you home."

Elizabeth followed Robert through the dining room, running quick hands over her skirt to brush away any stray crumbs. Spotting Charles at the door to the parlor sent a flush to her cheeks. Ruby shouldn't have said anything—now she'd never get the idea out of her head. She squinted her eyes and tried to picture him on the back of a horse, as he'd described in the garden. She couldn't quite manage it, though he did have the broad shoulders of one who bucked hay for a living.

When his gaze met hers, she lifted her chin and turned away. The last thing she needed was for him to think she might be interested.

As they settled into the room, she folded her hands in her lap. She would remain calm, quiet, and demure—even if it killed her.

Charles opened the case and drew out several file folders. "I have a complete accounting of your father's investments, dating back to ten years before his death. It seems he entrusted my uncle with the task of investing his savings, which included the bulk of your grandfather's estate."

It doesn't sound as if he should have trusted Silas McKinley with anything. Elizabeth nearly choked, keeping the words inside.

Her brother sat forward in his chair. "May I see them?"

"Of course." Charles moved to a seat closer to Robert and spread the papers across a low table. "These are the most pertinent records here. This document details the investments still current at the time of the earthquake."

Robert lifted the paper. "It looks like he invested in several buildings in the downtown area. Did any of these structures survive the quake?"

"They were all damaged in the quake, but completely destroyed by the fires."

Elizabeth sank back against her seat. "All of them?" So much for staying silent.

Charles glanced up, lines forming around his brown eyes. "Yes."

Robert folded both hands and rested his chin against his knuckles. "Insured, as your uncle claimed?"

The attorney paused, a twitch obvious above his jaw. "Yes, but since the structural damage was done during the earthquake, fire insurance doesn't apply."

The breath leaked from Elizabeth's chest. Mother would be ruined. "You said your uncle was a partner in these investments."

"And he suffered losses as well."

Robert flipped through the stack of papers. "I'd heard some of these insurance decisions were being challenged in court. Have you confronted the insurance companies about covering these losses? Certainly they're duty-bound to cover some of the investments. I walked the city during those three days of fires. The buildings may have been damaged by the initial shock, but it was the flames that gutted the structures—that and the army using dynamite to clear firebreaks."

"Many of the companies are paying 100 percent of the claims, regardless of the situation. I'm afraid yours isn't one of them." Charles ran a hand across the back of his neck. "Some denials are being con-tested. A few have been overturned."

"But not ours." Elizabeth swallowed down the burning sensation growing in her chest.

The attorney opened his mouth, as if to say something, but closed it again. He shook his head "It's mostly larger accounts—the banks, the railroad, the newspapers."

The words settled in the pit of Elizabeth's stomach.

Robert rubbed the bridge of his nose, falling silent.

Elizabeth scooted forward in her seat. "Why can't we take our case to court? You'd represent us, wouldn't you?"

The shadows deepened around the attorney's eyes. "I wouldn't recommend it. The court fees alone would eat up any gains you might see."

His words doused any flicker of hope she'd mustered. She lowered her eyes, the smothering truth dropping over her like a blanket. No matter what Ruby said, men like the McKinleys weren't concerned with people like them. Hadn't he already said as much?

14

*C*harles sat in the rear of the gallery, scribbling his observations on a notepad. After two weeks of busy work, Spencer had finally allowed him to observe. Not from the defense table, but definitely an improvement.

The senior attorney strutted past the jury box, gesturing as he spoke. "The photographic evidence clearly shows the building in question was damaged by the earthquake." Spencer laid both hands on the rail and leaned toward the jurors, his extreme height bringing him to perfect eye level with the front row of men. "I'm sure many of you—like myself, and most of the good folk here in this courtroom—walked the streets of San Francisco on that horrific day. We saw our beloved city hall in shambles. We saw neighbors' homes pulled apart like dollhouses. We saw whole buildings toppled by the shaking. Do you remember how you felt that morning? Were you thrown from your beds? Did you fear for your loved ones?" He lowered his head, voice shaking. "I know I did."

"You may have strolled past the Wright Building on that first morning before the fires ever began—a building rocked off its foundation by the same shock that sent us running into the streets." He swiveled on his heel and spread his arms wide. "What happens to a building thrown from its moorings? Can it ever be righted? Or is it like Humpty Dumpty from our children's nursery rhymes?"

Smiles and faint laughter trickled through the jury box and the audience in the gallery.

He cleared his throat. "Mr. Morrison wants the Williamsburgh City Fire Insurance Company to be 'all the king's horses and all the king's men.' But you folks remember how that ended."

Spencer pointed to the large map of the fire zone, standing prominently in the center of the courtroom. "The fires didn't even reach the building until the third day of the conflagration. The building was a complete loss days earlier. In fact, I'd argue that the fires did the plaintiff a favor. Cleaned the slate, if you will." He faced the jurors once more, his dark brow lowering over his eyes like an executioner's hood. "Many people lost lives and property in the days that followed. They are the ones who deserve compensation. I put forth that Mr. Morrison is trying to seduce the Williamsburgh Company into providing capital for his next construction project. I ask you, good men of the jury—as we demonstrated earlier, haven't the adjustors already shown the utmost compassion? They cannot be expected to cover every whim and whiffle of his imagined slights."

The plaintiff—a sallow-faced man in a gray suit—bristled under Spencer's smooth-voiced accusations. He turned and whispered into his own attorney's ear, but the counselor waved off his attention.

A sour taste rose in Charles's mouth. The firm seemed to be fighting on both sides of this battle—wherever the money lay.

Spencer continued his posturing and orating for thirty minutes, the jury leaning forward and consuming his words like a flock of baby birds waiting for tender morsels. By the end of the day, the jury found for the insurance company, and the building's owner left penniless.

The man shambled past, face sagging, and Charles's spirits sank. *Corruption is the lifeblood of this city. How long can I skirt around the edges of the firm's business before I'm forced to try one of these cases?* He strode up the aisle to meet Spencer. Had the man grown an inch during the deliberation?

Spencer passed him a box filled with files and briefs. "Time to put this case to bed, McKinley. Can you handle the task, or does your uncle need to walk you through it?"

Charles's fingers clenched on the edge of the box. "You must be proud."

The man jutted his chin. "We can't stand by while shysters like him shake down legitimate businesses. That money belongs to those who can rebuild this city and make it something great."

"And here I thought it was about justice." Charles shoved the box under his arm.

Spencer snorted. "There's a fine line between justice and business. You need to decide which side of the line you're going to settle on." He smoothed his lapels before striding out of the courtroom.

A long exhale escaped Charles's lips. He'd ridden to court in Spencer's auto, but he'd rather return via streetcar. At least he'd be riding with people worthy of his respect.

&

"You're dismissed." Elizabeth smiled as the words left her lips, her spirits lifting with the girl's happy voices.

The children chattered and giggled as they gathered their things and left the classroom, a few stopping to ask questions or express their thanks.

As the room fell silent, Elizabeth drew a deep breath, another class complete. Each one seemed a little easier, as she grew accustomed to her students' odd ways—or them to hers, perhaps. She gathered a few scraps left lying about the room, tucking them into the ever-expanding rag bag. Perhaps she should teach them to quilt, while she was at it.

She glanced out the window at the street below. Sometimes the Mission seemed like a fortress, wholly separate from the buzzing activity outside. *What is Charles doing right now?* Her traitorous thoughts focused on the young attorney more often than she'd like, ever since the conversation in Ruby's garden. How unusual to find a young man who didn't mind her outspoken ways. Learning he wouldn't be volunteering with the Mission had pierced her with unexpected disappointment.

Content the classroom was in order, Elizabeth switched off the light and closed the door. She headed to the kitchen. Mrs. Lee, the cook, had bought several bushels of apples and said Elizabeth could help herself. It would be the perfect snack to tide her over until dinner. An apple for the teacher.

Even with teaching occupying much of her time, restlessness stalked her. For years, she'd arranged her life around the piano, every free moment in preparation for her next lesson with Tobias. She pushed his image from her mind. Would she ever be able to think about music without resurrecting unwanted feelings? It seemed safer to dream about handsome cowboy attorneys—even if they were off-limits.

Mrs. Lee bustled around the kitchen, directing three girls through the evening meal preparations. Tien Gum gathered the plates for supper. She offered Elizabeth a quick smile as she balanced the stack against her hip.

A rush of warmth raced through Elizabeth's chest. *How close we came to losing her.*

She scooped up one of the apples from the barrel, the lilting sound of music giving her pause. Interspersed with the various noises of meal preparation, faint notes carried through the room, sending a vibration through Elizabeth's soul. *Piano.*

She peeked inside the dining hall, her gaze settling on the back of an ancient upright piano in the corner, the player hidden on the far side. The gentle melody continued, hesitating for a moment as if the player searched for inspiration, but then growing in confidence. The haunting tune pulled Elizabeth forward, the familiar notes of "Amazing Grace" spiraling through the room. She crept around the edges of the far table, holding to the shadows until she could see the form sitting at the stool.

Little Yoke Soo bent over the keys, her slight form swaying with the music.

Elizabeth pressed her back against the wall. *She's so young.*

Yoke Soo's tiny hands curved above the keyboard. A smile toyed at the corners of her lips, as if the hymn—or the simple act of playing it—brought joy.

Elizabeth reached for a chair. It wasn't often one encountered such talent, and even more rare to find it in one so small. How many times had Father told her as much? She tugged the chair away from the table, its legs squeaking against the floorboards.

The music halted abruptly. Yoke Soo jerked her head upward, her braids swinging with the motion. She jumped from the stool and moved toward the door.

"No, wait." Elizabeth stepped forward. "Yoke Soo, it's me."

The child stopped, her eyes wide. "Miss, I'm sorry. I know I'm not supposed to be playing."

"Why not?" Elizabeth walked to the girl's side. "It was lovely."

"I should be spreading the tablecloths. I thought I'd just play one song."

"You got lost in the music." Elizabeth's fingertips tingled. How often had she experienced the same, only to discover hours had passed? "You're very talented."

Yoke Soo shook her head. "I'm not good enough."

Elizabeth squelched a laugh before it escaped from her mouth. "Who told you that?"

"Mrs. Woolsey, the piano teacher. I like to play what I hear in my head. She wants me to play the book."

A shiver raced across Elizabeth's skin. "You played 'Amazing Grace.' Isn't it in the hymnal?"

"Not the way I hear it."

Which explained its beauty. "You have a lot of natural talent, Yoke Soo. It's a gift from God. Your instructor is helping you develop your skills so you can be even better."

The girl's lip curled. "I don't want to play like…" Yoke Soo glanced behind her, as if fearing the woman might sneak out of the shadows. "Mrs. Woolsey's songs have no life." She shrugged her narrow shoulders.

"When is your next lesson?"

"Tomorrow morning." She looked down at her fingers. "She'll be mad, again. I can't play the hymn like she wants."

"Which one?"

Yoke Soo pulled the hymnal from the rack and gestured at one of the pages.

Elizabeth chewed her lip and glanced at the chipped keys. "Come here." She sat at the piano. "They'll be setting up for dinner soon, but I can play through it for you at least once."

Yoke Soo's face brightened. "You play?"

Elizabeth tucked her skirts under her as she perched on the stool. "Our secret, yes?"

The child nodded, pressing her lips closed.

Elizabeth leaned forward to see the notes in the dim light. Her hands stumbled over the fingerings at first, but as her muscles warmed up, the music flowed.

Yoke Soo stared into the distance as she listened, not bothering to watch Elizabeth's fingers.

Elizabeth pushed through even as a hole opened in the pit of her stomach. Why had she given this up? Hadn't Tobias stolen enough from her?

When she reached the end of the song, Elizabeth dabbed her wrist across her eyes and turned to Yoke Soo. "Do you want me to play it again?"

The child smiled. "No." She stood next to Elizabeth, placed her hands on the keys, and repeated the song verbatim.

Elizabeth's breath caught in her chest. "You . . . you've never played it before?"

"Never right." She beamed. "Miss Woolsey will be happy."

Elizabeth shook her head, slowly. "I'm impressed."

The girl dropped her gaze to the keyboard. "I hope she will be."

15

The restaurant's chandeliers spilled light down onto the well-heeled guests as waiters bustled from table to table delivering local delicacies and pouring fine wines. Charles ran a quick hand over the front of his suit jacket, finally thankful for his uncle's gift. He'd never have dared enter such an establishment in his normal clothes.

Uncle Silas passed a folded bill to the maître d´, his hushed voice obscured by the din of the lunch crowd.

The heady scent of roasted quail permeated the atmosphere, and Charles's mouth watered. If he'd learned one thing during his weeks in the city, it was that San Franciscans knew how to eat. He hadn't expected this lunch invitation from his uncle, but he certainly wasn't going to argue with the man. After scraping together a few bachelor meals at home, or visiting the cafe down the street from the office—he wouldn't complain if his uncle offered to buy a sandwich in the park.

They followed the tuxedoed gentleman to a table in a quiet corner with a good view of the square below. Charles's uncle took the first seat. "How are you settling in?"

Charles held his breath for a moment. Not well, but he knew what his uncle wanted to hear. "Fine, sir. Splendid. I'm honored to be working with Mr. Spencer."

"Spencer's a firm taskmaster, I'm aware. But you needed a little discipline, and I knew he could provide it." Uncle Silas reached for his water glass.

Charles shifted in his chair. How long before he could have a conversation with his uncle without feeling like a petulant two-year-old? Perhaps never. "Yes, sir."

His uncle folded both arms across his chest. "You know I have big hopes for you, but it won't come without a price. First, we need to polish your image a bit—no one need know you came from simple folk. Act like the man you want to be, not the man you were raised to be."

Charles managed a nod. *Or the man* he *wants me to be?* "I must confess, I'm a little stymied about the insurance cases. If you don't mind me saying, it seems like we're only defending those property owners who could easily afford to replace their losses—and Spencer argued a case for an insurance company, as well. It feels like a conflict of interest."

"Spencer works the cases he's given, like every other attorney at the firm. We're a business. We work for the clients." His uncle's voice deepened.

"What happens to potential clients who can't necessarily afford our fees?"

"If they can't afford to pay, they're not potential clients. We don't take on charity cases."

"What if it's a case you believe in?" *Or a client you can't keep out of your thoughts?*

Uncle Silas dragged knobby fingers through his whiskers. "I've supported a few causes for the sake of the city." He laid both hands on the tablecloth. "I know you think I'm a curmudgeonly old man with a nose for money, but it's not true. If I only concerned myself with amassing a fortune, I'd be one of those railroad barons up on Nob Hill. San Francisco will be the Paris of the West when I'm done with it. But that requires capital and influence. We've got to clean up the neighborhoods, make them safe for decent families and businesses." He shook his head. "Look at it now. Streets filled with rubbish, crawling with rats. Shoddy buildings going up piecemeal after the quake." Uncle Silas picked up the menu. "The fires provided a clean slate. I refuse to let 'em slap the buildings up willy-nilly with no sense of civic pride."

Charles took a sip of water. "I respect that, but maybe if we assisted those in need—"

"We'd have a city of beggars and pickpockets. You need to wise up, Charles. The only people capable of rebuilding this city are the businessmen, the politicians, the railroads. It's time to shed the image of the grizzled prospectors and embrace our future." He narrowed his eyes. "And you could be an integral part in it."

Charles's pulse accelerated. Leading the city into the future? No more bowing to the likes of Spencer? "I'd relish the opportunity."

"Then start imagining your future as a man of influence, not a servant to every lowlife that rolls out of the gutter." He lifted a brow. "Or every arrogant attorney determined to place you under his thumb."

A shiver trickled down Charles's spine. Spencer had been a test.

Uncle Silas leaned forward, pinning Charles in his gaze. "This afternoon, you'll practice as such."

"This afternoon?" Charles frowned, his mind racing through the day's schedule. He'd expected to be sorting files all afternoon, and likely most of the evening, too.

An unfamiliar voice boomed from behind him. "Silas—there you are!"

A smile crossed Uncle Silas's face as he rose. "Governor, right on time, as always."

Charles sprang to his feet, sending several pieces of silverware skittering across the table along with any sensible thoughts.

His uncle stepped forward, as if unaware of Charles's gaffe. "James, may I present my nephew, Mr. Charles McKinley?" He shot Charles a pointed look. "Charles—Governor James Gillett."

The tall man extended a hand toward Charles. "Mr. McKinley. Your uncle has told me much about you."

Charles's mouth went dry as he gripped the governor's hand. "It's an honor, sir." He had the feeling he'd be repeating that phrase many times in the months to come.

Elizabeth pressed the book to her chest as she listened from the kitchen door. The sounds of Yoke Soo's playing echoed from the dining room. The simple arrangement blossomed the second time through, the notes weaving together into a tapestry much richer than what was set out in the hymnal.

"Stop." The teacher's voice snapped, her harsh tone carrying out to the kitchen. "What are you doing? That's not what's written."

"It's how it should be written."

"Don't give me any of your impudence. You're hopeless. Begin again, and only play what's on the page."

Elizabeth sighed. She hadn't done Yoke Soo any favors by demonstrating the song for her. She peeked around the corner.

Yoke Soo's head hung low. She reached for the keys.

"Sit up, child. You can't play like that." The matron poked the girl's spine with a wooden pointer.

Jerking upright, Yoke Soo pursed her lips and began to play. She held to the arrangement for a few bars, but a countermelody sneaked in at the midpoint.

The rod snapped down onto her fingers, sending a discordant jumble of notes jarring the morning air. Yoke Soo yelped, drawing her hands to her lap.

Elizabeth's heart jumped, her breath catching in her chest.

"If you play it like that again, I'll close the lid over your knuckles. Now read the notes."

A pounding rhythm arose in Elizabeth's ears. She jumped forward. "Excuse me—"

The teacher spun around. "We're in the middle of a lesson."

Hurrying forward to Yoke Soo's side, Elizabeth stepped between the pair. "I don't know what you think you're doing, but I certainly wouldn't call it teaching."

Yoke Soo hopped up from the stool and hid behind Elizabeth's back.

Mrs. Woolsey's eyes shot wide. "Who are you to tell me my job?"

"I can't believe Miss Cameron would authorize this sort of instruct—no, I can't call it that. You're bullying this child."

"She's playing dumb to make me look the fool." The woman's lips pinched, a myriad of tiny wrinkles forming around them.

"I think you're doing fine all by yourself." Elizabeth turned to Yoke Soo. "You're done here, sweetheart. Go on in the kitchen and see if cook has any toast left from breakfast."

The piano teacher drew up to her full height with a huff. "I'll be speaking to Miss Cameron about this."

Elizabeth folded her arms. "Please do."

Ʌ

"Haven't these children been through enough?" Elizabeth stood in front of Donaldina's desk, her voice quavering with tension. "They should feel safe here. I can't believe you'd allow such methods."

Donaldina swung around, eyes sparking. "I don't allow it. I believe these girls have survived enough abuse in their young lives." She sunk into her chair. "When Mrs. Woolsey told me what she'd done, I dismissed her on the spot."

Elizabeth's breath caught. "You did?"

"But now we're faced with the task of replacing her. It takes a certain type of individual."

Elizabeth sank into the seat near the window, her mind drawing back to the weeks after her father's death. Piano had been her lifeline, grief finding an outlet through her fingers. Some of these girls would need the same. She squeezed her hands into fists, burying them in her lap. "Let me teach it, then."

Donaldina's brows drew together. "You play?"

A lead weight lay on Elizabeth's chest. The time had come to cast it off. She stood, her knees rubbery. "I'll show you."

The dining room tables were set for lunch, the mingled scents of ginger and garlic flavoring the warm air. Elizabeth sat at the piano, her heart pounding. Other than playing for Yoke Soo last night, she'd avoided the Mission piano like it was tainted. Just the feel of the woodwork brought a shiver to her skin, as if Tobias stood just behind her shoulder. She closed her eyes, banishing his memory. *I've given enough of myself to you. You can't have this, too.*

Without opening her eyes, she touched the ivory keys, their cool smoothness a treat to her fingertips. With a deep breath, she launched into the first phrase of her favorite Brahms sonata. The notes curled and danced in the quiet dining room. This sturdy upright was nothing in comparison to a concert grand, but the sounds fed Elizabeth's hungering soul.

Her muscles recalled every pattern and variation. Elizabeth bent forward, leaning into the keys.

After a few moments, she forgot Donaldina listened. The music poured forth, the trickle becoming a stream and then a torrent. For months it had been held behind a dam of her own making. The sounds carried Elizabeth along, her foot finding the pedal.

She drew out the ending, not wanting the music to fade. Striking the final notes, she held her breath, listening to the tones diminish. Silence followed, rich with unspoken words. Gooseflesh climbed her arms. *I'd forgotten. How could I forget?* A squeal woke Elizabeth from her trance.

Yoke Soo flung herself against Elizabeth's side. The room teemed with girls, all of them clapping.

Donaldina smiled. "You're a woman of secrets, Elizabeth King." She turned to address the children. "What do you think, ladies? Should Miss King be our new music teacher?"

The students cheered.

Elizabeth cuddled Yoke Soo to her chest, the little girl's warmth driving away the chill. *A woman of secrets.*

16

*C*harles turned in front of the cheval glass as the Chinese tailor pulled and tugged at the jacket.

"Much better, yes?" The man bobbed his head, a braided queue dancing along his back. "I give you more room here." He gestured to Charles's shoulders and then to his arms. "And here."

Charles nodded, brushing a loose thread from his sleeve. "I appreciate your fine work."

Lim Sang folded both arms, tucking his hands into his sleeves. "It is an honor to serve."

A bell jingled as the door swung open, a familiar figure crossing the threshold.

Charles straightened. He hadn't seen Miss King since the episode at her sister's house.

Lim Sang hurried to greet her. "Miss King, welcome. How is everything at the Mission Home?"

"Everyone is fine, but I'm in need of more of your nice thread." Elizabeth held up a fabric swatch. "We're making new seat cushions, and I don't have anything to match this. I knew you could help me."

Accepting the swatch from her hand, the man smiled. "I think I have just the thing. If you'll excuse me for a moment, Mr. McKinley?" He bobbed his head at Charles before ducking behind the counter.

Elizabeth raised a brow. "I'm surprised to see you here. I didn't know you frequented Chinatown shops."

"His work came highly recommended." *And cheap.* Charles ran a hand down his lapel. After weeks of feeling like a hog-tied calf, the new fit was welcome relief. "How is the teaching coming?"

The young woman averted her eyes. "It's been a learning experience, but the girls are eager pupils." She moved over to the window, where the storekeeper displayed an array of fabrics. Her simple dress seemed a sharp contrast to the gown she'd worn the night they met. *She could wear a flour sack and still catch every man's eye.* His heartbeat doubled its pace. There had to be a way to see more of her, even though he couldn't serve at the Mission. "I haven't had much of an opportunity to explore the city since I arrived. Lim Sang was just telling me of a lovely Japanese garden in Golden Gate Park. I don't suppose you get out much, either."

Elizabeth lifted her gaze. "No, but I visited the tea garden when I came for my brother's wedding. It's beautiful."

"Oh." So no need to invite her, then. "If you say I should, then...I will." He closed his mouth lest he stammer something else.

"I don't imagine you have a lot of free time."

"No, but I'd like to see something besides the office and the courtroom." And he'd love to see it with her. "Visiting your sister's home last week was a treat."

She smiled. "I hope Robert and I weren't too hard on you."

"Not at all. I expected worse, actually—something along the line of tar and feathers, especially once you saw the accounting of your father's estate."

She ran a gloved hand across a bolt of silk on the worktable. "You can't be blamed. You didn't cause the earthquake, after all."

"No, I'm innocent of one offense, at least."

"And you didn't make my father invest in those buildings."

"True."

She nodded, lifting her shoulders in a slight shrug. "I guess I have no evidence against you then, do I, Counselor?"

"But it will take more to redeem me in your eyes."

She blinked twice, her lips pursing. "Why do you care how I view you?"

A quiver ran through his gut. "I'd like for us to be friends." He glanced around the shop, glad the owner had not yet returned. "I spend all day around lawyers." He tried not to make a face. "You wouldn't believe what a boring lot they are."

"Present company excluded, I suppose." A mischievous glint brightened her eyes.

"If you say so." He took a step closer. The tailor would return any moment and his opportunity would pass. "I enjoyed conversing with you at your sister's home—before we quarreled. You're unique, Elizabeth."

She squinted at him. "Is that a compliment or an insult?"

He chuckled, the tension easing from his chest. "A compliment." Time to wade into deeper waters. "I respect the work you're doing, and I wish I could be more involved. I hope you know that." He shook his head. "But for the time being, I'm at my uncle's mercy. I can't stay in the city without his support."

Her gaze softened. "I suppose I understand. Perhaps when you've achieved some status, you'll be able to follow your dreams."

"That's my hope." If only she realized how quickly his dreams were changing to include her.

Lim Sang returned, a small wooden box clutched under his arm. "So sorry to keep you waiting. My back room is sadly disorganized." He laid the box on the table and opened the lid. Digging through it, he retrieved three spools and set them in front of Elizabeth. "What do you think of these?"

She picked them up, comparing them to the swatch. "They're perfect. How much do I owe you?"

He waved his hand. "No charge. It is my honor to support the Mission. Miss Cameron introduced me to my wife. Did you not know?"

A smiled danced across Elizabeth's face. "No, I didn't. How wonderful for you."

"Now I support the Mission in what little ways I can. You need more thread, you come see me." He patted the tabletop.

Charles paid for the alterations and hurried to catch Elizabeth as she left the shop. "May I walk you home?"

"It's only three blocks." She smiled. "But if you'd like…"

He took the wicker basket from her arm and fell into step beside her.

"It's romantic, isn't it?"

"Yes." Charles jerked alert. "Wait. What is?"

"Lim Sang marrying one of the Mission girls. Donaldina as matchmaker."

"Oh." Charles mulled over the statements. It sounded more like an arranged marriage. "I expect it would be difficult for most of the young women who come through the Mission doors to find love after everything they've experienced."

"It speaks well of his character. I've witnessed Donaldina's protective mothering. I don't believe she'd condone a marriage with someone she didn't approve." Elizabeth glanced sideways at him. "Most men seek women of impeccable character and reputation. Would you consider marrying a woman with a past?"

Charles stepped around a market stall. The conversation had veered into dangerous territory. "The girls didn't choose their situations. They're innocent of wrongdoing."

"Many wouldn't see it that way."

He considered her words. "I couldn't love a woman who cast off her virtue by her own free will—that would be far more difficult to ignore."

Elizabeth stumbled on the cobblestones outside the Mission. He gripped her elbow to steady her, but she took a step back and pressed fingers to her chest as if to catch her breath. "We should probably say good-bye here. I don't want to give anyone the wrong idea."

Charles glanced up at the large brick building. "If you wish. Has Donaldina located other legal representation?"

She stood staring at him with those impossibly large eyes. "She has yet to replace you. It's not easy to find someone."

"I'll make some inquiries." Charles fought the urge to take her hand. Three blocks had not been enough. "Elizabeth, I meant what I said. I'd like for us to be friends. I believe we have much in common."

"I could use a friend."

His heart lifted toward his throat. *Friends—remember that.* "Would you consider accompanying me to the Japanese Gardens this Saturday?"

Elizabeth's gaze dropped. "I don't know."

He rushed ahead. "If you're concerned about being unescorted, we could invite another—" he caught himself before saying couple. "Invite a friend or two. Or one of your siblings, perhaps? I could see if Henry from work might join us. We'll make a whole group."

"Let me think about it."

Charles's stomach sank. Was this her way of saying no? "Of course."

Elizabeth backed toward the safety of the steps. "Thank you for the walk." Her lips parted, as if searching for more words. She clamped them shut and offered a polite nod instead. Turning, she hurried up the steps and into the door.

☙

Elizabeth closed the Mission door and leaned against it, chest aching. If only she could go back and change her past.

"I couldn't love a woman who cast off her virtue by her own free will."

She gazed at the stairway leading to the upper floors where the girls slept. Innocents, all. Elizabeth's stomach churned. *Who was I to think I had anything to offer them?* She laid a hand on her midsection, her ribs pinching as if someone had drawn her corset laces inches too tight.

A knock sounded behind her, jolting her alert. Elizabeth caught her breath, turned, and opened the door a crack.

Charles stood under the overhang, her shopping basket dangling from his fingers. "I almost walked off with this."

"I—uh—I . . ." She swallowed hard. "Thank you. Apparently, I also forgot to lock the door."

His brow crinkled. "Is everything all right?"

She took the basket from his grasp. "Yes. Fine. I just can't believe I was so foolish."

Charles tipped his head to one side. "Don't be so hard on yourself, Elizabeth. We all make mistakes." He tapped the brim of his black derby. "I'll see you soon."

She stood in the doorway and watched the young attorney hurry down the sidewalk. He offered a quick wave before crossing the cobblestone street.

Elizabeth closed the door and clicked each lock twice, just to be certain. She leaned her forehead on the cool wood. *Yes, we all make mistakes.*

⁂

Charles sat cross-legged on the narrow bed as he flipped through the documents and reports. He opened a notebook and scribbled down a column of figures, but the numbers didn't add up. According to this list, there should still be plenty of money in the King family's account. He rubbed his fingers against his pounding temples.

He pulled out the fire insurance map. With a pencil, he marked each of the King investment properties—all well within the burned zone. Most of the structures in this area had received some type of payment from the insurance companies. Charles tapped one of the locations with the pencil. The settlement Spencer wrangled two weeks ago included an adjacent property.

He glanced back at the claim report. *"Building heavily damaged in earthquake, fire damage irrelevant. Displacement due to construction on made ground."* How was that possible? The neighboring building would have been on the same type of loose soil, and yet the company had agreed to a settlement.

Charles covered a yawn with the back of his fist. Stretching, he gathered the papers and returned them to the folder. He'd been going over the figures for hours. Perhaps Henry could shed some light on it in the morning. Charles didn't trust taking this question to Spencer, and asking Uncle Silas would be tantamount to admitting defeat.

He unbuttoned his vest and lay back on the pillow. Somehow, back in his law school days, he'd imagined an attorney's life would contain more excitement. Charles jammed fingers through his hair, massaging his scalp in an attempt to drive the ache from his head. Would politics be any better, or would someone like his uncle always be standing in the way?

Closing his eyes, Charles let his mind drift, a certain outspoken beauty never far from his thoughts. When he'd returned the basket, something in her countenance disturbed him. Perhaps she found the thought of spending an afternoon in his presence troubling. The sparks between them couldn't be denied—could they? He rolled to his side, gazing out the window at the city lights sparkling in the clear night. He'd misjudged women before.

With a groan, he pushed himself off the bed and drew down the blind. He'd best get changed before he fell asleep in his clothes. Again.

The discrepancy in the sums plagued his thoughts, even as he pulled off his shirt. If he could prove just one of those buildings was deserving of compensation, it might go a long way toward changing Elizabeth's poor opinion of him.

17

$\mathcal{E}$lizabeth stood at the window as Yoke Soo played through the hymn a fifth time. A shiver raced through her heart, like a bird breaking free of a dense thicket. "You always play it differently. Why is that?"

Yoke Soo shrugged. "I don't feel the same as I did a few minutes ago."

"What's changed?"

"I'm hungry."

Elizabeth laughed. How often had she made similar arguments to her tutors? Eventually they'd succeeded in explaining the intricacies of the written music to her, though she still enjoyed playing by ear. "Yoke Soo, the music you play—it's like a treasure."

The child bobbed her head. "Yes, Teacher."

Drawing a chair close to the piano, Elizabeth smiled. "If you want someone to be able to find a treasure, what do you do?"

Yoke Soo scrunched her nose. "I can play it for them." She laid her fingers on the keys.

Elizabeth lifted a hand. "Not right now. Let's imagine it's a buried pirate treasure. How would someone find it?"

"A map?" Yoke Soo swung her legs back and forth.

"Right." Elizabeth picked up the hymnal and let it fall open in her hands, the pages ruffling. "Each of these songs is a treasure. If you want to discover them—just like the person who wrote them—you have to follow the map."

Yoke Soo fanned the pages. "So many."

"People have composed music for as long as anyone can remember. These are just a few special ones people wrote for God."

Yoke Soo swung around, spinning the stool toward Elizabeth. "I have songs."

"You've learned many songs, as best I can tell."

"No. My own God songs, from here." She patted the front of her smocked blouse. "Can we write down my songs? Then if someone steals me away—like they almost did with Tien Gum—my songs won't get lost, too."

"We won't let that happen. Miss Cameron is watching out for you. So am I." A quiver raced through Elizabeth's stomach. When had this gentle lesson gone awry? Children shouldn't have to live with such fears. "I can help you write down your songs. But first you must focus on reading music."

Yoke Soo grasped the hymnal and thrust it onto the rack, turning to the first page. "Teach me."

Elizabeth leaned against the old instrument. "I will. And then you'll be able to play every song in the book, whenever you want."

"Let's play them all."

❧

Charles wove through the busy lunch crowd at O'Malley's, aiming for the small table in the back. After the late night and hectic morning, the smell of food set his blood humming.

Henry sat in the rear booth, a chicken leg in one hand, a copy of *The Call* in the other.

"I thought you'd be here." Charles grinned. "Where've you been all morning?"

His friend gestured at the empty seat with the drumstick. "Join me."

Charles slid onto the bench, discreetly patting his pocket to check on his billfold. Henry had yet to pay for a meal.

The clerk swiped a napkin across his face before answering. "I've been stuck at the Hall of Records. They're still dealing with all the paperwork lost in the fires. Such a mess. They've been processing permits for buildings and property without access to any deeds of ownership. It's a clerk's nightmare, let me tell you."

Charles gave the waitress his order before turning back to his friend. "I've got my own records headache, I'm afraid. I need your expertise."

Henry's face lengthened as his brows shot up. "My expertise?" He straightened his vest. "I rather like the sound of that. What've you got?" He pushed his dishes to the side.

Charles opened the briefcase and withdrew the stack of files. "I've been examining the King family's accounts. In 1894, Dr. William King—under my uncle's advisement—invested in multiple buildings around the city." He opened the files and drew out several sheets of paper. "The investments paid out well for a time, but all of these structures were lost in the quake. None received compensation from the fire insurance companies."

Taking the documents from Charles's hand, Henry scanned them with a sigh. "Unlucky fellow. He must have been ruined."

"He passed away a few years ago, but his family was left with nothing. The proceeds should have provided for King's widow and his grown children."

"It's remarkable we didn't all lose our shirts in the disaster." He jabbed a finger at the folded newspaper. "Regardless of the complaints we read in the papers, most of the insurance companies have paid in full, whether or not their contracts included earthquake exclusion clauses. But some of the foreign companies, and those less solvent, haven't been as forthcoming."

Charles sat back, his chest deflating. There had to be something he could do for Elizabeth's family. "How was my uncle not ruined? He made sizable investments in the same properties."

The clerk chuckled. "Your uncle has a sixth sense. He lost some investments, but he came out smelling like a rose. Now the firm is raking money in hand over fist. Do you know how many building permit requests have passed through our doors since the earthquake? I process dozens every day."

"Building permits? Why are we handling permits?"

"The seal from our office goes a long way toward getting it approved with city hall."

Charles's throat tightened. "Mayor Schmitz and attorney Abe Ruef were indicted on something similar last year."

"For graft. Your uncle's too smart for such nonsense. Everything's aboveboard."

"And representation from McKinley and McClintock doesn't come cheap." The three bites of meatloaf sat in Charles's gut like a cannonball. "He's filling the coffers."

"And Mr. McKinley gets to have his hand in what goes where. He's rebuilding this city, one property at a time." Henry lifted his glass. "A city built to his specifications—and they're paying him to do it."

A chill swept over Charles, like stepping into an icy rain. Should anyone have such power? He frowned and tapped the folders. "But what about this case? How can one building receive compensation and its neighbor be denied? The insurance policies appear identical."

Henry shrugged. "You're the attorney. My guess is, it depends on who's doing the fighting and how much money they've got."

Charles jammed fingers through his hair. "If my uncle has a stake in these buildings, why isn't he protecting his investments?"

"Have you asked him?"

"Every time I mention the case, he changes the subject."

Henry took a swig of coffee. "Perhaps he doesn't want to be reminded of his losses."

As the server arrived to clear the dishes, Charles returned the paperwork to his satchel. Perhaps it was time to put the case away, as well. Elizabeth was the main reason he'd spent so much energy on it and considering the look on her face when he left yesterday, she wanted nothing to do with him.

So why couldn't he let it go?

Elizabeth ran the broom under the classroom sewing tables, catching the stray threads into a nice pile. "I don't know, Ruby. He's nice, but I'm not looking for romance. I want to focus my energy here."

Her sister folded the long curtain panel she'd been stitching for demonstration. "Why can't you do both? He's a handsome fellow, and he's sympathetic toward the underprivileged. Like you, he's interested in politics. I can't imagine someone better suited."

Elizabeth shook her head and continued sweeping. The one difficulty with inviting your sister to help was enduring an overly helpful sibling.

Ruby opened her sewing basket and jabbed a needle into the silk pincushion. "I think you should accept his invitation. If not to the Japanese Tea Garden, somewhere else. Perhaps you could join Gerald and me at a play or a concert." She smiled. "Abby still wants to take Robert to the Sutro Baths. Can you imagine us all swimming? It would be fun."

"I didn't come to the city for merrymaking and romance. I came to serve."

"So did I, in case you've forgotten." Ruby folded both arms across her chest. "God had other plans."

"You always say as much." Elizabeth blew out a long breath. "I thought His plan was for me to become a concert pianist. That's what father wanted. He told me to use my gifts."

Ruby sat on one of the student chairs. "You never told us what happened—why you backed away from your music."

Elizabeth closed her eyes for a moment. Tell Ruby about Tobias? Never. "I needed a change. I came here to serve God. I'm putting everything else behind me."

"You can't live a life of seclusion."

"Donaldina has made this her life's mission and never married. Why shouldn't I do the same?"

Ruby's pale brows pulled together like so many gathered stitches. She walked to Elizabeth's side and took her arm. "Gerald and I pray for you every night. I don't know what you're going through, but I feel like you're hiding yourself here. I wish you'd talk to me. Or to someone—Abby or Donaldina."

Elizabeth bit her lip. "I appreciate the prayers, Ruby, but I know what I'm doing." She squeezed her sister's hand and released it. "I'm even playing the piano again. I'm tutoring some of the girls."

"I'm glad." Ruby brightened. "I know how you delighted in it. And you're right—father's greatest joy was hearing you play. He adored you." She touched Elizabeth's face. "How he'd love to see you now."

The words pierced Elizabeth's heart. *No, he wouldn't. He'd hate what I've become.* She glanced around the quiet classroom. Perhaps in time, with effort, she could once again be worthy of his love.

Kum Yong knocked on the door frame.

"Come in." Some of the tension eased from Elizabeth's shoulders. Finally, something to distract her sister's attention.

Kum Yong greeted Ruby with a hug before turning to Elizabeth. "The annual board meeting is coming up—the first in the new building. Miss Cameron wants to make it special." She brought her hands together in front of her chest. "We were hoping you could help."

"Of course." Elizabeth straightened. "Perhaps the girls could sew some banners for the occasion. And the curtains and cushions should be ready by then."

Kum Yong shook her head. "We're talking about a concert, Elizabeth. Recitations, songs, poems. Anything you think they'd enjoy."

Ruby's eyes danced. "Sounds like fun. Elizabeth, it's a perfect use of your gifts."

The hairs on the back of Elizabeth's neck stood to attention. A concert? "The students would enjoy the diversion. Perhaps Yoke Soo could play the piano. It would be a good incentive for her to keep working at reading sheet music."

Kum Yong smoothed her white blouse. "Donaldina wants you to play, too." A grin darted across her face. "She wants the board to know the wonderful talent we have in our teachers."

"They're coming to see the students, not me."

"You *must* play." Kum Yong folded her arms. "The girls are so proud—they want to show you off."

Ruby laid the folded curtains on the front table. "Pray about it, Elizabeth. He'll lead you."

Sinking into one of the seats, Elizabeth fought the sensation of being lost at sea. *That's what I'm afraid of.*

A spark of mischief glinted in Kum Yong's dark eyes. "There's one other thing Donaldina asked me to tell you. We're taking the children on a surprise outing tomorrow to the beach."

Elizabeth glanced up, her heart lightening. "Is it safe, considering what happened to Tien Gum?"

"We're bringing along chaperones. The board has sent money for train tickets."

A smile darted across Ruby's face. "Gerald and I could come, if it helps."

Warmth spread through Elizabeth. The day sounded better and better. The beach, the children, and her family? Maybe she'd met with God's approval after all.

Kum Yong tipped her head, her lips curving upward. "Miss Cameron invited Mr. McKinley, too."

Ruby covered her giggle with the back of her hand.

Elizabeth closed her eyes. "Of course."

18

*C*harles lifted two baskets from the back of the Larkspurs' automobile, the sun warming his shoulders as gulls wheeled on the light breeze. The sea air chased away the tension of courtrooms, cases, and surly supervising attorneys. Trading heaps of paperwork for mounds of sand sounded like an undeserved gift. "I've never ridden in a car driven by a lady before."

Ruby gathered a large canvas bag from the rear seat and grinned, a silk scarf holding her hat in place. "I am a King sister, after all. We're a rather unconventional bunch."

Gerald chuckled, hoisting a blanket over his shoulder. "Truer words have never been spoken, though I think your baby sister might take the prize in that contest. Marching in suffrage rallies, performing in concert halls, rescuing Chinese slave girls—what will she attempt next?"

Charles stopped, sand already finding its way into his shoes. "What did you say?"

Gerald paused as his wife hurried off to join the others. "Which part?"

"Concert halls?"

The good doctor cocked his head, as if conducting an examination. "Elizabeth's a concert pianist. Or rather, she was. Hasn't she told you?"

"A concert pianist? Elizabeth King?" He thought back to the beautiful piano in their home in Sacramento. Not to mention those long graceful fingers. Charles shook away the stray thought. No need to let his mind go there. "Why did she stop?"

"You can try asking her, but Ruby says she won't talk about it." The corner of his mouth lifted. "Perhaps you'll have better luck."

Charles clamped one of the baskets under his arm. "I'll do that." He shook his head. "The woman is one surprise after another."

Gerald patted his shoulder. "I think you'll discover that's true of every woman, Charles."

The two men strolled out to Ocean Beach, the children already running through the sand and squealing in play.

Charles pulled in a deep breath of ocean air. "It must be a relief for them, escaping the walls of the Home. Being normal children for a day?"

The doctor nodded. "They have a difficult life, in some ways, but so much better than before."

Near a clump of sea grass, Elizabeth organized the picnic hampers. Charles joined her, adding his two baskets to the collection.

She straightened. "There you are. I thought perhaps you weren't coming after all." Her words sounded clipped, as if it would have been a relief if he'd never arrived.

"These belong to your sister. She said something about Gerald's mother packing enough for armies of children."

The words coaxed a smile to Elizabeth's face. Her white lace dress fluttered in the breeze. "I'm sure with all this fresh air and exercise, they'll be famished by lunch time."

"As will I. I hope they'll share." Charles patted his stomach, desperate to keep her smile intact. He turned and glanced down the shoreline. Miss Cameron strode along the water's edge with several of the older girls.

A youngster raced up to Elizabeth, sand flying from under her bare feet. "Teacher, teacher—come see! There are little crabs."

"Crabs, you say?" Elizabeth bent down to speak to the child. "Then maybe you should watch out for your toes."

"Come see." The girl ran off, swinging her arms like a broken windmill.

Elizabeth set down the hamper and moved to follow.

"I'll join you." Charles had resolved not to chase her around like a puppy dog the entire afternoon, but the day was young. "After all, you might need protection from dangerous crustaceans." He hooked his fingers in the top edge of his vest and smiled.

"If you'd like." She shrugged. "It's a public beach."

Not exactly an invitation, but he followed regardless. "You're going to have to help me with the children's names. That is, if they'll even speak to me."

"They'll speak to you. You're the hero who rescued Donaldina from jail."

The woman's dimples would drive him to distraction. He focused on the children, three of the littlest darting in and out of the water under the watchful eye of a young Chinese man. One of the girls grasped the man's wrist and tugged him toward the water, giggling.

Elizabeth paused at the water's edge. "This is Yoke Soo, Ah Cheng, and Ah Lon." She nodded at each before gesturing to the man. "And this is our friend, George Wu. George, I'd like you to meet Mr. Charles McKinley. He's the attorney who assisted with Tien Gum."

Still holding the child's hand, the man bobbed his head. "Mr. McKinley. A pleasure to meet you."

Elizabeth turned to Charles. "George owns the apothecary shop on Stockton Street."

"I'm honored to meet you. I haven't visited many of the shops, yet." Charles nodded. "I'm sure Miss Cameron appreciates your help today."

George smiled down at the little girls. "This is pure joy to me. I'm not married, so for now—these are my children."

Yoke Soo splashed her feet in the water. "It's so cold I can't feel my toes!"

"Don't go in too far. The waves will carry you off." George swooped her up and carried her to the sand, the other two following.

Elizabeth's hands were both captured by children within moments, but she stepped back from the waves. "Oh, no, you don't. I'm not going in there."

"Please, teacher, please!" The girls tugged on her arms.

Charles chuckled. Elizabeth would have a difficult time staying out of the water if her students had anything to do with it. "Did you bring a bathing costume?"

She freed herself and shooed the girls back to their play. "I was told this beach was too cold for swimming. But I wore my sandals." She lifted the hem of her dress, showing the black leather slippers with lilac ribbons. "I'll let them convince me in a while."

"I never understood why women wore those. What's wrong with feet?" Charles pulled off his shoes and socks, rolling up the legs of his trousers.

She smiled and held out her hands. "I'll take your shoes. You take the girls."

He tucked the socks inside and handed them to her. "That's very kind." He clapped his hands. "Come on, girls, I'll be the lifeguard."

Little Ah Cheng grabbed Charles's leg and held on. Yoke Soo claimed the other. Charles lifted each girl high in turn, as if he were pulling his foot out of clinging mud with each step.

He glanced back to see Elizabeth standing on shore, his shoes pressed against her chest, one hand shading her eyes.

Even with his feet turning to ice, heat coursed through his body. The evidence was conclusive. She was, without a doubt, the most beautiful woman he'd ever seen.

&

Elizabeth placed Charles's shoes beside the blanket, taking a moment to run her fingers along the warm leather. The clothes he wore today confirmed what he'd told her about his upbringing. The trousers were well-worn—appearing almost soft to the touch. The cuffs on his jacket were frayed around the edges, too. *So different than what he normally wears.*

Now as she watched the children frolic with George and Charles in the surf, she regretted not bringing a bathing dress. Charles was right. Why must women wear stockings and shoes in the water? The girls were splashing with their bare toes and having the time of their lives.

Kum Yong joined her, flopping down onto one of the blankets. "This is what Heaven will be like, I am most certain." She laughed, the sun and wind tinting her cheeks pink.

"I agree." Elizabeth stretched, the cool breeze sending shivers across her skin. "Sunshine, fresh air, and no fog."

Kum Yong opened the nearest basket. "And plenty of good food. Are these cookies I smell?"

Tucking her skirt under her, Elizabeth knelt on the blanket. "Probably. Ruby brought two baskets. Her mother-in-law likes to bake."

Kum Yong closed the lid. "I dream of my own kitchen, sometimes. And a nice mother-in-law."

"Don't you need a husband for that?"

Her friend ducked her head to hide her smile. "Yes. Maybe. I suppose so."

"Did you have someone in mind?" Elizabeth sat up straight. Kum Yong rarely spoke of herself.

"No." The young woman's gaze flickered toward the shore. "Forget I said anything."

Elizabeth followed her gaze. "George Wu?" Her heart twirled upward like leaves in a whirlwind. Why hadn't she considered the possibility before? "Does Donaldina know?"

"You mustn't say anything. Elizabeth, please." Kum Yong covered her face with her hands. "It's nothing. Just a dream."

"A beautiful, sweet dream." Elizabeth leaned back, bracing her palms in the sand and crossing her ankles in front of her. "I would give anything for such a dream."

"What of Charles?"

Elizabeth's heart dropped toward her stomach. "I make poor choices when it comes to men. I think I'm safer on my own."

Charles lifted one of the girls and spun her around in the air. The squeals carried across the sand to where she and Kum Yong sat.

A good man. He'd make a good father, someday.

George stumbled out of the surf, laughing, as Yoke Soo flicked water toward him with her toes.

When Kum Yong sighed, Elizabeth clambered to her feet. "That's it."

"What?" Kum Yong's eyes widened as Elizabeth grabbed her hands and puller her up as well.

"I'm not going to let you sit here and pine away all afternoon. You're going to have some fun." Elizabeth yanked her friend forward, jogging toward the shoreline.

The expression on the men's faces was worth getting her skirt wet. Elizabeth darted into the waves, one hand holding her skirts above her knees, the other dragging a giggling Kum Yong.

The three children squealed. Ah Cheng reached her arms in and flung handfuls of water at them.

"Oh, no you don't, little miss." Elizabeth dropped Kum Yong's hand and snatched the little girl up, swinging her over one shoulder. Drips of icy water caught her neck as Ah Cheng grabbed her and held on for dear life.

Charles grinned. "I thought you weren't coming in."

"I said I wasn't coming in, *yet*. I needed motivation."

He gave Elizabeth a sideways glance. "What got you moving?"

"Seeing all the fun you were having. I don't like being left out."

Kum Yong shrieked, splashing away as the little ones chased her through the shallow water.

George laughed, a huge smile spreading across his face. He tucked his hands into his sleeves and watched Kum Yong play with the children, a softness crinkling around the corners of his eyes.

Elizabeth's heart warmed. Kum Yong might not be alone in her dreaming. She swung Ah Cheng down, landing her on her feet with a gentle splash. "Kum Yong is getting away. Why don't you go help?"

The girl hurried off, joining the group further down the beach. George followed a few steps behind.

Elizabeth stood still, the water lapping at her ankles. She unpinned her hat and took it off. Closing her eyes, she let the sunshine warm her face even as her toes ached from the cold. For one blessed moment, her past with Tobias was a million miles away—perhaps even washed clean by the tortuously cold water. Let Kum Yong go find romance. She'd be perfectly content to bask in the California sun.

He'd never seen a painting near as beautiful as the actual sight before him.

Elizabeth stood silhouetted against the horizon, wisps of her blonde hair floating on the ocean breeze, her head tipped back as if admiring the grandeur of God's creation. She'd released the hem of her dress and it rose and fell with the rippling water.

Charles's heart pounded, like the current against the sand. How could he not fall in love with this woman? She was everything he'd ever wanted. When she'd tossed aside convention to jump into the waves with the rest of them, it took everything he had not to capture her in his arms.

He stepped close behind her. "I could stay here forever."

"Me, too." Her voice was nearly lost in the sounds of the surf.

Reaching forward, he grasped her fingers. "Elizabeth..."

She jumped, yanking her hand away. "What are you—" Her words cut short as she flailed her arms, eyes widening.

Charles reach out to grab her, but arrived a second too late.

Elizabeth tumbled face-first into the surf. She popped up sputtering, silt dripping from her chin.

He reached down to assist.

She knocked his hand away. "Don't." She spit the word toward the foamy brine. Pushing up to her knees, the sandy seawater cascaded off the front of her no-longer-white gown. "I can't believe I just..." She shook her head, several locks of hair coming free and hanging bedraggled over her shoulders.

"Elizabeth!" Ruby came running. "My goodness! What happened?"

"I—I slipped." She cast a burning glance at Charles.

He crouched at her side. "Please, let me help you. It's my fault, I startled you."

After wiping a muddy palm across her chin, she nodded. "All right."

He gripped her arm and helped her stagger to her feet, the dress hanging sodden against her legs, like she'd washed up from a shipwreck. "Your dress—I'm so sorry."

"You didn't push me in, Charles. I stumbled."

"You wouldn't have if I hadn't…" The words stuck in his throat. Had he really tried to hold her hand? "If I hadn't surprised you."

She leaned against his arm as they floundered through the shallow water back to the beach. "I'm so clumsy."

Ruby reached out to grab Elizabeth's other hand and help her to dry land. "Elizabeth, where's your hat?"

Elizabeth's hand flew up to her hair. "I took it off, just before I fell." She spun around. "Oh." She pointed to the waves, the flowered hat bobbing on the surf like a brightly colored duck decoy.

"I'll get it." Charles rolled his pant legs higher above his knees.

"It's too far." Elizabeth's voice quavered. "It'll be halfway to China soon."

Charles set his jaw. "I can retrieve it. That's the least I can do."

"Don't be ridiculous. You've done enough."

Her words froze him worse than the water pulling at his ankles.

As Ruby helped Elizabeth back to the blankets, Charles gazed out at the waves in frustration. The bobbing hat drifted further away, much like his chances with Elizabeth.

℞

Elizabeth collapsed on the sand, the drenched clothes pulling her toward the earth. A shiver coursed through her limbs.

"You're going to freeze." Ruby shook out of one of the blankets and wrapped it around her shoulders. "What were you thinking, going out there in your clothes?"

"I wasn't planning on swimming. The wave sucked the sand out from under my feet."

"Pity Charles didn't catch you." Ruby clucked her tongue.

Elizabeth lowered her head to her knees. "Why do things like this always happen to me?" She muttered the words into the damp wool covering.

"Should I drive you home? You can't stay in those wet things."

"I think Kum Yong packed some extra clothes for the girls. I can borrow something. Just let me catch my breath."

Her sister's jaw dropped. "You can't wear one of those—those costumes."

"Why not?" The girls' loose white tunics and trousers looked like the epitome of comfort. "If they're suitable for the students, why shouldn't I wear them, too?"

Ruby wrinkled her nose. "I suppose." She chewed her lip for a moment. "I'll go find her."

Elizabeth shivered in the cool breeze. She had no one to blame but herself for this indignity. Just when she thought she'd finished reliving the past, a man's touch sent her back into chaos.

In the distance, Charles walked along the shore, the water lapping at his bare feet. His shoulders hung like they'd become disconnected from his frame.

A lump grew in her throat. There'd been no denying the expression on Charles's face the moment their eyes met—not so different from the ones Tobias used to melt her defenses. Elizabeth pushed her hands up into her hair as the memories battled for her attention. Tobias's eyes held other desires, too—possession, ownership, control.

She'd never give herself to another man. Tears spilled down her cheeks. Charles deserved someone better. She must find some way to explain as much to him without revealing herself.

Ruby returned, Kum Yong in tow.

Kum Yong's brow furrowed. "Elizabeth, I'm sorry I ran off and left you."

Elizabeth pushed up to her feet, scrubbing the blanket across her face to obliterate any tear tracks. "As I keep telling people, this is no one's fault but my own."

Her friend dug through one of the canvas bags and drew out some wrinkled trousers and a long blouse. "I think these will fit. Good thing you're small."

"Where can I change?" The beach offered little hope for privacy.

"We'll hold up the blankets." Ruby lifted the one Elizabeth had been sitting on moments before.

Elizabeth groaned, but the cool air left little room for argument. Ducking between the blankets, she unfastened her skirt and shirtwaist with stiff fingers and slithered out of her stockings. "I've got sand in my corset lacing."

"Take it off." Kum Yong shrugged. "No one will notice. You can keep a blanket around you."

Ocean air swept in between the blankets. Elizabeth shuddered as she stripped out of the sodden layers, dropping the corset and petticoats to the ground with the rest. Leaving her damp chemise and drawers, Elizabeth tugged the long top over her head. She stepped into the loose trousers, stifling a giggle. "It's like wearing nightclothes. I could get used to this."

Her sister pursed her lips. "Don't you dare. You're unconventional enough, little sister. Let's not set tongues wagging."

Elizabeth ran her hands down the embroidered material, softened by countless washes. "Why don't we all dress like this?"

Kum Yong smiled. "I can't see you giving up your fine shirtwaists."

Ruby frowned. "You can't parade around the beach like that. It's okay for the little girls, but people will stare."

"It's not so different from the bathing costumes." Elizabeth gathered her unmentionables from the sand, wrapping them in her damp gown.

"Here comes Charles." Her sister started to lower the blanket.

"Give me that!" Elizabeth grabbed the covering.

Ruby laughed. "I knew you were bluffing." She turned to welcome the man.

Elizabeth sank down onto the sand. She should have taken Ruby's initial offer of a ride home. Sitting here wrapped in a blanket all afternoon bordered on ridiculous.

Charles sat beside her. "Are you going to be all right?"

She nodded, pushing aside any vestiges of pride. "I think I'll stay away from the water, though." Her teeth chattered, whether from cold or nerves.

"Is there anything I can do?"

Ruby's lips curved upward. "You can stay and keep Elizabeth company while I take her wet things to the automobile. Kum Yong and some of the older girls will get the food ready."

"Should I take them?" Charles held his hands out.

"No!" Elizabeth drew the bundle close to her midsection. The idea of this man handling her undergarments sent prickles racing across her skin.

Ruby laughed and reached for the dripping pile. "I'll do it."

As everyone else drifted away, Charles sat back and stretched his legs across the sand. "I'm sorry I startled you."

She laid her cheek against her knees and gazed at him. The tiny lines forming around the corners of his mouth plucked at her conscience. Was he really so troubled?

"I saw the panic on your face when I reached for your hand..." He lowered his eyes. "I won't touch you again, if you don't wish it. I promise."

A tendril curled around her heart. Is it what she wanted? "You caught me off guard."

Charles bent his knees and dug his feet into the sand. "I must confess, Elizabeth—you fascinate me. I'm completely mesmerized." He met her gaze, unwavering this time. "But if you're not comfortable with my attention, I won't pursue you further."

A shiver coursed through her at his frank words. "I've never done anything to encourage you."

"All my life, I've met women who are obsessed with little more than parasols and parties. You threw yourself into the mission work with no concern for yourself. You face down men like my uncle without flinching." He grinned. "You talk politics like a man."

"Is that supposed to be a compliment? Can't a woman speak politics?"

"Certainly, but I've met few who do. And fewer still who have the courage to disagree and argue their stance." He took a deep breath. "All of that, and you're beautiful, too." A light danced in his eyes. "Especially right now."

A hot flush crept up her face. "Don't make fun."

"I'm not. You're like a mermaid, washed up on the beach." He gestured to her head. "With seaweed in your hair."

"What?" Elizabeth dug her fingers through her locks, grasping the slimy strand and yanking it free. She flung the green offender to the sand. "I can't believe this."

"Still lovely." He grinned.

Elizabeth blinked back tears and turned away. The man's assertions were ludicrous. Sweet, but ludicrous.

Children sat in groups around the beach, lounging on blankets, some of the littlest curled up for naps. Two of the older girls helped Kum Yong distribute picnic food. Down by the water's edge, a small group gathered. Donaldina and George had joined in, everyone holding hands in a long chain, jumping the waves in unison.

As much as she'd like to know the handsome attorney better, she couldn't take the risk of her secret being revealed. "It won't work, Charles. I'd only disappoint you in the end. You have a bright future ahead of you." She lifted her head. "You'll be mayor, or maybe even a congressman—you'll change the world. I won't stand in the way."

His brows drew down. "You wouldn't."

"Each point you offered confirms we're not a good match. I'm contrary, argumentative. I like to have my own way. Can you picture me at state dinners or political rallies? I'd be a disaster." She ran her fingers through her hair, twisting it into a loose knot at the nape of her neck. "You need someone who can love and support you. Someone with a spotless reputation and delicate manners. I spend my time with former prostitutes and opium addicts whose sins pale in comparison to my own."

Charles shook his head. "I've no desire for a simpering wife who'll agree with every word I say. I'm searching for someone who will challenge me and help me remember why I went into law in the first place." A smile crept to his face. "I'm searching for you."

"Look at me." Elizabeth dropped her hold on the blanket and gestured to herself, odd garb and all. "I'm no one's idea of a perfect woman."

Charles's gaze never wavered. "Elizabeth, you don't get to decide my opinion of you. If you don't return my feelings, I understand. I wish I could somehow separate myself from your distrust of my uncle, and my connections with your family's financial state, but I cannot. We each bring complications and stumbling blocks to our path, but I believe we can overcome these obstacles—together."

She cupped a handful of sand, letting it slip through her fingers. "It's not your uncle or your job, Charles."

"This'll be my closing argument, then." He laid a hand on his heart. "If you want me to walk away and not bother you again, tell me. But, I'm praying you'll give me an opportunity to prove myself worthy."

She could set him free with one statement, but the words died in her throat. She couldn't lie to him—not about this. Elizabeth studied the firm line of his chin, tracing it up to his earnest eyes. Her chest ached, as if she'd spent the entire conversation holding her breath. If she confessed her feelings now, would she be able to hide the other truths? The ugly ones? "I do care for you." Her voice quavered. "But it frightens me. I don't think it'll be enough."

"It's enough for now." A smile spread across his face.

Prickles raced across her arms. Why did her heart leap every time he smiled? *Father, help me.*

"Will you accompany me to the Japanese Gardens, then? Say, Friday afternoon?" He glanced around the beach. "Perhaps without the few dozen chaperones?"

A weak laugh bubbled its way up her throat. She tucked a lock of hair behind her ear. "I will."

19

Elizabeth stood in front of her small bedroom mirror, fussing with the lace cravat covering the neckline of her blue shirtwaist. Why hadn't she telephoned Charles to cancel this outing? The rice and vegetables from lunch sat in her stomach like a rock. Perhaps she hadn't canceled because she'd spent the week dreaming about walking flowered paths with the attractive man by her side.

Now the day had arrived foggy and cold, as if the truth hung suspended in the air. She couldn't pretend she was like any other young woman out to snare a fellow. She had no business being seen with a respectable man like Charles McKinley.

A gentle rapping on her door broke Elizabeth from her worries. Kum Yong peeked into the room. "I came to—ooh!" Her mouth curled around the vowel and drew out the sound. "You look so pretty!" She tiptoed inside and closed the door. "Is this the big day?" Kum Yong clasped her hands in front of her chest, bouncing on her toes.

"You look like a little girl when you do that." Elizabeth couldn't help but smile. Her friend's joy was contagious. "I think you're more excited than I am."

"How could you not be excited?" Kum Yong sat on the edge of Elizabeth's bed.

Elizabeth picked up a pair of earbobs from the box on her dresser. "It's just nerves, I expect." She sat next to her friend, rolling the jewelry in her palm. "If George asked to court you, would you accept him?"

Kum Yong fiddled with the cuff of her sleeve. "I never should have told you."

"I'm glad you did. Now I can speak to Donaldina."

"No!" Kum Yong jumped from the bed. "You mustn't. It's unseemly for me to express interest. It must come from him." Her shoulders fell. "And that's not likely."

"Kum Yong, it's a new century. A woman can have opinions of her own." Elizabeth clipped the baubles to her earlobes. "And unlikely? Why?"

"He only comes to see little Yoke Soo. He rescued her, so he feels responsible." She shrugged. "He doesn't come to see me."

"Perhaps." Elizabeth stood and stretched. "But I saw how he looked at you when we were at the shore."

Kum Yong's brows drew low over her eyes. "Don't say such things."

"Why not? You said as much of Charles."

Another knock made both of them jump. Elizabeth stifled a giggle as she walked to the door.

Tien Gum stood in the hallway. "Your young man is downstairs, Teacher."

My young man. A chill raced over Elizabeth's arms. "Thank you, Tien. I'll be right down." She closed the door and leaned her forehead against it. "What do I do?"

Kum Yong placed a hand on her shoulder. "You have fun for the both of us."

Elizabeth nodded and turned to face her. "You're a good friend."

"And I hear everything, later. Yes?"

Elizabeth squeezed Kum Yong's hands. "If it goes well, yes." She snatched up her reticule, took a deep breath, and opened the door. Willing her feet to move, she walked down the stairs.

Charles waited near Donaldina's office. "I was afraid you might have changed your mind."

Elizabeth bit her lip. *Was it too late?* "You didn't reconsider either, I see."

He grinned. "Of course not. The man in the corner market almost convinced me to bring you flowers, but I wasn't sure if you could display them in your room."

"I'm glad you didn't. The girls would gossip about it for weeks." She glanced around the empty hall. "In fact, we should hurry out. Tien Gum is probably making the rounds as we speak. Pretty soon we'll have an audience."

Charles offered his arm. "I wouldn't want to make you the talk of the Mission."

"The damage is already done, but we don't need more eyewitnesses to confirm it."

"What about the locks? It seems to be a ritual around here." He opened the door.

"Kum Yong is waiting." She inclined her head toward a group of potted palms. "She just doesn't want us to know."

"Oh, I see. How kind of her to give us privacy. Almost."

They walked outside and pulled the door shut. Within moments, the locks clicked into place.

Elizabeth's fingers trembled as her hand looped through Charles's arm. Now, if only she could manage to get through the outing with no disasters.

The fog hung over the Japanese Tea Garden in Golden Gate Park like a wool fleece, closing out the world's disturbances and absorbing every sound, every footstep. Charles squeezed Elizabeth's arm where it looped through his own, relishing the warmth of her body on this chilly day. "I'm sorry I couldn't arrange for sunshine. I did my best."

"I prefer this. It feels like we're alone in the park. It's as if all of life's problems were left outside the gates." She lifted her chin.

Charles smiled. "So, no paperwork, snobbish attorneys, or stoic judges for me. What have you left behind?"

Her dimple showed. "Tangled bobbin thread, girlish squabbles, and students whispering to each other in a language I don't understand..."

"You like your work, don't you?" He gazed down at her gloved fingers, resting on his sleeve.

"I love it. Even more so, now that I'm teaching piano." She adjusted her small-brimmed hat, tipping it slightly so she could glance up at him.

"I understand you're putting together a concert."

"Just a little exhibition for the board and the donors. The girls will sing and recite. Our little piano prodigy, Yoke Soo, will play a piece."

"Any chance you'll be performing, as well? I'd love to hear you play."

Elizabeth blushed. "Donaldina is petitioning me to, but it seems rather self-serving. We're celebrating the Mission and the girls. I shouldn't be in the spotlight."

"I can't think of anyone I'd prefer to see on a stage."

"My stage days are over."

"Why is that?" The nosy question slipped out before he could stop himself.

She glanced up at him, her blue eyes luminescent in the bright fog. "I made certain mistakes I needed to leave behind." She lowered her gaze, concentrating on the pond. "I came to the Mission not just because I wanted to help the Chinese girls." She lifted one shoulder in a half-shrug. "I thought they could help me, as well."

Her honesty took him off-guard. "Have they?"

"I believe so. I'm more sure of myself." A smile broke through, like a shaft of sunlight piercing the fog. "I've stormed into brothels and opium dens with Donaldina—far more frightening than walking onto a stage. Or facing myself in the mirror."

"Then perhaps it's time for you to reconsider the stage."

Elizabeth shook her head. "No, not yet. Probably not ever."

They walked to the far edge of the pond, pausing under a dogwood tree, the wind ruffling its leaves in a steady rhythmic sound. Charles glanced down at Elizabeth's thin wrap. "Are you warm enough?"

She rubbed her arms. "It's a little chilly."

He gestured to a bench protected by an ornate wall. "Why don't we sit for awhile? There might be less wind."

Elizabeth released his elbow as she took a seat on the bench. "Yes, this is better."

Charles ran his hand over his sleeve where her fingers rested a moment before. "I'm glad you came. I know you could come up with a thousand arguments why it's not a good idea."

"You're the one with arguments, Mr. Attorney. I only needed one."

He sat down, studying her gaze. Why did he have such trouble reading her? "And which one is that?"

"I'm not the right woman for you."

"We've been over this already. I've dismissed the argument."

She placed one hand on her hip. "You're not the judge, here. You can't dismiss me."

He couldn't help but smile at her petulant pout. "You're correct. I'm sorry." He gestured for her to continue. "Go ahead—what were you saying?"

Her exhale ruffled the fringe of hair above her brows. "You're allowing me to reopen the case?"

"I'm encouraging you to do whatever pleases you, Miss King." He leaned back and folded his arms. "And just so you know—you're quite partial to making opening statements and arguments as well."

Her mouth closed slowly as if he'd deflated her thoughts.

His stomach tightened. "That probably sounded a bit patronizing. I'm sorry."

"No." Lines crinkled across Elizabeth's forehead. "You're right. I've just never considered it before."

"You should go to law school. We could open our own firm. McKinley and King."

"Or King and McKinley." The dimple showed in her cheek. She pressed her palms against the seat.

Or McKinley and McKinley. The thought stilled his heart. How easy it was to picture her as his wife. Without thinking, he reached for her fingers.

She jerked, scooting back along the bench. "Please, don't."

A chill swept over him. "Don't touch you?"

"You said you wouldn't." She folded her arms and tucked both hands out of sight.

"I was just trying to…" Trying to what? He bit his lip. Trying to touch her. The very idea overwhelmed his senses. "Why are you so easily startled? You held my arm earlier."

Her brows dropped low over her eyes. "You offered, I accepted. It's not the same thing at all." She shook her head. "You can't just—I'm not the sort of girl who likes being caressed at a man's whim. I won't have it."

A wave of heat rushed through his system. "I'm sorry. It wasn't like that."

"I know exactly what it's like. I've been around men enough to know." She stood up and walked a few steps away.

The haunted look in her eyes paralyzed him. What had Elizabeth endured to make her so wary? After a long moment, he pushed himself up to follow. "Elizabeth."

She paused near the moon bridge, her arms still pressed against her ribs.

Charles stopped, well out of reach. "I don't know what's wrong, but you can trust me." He placed his hands in his pocket. "Is this better?"

Instead of answering, she closed her eyes. "What must you think of me?"

He could almost hear Professor Davis's lecture about loaded questions. Charles considered his options. "I think you're frightened. I think…" Her lowered head reminded him of his sister, Josephine, the night she'd shown up at the door with blood on her hands. Scenarios raced through his mind, each one more daunting than the last. "I—I'm guessing you've been hurt before." He braved a step forward. "Look, I've seen you wet and covered in silt. I've seen you laugh, cry, and be angry as a cornered cat. Nothing about you will shock me or drive me away."

"You don't know." She leaned on the wooden post.

He rubbed his jaw, the pain in her stance tearing at him. What could he say to earn her trust? "I told you what happened with my sister."

"Not all of it. You said she was hurt by someone and the courts failed her."

He drew a deep breath. The story rarely strayed far from his mind, even though he'd spent years trying to bury it. "Her husband used to beat her—torture her, really. I've never met a more cruel or arrogant man. Once, after nearly killing her, he left to feed the stock. She believed he'd finish the job when he returned." He fell silent, the discussion punching holes in the protective wall he'd built around his memories.

Elizabeth's eyes widened. "What happened?"

"She took the shotgun from over the door and waited." A lump rose in his throat, choking his words. "As soon as he came through the door, Josephine shot him through the chest."

Elizabeth covered her mouth with trembling fingers.

Charles forced his hands back into his pockets. Every time she made that face, his instinct screamed for him to take her into his arms. "As I said, I don't think there's anything you could say that would shock me at this point."

She lowered her eyes, gripping the post. "Where is she now? Your sister."

"The state mental hospital in Ukiah. Uncle Silas succeeded in moving her there, out of the prison system."

"Do you ever see her?"

"Once a year." He blew out a long breath, fixing her in his gaze. "So you see, I understand people have scars. But I'd love it if you could trust me."

She stood silent at his side for a long moment. "I'll try."

Charles's heart leaped upward in his chest. He locked his elbows rather than risk spooking her again.

A smile softened her face. "Now are we going to climb this silly-looking bridge?" She gestured to the odd bridge arching over the goldfish pond like a massive barrel sitting on its side. "I'm afraid it might require mountain climbing equipment."

"I think we should." He lifted his chin. "Why not? We've already conquered some pretty steep hills today."

Charles spread the files on the table, a tremor racing through his gut. His first day in court as a lead attorney, and Spencer issued him a case a monkey couldn't lose. So why did he feel like a child starting kindergarten?

"All rise." The bailiff's voice echoed through the room. Few were present to answer the order, the public finding little of interest in the dry financial case.

Charles stood in a swift motion, his leg bumping the table and sending several forms scattering to the floor.

William Smythe, the defense attorney, cast a raised brow at Charles.

"Judge C. P. Percival, presiding." The bailiff droned the words as if he'd repeated them countless times during his career.

The judge claimed his seat and shuffled his own set of papers with little emotion. Glancing down his nose over a pair of gold-rimmed spectacles, he studied the room in similar fashion. He nodded to Smythe before turning his gaze on Charles. "New here, are you?"

Charles forced himself to take a breath. "Yes, sir."

Judge Percival glanced down at his notes. "McKinley. Of McKinley and McClintock." He lifted his gaze, deep grooves forming on either side of his mouth. "Impressive bloodline."

His stomach lurched at the official's condescending tone. "Yes, sir."

"It won't get you any special treatment here."

"I don't expect any, sir."

The judge adjusted his glasses, tapping a pen against the desk. "The case looks straightforward. In my experience, these sorts of minor disputes are resolved in short order. We should be out in time for lunch."

The judge took a sip of water before launching into the perfunctory reading of the case notes, his voice echoing through the cavernous room.

Charles glanced down at the table, sliding the pages from side to side with one finger. Several were missing. His pulse accelerated. As the judge continued speaking, Charles flipped open his briefcase. No other files remained, except for the King family's which he'd practically committed to memory at this point.

Judge Percival glanced up from the sheet, staring over the edge at Charles. "Mr. McKinley, is there a problem?"

How many times had he endured this nightmare during law school? Any moment now, he'd wake up in a cold sweat. Charles rose to his feet without removing his gaze from the tabletop. Willing the forms to appear didn't seem to be effective. "Sir, I seem to be missing a few of the key documents."

Silence fell over the courtroom, pressing down on Charles like a vise.

The judge yanked off his spectacles. "Do you often show up to court unprepared, Mr. McKinley?"

"No, sir. Never, sir." The hairs lifted on the back of his neck. Those records had been complete when he left the office this morning. He'd checked them twice.

"Do you need a short recess?"

Charles bent down and sorted through his belongings while panic clambered up his throat. "I'm not—not sure, Your Honor." He peered under the table. One paper rested on the wood floor. He scooped it up and added it to the stack, but it failed to explain the others.

Mr. Smythe chuckled. "Might check your pockets, son."

No matter the ridiculous nature of the insult, Charles patted his coat pockets with no luck. Had he forgotten them at the office? Heaven forbid he left any on the streetcar. He shook his head to scatter the panicked thoughts crowding his brain like pigeons chasing breadcrumbs.

"Mr. McKinley?" The judge's voice graveled from the bench.

"I—sir—Your Honor…" Charles laid both palms on the table, focusing his eyes on the stack of pages. *The files were here. And now they're not.*

The defense attorney blew a noisy exhale. "Your Honor, if opposing counsel is choosing to stall in order to bring confusion—"

"I'm not stalling." Charles shot the man a glare. "I just need a moment to collect my thoughts."

The smug expression on the man's face chilled Charles's heart. The plaintiff's case was so simple a first-year law student could argue it. And yet, the defense attorney reclined like a bored child in a church pew.

Turning, Charles studied the gallery.

Spencer sat in the back row, arms folded across his chest, his ever-present smirk growing larger by the second.

Charles spun forward to face to the judge. "Your honor, may I request a moment to speak with my associate?"

The man grunted, waving his fingers in dismissal. "Be quick."

Charles charged down the aisle, wrestling his emotions into check. "What have you done?"

"Using me to cover for your own incompetence, McKinley? A desperate act." Spencer's eyes narrowed to slits as he leaned forward. "You aren't worthy to carry the McKinley name. It won't take long for the partners to arrive at the same conclusion."

"Where are the missing documents?" Charles balled his fists to prevent himself from grabbing the man's shirtfront. Or better yet, his throat.

An oily smile spread across the attorney's face. He gripped his knees, dropping his voice to a whisper. "Perhaps you should ask Smythe."

Acid crawled up Charles's throat. The image of the lawyers shaking hands after the insurance agreement flickered through his memory. Charles straightened and faced the front of the courtroom.

Smythe pressed his fingers together like a tent in front of his mouth, an unmistakable gleam in his eye.

"You—you gave him the files?" Charles swung back to the senior attorney. "Is it worth losing a case just to ruin me?"

Spencer's brows lowered over his small eyes. "Don't throw around accusations you can't substantiate." He shrugged. "Besides, even if I had—I'm not the one losing a case."

"It's our firm's case. We're on the same team."

"There's no team. There's you and me." Spencer pinned him with a glare. "I thought you'd figured it out."

Charles strode to the bench, pushing down the anger brewing in his belly and focusing his mind. "I'm ready to proceed, Your Honor. Thank you for your indulgence."

"My indulgence is limited, Mr. McKinley. Let's have no more interruptions."

"No, sir. There won't be."

∾

Elizabeth stood at the door and smiled at each departing student. "Good work today, Qui N'gun. Your shirt is really coming along, Ah Cheng." She couldn't help darting glances at Ruby, gathering loose fabric scraps for the class bag.

Unspoken questions glinted in her sister's pale eyes. Ruby would want to know what had happened with Charles, and what Elizabeth hoped for the future. The truth was Elizabeth had the same questions—and a startling lack of answers. Her stomach grew queasy at the thought. She'd been honest with Charles about her feelings, but she could never be honest about her past. How long could she keep it secret?

Ruby lifted a castoff piece of pink silk. "This material is lovely. Wherever did you find it?"

As the room emptied, Elizabeth returned to the sewing tables. "One of our donors brought several bolts last time she was here. I believe it was left over from their dressmaker's shop. She loaned us an extra machine, too. We're very fortunate." Elizabeth tucked away a forgotten spool of thread. "She's paying some of the older girls for piecework. It's a wonderful opportunity."

"You've done well." Ruby retrieved a scrap from the floor under the last table. "I'd never have believed you'd give up piano to teach sewing."

"I'm still playing. Wait until you hear Yoke Soo at the musicale. She's so tiny, it's difficult to believe how accomplished she's become. She could have an astounding future on the stage."

"Children are like blank slates waiting to be filled. You're teaching them not just piano and sewing skills, but that God loves them and has a special plan for their lives. Can you imagine if we stepped back and let God write on our slate instead of filling it with our own mistakes?"

Elizabeth sorted through the paper patterns and added them to the drawer. "It's not like you've made so many mistakes. Your slate is filled with good things. Two men you've loved. The patients you've helped. Your work in the refugee camps."

Ruby wandered over to the window and gazed down at the city. "I've had my share of blunders. Mostly because I try to control everything myself." She sighed. "I still worry after Gerald's heart condition and the threat of the cancer returning."

"That's hardly a sin. In fact, I think it would be abnormal if you didn't worry."

"Perhaps, but God has called me to trust Him—no matter the outcome. It might not be robbery or murder, but it's still turning my back on His love."

"Many of us have worse marks on our pasts. Mine would make you look like an angel." Elizabeth snapped her mouth shut, the careless words hanging in the air between them.

Ruby's brow rose. "What does that mean?"

"Nothing. Never mind."

Ruby pulled out two of the chairs. "You've been speaking in riddles ever since you arrived in the city. I think you want to tell me, but you're finding it difficult." She ran her fingers along the table's edge. "Does it have to do with why you gave up your concert career?"

"I can't, Ruby. I just can't." Elizabeth ran a hand along her throat, fighting the choking sensation.

"I know you're running from something—or someone." Ruby's gaze softened. "You didn't sacrifice your dreams, you flung them away."

Elizabeth blinked hard to prevent the tears threatening to dissolve her. When had her sister grown so perceptive? She crossed the room to stare out the window.

"It's as if someone stole your affections and you haven't recovered." Her sister's words cut through the quiet classroom.

Elizabeth pressed fingertips to her closed lids before the tears spilled over. "He didn't steal them. I gave them freely."

Ruby stood, closing the space between them in a breath. "Who was it?"

"I can't tell you."

"I suppose it doesn't matter." She wrapped her arms around Elizabeth. "What happened? He spurned you for another?"

Elizabeth shook her head, swallowing hard. "No, that's why I left Sacramento. I had to get away from him."

"Is he dangerous?"

"No." Elizabeth's knees weakened. She wanted nothing more than to fall into Ruby's arms. As the secret crumbled away, so did her strength. "He's...he's married."

20

Charles dragged himself off the busy street and into the Flood Building. The trial had gone from bad to worse, the missing documents giving Smythe the ammunition he needed to demand a dismissal. Judge Percival seemed more than happy to bang the gavel and send them all home. The day's failures settled in Charles's gut like a lead weight.

Clemmons grinned as he folded back the lift's accordion gate. "Good to see you, Mr. McKinley. How's the day treating you, sir?"

The operator's effusive greeting grated against his last nerve. "Eugene, tell me—how do you manage to be so lively, day after day? Don't you ever get tired of all life's ups and downs?"

"Ups and downs *are* my life." He chuckled. "Actually, I'm a blessed man, sir. Can't complain. Steady job, loving wife, a bouncing baby boy, and a faithful God."

Some of the tension melted from Charles's shoulders. "A baby? New one?"

"Yes, sir. Two weeks, now. Thank you for asking." He inclined his head. "Healthy and loud, if you know what I mean."

"I can imagine. You're a lucky man."

"Yes, I am. Career ups and downs—they don't matter none. It's all about loving the people God gives you." Eugene slowed the car as it approached the ninth floor.

"I appreciate your wisdom."

"Ha! I don't imagine I have much to speak of, but I appreciate the conversation. Most folks don't take the time."

Charles stepped out, gazing back at the wiry man. "Perhaps not. And as you say—it's the ones God gives you who count."

Eugene tipped his hat as he closed the gate.

Charles's footsteps lightened as he hurried down the hall. As had become his habit, he touched the stenciled names on the window before pushing through the door and heading for his desk. He called a greeting to Henry and waved to a few others as he maneuvered through the rows.

More cases waited in his future. Losing one because of a dishonest coworker wouldn't derail him for long. Let Spencer think he held the upper hand. The man also went home to a cold, lonely house each night.

Charles thought back over his trip to the Tea Garden with Elizabeth last week. She'd confessed feelings for him—perhaps not a pledge of undying love, but definitely a step in the right direction. He set his briefcase on the desk and plopped into the chair with a sigh.

Henry appeared, one eyebrow cocked. "I didn't expect you to be looking so pleased with yourself. Spencer called from the courthouse, and your uncle looks like he's been sucking lemons."

"I'm not surprised. The case was an unmitigated disaster."

"What happened? I thought he said you couldn't lose this one."

Charles lowered his voice. "I stumbled into Spencer's trap—but you didn't hear this from me. I'll find a discreet way to counter his actions."

Henry perched on the corner of the desk. "Let me know how I can help. I've got a few axes to grind with the fellow, myself."

"Perhaps we can put our heads together later." Charles glanced toward the rear of the office. "Assuming I survive the rest of the day."

One of the law clerks appeared at Charles's desk. "Mr. McKinley would like to see you, Mr. . . . um . . . Mr. McKinley." Red splotches dotted the man's cheeks.

Henry rapped the tabletop with his knuckles. "And here it comes. Good luck."

"I'd like one day where I didn't get called in for a scolding." Charles straightened his tie. Heading to his uncle's office, he rehearsed responses. *What's one case, Uncle? Missing documents? Could happen to anyone.*

Uncle Silas glanced up from the stack of files, pen clutched in his right hand. "Charles—have a seat." He returned his focus to the paperwork, scratching his signature on several typed forms.

Charles drew up the now-familiar wooden chair, readying himself for the impending dressing-down.

His uncle pressed the blotter over each signature. He added the neat pile to the box on the desk's corner and folded his knobby hands over the green desk pad.

Charles held his breath, resisting the urge to jump into excuses before the tirade ensued. His uncle's silence disturbed Charles more than the lectures. Was the man considering all the money he'd wasted on his nephew's schooling?

"Charles. I know why you went into law." Uncle Silas rubbed a hand across his brow.

He's going to fire me. The hairs on the back of his neck stood to attention.

The man's eyes softened. He propped elbows on the desktop, folding his fingers into a steeple before his mouth. "You were only ten when your sister murdered her husband."

Coils twisted around Charles's windpipe choking off his voice. "She defended herself." He scooted to the edge of his seat. "You know that. You represented her."

"Against my better judgment."

The words landed like a sucker punch. "What's this about, Uncle?"

"We all take cases we regret. We do the job. We fight for the client regardless of our personal feelings." His eyes narrowed. "If you can't get your heart out of the way of your job, you'll end up clerking for the rest of your career."

"Are you saying you didn't believe Josephine's story?"

"I believed her." Silas lowered his palms to the desk. "That's beside the point. I fought for Josephine's freedom, in case you've forgotten."

Charles swallowed, a familiar bitter taste welling up on his tongue. "I'll never forget."

Uncle Silas pushed back from the desk and came around to stand beside it. "Charles, I did the best I could for her. You know that. I saved her from a lifetime in prison."

A curt nod was the best Charles could muster.

Uncle Silas reached into his pocket, drawing out a gold watch. Glancing down at the face, he clicked his tongue. Snapping the lid shut, he returned his focus to Charles. "I expect the same level of commitment from you on every single case you try for me."

"Sir, about today..."

His uncle waved off Charles's words. "You misunderstand me. Today's case was a throwaway, Charles." He huffed. "I'm talking about your loyalty to me. To this firm."

A swirl of confusion gripped Charles. What was he talking about? "I don't understand. Why would you question my loyalty?"

His uncle pinned him with a gaze that could freeze the Sahara. "Where are the King files?"

"In my briefcase. I've been trying to figure out a plan to improve their situation." He cleared his throat, his mouth drying further by the second. "I've gotten to know the family. We've grown... close. I'd like to assist them."

Uncle Silas dropped the watch into his pocket, never once releasing Charles's gaze. "Return the file to the company drawer. I'm taking you off the case, effective immediately."

Charles's heart sank toward his shoes.

"I want to hear no more about it. The case is dead, do you understand me?"

"Yes, sir." He fought to keep his spine straight. What would he tell Elizabeth?

"And Charles, the Cameron woman telephoned again." The lines around his uncle's mouth deepened.

Could this conversation get any worse? "I'm sorry, sir. I told her I would send her some names of possible attorneys."

"I informed her you'd represent the Mission Home."

Charles sat back in the chair, his mouth falling open. Had his uncle suffered a stroke? "You did? I will?"

"I'm not completely without emotion, Charles. Obviously, you're not cut out for property law. Though I'm concerned for your reputation, some *pro bono* work might play well in the newspapers as we prepare you to run for city council."

"City council?"

"Why must you repeat every word I say? We need to brush up your elocution. Talking like a parrot won't fly in front of a crowd of voters. Now, on your feet."

Charles lurched up, his mind whirling.

"Call on Miss Cameron this morning. She has several upcoming cases that require your attention." He headed for the door.

"I will, sir." Charles swallowed. He gazed at his uncle's back, remembering the days he'd stood up in court for Josephine. "And Uncle…"

Uncle Silas turned back, gripping the brass doorknob.

A tremor passed through Charles's chest. "Thank you."

❧

"Married?" Ruby sank into one of the classroom seats, the color draining from her face.

Elizabeth laid her palms against her burning cheeks. "You must never speak a word to anyone, Ruby. Now you understand why I had to leave."

"Why didn't you put a stop to it? How did this even come about?"

"You don't want the details. It should never have happened." Elizabeth strode to the window and lifted the sash, desperate for a breath of air. She'd never spoken of Tobias to anyone, and the confession brought every shred of guilt rushing back like a freight train.

"But you were traveling so much, performing all over the region. Wasn't that enough to get you 'away'?"

Elizabeth closed her eyes, trying to forget the first night. The hotel. How surprised she'd been when he showed up in her room. Was she surprised, really? A cold sweat washed over her.

"I—I…" She ducked her head, tears squeezing between her closed lids. She couldn't keep the secret anymore. "That's where everything went wrong."

"Then it's…" Ruby's lips pulled downward, "your instructor?" Elizabeth dug a handkerchief from her pocket and nodded.

"He's older, isn't he?" She paused and shook her head. "Lots of girls feel affection for their teachers. You two worked closely for years."

"Ruby, it wasn't infatuation." She swallowed, nausea rolling in like a wave. "I'm not a child sweet on the teacher. I can't wave my hands and explain it away." Hot tears rolled down her cheek, collecting on the edge of her jaw.

Her sister's color faded until her complexion resembled ivory piano keys. She gripped the edge of the table. "I don't know what to say." Her voice faded to a husky whisper.

"Say the truth. You hate what I've become. I'm ruined. I'm beyond redemption. I came here to make restitution for my sin, but no matter how hard I work, no matter how many girls I rescue from prostitution—it'll never make up for what I've done. These girls—" Elizabeth gestured to the door through which the students had left. "They were forced into their lives. I walked in on my own accord. I'll never fix that. I'll never be worthy of God's love."

"Oh, honey." Ruby jumped up and hurried to her side, drawing her into a crushing embrace.

Elizabeth buried her face in Ruby's shoulder, releasing the tears she'd restrained for months.

Ruby stroked her hair. "I would never turn you away, Elizabeth. And you're never beyond God's love."

Her sister's heartbeat sounded against Elizabeth's ear. For just a moment, she was a little girl again, young and innocent. Ruby had always bandaged her skinned knees and elbows, more of a mother than Mama had ever been. But this was one wound she couldn't treat. "I'm sorry I've disappointed you."

Ruby exhaled a noisy sigh. "Elizabeth, we all sin and fall short. God forgives, so who am I to hold your sins against you?"

Elizabeth gulped back a sob.

"Is this what's kept you from accepting Charles's affection?"

Elizabeth drew back, wiping her face with the handkerchief. "I thought I could pretend nothing had ever happened." A growing ache settled in her temples. "But the more I care for him, the more it hurts. It wouldn't be fair. I'll never be able to love again."

"Don't say that." Ruby drew Elizabeth over to the window. "Think about this city. Two years ago, these buildings were shaken off their foundations and burned to the ground. If you'd been here, you'd never imagine it could recover." She touched the glass. "Look at it now. New buildings rising on every street. Homes, banks, factories, stores, schools. God grows new life out the ashes of our failures. No one knows that better than me."

"I'm trying to pull my life together, Ruby. I'm trying." Elizabeth sniffled, barely able to draw a breath through her nose. "It's all I can think about."

Ruby leaned her head against Elizabeth's. "You need to let God repair you, little sister. He's the healer. You can't do it yourself."

It couldn't be that easy. Elizabeth gazed out at the burgeoning city. God wasn't rebuilding it—the people were doing the work. She took a deep breath, trying to still the tremors chasing each other through her chest. "You'll keep my secret, won't you? No one can know what I am."

"What you are is a child of God." She rubbed Elizabeth's back. "And it's your story to tell, not mine."

Elizabeth's shoulders drooped. "I'm not telling anyone else. I can't."

"I'll ask God to heal your heart and to show you exactly how much He loves you. And also how to proceed with Charles, because I don't think God wants you to live a life of servitude out of guilt and shame."

"I love serving here. I don't mean to sound like it's a burden. I could be happy doing this forever."

Ruby squeezed Elizabeth's fingers. "But He may not mean for you to do it alone."

Elizabeth thought back to her outing with Charles. Had she met someone like him a few years before, things might have turned out differently. No matter what her sister said, it was too late to walk that path again.

Ruby returned the chairs to their places. "I need to go. Gerald will be home soon and I'd like to be there." She tucked a loose ringlet behind her ear. "And since you trusted me with your secret, how about I return the favor?"

Elizabeth studied Ruby's face. "What kind of secret could you have?"

"A happy one." Ruby's eyes glistened with tears. "Something I don't really deserve, since—unlike Abby—I was too timid to pray for it." She touched a hand to her midsection. "But God provided, anyway."

Elizabeth's breath caught in her throat. "Are you..."

Ruby nodded. "Gerald and I are expecting a baby."

જી

Charles hopped off the streetcar, checking both directions before striding across the cobblestone street. The sun warmed the wet stones, sending steam rising into the air.

His uncle's startling turnaround still made his blood hum. What had Miss Cameron said to change his mind? Or had it merely been a maneuver to get his nephew out from under Spencer's thumb? No matter the cause, Charles hadn't felt this excited about the job since the day he arrived in San Francisco.

He pressed his lips tight to prevent a goofy smile from claiming his features. Using his legal training to assist in the rescue work fulfilled one of his fondest desires. And being near Elizabeth—he couldn't think of anything he'd like better. He'd been praying for God to clear a path for them, but instead God had built a highway.

Hurrying up the steps, Charles rang the bell.

Elizabeth opened the door, eyes wide. "Charles. I wasn't expecting you."

The grin won out. "Miss Cameron is expecting me." He ran a hand across his vest front. "You're looking at the new Mission attorney."

"What?" Her brows shot upward. "I thought you weren't to have anything to do with us."

"I'm struggling to believe it myself. May I come in?"

"Of course." She backed up and swung the door open.

He stepped through and watched as she closed it, fastening the locks. "Don't you ever get tired of living in a fortress?"

"I've grown accustomed to it. It's for our girls' safety. I can come and go if I get fidgety." She shook her head, slowly. "I'm shocked at this sudden turn of events."

He couldn't resist taking a step closer, careful to keep his hands behind his back. "But not dismayed, I hope. We've moved past that, right?"

"How could I be anything but pleased? Donaldina needs all the help she can muster. Your knowledge and skills will be invaluable."

His chest deflated slightly. Couldn't she see beyond work? "And we'll be able to spend more time together."

Elizabeth's gaze dropped to the floor. "An added bonus."

The hairs on his arms lifted. Their outing had gone well, minus one little altercation. Had she gone off the idea? Charles cleared his throat. "I suppose I should get on with business, then."

"Donaldina's in her study." She backed a step and gestured to the small office. "She'll be glad to see you. I'm in the middle of a piano lesson, so I'd better get back to it."

Her stiff posture knocked some of the wind out of his sails. Would he never succeed in reading women? She strode out of the room, leaving him standing in the hall.

He approached Miss Cameron's office and tapped on the door.

"Come in, Mr. McKinley." The muffled voice called out.

Charles peeked inside. "How did you know it was me?"

Miss Cameron sat at one of the chairs by the window, a cup of tea in her hand. Another cup and saucer sat waiting on the small table. "Your uncle telephoned to say you were on your way." She smiled. "He seems like such a nice gentleman. He even promised a donation to our cause."

"My uncle?" Charles ran fingers over his jaw. "I'm pleased to hear you say so."

"Come join me. I'll pour the tea."

He sat down, removed his derby and placed it on his lap. He'd never been much of a tea drinker, but it seemed appropriate for a Chinese Mission. Perhaps he'd learn to appreciate it.

Miss Cameron poured a stream of the fragrant liquid into the tiny cup, her gaze never leaving his face.

Charles accepted the drink, trying not to squirm under her scrutiny. "My uncle said you have upcoming court dates."

"Yes, but I want to discuss something before we begin." She set the pot down on the table. "Some of my daughters have informed me you are courting Miss King."

The mouthful of tea stalled in his windpipe. He coughed several times before arranging an answer. "I've expressed interest in seeing more of her, but she's been cautious. I don't wish to rush things."

"That's wise." Miss Cameron shifted in her seat. "I don't mean to meddle, but I've grown quite fond of Elizabeth and I don't wish to see her hurt."

"Yes, ma'am." He set the cup into its saucer and leaned forward. "And trust me, I have nothing but the purest intentions."

She chuckled. "I may be an unmarried woman, Mr. McKinley, but your words sound a touch naïve. But let's leave such talk for another time."

Charles nodded, content to push aside uncomfortable thoughts for the moment.

"I've been given a note requesting our help. Two girls wish to escape their lives in the cribs and take refuge at our Home." Miss Cameron unfolded a slip of yellow paper and passed it across the table.

"Cribs?"

"The worst of the Chinatown brothels. The girls stay in tiny, crowded cells with bar-covered windows. They are required to call out to men who pass in order to entice them into the establishment. They're sometimes referred to as 'sing-song girls.'"

Charles's skin crawled. No wonder Uncle Silas feared for his reputation.

"George Wu gave me the note this morning. The request came from an actress with the Chinese theater. According to George, one of the women is the actress's sister—and with child. They'll be wearing yellow ribbons in their hair so I can identify them. Officer Kelley is securing a warrant." She lifted her eyes to meet his gaze. "Are you interested in joining us? It would give you the opportunity to see a rescue in action."

"I'm honored. Are you sure I won't be in the way?"

"Not at all. I believe it will give you a better understanding of what we're up against when we go to court to fight for these young women. Slavery is not pretty, and the judges need to understand such."

A jolt of adrenaline shot through his veins. "This is the reason I went into the legal profession. After spending the last month deciphering property cases, your words are like music to my ears."

The missionary sat back in the chair, a smile spreading across her face. "Then I believe, Mr. McKinley, you may have found your calling."

21

*E*lizabeth pulled the woolen cloak snug around her shoulders to hide the trembling in her arms. The streetlight's glow didn't extend into the dark reaches of the Chinatown alley, and the idea of traipsing through the gloom triggered a now-familiar flutter in her stomach.

Charles's presence, like a rock at her side, steadied her nerves. Though his square jaw and broad shoulders indicated a man of confidence, the fingers tapping a steady rhythm against his leg suggested otherwise.

She pressed her lips into a line to prevent a smile. She understood his apprehension. Every rescue seemed to deliver a new set of unexpected hurdles. Just because he could wrangle a horse as easily as a witness didn't mean he knew how to handle a brothel owner.

The sudden change in his status baffled her. His expertise would be a godsend for the Mission, but having him underfoot would create its own set of problems. How could she prevent her heart from melting into a puddle every time he appeared?

Donaldina gestured for them to follow, refusing to break the silence she'd instituted a few blocks away.

Kum Yong brushed Elizabeth's elbow. She mouthed the words, "Stay close."

Elizabeth nodded, biting her lip. One step out of line this time and she wouldn't see another rescue for months. Donaldina's warning still rang in her ears.

The windows were covered with steel mesh. Donaldina pointed to a red door, barely visible in the dim light. "Officer Kelley, if you don't mind?"

"Yes, ma'am." He banged on the heavy door with his stick.

A flurry of voices spilled forth as the door cracked open and revealed a sliver of light. A few of the Cantonese words caught Elizabeth's ear, but she was thankful Kum Yong came along to interpret.

A sour-faced old man filled the open space, a round cap pushed low over his head. His gravelly voice snapped back, arm gesticulating as he spoke. "No girls. No girls."

"Likely story." Officer Kelley scowled. "Now move back. We've got a warrant, and we're coming in whether you like it or not." He lifted the rolled document in his fist.

Kum Yong translated, her chirruping voice an odd contrast to the policeman's surly tone.

The Chinese man held both hands forward. "No. No enter."

Donaldina huffed. "He's stalling as they move the girls out the back. Go now."

Officer Kelley barreled in like a Pamplona bull, knocking the man to the side and clearing the path.

Donaldina followed, striding through the dank tenement as if she owned the place. "I've been here before. They know what we're after."

A group of men glanced up from a table, ivory mahjong tiles spread on the surface before them. An oil lamp cast a ghostly glow across their faces.

Kum Yong and Elizabeth hurried past, searching each corner of the room. Remembering her first experience, Elizabeth checked under every table. Charles stayed a step behind her, his attention darting around the dwelling.

In a cellar, they located a cluster of young women cowering in a closet. Elizabeth helped them file out into the hallway, but each girl cringed away with wild eyes, murmuring frantic words she couldn't understand. "How do we know which girls we're after?"

Donaldina scanned the group, her eyes settling on a pair of girls clinging to each other, matching ribbons in their dark hair. "Those two." She glanced around before pushing open one last door. "Bring them in here. We'll speak in private."

Elizabeth and Kum Yong reached for the girls' hands, but they cried out and pushed further into the group. Elizabeth's throat ached. Why was this always so difficult? She pressed a friendly smile to her face as Kum Yong murmured quietly in Cantonese. With wide eyes, the two nodded and stepped free of their friends.

Donaldina turned to Charles. "You and Elizabeth stay with the rest, and keep an eye on them. I don't want anyone moving until we're sure we have the right girls."

The gathering of women resembled a caged flock of tropical birds, their brightly colored *cheongsams* suggesting a cheerier life than they'd probably experienced.

Elizabeth moistened her lips. "Do any of you speak English?" She offered one of the Cantonese greetings she'd learned from her students.

One of the girls wrinkled her nose and spewed a harsh stream of words back.

"Do you usually receive such a welcome?" Charles asked.

She sighed. "Not always so pleasant."

The door swung open and Donaldina came back into the hall with Kum Yong and the two women on her heels. "These are our girls. Time to go."

Elizabeth gave one last glance at the rest waiting in the hall. "Kum Yong, can you speak with them? Find out if any more wish to join us?"

Kum Yong approached the line of girls, holding out her hands and speaking softly. The young women shook their heads, turning away.

As the Mission group departed, Elizabeth walked between Donaldina and Charles, her mind caught on the ones left behind.

Circles darkened the area beneath Charles's eyes. "I don't understand why some girls turn away what you're offering to them. I'd imagined them leaping into your arms."

Donaldina sighed. "We all suffer our own chains. The Lord holds out the gift of new life, but many turn Him away, not trusting the offer." Faint lines etched their way across her forehead. "Freedom is not achieved for these girls when we whisk them away from their captors, nor even in the courtroom. The victory is won through patience, gentle comfort, and compassion. Only then can they grasp the unending depth of God's love."

A chill traveled through Elizabeth, like someone performing an icy-fingered *glissando* down her spine. If God had given her the gift of freedom, why did she live under the shadows of the past?

⁂

Energy pulsed through Charles's veins as he escorted the group back to the Mission. He glanced behind them, half expecting to see a Chinese tong member in pursuit, but few people seemed to pay them any mind as they climbed the hill on Sacramento Street.

Elizabeth's face glowed in the morning light, her blue eyes fixed on the two girls clinging to Kum Yong like seaweed on the rocks.

He leaned close. "So, what happens now?"

Elizabeth met his gaze "Donaldina and Kum Yong will get the girls settled. Then, within a day or two, they'll need to appear in court so Donaldina can obtain official custody." A hesitant smile toyed at her lips. "I imagine you'll take part."

"Yes, of course." He brushed a hand across his chin. "I'll get the paperwork ready."

"And we return to work. Meals, lessons, sewing." She made a face. "Preparation for the musicale."

"Aren't you looking forward to the grand event?"

"I was until the girls insisted I join in."

His heart lifted. "I finally get to hear you play."

She shot him a glance from under long lashes. "If you attend."

"I wouldn't miss it for the world. No, for two worlds."

Her chest rose and fell in a large sigh. "I wish I felt the same. I haven't played in front of an audience in months."

Charles jammed his hands into his pockets in an attempt to keep them still. "There's a florist stall two blocks away from my apartment. Would it be appropriate to bring flowers? For the girls?"

Her brows ratcheted upward. "For all of them?"

"I'll buy a large bunch and hand them out one by one." And an extra bouquet for Elizabeth. No one would protest such an act, especially after she impressed the donors with her inspired performance.

As they approached the steps, Charles hung back. "Elizabeth, wait a moment, please."

She paused, her gaze following the others as they entered the building.

"Tell me how you felt after your first rescue."

She smiled. "Like I could do anything—dance, shout, fly." She pressed a hand to her lace shirt. "And a little shaken, too."

"I can't imagine going back to the law office quite yet." The morning's excitement gave him a burst of courage. "Come out with me. You said Donaldina and Kum Yong wouldn't need your help. Let me treat you to breakfast on the town."

"Breakfast?" Elizabeth's lips parted. "I'm not sure. How would that appear?"

"I thought you prided yourself on being unconventional. And who would even notice in a city this size?" He grinned. "There's a bakery down the street. If you don't want to go to a restaurant, we could buy some sweet rolls and walk to Union Square."

Elizabeth's face softened. "I—I'd like that." She glanced at the door. "Let me inform Donaldina. I'll be right back." She touched his hand before hurrying up the steps.

Charles faced the street, delivery wagons rattling past at a hurried clip. *Thank you, Lord. Thank you.*

Elizabeth traded her heavy cloak for a lighter jacket and hurried out to meet Charles, an unfamiliar melody lifting her spirits. No matter her fears, it grew more difficult every day to ignore her growing feelings for the man. Ruby said God would give her a new beginning. She'd certainly done her part—throwing herself into His service. Even if the memories continued to haunt her, it didn't mean she had to live in their shadow.

She and Charles stopped at the bakery, laughing together as they savored the fragrance of fresh-baked bread. Buying a box of sweet rolls, they walked the five blocks to Union Square. The thinning fog promised a sunny day ahead. Elizabeth tipped back her hat to allow the sun to warm her face as they wandered down the sidewalk toward the park. "It's good to get out."

Charles tucked the parcel under his elbow. "Between the seclusion of home life and the tension of rescues, you must feel isolated at times. It'd be healthy for you to get out and take in some air." He smiled. "And perhaps remind you the city is not as ugly as it seems." He held out his arm to her as they walked.

Elizabeth's fingers tingled as she looped her wrist around his elbow, his bicep firm under her fingers. With her white gloves, she couldn't feel the texture of his sleeve, but it didn't stop her from imagining it.

Charles gestured to the nearly completed St. Francis Hotel. "The city seems to be changing every day."

"Ruby says God's bringing new life from the ashes."

"I like that. Does she often have words of wisdom for you?"

"Always. Whether I want to hear them or not." She tightened her grip, relishing his warmth on the cold morning. "You made a grand impression on her, you know."

"Well, there's one of the King siblings, anyway."

She laughed. "In case you've forgotten, you mistook me for a maid on your first visit."

He scrubbed a hand across his forehead. "Yes, and I'll never live it down."

"Ruby is a better judge of character. She's quite intuitive about people. I suppose she learned during her years of nursing." The light breeze toyed with the tassels on Elizabeth's cloak.

"And she's put in a good word for me?"

A flush crept up Elizabeth's neck. Perhaps Ruby wasn't the only perceptive one. "Yes. You could say so."

Charles squeezed her arm against his side. "I'm glad to hear it."

They crossed Post Street and wandered into Union Square, the tall column of the Dewey Monument spearing the sky above. Stopping at a bench, Elizabeth spread her wrap over the damp seat.

"Has the excitement of the morning worn off yet?" She scooted to the end, giving Charles plenty of space.

Charles grinned. "I'm not certain it will." He sat down, opened the bag, and held it out to Elizabeth. "I dreamed about this sort of work when I decided on law school. Instead I got dusty books and stuffy courtrooms."

Elizabeth selected a roll, setting it on a napkin. "But you have your eye on political office, right?"

"It would be nice. Lawyers can help in some situations, but when the laws are fundamentally flawed, it's difficult to watch people suffer. Like your students, for instance."

"How would you help them?" She broke off a corner of the pastry and popped it in her mouth.

"There's a deeper issue at work. We have a large population of Chinese men, but the unfair immigration laws make it difficult for them to bring their families over. You have a group of bachelors living in tight quarters, with little hope of bettering their own lives or the lives of their families back home."

Elizabeth's throat tightened. "That's no excuse for how they treat the girls."

"Of course not. And not all do. You've met honorable men in Chinatown."

"Yes, like George." She smiled, thinking of Kum Yong's burgeoning feelings toward the apothecary. "And Lim Sang, the tailor. I'm sure there are many others."

"But I believe there are probably many more men who'd like to be honorable, but they feel they have no options. If we could change the immigration law, among other things, we could provide hope for their future. They could have real lives—not just being second-class servants of San Francisco society, but full-fledged participants in making this city better."

The intensity with which he spoke stirred the fire in her own heart. She could picture him standing on the back platform of a train, addressing voters in towns across California. Here was a man who would change the world—a future mayor, or even governor. "But first we have to get people past their fear and hatred."

"True."

She sighed. "Even my brother, Robert. He says he doesn't dislike the Chinese, but you can sense it in his words and his actions. He wasn't like that as a child."

"Perhaps he's had a bad experience since coming to the city."

Elizabeth frowned. "Maybe. I know it's a sore point between him and Abby. She met Donaldina and Kum Yong after the quake, and they were a great help to her as she escaped the fires."

"He's not alone in his thinking."

"I wish we could change that. Help people see the Chinese in a better light."

"Miss Cameron does so with her speaking engagements. Perhaps you could join her sometime. Maybe the girls could perform some of the pieces they've learned for the musicale."

"Don't remind me. I'm nervous enough about it." She slipped off her gloves and crumpled them in her hands.

His brown eyes gleamed, tiny crinkles forming around the outer corners. "It will be wonderful. A gift for the donors and the board. They'll be like proud parents there to watch the girls shine."

Elizabeth tipped her head back, watching a bird wing its way across the square. Charles was right. She should get out more often. The trip to the beach and the garden had both been good for her soul. But even more so, sharing a meaningful conversation with this man, she could feel her vitality returning.

What would life be like with someone like Charles? He had the potential to change the world with his ideals and his words. Add on his handsome features and passion, and he'd inspire women and men alike. But for this one moment, he seemed to care only about her. The thought set a fire burning in her chest. Some secrets were worth concealing.

22

Charles walked Elizabeth home, every stride taking them a step closer to the end of a delightful morning. The sun's rays shone straight down between the tall buildings, suggesting they'd whiled away several hours. The combination of no sleep and the night's excitement had loosened his tongue and seemed to have done the same for Elizabeth, but now she leaned heavily on his arm, an easy silence ruling the moment.

The quiet allowed his mind to wander dangerous paths, fatigue weakening his defenses. If he wasn't careful, he'd pull Elizabeth close and kiss her lips, right here in the middle of the busy sidewalk. Unfortunately, such an action would ensure an end to their fragile truce. Whatever she'd endured in the past, he needed to earn her trust, and he was willing to wait a lifetime to obtain it.

Hopefully, she wouldn't keep him at a yardstick's distance forever.

They paused at the Mission Home steps, her blue eyes rising to meet his gaze. "You should see your face right now. I'd love to know what you're thinking."

"No. You wouldn't." Charles's throat tightened. "No matter how I try, I can't keep every thought pure."

Her arm tensed in his grasp.

He stepped back. "Please, don't be concerned." Perhaps if he retreated, she wouldn't flee.

Elizabeth tightened her grip on his sleeve, a hesitant smile replacing her strained expression. "I'm not." She slid her hand upward until it rested on his collar bone.

His breath hitched in his chest. "Really?" He laid his fingers atop hers, weaving them together.

"It's probably still wise not to startle me."

"I wouldn't dream of it." He lifted her wrist to his lips, the scent of lilacs on her skin overpowering his senses. "Too startling?"

As if in answer, Elizabeth leaned into his chest, resting her ear against his shoulder.

Interpreting her touch as a signal, he reached out and brushed a knuckle across her cheek. Either the street had grown quiet behind him, or he'd lost all knowledge of anything outside their tight circle. He lowered his head until his brow rested on her temple. The fragrance of her skin proved intoxicating. "May I—"

"Yes." Her breath warmed his skin as she touched his unshaven cheek.

Heart seizing, Charles bent to press a kiss to the dimple he'd long admired.

She turned to meet him, her lips grazing his with an irresistible, sweet softness.

"Elizabeth..." His throat grew parched and he claimed her lips, this time with intent. The pastry's sweetness lingered on her mouth, tantalizing him beyond control. Charles lifted his chin to her forehead, determined to slow his pulse before he proved her right about men's desires.

Her hand traveled up his shoulder to the nape of his neck, her fingertips caressing the bare skin between his collar and his hairline.

When she stepped away, Charles sucked in a quick breath. How had they gone from not touching to a first kiss in the span of a few moments? No matter, he wasn't going to question her.

Her eyes glistened, a smile playing around her mouth.

The mouth he'd just kissed. He fought every urge to pull her back for more, swallowing hard to break himself from the trancelike moment. "I—I should go." He hitched a thumb toward the street behind him.

She nodded, her palm pressed to her cheek. "Yes. I should get ready for class."

His gaze darted up to the heavy door under the portico. Hopefully, everyone had been too busy to notice anything unusual on the front stairs. Next time they kissed, he'd choose somewhere more discreet. *Next time.* The thought brought a sweet ache to his chest.

He touched the brim of his hat. "Until next time."

❧

Elizabeth closed herself in the bedroom and sank down on the edge of the mattress, legs trembling. The sensation of Charles's lips lingered on her own. A few days ago, she'd promised herself to either tell him the truth or push him away. Neither option ended with a kiss.

She leaned forward, resting both forearms against her knees. How quickly stray thoughts became actions. Was this a new life—or an old one coming back to haunt her?

A gentle tap at her door caught her attention.

Elizabeth hopped off the bed and strode to the door, pulling it open.

Yoke Soo stood in the hall. "Teacher, aren't we doing lessons today?" Her voice quavered.

Elizabeth glanced at the timepiece clipped to her bodice. "Oh, no. I'm sorry, Yoke Soo. I lost track of time. You begin practicing. I'll be right there."

The little girl nodded and skipped off.

Elizabeth rushed to check her reflection in the hand mirror. No one must know what happened between her and Charles. She ran a finger across her lower lip, stomach quivering. Until next time, he'd said. A second kiss? She closed her eyes, her longing intensifying into a crescendo. How many could she enjoy before she lost all grip on reality?

❧

Charles jogged down Market Street, his spirits too high for a leisurely pace. In two days time, his life had been turned on its ear. Everything had snapped into place—career, goals, and the woman of his dreams. The Lord must be smiling on him. As if in agreement, the sun finally broke through the fog, swaths of California blue showing in the sky above.

He didn't care what Spencer tried today. None of it mattered. He'd kissed Elizabeth King. The recollection sent blood surging through his veins.

After hurrying into the Flood Building and chatting with Eugene, Charles strode to the office. Nodding at everyone he passed, he laid his satchel on the desk. First thing, he needed to submit the guardianship petition. The sooner he set the process in motion, the safer the girls would be.

The swivel chair rocked as he sat down and opened his bag, retrieving the notes he'd written about the two rescues. He should add more background about the girls' situation before delivering it to the judge. Looking for a pen, Charles opened the desk drawer, but a misplaced folder jammed its forward momentum. Charles frowned— he never placed files in the top section. He jerked the manila folder loose and squinted to read the name on the tab. One of the King family's accounts? He'd put all of those in the main cabinet yesterday.

The rhythmic hammering of a nearby typewriter clattered its way into his thoughts as Charles flipped through the records—more contracts and expense sheets. Uncle Silas had insisted these documents be put away. How had one ended up in his desk? A whisper of doubt ribboned its way through his chest. Glancing toward Spencer's office, Charles jammed the papers into the folder and tucked it under his arm. How low would the man stoop to discredit him?

Charles opened the long company drawers and thumbed through the folders, searching for William King's name. After three times through the contents, he straightened, tension coiling around his throat. There were dozens of reasons why the main body of paperwork could be missing from the collection. He lifted his gaze and scanned the busy office. Perhaps someone had need of them.

"The case is dead." Uncle's words whispered in his brain.

Charles tucked away the remaining file under his jacket. If the King family's information had gone missing, he didn't want to lose the one surviving piece of evidence.

23

*E*lizabeth sat in Abby and Robert's light-filled kitchen, the pressures of the past week melting from her shoulders as she listened to Abby talk about their new home.

"The ads kept referring to Parkside as the sunny slope of the Sunset District, but I think I've seen more fog and wind than I ever did while living with Gerald and Ruby." Abby held a watering can over a row of plants in the small window above the sink.

"It's lovely, though. You're practically living in the country."

"New homes are going up all around us, but there's still a dairy farm at the end of the street. I always say good morning to the cows when I walk to the streetcar stop."

Elizabeth laughed. Of course, her sister-in-law talked to cows. Abby's sweet disposition and love of nature showed in everything she did. "Then it's the perfect place for you, isn't it?"

"I've planted a few fruit trees in the backyard, but I'm not sure how well they'll do in the sandy soil. I do love the fresh air off the ocean, though. Robert thinks I'm silly for saying so, but I don't think the air in the city is as healthy."

Elizabeth gazed out the window to the spacious backyard. It would be the perfect place to raise children, if Robert and Abby were ever blessed. A lump grew in her throat. God certainly wouldn't keep this from them, would He? "How often do you get into the city?"

"Not as much as I'd like. I've joined an improvement organization and we're trying to accomplish some things before the neighborhood gets too built up. We're planning for schools and parks and such. Maybe a library."

"Parks? The whole place looks like a park to me." She lifted her cup. After weeks of drinking tea at the Mission, the coffee's rich fragrance was a treat.

Abby wrinkled her nose, making her freckles dance. "You should see the planning maps. This area will look just like the rest of the city in a few years."

"The poor cows."

Robert entered through the back door, a grin lighting his face. "There are my girls."

Abby jumped to her feet, welcoming her husband with a quick kiss. "I thought you were at the hospital all day."

"So did I." He pulled off his hat and hung it on a hook by the door. "But the director cancelled the afternoon meeting, and Dr. Lawrence had everything else under control. I hope you two don't mind me crashing in on your day."

"Not at all." Abby beamed. "It's nice you can see Elizabeth before she heads back."

Robert took the seat across from Elizabeth. "I wish I could give you a ride home. We're still saving for an automobile."

"I don't mind riding the streetcar. It's a lovely trip."

"Why don't you spend the night? You could go back in the morning."

Elizabeth bit her lip. Donaldina had asked her and Kum Yong to call on a Chinatown family this evening. Their daughter had run away to the Mission to avoid a marriage proposal, and Donaldina hoped to convince the parents they had other options. "I need to get back."

Robert smiled as he accepted the cup of coffee Abby set in front of him. He turned to Elizabeth. "How is the teaching? Are you able to get through to those girls at all?"

Those girls. Elizabeth bristled. "It's going very well. They're fast learners and hard workers."

Abby sat next to Robert. "Elizabeth is teaching piano, now, too. She says one of her little students is quite the prodigy."

"Yoke Soo can play almost anything she hears, and she composes, too." Elizabeth wrung her fingers under the table. Robert's countenance had darkened upon first mention of the Mission Home. "I hope you'll come to the musicale on Friday. You really should hear her play."

He shook his head. "I don't think so. I've got patients to see."

Abby's brows drew low. "Robert, Elizabeth is performing, also. I've yet to hear her play in concert."

Elizabeth's stomach tightened. "What is it about my work that bothers you so much?" She shook her head. "Papa treated patients of all races. Why do you feel differently?"

He took a sip of the coffee, his focus fixed on the dark brew. "I don't turn away Chinese patients."

Abby frowned. "You don't spout many of the harsh things others say, but your demeanor suggests you disapprove. And you've dissuaded me from visiting with Kum Yong."

"You two are going to team up against me, aren't you?"

Elizabeth reached across the table to touch her brother's wrist. "Whatever it is, I'd like to know."

"As would I." Abby grasped her locket, sliding it along the chain.

He sighed and raked a hand through his hair. "Back in medical school, I volunteered for projects that took us into Chinatown. We'd offer free treatments for the children. We even saw girls from the brothels." His lips rolled together, and he closed his eyes for a moment. "I saw more cases of syphilis than I cared to count." He pressed fingers against the bridge of his nose. "But that was before we encountered our first case of the plague."

Elizabeth scooted back a few inches from the table. "Plague? Bubonic plague?"

He nodded. "There had been some cases earlier in the year, and the health officials put Chinatown on quarantine. No one was allowed in or out."

"Is there no treatment?"

"There's an antitoxin, but it's only effective in the early hours after infection. The Chinese were so fearful of the doctors who were trying to help, they hid the patients away." Robert ran fingers through his hair. "I held a young girl as she died. She'd spent a year in the cribs. When she sickened, they carried her out into the gutter and left her there—like one of the plague rats that crawled out into the street to die. She was too far gone by the time we got to her." He gripped his cup and drew it close. "The girl actually had appendicitis, not plague. Had she been treated, she might have survived. But she was no more than an animal to them. Less than that, even. She was rubbish. Twelve-year-old rubbish."

A tiny cry of dismay sounded from Abby. She dropped her forehead to Robert's shoulder.

"I know they acted out of fear." He swallowed, his voice cracking. "But if I'd just seen some compassion in their eyes for this girl…"

Elizabeth's throat squeezed. "Those girls are the ones we're trying to save."

His eyes darkened. "You save one, they bring in two more. I've been to Angel Island where they process the immigrants coming in on the ships. The women know the questions—they know what to say. They show their papers and walk straight into the lions' den. That's where it needs to stop. Don't allow any more girls in." He lifted his hands. "Don't let the Chinese in at all. They don't care about each other. They don't care about us. Why should we care for them?"

Abby squeezed his arm. "Because God asked us to, Robert. 'Inasmuch as ye have done it unto one of the least of these my brethren, ye have done it unto me.' Who are 'the least' if not the strangers we take in to our shores, the sick you treat in the hospital, and the children cared for at the Mission?"

"They don't even know God, Abby."

"Some do. And how will they learn, unless they see Him through our actions? We were strangers, but Christ took us in. Don't you believe He means for us to do the same?"

Robert sat back, his jaw slackening. After a long moment, he drew Abby into an embrace. "You're right, of course."

Tears blurred Elizabeth's vision. God must have tailor-made Abby as the perfect complement to Robert's bullheaded ways. *Is it the same with Charles and me?*

Abby placed her palm against Robert's cheek. "I wish you'd explained earlier."

"I didn't want to spoil your image of Kum Yong and her people."

Elizabeth set her cup on the table. "Come to the concert, Robert. It might give you an opportunity to see the Chinese in a new light. If you could understand how the girls care for each other, and how they love God, it might open your heart to what could be."

He ran a hand down his wife's back. "We'll be there."

✑

Charles sprawled on the bed, the overpowering odor of fresh bread wafting into his apartment from the cafe below. The first week or two, he'd loved waking up to the fragrance. Now it turned his stomach and saturated his clothes. He leaned over and lit the small lamp on the nightstand.

Cold sweat clung to his chest, the specter-filled images of his dreams refusing to be banished by the light. Whispers of missing case documents, misrepresented figures, and vanishing money haunted him... and somewhere in the back of his mind—Elizabeth. He rubbed the sleep from his eyes. The details faded, but a helpless disquietude remained.

Lowering his feet to the floor, Charles wandered over to the coat rack and retrieved the file from his bag. Uncle Silas had told him to leave the case alone, but something didn't seem right.

He flipped open the folder and ran his finger down one of the contracts. Both William King and Uncle Silas had invested in the building. Nothing stood out in the paperwork to suggest anything out of place in the transaction. He flipped through the pages, his hand stilling on the last sheet. Uncle Silas had sold his portion of the investment on April 16, 1906, completely divesting himself of the property. Two days before the disaster? How fortunate.

Charles's stomach knotted. His uncle boasted good instincts for business decisions, but this seemed oddly prophetic. He scanned the figures. Uncle Silas walked away from the building with thousands of dollars, days before it crumbled to the ground.

He flipped to the next page, focusing on the lines of text. What unlucky soul bought him out? The man must be incensed at his uncle's good fortune. Charles's gaze locked on a familiar name.

The estate of William King, M.D.

Charles lowered the papers, a weight settling into the depths of his belly.

꩜

The courthouse was quiet this morning, as if the powers-that-be had decided to begin the weekend a day early. Judge Simpson completed the guardianship forms in record time, waving Charles out the door with hardly a civil word.

Drawing on the chain of his pocket watch, Charles glanced at the time. Donaldina had offered a standing lunch invitation at the Mission, and he'd been able to claim it twice in the past week. The unusual food had been disconcerting to him at first, but after a few meals he'd grown to appreciate it. And the company couldn't be surpassed.

His mind wandered back to the morning's discovery, his throat tightening at the thought. As best as he could decipher, Uncle Silas had done no wrong. He'd just been lucky. His shoulders sank an inch. Too lucky. How would Elizabeth react if Charles's uncle was somehow responsible for her family's destitution? He had to keep it secret until he had more information.

Lord, this could change everything.

It took him twenty minutes to reach the Mission. The girls had grown accustomed to his presence, so Kum Yong waved him through to the dining room. The sounds of piano flowed through the front hall, calling him forward. He moved toward the sound, bracing one arm against the doorframe between the hall and the large dining room.

This time it wasn't Yoke Soo at the old instrument, but the young teacher he'd grown to admire.

He laid his head on the frame, letting the strains of "Amazing Grace" wash over him. He could almost hear his mother singing at the kitchen washbasin.

Elizabeth moved with the song, leaning in toward the piano, eyes closed. Her fingers spread across the keyboard, adding harmonies and counter melodies as effortlessly as a bird taking to the sky. The song built, chords upon chords, until Charles's lungs felt like they'd burst from his chest.

A single bobbled note brought her to a halt. With a frown, she reapproached the section, working through it in a new way. After repeating the same segment several times, she continued, the music flowing like water down a mountain stream, bouncing and trickling over stones and creating something ethereal in its transitory existence.

As she played the final chord, Elizabeth held her position, her face glowing with a serene beauty he'd never experienced.

The reverberations faded and Charles straightened, his applause shattering the momentary silence. "That was extraordinary. Inspired."

She jerked her gaze up to meet his, the sedate expression vanishing in an instant. "I didn't know you were standing there." Her brow wrinkled.

"I couldn't help it. I hardly dared breathe, listening to you play."

Elizabeth closed the hymnal. "It was just a little hymn, not a Bach fugue."

He approached from behind, placing both hands on her shoulders. "Little hymn? It's my favorite."

"It was my Papa's, too." She sighed, leaning her head back against his chest to gaze up at him. "He always asked for it."

"Then it must be special to you, too."

She stood. "I hadn't played it since he passed away. Not until a few weeks ago."

Charles glanced around to make sure they were alone before taking her hand. "Why so long? Was it painful to remember him?"

"Somewhat." She dropped her gaze, even as she pressed her palm against his. "But more because my teacher didn't approve of church music."

"His loss." Charles tugged her a step closer. Private moments were a rarity in the Mission House. He wanted her as near as she dared. "Now you can rediscover old favorites."

Her lips curved upward. "And new favorites."

Charles stepped back as two girls entered from the kitchen with armloads of plates. He turned his eyes back to Elizabeth. "Will you play it at the musicale?"

"I thought I'd play it in my father's memory. Ruby and Robert will both be in attendance. I'm sure they'll remember."

"The hymn is quite fitting for the Mission's work, as well."

She tipped her head. "You're right. 'I once was lost, but now am found.'" Elizabeth turned her gaze on the girls setting the tables.

"And penned by a former slave trader."

Her eyes widened. "Truly?"

"Didn't you know?"

"As I said, I haven't played the hymn since I was a child. I—I've barely stepped foot in church since my father died." She lowered her voice to a whisper. "Don't tell Donaldina."

Something squeezed in his chest. "Why did you feel drawn to this work if you're not a believer?"

"I didn't say I didn't believe. I just…" She shrugged. "Life grew hectic. I focused on lessons and Tob—" Her face darkened. "…And piano."

A knot formed in his stomach. He'd seen the expression before—when she insisted she wasn't the woman for him. "You must feel God's love at work in this place."

Her face softened. "Every single day. And that's what I want to be a part of."

As the students returned to the kitchen, he leaned down and kissed her cheek, wishing he dared for more. "And so you are. I have some papers to deliver to Donaldina. May I join you for lunch?"

She nodded, a shy smile dancing across her dainty face.

Warmth rushed over him, and he squeezed her talented fingers in response. A quick visit to Donaldina's office, and he'd be back at Elizabeth's side. He pushed down the silly schoolboy emotions threatening to consume him. He was here to work, not bask in a woman's presence. *Help me remember, Father.*

Donaldina glanced up from her desk as he entered. "Mr. McKinley. How are you this fine day?"

He grinned. "Call me Charles, please. As I've learned over the past months in this city, Mr. McKinley is my esteemed uncle."

Donaldina rose from her seat. "My Scottish father was an imposing shadow in which to live, as well." She eyed the papers in his hand. "Do you have something for me?"

He extended his arm, laying the records on her desk. "The guardianship records for your two newest wards. The judge didn't even blink."

"They usually don't, unless someone contests the claim. We've been fortunate since Tien Gum."

"About that . . ." Charles hated to bring the specter of bad news.

"Oh, dear. This looks like something I should hear sitting down." She waved him to the little seating area by the window. Claiming her usual chair, Donaldina folded her hands in her lap. "What have you heard?"

"Her owners—for the lack of a better term—claim you are holding her captive against her will."

"That should be easy enough to contradict. As much as I'd rather Tien Gum not be subjected to more scrutiny, I'm certain she'd answer to a judge on such an assertion."

"It might not be so simple." Charles set his jaw. "When you retrieved her, you did so with no warrant, no police supervision. There's some talk at the courthouse that your entire operation might be illegal."

The color washed from Donaldina's face. "We've conducted Mission work here since 1874."

"And you have a strong relationship with the courts and the city government. I'm not overly concerned. But they could make life difficult for a time."

Donaldina sat back against the chair with a sigh. "So, business as usual, then."

He chuckled. "I suppose so."

Elizabeth tucked her wrist around Charles's arm for warmth. After an early supper at a new cafe, they'd taken the cable car to Golden Gate Park. She gazed up at the massive glass conservatory with a sigh.

"This is our third visit to the park this month."

She squeezed his arm. "And we've discovered something new each trip. I think this is the prettiest."

"You said as much about the Tea Garden and rowing at Stow Lake." He chuckled.

Elizabeth cocked her head. "And it's true. They're all lovely. Who knew this kind of beauty could exist in a city capable of such tragedy?"

He laid a hand over her fingers, his eyes crinkling about the corners. "Perhaps something shaped by sorrow has that much more beauty to offer."

She laid her head against his shoulder. Truth rang in Charles's words. Had she experienced a day like this a few years back, the joy wouldn't have been nearly so sweet. "I wish we could remain like this and never return to dark places and times."

"I don't believe you'd turn your back on your students. And I've my own calling to live up to." He slid his arm behind her back.

"Stop thinking as a lawyer for a moment. You must have a poet's heart in there somewhere." She patted his shirtfront.

A wide smile spread across his face. "I had to memorize some Keats when I was in high school. 'How beautiful, if sorrow had not made Sorrow more beautiful than Beauty's self.' Of course, I couldn't say I understood it. I've always preferred people to say what they mean."

Elizabeth gazed at his earnest face, memorizing each detail from the black rims on his irises all the way to the tiny cleft in his chin. She wouldn't change a thing. Turning to survey the meticulous grounds, she sighed. "I suppose what I'd really like is to bring all the girls here and witness their reaction to this astounding place."

"That would be a treat, wouldn't it?" He tugged her closer. "But for the moment, I'm enjoying not sharing your attentions." He leaned down and placed a kiss on her lips.

A shiver raced through Elizabeth. *Too good. Too perfect.* She drew a breath, pulling all the pleasure of this moment into her chest for safekeeping. She could fall into Charles's caresses and forget anything she'd ever been or done. She braced his rough jaw in her palm, responding to his kiss with hunger.

Charles nuzzled her neck. "It's difficult to see you at the Mission and not be able to touch you. Do this."

Her breath caught as his lips touched her throat. "I know what you mean."

A woman strolled by with a French poodle, her face pinched into a frown.

Elizabeth gently pushed Charles back, though every fiber in her being resisted. "We should be careful, even here. People are watching."

"Let them." He shot a glance over his shoulder as the lady flounced away. "I've found the most beautiful woman in the world, and I plan on kissing her every opportunity I can muster."

Heat rushed to Elizabeth's cheeks, even as delight curled around her. "Remember, Mr. Future Mayor, you have a reputation to protect. We don't want people thinking you hang around with loose women."

He chuckled and drew back. "Loose women? I hardly think you qualify for such a title. You wouldn't even let me touch your hand for the longest time."

A bitter taste rose in her mouth. "You don't know everything about me."

"I hope to, one day." Charles ran a finger along her earlobe.

Elizabeth closed her eyes. *Be careful what you wish for.*

24

The dining room sparkled from days of scrubbing and polishing. Bunting and banners decorated the walls, the seats arranged in neat rows facing the improvised stage. Elizabeth took a deep breath in a vain attempt to slow her racing heart. If only she could hide in the basement until all the guests departed. Why had she agreed to perform?

A rumbling cut through the morning air. In the kitchen, girls shrieked.

Elizabeth jumped from the piano stool and hurried out to the main hall. "What was that?"

Students poured into the room from the kitchen and classrooms. Yoke Soo grabbed Elizabeth's skirt. "Teacher? Was it the earthquake?"

Donaldina came out of her office. "Girls, girls. It's only thunder. Now let's get back to our preparations." She clapped her hands together. "Off you go."

The buzzing voices echoed through the hall and stairway as the children made their way to their rooms.

Donaldina laughed. "Everyone is jumpier than jackrabbits this morning."

Elizabeth walked to the window and craned her neck to study the darkening sky. "What a day for a storm. Hopefully it's not a sign of things to come."

"Not you, too." Donaldina shook her head. "Today will be a treat. The board is delighted. You'll probably be inundated with requests to play for various other functions."

"I'm not even comfortable playing today." She grabbed handfuls of her skirt rather than be seen with clenched fists. "I came here to get away from concert life."

Donaldina placed an arm around Elizabeth. "God has given you a gift, child. I don't think He intends for you to run away from it."

Elizabeth's shoulders loosened. One performance. After that she could relax and get back to work.

"I hope your young man will be joining us."

Heat rushed to her cheeks. "If you mean Charles, then yes. He will be here."

Donaldina squeezed her arm. "He's a nice fellow. I'm glad to see you so happy."

A quiver ran through Elizabeth's stomach. "I'm not certain I deserve to be so happy, but I am."

"Remember, every good and perfect gift is from above." Donaldina glanced around the dining hall. "The guests will be arriving soon. Will you check in the kitchen and see if Mrs. Lee has all the help she needs?"

"Certainly." Elizabeth hurried through to the kitchen, pleased to find Mrs. Lee in her element—organizing the children like troops prepared for battle. After checking on a few other details, Elizabeth climbed the stairs to her room for a few moments of quiet.

Closing the door, she surveyed the tiny space. Over the past few months it had become home. Yoke Soo's drawing sat propped up against her jewelry box. New curtains graced the narrow window. A rag rug softened the floor by her bed. Elizabeth sat on the mattress's edge, marveling at everything she'd experienced in her time here. She'd volunteered in an attempt to make amends for her mistake, and instead she'd been blessed beyond all expectation. Perhaps God was pleased with her choices. Not only had she left Tobias, but she'd worked hard since coming to San Francisco. She'd added a third sewing class, all of whom were well on their way to becoming excellent seamstresses. She'd set Yoke Soo on the path to reading music. She'd helped with several rescues. And today, the girls were ready for the musicale because of her instruction and encouragement.

Donaldina was correct. The board *should* be pleased.

Elizabeth spent the next twenty minutes fixing her hair, teasing it into a perfect Gibson Girl knot. The bodice of her blue gown pinched under the arms. She'd grown accustomed to the simple attire of a schoolteacher—shirtwaists, walking skirts, vests, and tailored jackets. She held the small mirror up above her head, trying to get a good aspect on the dress. *Ridiculous. Why did I love this so much?* She pinned a lace panel across the neckline. It wouldn't do to show too much skin.

Smoothing her hair one last time, Elizabeth managed to ignore her clammy palms. Heading downstairs, she greeted several of the students as they hurried about the house in their Sunday finery.

Tien Gum waved at Elizabeth, the brilliant jade green of her dress bringing out the sparkle in her dark eyes. She'd be singing a duet with one of the other young women, and Elizabeth couldn't wait to hear the audience's reaction.

Elizabeth peeked into the dining hall and scanned the decorations. Between the banners and the fresh flowers, the room looked ready to receive the president, not just a collection of supporters and donors. She couldn't resist a smile. The new home gleamed.

"They're coming!" Yoke Soo stood in the covered doorway under Kum Yong's watchful eye. "People are coming!" Her red tunic reflected the joy and excitement in her face. Yoke Soo bowed to the newcomers—an older couple. "Welcome to our new home." The child straightened, beaming like a street lamp.

Elizabeth hurried back to check on the choir. Dressed in matching white robes, the pupils chattered to each other like a flock of starlings. "Girls!" Elizabeth waited for their attention.

The children quieted, turning their wide-eyed gazes to their music teacher.

"We're all excited, I'm sure. This is a day we've looked forward to for quite a while." Elizabeth touched the backs of the two young women on either side of her. "I am so proud of you, I could burst my buttons."

The students giggled, their bright faces sending a thrill through Elizabeth's chest.

"But, today isn't about impressing the donors. It's about thanking them and God for providing this beautiful building, and making it possible for all of us to have new lives." A lump rose in her throat, choking off her words for a moment. "I'm so glad mine is with you." Her voice cracked, pitching upward.

Many hands reached out to touch Elizabeth's arms and shoulders, as they dissolved into an impromptu mass hug.

She laughed as they nearly knocked her over. "All right, enough. We need to focus on the program ahead. Remember what we've practiced."

"Teacher, teacher." Little Ah Cheng tugged at Elizabeth's skirt.

Elizabeth crouched down to hear the child over the buzzing conversations.

"Teacher, I don't feel so good."

❧

Charles huddled under the black umbrella as he made his way down Sacramento Street, the oiled silk doing little to keep the blowing rain from soaking him through. He crushed the armful of bouquets to his chest, not that they'd mind the added moisture.

He'd anticipated this day for weeks. Elizabeth deserved every accolade the Mission supporters were likely to heap upon her. Who could help but be impressed with what she'd accomplished in such a short time?

The weather carried his thoughts back to the day they'd met. He could never have imagined she'd become an enduring fixture in his life. And if Charles had his way—he'd never leave her side. How long should one wait before issuing a proposal? If he thought she'd say yes, he'd drop to one knee in front of the entire gathering.

Up ahead, Elizabeth's brother and sister-in-law climbed the steps to the Home.

Charles hurried to catch up to them. "Dr. King, Mrs. King—how nice to bump into you." He tucked the flowers under his arm.

Dr. King stepped back so Charles could join them under the cover. "Mr. McKinley, I'm surprised to see you here. I didn't realize you still had dealings with the Mission."

Elizabeth obviously hadn't mentioned their relationship to her brother. Charles folded the umbrella and left it in the corner to dry. "I'm volunteering my time."

A twinkle in Mrs. King's eyes suggested she might be more aware than her husband. "Of course you are. And why wouldn't you?"

The door swung open, little Yoke Soo rushing out to greet them. "Welcome to our new home!" She chirped the words like a little songbird. "Come in, come in!"

Kum Yong followed on the child's heels. "Abby, my friend." She grabbed Mrs. King's hand and tugged her inside. "I'm delighted to see you."

The doctor's wife threw her arms around the smaller woman, the vibrant show of affection surprising Charles.

Yoke Soo tugged on Charles's pant leg. "Welcome, Mr. 'Kinley."

He scooped her up, the mispronunciation making her more endearing. With her brilliant red tunic the child resembled a ladybug. "I can't wait to hear you play piano today."

Her eyes widened at the sight of the flowers. Her fingers touched the tender blossoms. "For me?"

Charles chuckled. When did women learn the art of politely waiting to be offered a gift? Apparently, not at age six. "I brought one flower for each of you."

She buried her nose in the bouquet. "Then you brought too many."

He ducked close to her ear, lowering his voice. "And an extra bunch for your pretty teacher. But it's a secret. I don't want the others to be jealous."

Yoke Soo grinned and patted his cheeks. "She likes you."

He couldn't resist giving the little girl a squeeze. "I'm glad to hear it." He lowered her to the floor so she could continue her duties.

Robert's mouth quirked upward. "Looks like you've made a few friends, Mr. McKinley."

Little do you know. "Please, call me Charles. I'm only Mr. McKinley at the office."

The doctor nodded, removing his dark hat. "I know how you feel. And you must call me Robert. Would you like to sit with us? Gerald and Ruby should be arriving shortly."

Charles nodded. "I'd be honored. Could you save me a seat? I need to speak with someone first."

"Not too long—there's sure to be a crowd." He glanced down at the massive bunch of flowers. "You want me to take those in for you?"

"That would be helpful, thank you. I'll just be a moment." He needed to find a certain young lady and wish her the best. Probably best to do so without flora in hand.

༄

"Oh, dear." Elizabeth touched Ah Cheng's warm forehead. Scooping the child up, she hurried to the dining room.

Donaldina met her in the doorway. After Elizabeth's brief explanation, Donaldina sighed. "Have Kum Yong put her to bed. It doesn't look too serious. We can take turns checking on her during the program." She brushed a kiss to Ah Cheng's hair. "Get some sleep, sweetheart."

Ah Cheng laid her head down, wrapping arms around Elizabeth's neck.

Elizabeth stroked her back. "I'll take her up. Kum Yong will need to translate for your opening comments." Several of their friends from Chinatown had agreed to join them for the day, so Donaldina had decided to offer the program in English and Cantonese. "The music doesn't start right away."

Donaldina pursed her lips. "Hurry back. I want to introduce our newest teacher. You're responsible for pulling this whole day together."

With a quick nod, Elizabeth shifted Ah Cheng higher on her hip and headed for the large staircase.

Charles caught her before she'd reached the first tread. "Is everything all right?"

The earnestness in his eyes warmed her as much as the girl's body leaning against her shoulder. "Ah Cheng has a slight fever. I'm going to tuck her in and then come right back. Have you gotten a seat?"

"I was tempted to claim front and center so I had the best view of the music teacher, but I thought better of it. I'll be sitting with your family." He grasped her free hand and pressed a quick kiss to her fingers. "I wanted to wish you the best."

A tingle went up her arm in response to his touch, her mind returning to yesterday's kiss. Kisses. A wave of heat climbed her neck. Best to keep her mind focuses on today. Elizabeth patted Ah Cheng's back as she climbed the stairs.

"Don't want to miss show," the little one murmured.

"We'll tell you all about it. I'll send Yoke Soo to cheer you up, later. Would you like that?"

The girl had already drifted off, her head nestled in the crook of Elizabeth's shoulder. Elizabeth tucked her into the low bed. Perhaps Robert or Gerald could look in on her before they went home.

Backing out of the room, she left the door ajar and hurried downstairs. She hadn't missed the opening words after all. Some of the guests were still getting situated. A tap on the front door caught her attention.

Elizabeth smoothed her gown and pulled the door open. "Welcome. We're just about to start."

The familiar figure on the front step stared out from under a dripping umbrella.

Tobias. Weakness engulfed Elizabeth, her legs suddenly no stronger than blades of grass. "Wha-what are you doing here?" She blinked several times, clearing her eyes.

He removed his hat, pressing it to his chest. "I could ask you the same. I never realized this was where you were hiding yourself."

A thousand bees buzzed in her ears. "Why else would you come?"

He lifted one brow, his catlike eyes gleaming. "Don't flatter yourself, Elizabeth. I'm a donor. My name was on the invitation list." He stepped to one side, revealing a raven-haired woman behind him. "I'm sure you remember Mrs. Carver."

Elizabeth backed up, her vision tunneling like she'd been dropped to the bottom of a dark well. *His wife.*

25

"*A cultured pianist shouldn't involve herself in political causes.*" Tobias's words from years before echoed in her mind. To see him standing on the doorstep of the Presbyterian Mission stole the breath from her chest.

"May we come in?" Tobias's brow lifted. He'd obviously recovered from the shock.

If only she could do the same. "Of course. Please, enter." Elizabeth stepped back as her former teacher and his wife walked through the door.

"Marie, you remember my prize pupil, don't you?" He turned to his wife.

The woman's eyes narrowed. "Miss King, wasn't it?"

Elizabeth's thoughts dissolved into a puddle on the floor. *Father, help me.* As if God would intervene in her disgrace. She bobbed her head, since no words would make it past her lips.

"What a surprise." The woman directed a piercing glare at her husband. "Tobias, were you aware Miss King was in San Francisco?"

"I believe her mother may have mentioned it in passing." He ran a hand over his lapel. "Very impressive, Elizabeth. I wouldn't have believed you suited for missionary work."

Elizabeth swallowed, her mouth as dry as cotton batting. "Life is full of twists and turns, Mr. Carver." His name felt foreign on her lips. She leaned against the oak door for support.

Mrs. Carver glanced toward the dining hall. "It sounds as if things are getting underway. Perhaps we should find our seats, Tobias."

"Yes, my dear." He inclined his head to Elizabeth. "I look forward to hearing your performance. It's been far too long."

Her hand remained glued to the doorknob as she watched them proceed through the hall. She could leave now. Step out into the street, catch a cable car, and disappear. Elizabeth's mind jumped from Charles to Donaldina to her family—all waiting in the other room. *God, I thought I'd paid for my sins. Wasn't it enough?*

᠅

Charles sat next to Robert and glanced down the row at the rest of Elizabeth's family.

Ruby waved and smiled. Obviously, Elizabeth had shared the news with one sibling, at least.

The room overflowed with well-dressed men and women, all speaking in hushed tones. The woman sitting in front of Charles sported a massive hat, the peacock feathers trailing back to tickle his knees.

Donaldina took to the stage and waited for the room to quiet. "Greetings to you all. We're so pleased each of you could join us today for our musicale—something we hope to make an annual event." She paused as Kum Yong translated her words. She introduced several important individuals, including the head of the Missions board, the pastor of their supporting church, and some representatives from Chinatown.

Charles scanned the room and noticed several familiar faces, including George Wu's. Elizabeth would be pleased by the turnout. Every chair was occupied and additional men lined the walls, having sacrificed their places for ladies.

Donaldina spoke for about ten minutes, regaling the assembly with stories of how the family had fared since they'd moved into the new building. "Many of you joined us on our opening day, and I hope you notice the beautiful new curtains, cushions, and wall-hangings, designed and stitched by our students with the help of our sewing teacher, Miss Elizabeth King." She turned and glanced behind her. "Miss King?"

The room remained silent.

Charles shifted in his seat. Had Elizabeth been delayed with the ill child?

Kum Yong moved to the back of the room and disappeared into the kitchen. A moment later, she reappeared, Elizabeth in tow.

He leaned forward, Elizabeth's ashen color unsettling. Could she be so nervous? She'd played concerts in large auditoriums, why would a simple musicale frighten her?

Elizabeth's sister, Ruby, whispered to her husband. Had she noticed as well?

Lord, give her strength. Charles forced his muscles to relax. He could do little to help besides pray.

Donaldina took Elizabeth's arm, as if to steady her. "Miss King came to us three months ago. After attending one of our presentations, God prompted her to leave behind her life as a concert pianist and join us as a humble teacher."

Elizabeth's gaze flickered and she glanced down, red blotches appearing on her cheeks.

"Miss King has taken on both our sewing classes and our piano students. I know you'll be pleased by what you hear today." She patted Elizabeth's hand. "Not only is she immensely talented and giving—our girls love her, as well."

As Kum Yong translated Donaldina's words, Abby leaned past Robert and whispered. "Charles, do you know what's wrong?"

He shook his head. "She was fine a few minutes ago." Charles sat back and studied the woman he loved. Her pallor sent a quiver through his chest. Was she prone to fainting? He'd never have believed it before today.

A smattering of applause followed Kum Yong's words and Elizabeth inclined her head to the crowd, retreating to the piano stool.

Donaldina and Kum Yong took their seats in the front as Elizabeth began to play. Strains of "Come Thou Fount of Every Blessing" filled the room and the students filed in, forming three long rows, the littlest in front.

Charles studied the group, trying to put a name to each girl. He could only match a few, mostly the young ones. Tien Gum's smile sent a flood of warmth through his limbs. How far the young woman had come from the sobbing waif in the courtroom. If Elizabeth and Donaldina hadn't retrieved her, the child's life would be very different, indeed. How wondrous to be part of their work.

As the pupils finished their hymn, Tien Gum stepped forward. The smile never left her face as she recited the Twenty-Third Psalm, first in English and then in Cantonese.

A respectful murmur of approval rippled through the audience.

The musicale continued with the choir singing two more hymns, and several children reciting scripture and poetry.

As the audience applauded the previous selection, Elizabeth stood from the piano stool and retreated to a bench off to one side.

Little Yoke Soo marched out of the kitchen in her brilliant red costume and walked over to the piano. She turned to face the audience and dropped a perfect curtsy. "I will play for you my Jesus song, like the ones we sing from the big book. My teacher is helping me learn to read those songs and to write down my own." She glanced at Elizabeth, a smile dancing across her tiny features. "I hope one day to play big concerts like Miss King."

Elizabeth smiled, nodding to Yoke Soo.

Yoke Soo climbed up on the stool and got herself situated while the audience murmured over the child's sweetness.

Everyone hushed the instant Yoke Soo touched the keys.

The notes flowed through the room like water sliding over the ocean sands and rolling small rocks in its wake. Yoke Soo leaned her shoulders toward the old wooden piano, encouraging it into sounds and stories no one would have believed it capable of producing. The delicate tune pulled at Charles, drawing him into her world—at least for the moment.

Mouths fell open about the room as the crowd soaked in the simple, sparkling tones of Yoke Soo's Jesus song. Minutes passed with no whispers or feet shuffling or chairs squeaking.

As she reached the final chord, the sounds faded from the room. A long moment of silence passed until a short man in the front row began the applause. His slow clapping migrated through the room as everyone joined in. Several women stood to their feet, the rest of the audience following in short order.

Yoke Soo sprang from the bench—a child once again—and threw herself into Elizabeth's embrace.

Tears ran down Elizabeth's face as she pulled Yoke Soo close, rocking the little girl in her arms. Her lips moved as she whispered quiet words into the child's hair.

Charles clapped until his palms stung—for Yoke Soo, for the Mission, but mostly for Elizabeth. Her tears cut at his heart. How precious she was to invest so much of herself in this little child.

As Yoke Soo disappeared back into the kitchen, Donaldina rose to address the room. She dabbed at her eyes with a handkerchief. "I've heard her practice the beautiful piece, and every time it's been a little different. This evening—hearing it with you—I was most touched by your outpouring of emotion and appreciation. It's clear you understand what we are desperately trying to accomplish here. We cannot continue to allow young girls like Yoke Soo, Tien Gum, and all of the others, to be crushed by human failings. Not only do their captors sin when they force their desires on these children, but I believe we sin when we turn our backs. How often do people dismiss them because of their age, their status, their culture, or their race? No more. Each child of God is equally precious."

Charles bowed his head as the director prayed over the group. A few more songs from the choir and then Elizabeth would finish the concert with her piece. He bumped his foot against the bouquet sitting under his feet. He couldn't wait to congratulate her.

Elizabeth took a moment to dry her cheeks as Qui N'gun curtsied to the crowd. Because of Qui N'gun's poor hearing, her solo of "Blessed Assurance" had been a bit off-key, but her authentic passion still brought several women to tears.

Elizabeth knew Donaldina wanted her to say a few words before performing "Amazing Grace," but one glance at Tobias scattered every idea of a planned speech. How could she boast about her accomplishments when her sin stared her in the face?

Instead, Elizabeth crossed to the piano and lowered herself to the stool. She glanced to where her family waited, in the second-to-last row on the right. Gerald sat with his arm draped around Ruby's shoulders. Abby and Robert smiled beside them, Robert's brown hair tousled, likely from running his fingers through the damp strands. Elizabeth's gaze settled on Charles. The man's head tipped slightly to one side as he studied her from afar. He nodded in her direction, as if to show his support. His eyes spoke love, even from across the room.

Nausea twisted her stomach. Why had she let things travel so far with Charles? Had she forgotten what she was? She swallowed, directing her focus back to the instrument, her vision blurring. She'd been a fool to think she could walk away from everything she'd done.

"I wouldn't have believed you suited for missionary work." Tobias's words tore the strings she'd been using to bind the pieces of her soul together. He stripped away any hope of forgiveness and new life, leaving her with no shield from the audience's curious stares.

She laid her trembling fingers on the keys. One last task. She could play her father's favorite song. A deep calm penetrated her as she laid out the opening strains of the hymn. The notes reverberated off the walls, ringing through the decorated dining room like a carillon tower calling parishioners to worship. Within moments, someone began to sing.

Elizabeth sucked in a quick breath—she hadn't intended to lead a hymn sing.

Others joined in, and soon the entire group was lifting up the words of the old hymn.

Closing her eyes, Elizabeth surrendered to the moment. No longer a performance, she focused only on leading the singers. The fears and trials of the day faded. "Through many dangers, toils, and snares I have already come. 'Tis grace has brought me safe thus far and grace will lead me home."

Gone were Tobias's condemnation, Donaldina's praise, and Charles's affection. She pushed into the music. "When we've been *there ten thousand years bright shining as the sun, we've no less days to sing God's praise than when we first begun.*"

The final notes suspended in the air, fading into cherished silence. Her father's words echoed in her mind, "*My precious daughter, you have a gift.*" Elizabeth's breath came slowly, filling her chest as she waited for a single clap to shatter the stillness, like being jostled awake from the perfect dream.

If only she could remain in that quiet place for all eternity.

26

*E*lizabeth slipped into the outer hall, fighting a wave of dizziness. She'd survived the concert, but the rest of the evening lay ahead. She whispered another prayer, in case God still listened. If He truly cared about her, He'd send Tobias and his wife home to Sacramento before they could breathe a word to anyone.

Ruby hustled after her, cheeks flushed. "Elizabeth, what's wrong? You look as if the devil himself is on your tail."

A shudder raced through Elizabeth. "Might as well be." She glanced over her sister's shoulder to where guests were beginning to file from the dining room, the clamor of their conversations spreading through the building. "Ruby, he's here."

She frowned. "Who?"

Elizabeth grabbed Ruby's arm and pulled her to the corner by Donaldina's office door. "Tobias Carver. He claims he's a donor." She dug fingers into her hair. "He never would have supported something like the Mission in the past. I can't believe this is a coincidence."

"Why would he do such a thing? Is he hoping to entice you back?"

"I don't know. He was so angry when I left." Her throat squeezed. "I can't imagine he wants anything to do with me."

Charles appeared, his eyes scanning the hall.

Elizabeth pressed herself into the doorway, behind the potted palm. "Please, Ruby. Tell me what to do."

Her sister bit her lip. "You could pull him aside and insist he leave."

"Every time I see him, I feel as if I will be ill."

Charles caught her gaze and waved from across the hall. Clutching a large bouquet of flowers to his chest, he weaved through the guests cluttering the room.

Elizabeth slid a fingertip under her lashes to vanquish any stray tears.

"There you are. You disappeared so quickly, I was concerned." Charles leaned down and pressed a kiss to her cheek. "Congratulations." He held the flowers out to her.

"Thank you." Elizabeth grasped the blossoms, her hands trembling. As she spotted Tobias and his wife entering the room, her heart leaped. "I—I've a vase in my room. I'll run up and put them in water."

His brows drew down. "You can't leave. Everyone is waiting to meet you."

Elizabeth's thoughts raced. How could she escape without raising suspicion?

Tobias had joined Robert and Abby, leaning toward her brother with a glint in his eye.

Ice chilled through Elizabeth's veins. She thrust the flowers back at Charles's chest. "I need to speak to Robert. Please, excuse me." She pushed through the crowd of well-wishers until she reached Robert's side.

Her brother turned with a grin. "Elizabeth, Mr. Carver was just telling me—"

"Robert, Abby, I need your help." She grasped her brother's sleeve and tugged, pulling him off-balance a step. "I'm sorry, Mr. Carver, but I must steal him away."

"All right, hold on—" Robert turned to speak to Tobias, but Elizabeth was already propelling him toward the stairs.

Abby followed a step behind. "Elizabeth, what has gotten into you?"

"One of our children is ill. I want Robert to take a look."

His arm stiffened. "In that case, let me get Gerald. He keeps a medical bag in the car."

"I'll send someone down for him. You must come now." Elizabeth yanked his arm like she used to when she was a little girl.

Abby touched Elizabeth's sleeve. "I'll get him. And Ruby, also. You two go ahead."

The crushing fear eased a bit as Elizabeth thundered up the stairs, her brother in pursuit. "Thank you, Robert."

"You should have said something right away. How long has she been ill?"

Turning into the third floor hallway, Elizabeth paused to catch her breath. "Just before the program. I think she's had a runny nose for a day or two."

Robert halted. "A runny nose? You're panicking over a little sinus congestion?"

She bit her lip. "And a fever. She was quite upset when I put her to bed." Elizabeth tapped on the door before turning the knob and stepping into the bedchamber.

Ah Cheng popped up in the bed. "Teacher! Yoke Soo gave me a flower. She says your sweetheart brought them."

Robert pinned Elizabeth with a pointed gaze.

A prickle raced down her neck. "It's the fever talking."

"Right." He stepped over to the bed and crouched at the child's side. "Hello. I'm Dr. King. How are you feeling?"

"A little better, but my head hurts. Teacher, did I sleep through the whole show?"

Elizabeth sat at Ah Cheng's feet, trying not to think of what Tobias might be doing downstairs. "Yes, you did. You must have needed the rest to get better."

Her brother laid a hand on the girl's forehead. "She does have a slight fever. But hardly worth fussing over."

Gerald appeared in the doorway, Ruby peering in over his shoulder. "I hear someone missed her singing debut."

Elizabeth sighed. "I'm sorry to worry everyone. Robert thinks it isn't serious."

Robert tipped Ah Cheng's head back, looking into her mouth. "Gerald, can I get a tongue depressor from you?"

Elizabeth's brother-in-law placed the black medical bag on the mattress's edge and clicked it open. Withdrawing the small wooden stick, he passed it to Robert. "What are you seeing?"

"I think..." Robert grasped the child's chin, holding her mouth open toward the light. "Yes. Koplik's spots. Definitely."

Gerald grasped Ruby's arm. "Go downstairs, now. You shouldn't be up here."

"Is it bad?" Elizabeth's stomach dropped. She'd only intended to divert her family away from Tobias. She hadn't anticipated Robert finding anything. "I thought you said it was congestion."

Gerald dug through his medical kit as Ruby hurried out. "Koplik's spots mean one thing, Elizabeth. Measles."

⚬

Charles clutched the bouquet, his throat thick. He sensed people milling about the room, but his focus remained fixed on the stairway.

Kum Yong approached. "It was kind of you to bring flowers for the girls." Her voice sounded distant, and he managed a nod in response.

"Should I put those in water for Elizabeth? I think she's seeing to Ah Cheng. She should return in a moment."

Her words knocked him from his stupor. "The little one who was sick?" No wonder Elizabeth seemed distracted. A weight settled in his stomach. "Is she worse?"

The young woman lifted her shoulders. "I don't believe so. I checked after the program began, and she was sleeping comfortably. But Elizabeth wanted the doctors to see to her while they were here. It's not often we have physicians in the Home."

A gentle coolness swept over him. "Of course. I hope it's nothing serious."

"As do I." She took the bouquet. "Why don't you greet some of the donors? They'd like to meet the attorney who speaks on our behalf."

"I will. Thank you." In his worry over Elizabeth, he'd forgotten his own responsibilities. As Kum Yong disappeared toward the kitchen, he joined the throng in the hall.

A good-looking couple lingered near the door, apart from the others. He wandered toward them. "Hello. Please, allow me to introduce myself."

"I know who you are." The man hooked his fingers over the top edge of a wine-colored vest.

"Oh?" Charles swallowed his words. "Have we met?"

"One of the children pointed you out. She called you 'Teacher's sweetheart,' I believe."

His jaw fell. Elizabeth would not be pleased. "You know children—they get peculiar ideas in their heads. Actually, I'm the Mission's attorney, Charles McKinley."

"Tobias Carver." He shook Charles's hand, arm stiff, and jerked his head toward the woman at his side. "And Mrs. Carver."

"I'm pleased to meet you." The chill of the stranger's skin seeped into Charles's palm, lifting the hairs on his neck.

Carver smiled even while his eyes shifted. "We're pleased to be supporting such a fine organization."

"It's rewarding to see these girls escape slavery and begin new lives."

The woman's gaze wandered the room as if her mind were elsewhere.

Her husband continued. "I was surprised to discover Elizabeth here. I didn't realize she had any interest in spiritual endeavors, though she's always been drawn to hard-luck cases, I suppose. Women's rights and such."

"You know Elizabeth?" Hearing her name on another man's lips sent a prickle down Charles's back.

His nostrils flared. "Didn't she tell you? Elizabeth was my protégé. I taught her everything she knows."

Of course. The tutor who believed hymns were a waste of her time and talent. "You're her piano instructor?"

"Among other things." Carver thrust hands into his pockets and rocked on his heels. "I'll refrain from asking you about the sweetheart comment. I suppose a gentleman wouldn't deign to speak of such things. Might put a blight on a lady's reputation."

Mrs. Carver sniffed. "Tobias, let's go. The concert's over."

"In a moment dear, there are a few more people I'd like to greet." He met Charles's gaze. "If you'll excuse us, Mr. . . . McKinley, wasn't it?"

Charles nodded, not sorry to see the couple depart. He turned and watched as the Carvers made their way across the room, stopping to converse with several people. What was it about Tobias Carver that had unsettled him so?

A round-faced gentleman touched his sleeve. "Are you Charles McKinley, by chance?"

"Yes, sir." Charles straightened.

The man captured his hand with a grip akin to a vise. "Mortimer Byrd. I'm the head of the Building Trades Council."

Charles brushed away the previous meeting and prodded himself to smile. "It's an honor."

"I'm well acquainted with your uncle. In fact, he was just speaking to me about you, yesterday."

"Really?" Charles stepped back.

"He's very fond of you, obviously. Spoke highly of your work here."

My uncle? Charles scrambled for a suitable response. "He's quite concerned for the future of the city. Taking care of those less fortunate is a vital part of the process."

The man clapped his shoulder. "Well said. Silas intimated that you're seeking a city council post this fall. I'm glad to hear it."

"This fall?" He swallowed. "Well, nothing's been decided yet."

"If anyone can make it happen, you know it's Silas McKinley. When he throws his weight behind a candidate, people tend to step out of his way. Have you met my wife?" He gestured to a nearby woman, silver curls circling her face. "Mrs. Byrd, this is Silas McKinley's nephew, Charles—the one he was telling us about."

Her eyes brightened. "Mr. McKinley, such a happy coincidence. Miss Cameron was just speaking of you, as well." She adjusted the mink stole draped over her shoulder. "As director of the Missions Board, I'd like to thank you for your effort on our behalf. It's nice to see a young person who cares about his fellow man."

Director of the Mission Board. Head of the Building Trades Council. A light flickered to life in the back of his mind, his uncle's change of heart coming clear. "It's been an honor to work beside Miss Cameron and her staff. It's a fine thing they're doing here for San Francisco."

Motion on the stairs drew his attention. Elizabeth clutched the railing, her color resembling fireplace ashes.

Charles turned back to the Byrds. "I apologize for rushing away, but could you excuse me, please? There's someone I need to speak with before she disappears."

"Of course, dear." The feathers on Mrs. Byrd's hat bobbed in time with her head. "I hope we'll see much more of you. We'll send you an invitation for dinner."

"Thank you, that's very kind."

"Such a nice young man." Mrs. Byrd's voice carried over the crowd as he hurried toward Elizabeth.

He intercepted her near the bottom of the stairs. "How is Ah Cheng? Is she worse?"

Elizabeth's shoulders drooped, as if the day's excitement had taken a toll. "Measles, Robert says." She returned to scanning the crowd.

He fought the urge to draw her away somewhere private. She didn't appear up to socializing. "Everybody gets measles at one point or another, right?" When she didn't reply, he tried another tactic. "I met your piano teacher."

Her gaze jerked back to him. "Tobias? What did he say?"

Charles clasped her elbow, unsettled by the sudden sway in her posture. "Not much, but I can't say I liked the man. Should I?"

She breathed out a long exhale. "Absolutely not."

Elizabeth pressed her fingers to her throat as she stood midstair. The sensation of Charles's hand under her arm brought stability to her trembling soul, even as she watched Tobias working his way through the room. *I need to get him out of here.*

She focused on Charles, standing at her side. "Thank you for being here today."

"I wouldn't have missed it. You know that."

His smile melted the sliver of ice in her chest. "I do. And I want *you* to know something." She fought to keep her voice steady. "If anything happens—if something comes between us—I'll treasure our time together. You've given me hope for the future, even though I didn't deserve it."

His smile faded. "Elizabeth, I wish you'd tell me what's bothering you. Is it that man?"

"I can't. I'm sorry." She tightened her grip on his arm, wanting nothing more than to lay her head against his shoulder.

Tobias had crossed the room and was shaking Donaldina's hand. Elizabeth's throat squeezed until her breath remained trapped in her chest. "I need to go speak to Donaldina. Please…" She met Charles's fervent gaze. "Please, stay here."

"If that's what you want."

As if slogging through thick mud, Elizabeth forced herself to cross to where Tobias and Donaldina stood.

The missionary turned with a smile. "Elizabeth, there you are. How is Ah Cheng?"

Elizabeth's palms dampened as she pressed them against her skirt. "Robert believes it's measles." She glanced at Tobias, studying his eyes. Mrs. Carver had moved away to the opposite side of the room.

"Oh, dear." Donaldina shook her head. "I'll go and see her in a bit." She gestured to Tobias. "Elizabeth, you didn't tell me your former teacher was one of our donors."

"I didn't know myself, until today."

"Perhaps you'd like to give him and Mrs. Carver a tour."

Tobias's brows pinched together. "I'm afraid we've already stayed longer than my wife would like. She doesn't have the same appreciation for your work as I do." His scrutinizing gaze fixed Elizabeth in place.

"And where is your wife, sir?" Donaldina straightened. "I seem to have lost sight of her."

"I believe she went to speak to the director of your Missions Board. Apparently, she knows the woman, somehow. Old classmates or some such."

Elizabeth's heart banged into her ribs. She stepped away from Tobias and Donaldina, scanning the room. In the far corner, she spotted Ruby, Robert, and Gerald coming down the stairs. Charles turned to greet them. And less than ten feet away, Mrs. Emily Byrd, the Mission Board director, stood face to face with Marie Carver.

Elizabeth's breathing slowed as Tobias's wife's pointed a finger her direction. The woman's raised voice carried above the din of the crowd, her accusing words painting a vivid picture of Elizabeth's past.

Ruby jerked her head up, her hand flying to her chest. Her wide-eyed gaze found Elizabeth in an instant.

Charles clutched the railing, a dark cloud passing over his face.

Elizabeth backed two steps and stumbled, her stomach wrenching. *It's over.*

27

*E*lizabeth burrowed under the quilt, tears wetting her cheeks. Her skin crawled, like each set of staring eyes still followed her every move. The massive stairway had felt like a mountain, but she'd fled past her family like they weren't there. And Charles…

He hadn't even turned to look.

Lord, I did all You asked. I worked, I taught, I behaved myself. Elizabeth's stomach roiled. How many had overheard Mrs. Carver's words?

She'd be forced out. Donaldina would have no choice—Elizabeth was a blight, unfit to lead young girls into lives of righteousness. Every word of praise the missionary had uttered turned to ash in Elizabeth's mind.

Where would she go? Back home to Sacramento? There'd be no way to explain this humiliation to her mother. A throbbing pain settled deep in her core. She hadn't even loved Tobias, but now she'd lost the man she did. She yanked the quilt away from her face, lungs desperate for oxygen.

A tap on the door sent her under the covers once more. Donaldina so soon?

Ruby's voice reached her ears. "Elizabeth?" The door creaked, footsteps drawing close. The mattress shifted as her sister sat. "I don't know what to say, honey." She rubbed fingers down Elizabeth's back.

Elizabeth hiccuped. "Say it didn't happen. Tell me the entire room doesn't know my disgrace."

A quiet sigh cut through the air. "Perhaps not the entire room, but just about everybody who matters."

"Wh-where is Charles?" Tremors started in Elizabeth's midsection, radiating out to her arms and legs, as if she'd stepped outside in nothing but her drawers.

"I don't know. He was right behind me when Mrs. Carver made her scene. And then..." She lowered her voice. "He was gone."

Elizabeth's sobs stilled. She pulled herself into a ball as if it could protect her from people's gossip. "Robert?" She lowered the quilt in order to see Ruby's face.

"He's startled, of course." Reddened lids framed her sister's eyes. Her lip quivered. "And about ready to kill Tobias Carver."

Elizabeth sat up, the quilt puddling around her waist. She'd not considered Tobias's current role in this. "Is he still here?"

"Mr. Carver?" Ruby pursed her lips. "I imagine he's made himself scarce. His wife's behavior didn't reflect well on him, either."

"Somehow I don't think it's her behavior anyone is worried about."

Lines deepened around Ruby's mouth. "Come home with us, Elizabeth."

Her stomach lurched as she sat up. "What would Gerald think? And his mother?"

"They'd think you're the same woman you were yesterday and the day before that." Ruby stroked her leg. "Scripture says, 'For all have sinned, and come short of the glory of God.' We've all made mistakes, Elizabeth. Gerald and I would no more turn our backs on you than we would on each other."

"I wish everyone felt as you do. Charles will never speak to me again. He's the one good thing to happen to me, and I've lost him."

Ruby wrapped her arms around Elizabeth. "Give it time. There's no saying how he will feel when the truth settles in."

Elizabeth burrowed her head against her sister's neck. "I know already. He told me once he could never love someone who gave her virtue away of her own accord."

A quiet tap caught their attention. Donaldina stood in the doorway, her hand gripping the frame. "May I have a word?"

Ruby squeezed Elizabeth's wrist. "I'll be downstairs. The offer is open for tonight—and as long as you need."

"Thank you." Elizabeth whispered the words, her throat closing at the sight of her friend and mentor.

Shadows gathered around Donaldina's eyes.

Elizabeth swung her feet to the floor, the pillow crushed against her abdomen. Whatever Donaldina had to say, she deserved.

"I assume you've heard the woman's accusations."

Elizabeth lowered her head. "I didn't need to hear. I lived them."

Donaldina blew out a long exhale and sat down beside Elizabeth on the narrow bed. "You should hear them all the same, so you know exactly what you're facing. She could be exaggerating."

Elizabeth bit her lip and nodded.

"Mrs. Carver claims you were...intimate...with her husband. That you beguiled him."

Elizabeth rocked in place, the statement sinking into her chest.

Donaldina rubbed trembling fingers across the bridge of her nose. "He was your teacher, yes?"

Pushing down the agony, Elizabeth nodded, again. "For three years."

"Were you..." Donaldina closed her eyes, as if it would somehow protect her from the harshness of the words. "Were you *together* the whole time?"

"No." Elizabeth choked out the word. "I didn't—I wouldn't..." *But, she had.* She brushed the tears away with the back of her fist. "I idolized him. I never thought..." She lifted the pillow as if to smother the sickening words.

"What happened?"

"When I started performing, he grew sullen. Possessive."

Donaldina pressed her shoulders back. "Perhaps your success made him feel threatened."

"I don't know why it would."

The missionary traced the quilt pattern with one finger. "You were attaining your dreams. You no longer needed him as desperately."

Elizabeth thought back, her mind a blur of images she'd tried to bury. "I don't know. Maybe." She shook her head. "But that's when he came to me, and...he made the first overture." The odd word rankled in Elizabeth's mind, like the horrific experience had been a concert to be enjoyed. She shook her head, searching for a better description. "He demanded—orchestrated...everything."

Donaldina lifted her hands. "I'm not sure I need any more detail. I see where we're headed."

Elizabeth lowered her gaze, resisting the urge to duck back under the quilt. Seeing her mentor's face clouded with grief pierced her through.

"What made you leave?"

"I hated what I'd become. I knew my father would've..." her throat closed around the word. She swallowed and began anew. "Papa would've been crushed. It was always his dream for me to perform on the stage. I continued playing concerts, but my heart was no longer in it. It was no longer anywhere."

Elizabeth paused, sifting through the memories. "I told Tobias I couldn't work with him, or see him, anymore." She closed her eyes. "He said if I dared to perform without him, he'd see me exposed."

Donaldina rose from the bed and paced a circuit around the small room. "And then you came here?"

Elizabeth moistened her lips. "You said this was a place of new beginnings. A home where girls with the most soiled pasts could find new life." She drew her knees up and hugged them to her chest. Elizabeth lowered her voice to a mere whisper. "I wanted that."

The missionary halted, staring down at her. "Do you still?"

"With all my heart. I came here to offer my life back to God—if He'd have it. To make up for what I'd done." She drew her shoulders inward. "And now all my effort is for naught."

Donaldina sat down, the mattress springs squeaking. "Child, if you think you're to work off your sin, you've missed the point of the gospel. The new life comes free of charge. Nothing you do could ever earn you God's love."

"I don't deserve His love."

"None of us do, I'm afraid. That's why Christ went to the cross—to pay for our mistakes, so we could be washed clean. It's grace, nothing less."

The throbbing pain in Elizabeth's head scrambled her friend's words. "It doesn't matter now. Everything I've worked toward—the girls, the musicale—everything. No one will care. They'll only see what I did before." She glanced toward her trunk. "I'll need to pack my things."

Donaldina frowned. "You're not going anywhere just yet. We need to work some things out, first."

"But, Mrs. Byrd..."

"Mrs. Byrd demanded your resignation, but I'm not prepared to accept it. I want to pray about the situation, and she agreed to do the same." Donaldina patted Elizabeth's knee. "You pray as well, child. Think about what I've said. New beginnings are not earned, they're granted." She sighed. "The board meets in three days. You'll have your decision then."

"Three days?" Elizabeth balled her hands in the quilt. Why wait? There was no way they'd choose to keep someone like her.

"The good Lord took three days in the grave, I think you can handle three days with us."

"If you think it best."

"I do. We need time to wait upon His wisdom." Donaldina stood with a sigh. "Now, Ah Cheng is asking for you. Will you go see her?"

Elizabeth retrieved a handkerchief from her bureau. "Of course." At least the younger children wouldn't understand her shame.

&

In the darkness of the Mission Home's dining room, Charles leaned against the wooden piano and ran his fingertip across the chipped keys. Somehow Elizabeth and Yoke Soo coaxed beautiful music from the unsuitable instrument.

Unsuitable. Bile rose in his throat. She'd barely allowed him to touch her hand at first. Even now, she was the first to pull away when things heated up. Mrs. Carver's accusations didn't match the evidence. He pushed down two of the black keys, the discordant notes as jarring as the argument in his brain.

When Elizabeth jerked away from his touch at the Tea Garden, he'd feared she'd been misused at some point in her life. His stomach turned. Could he have so misjudged her?

His chest ached. *I love her, Lord. Please let this be a mistake.*

But, if the allegations were correct...

He straightened, pulling his coat closed and buttoning it. He needed to leave, before he pounded up those stairs and demanded an answer from her. His stomach clenched. There must be some other explanation. Mrs. Carver didn't seem in her right mind.

A single piece of evidence spoke louder than the witness's testimony—the expression on Elizabeth's face.

Charles slipped out of the dining room and made his way through the quiet hall. Most everyone had left. Kum Yong sat on a bench by the door, her head hanging low.

He paused, searching for something to say, but words failed him. When she glanced up and caught his eye, he nodded and touched the brim of his hat. Distant and cold, but it'd have to do. He closed the door behind him and listened as the locks clicked into place, the familiar sound taking on an odd finality.

Charles plodded down the street, burying his hands in his pockets. Tomorrow's court appointment provided a good excuse to stay away. Eventually he'd have to face Elizabeth, but he needed time to consider what he'd say.

A man lingered at the corner, his collar turned up against the wind. As Charles passed, the stranger tipped back his derby to look at him.

Tobias Carver. The name remained etched in his mind.

Carver lifted his brows. "I thought you'd left already."

"I could say the same."

"How is she?"

Heat seared through Charles's chest. "Why do you care?"

"I didn't intend for this to happen." Carver glanced down at the wet street, jaw slack. "Elizabeth was my protégée. I never wished to hurt her. I didn't realize Marie knew, or I wouldn't have brought her along. I just thought if I could see her one last time..."

"I don't want to hear this." Charles stepped back, but the man caught his arm.

"Please. Tell Elizabeth I'm sorry. I'd like to make it up to her."

Charles broke Carver's grip and grabbed his lapels. "I don't know what you're after, but Elizabeth wants nothing from you. Whatever happened—she's a different person now. She deserves better."

Carver's face twisted. "What we deserve and what we get are two different beasts. I should know."

Charles thrust the piano teacher away from him. "I'm the last man in the world who'd offer you sympathy."

"That's right. What was I thinking?" A glint appeared in Carver's eyes. "She was probably letting you think she's a sweet little church girl, wasn't she?"

Fighting for breath, Charles turned his back. His pulse hammered, every instinct telling him to pummel the man until he was no longer capable of spouting scurrilous words against Elizabeth. Striding down the street, he put a safe distance between himself and the source of his rage. An assault charge would not be the ideal way to start a political career.

❦

Elizabeth held her breath as she stepped into the dining hall, the smell of breakfast hanging in the morning air. Just yesterday, she'd entered as the triumphant teacher who'd earned everyone's accolades. Today, she was nothing. Worse than nothing.

A hush fell over the room. Every head turned, each student's eyes holding a mixture of emotions.

The hairs on her arms lifted, like a cat walking down a dark alley. She walked past the rows of tables, scanning the room for Donaldina and Kum Yong. Not finding them, she wandered into the kitchen.

Mrs. Lee fiddled with her apron. "Can I get you some breakfast, Miss?"

"No, thank you. I'm looking for Miss Cameron."

"She took a tray up to Ah Cheng a few minutes ago." A shadow flickered across her gaze. "If you'd like, I could make a tray for you. I wouldn't blame you."

"That's very kind, Mrs. Lee. But not just now." Elizabeth backed out of the kitchen and made her way to the nursery room. Pushing open the door, she paused.

Ah Cheng sat up, but Yoke Soo and Ah Lon lay tucked under blankets in their beds.

Donaldina sat by Yoke Soo's side.

A tingle raced through Elizabeth's chest. "More patients?" She crossed the floor and touched Yoke Soo's flushed cheeks, the child's downcast face pulling at her heart.

Donaldina sighed. "We rarely have just one ill at a time. I tried calling our doctor, but he's busy elsewhere. I thought, perhaps, your brother might attend to them?"

Elizabeth's stomach tightened. She hadn't spoken to Robert, yet. What must he think of her? "I can ask him."

"Thank you. I'm not feeling well, either, or I'd call him myself." Donaldina coughed into a wadded handkerchief.

Elizabeth crouched in front of her. "Are you coming down with it, too?"

"No, no." Donaldina frowned. "I think I've already had every childhood illness in existence. I'm just weary."

Elizabeth lifted a hand to check Donaldina's forehead. "You do feel warm." She bit her lip. "I'll telephone him, now."

Ten minutes later, she sat in the office staring at the telephone. What could she say to Robert? How could she act as if nothing had happened? She reached for the receiver. She'd start with Ruby. She was a nurse, after all.

When her sister answered, a lump grew in Elizabeth's throat. How wonderful to have one person who'd love you no matter what. "Ruby, it's Elizabeth."

"Oh, sweetie. How are you today?"

Elizabeth closed her eyes, pressing fingers against her forehead. "About as expected, I suppose. But that's not why I'm calling." She took a breath, organizing her thoughts. "We have more sick kids.

Donaldina wondered if I could contact Robert, but I can't bring myself to do so. I thought, maybe you and Gerald could come?"

Her sister remained silent for a long moment. "I can't come, Elizabeth. It's too risky for the baby."

Elizabeth's throat tightened. "I didn't think of that." She shook her head. She'd thought of little other than herself, recently. "I wouldn't want to put you in danger."

"You know I'd come in a heartbeat otherwise. I'll speak to Gerald. And if he can't come, I'll telephone Robert myself. You can't avoid him forever."

"I know." Elizabeth's shoulders fell forward. "I just couldn't face hearing the disappointment in his voice."

"He loves you, Elizabeth. We all do."

If only she could believe the same about Charles. He'd disappeared without a word. Elizabeth replaced the receiver on its hook and lowered her head to her hands. Her family might not turn her away, but the man she loved—with aspirations of political office—would have no choice.

28

Charles strode into the office, the long day at court hanging heavy on his back. Assisting Spencer required more energy and concentration than he could muster today. They'd won the ruling, but the situation left Charles with a queasy feeling in his gut. Another insurance case settled and still no money for the King family. His mind couldn't help wandering back to the suspicious file. He needed to check the company cabinet and see if the other folders had returned.

Henry met him at the door. "Hey, old man. I hardly see you anymore, now you're spending all your time down in missionville. It's the pretty little blonde, isn't it?"

Charles bit back a rude comment. "I'm serving the needs of the community."

"A politician's answer, if I've ever heard one." Henry rolled his eyes. "Speaking of which, your uncle is looking for you. Something about a banquet. Time for the golden boy to earn his keep, I believe."

"Did he say when?"

"Day after next. Make sure to bring your friends some leftovers, won't you?"

"I'll see what I can do." Charles strode to his desk, the allure of an elected position fading fast. He couldn't even manage his private life, how could he be expected to deal with city business?

"Charles!" His uncle's voice boomed across the office.

Charles closed his eyes for a brief moment. The other employees must be growing accustomed to his uncle summoning him into the inner sanctum on a daily basis. What had he done this time?

Henry smacked him on the back. "The master calls."

"Funny." Charles dropped his hat on the desk and smoothed his hair before heading back to another privileged meeting.

"Come in, come in." Uncle Silas stood by the bank of windows, a coffee cup clutched in his fingers. "I just heard from Horatio Byrd. Apparently his wife was quite taken with you." He hoisted a bushy brow. "You seem to have a positive effect on the ladies."

"Yes sir. I mean, no sir." He shook his head. What was the correct reply for such a ridiculous assertion? "I found the Byrds to be quite gracious."

"And well-positioned to assist you."

Leave it to his uncle to notice such things. "Mr. Byrd mentioned something about a council seat."

"It's short notice, I'll give you that. But with George Baher falling ill, a surprise seat has come open. I want you in it."

"Uncle Silas, I'm not sure I'm ready."

"Poppycock. You're a McKinley. And I'll be here to give you direction. You flash your smile and woo the ladies, I'll provide the oversight and direction. We can't lose."

We. "I've lived in the city less than six months. Certainly there must be some residency requirement."

"They're willing to waive it on my recommendation. Now, first things first. You'll be attending the Trades Council Annual Banquet on Tuesday evening. I'll introduce you to the key players, and we'll announce your intent to run." He turned and narrowed his gaze at Charles. "You do own a tuxedo?"

A cold sweat washed over him. "I'm afraid not."

"No matter. It's too late to order one from a tailor. You'd best go down to the Hastings, over on Post, and see what they have in stock." He studied Charles. "If only you didn't have shoulders like a quarryman." He huffed and gulped his coffee. "You'll need a top hat, too. Don't forget."

"I hate to admit this, Uncle, but I'm not sure I have enough to cover those purchases."

Uncle Silas waved a hand. "Bill it to the firm. We'll settle accounts later."

A long exhale escaped Charles's lips. "Whatever you say." He still owed the man for school debts and for the suit on his back. At this rate, Charles would never see more than a sliver of each paycheck until he was governor. Maybe not even then.

⁂

Elizabeth escorted Gerald up to the girls' room. "Miss Cameron has come down ill, too. She couldn't have measles, could she?"

"It's unlikely." Gerald gripped a medical bag under his arm. "But I'll see her when I'm done with the little ones."

Closing her fingers around the cold metal knob, Elizabeth pushed the door open.

Yoke Soo appeared to be sleeping, but the other two girls cuddled together on one bed, looking at a storybook.

"Girls, you're supposed to be sleeping in your own beds."

Ah Cheng coughed several times into her fist. "But teacher, she can't see the pictures from there."

Gerald chuckled. "I don't suppose it matters, if they're feeling up to it." He dropped to one knee beside the bed, lowering his bag to the floor. "Are you feeling better?"

"It itches." Ah Cheng scrubbed at the back of her neck.

"I'll leave some calamine with your teacher. It should help. Let me take a look." Gerald lifted the girl's hair and examined the rash on her back.

He sat back on his heels. "Neither case looks severe. I think they can stay here for the time being. I'll leave some creosote syrup for the cough, as well."

Elizabeth walked to the far side of the bed and touched Yoke Soo's shoulder. When the little girl's lids fluttered open, Elizabeth bent down. "The doctor needs to take a look at you."

Yoke Soo turned her dark-eyed gaze on Gerald.

He smiled. "It'll just take a minute." He placed a thermometer under her tongue.

Her eyes widened as he braced his shorter limb on the edge of the bed.

"Why is your arm like that?" She mumbled the words around the glass tube.

"Don't talk, Yoke Soo." Elizabeth touched her head.

He smiled at the girl. "I was sick. I'd have died if it weren't removed."

She pulled the instrument from her mouth. "What I have?"

"Oh, no. Nothing like measles. You're going to be all better in a couple of weeks."

"Piano would be hard." She tipped her head, studying the doctor. "Do you miss your hand?"

"Yoke Soo." Heat rushed up from under Elizabeth's lace collar.

Gerald touched Elizabeth's wrist. "I don't mind questions." He turned back to Yoke Soo. "I'll answer you, but you must keep this in your mouth until I take it out. No more talking for a whole minute. Agree?"

The child bobbed her head, placing the thermometer back in her mouth.

"Yes, I miss it. Every day. Sometimes I even forget it's gone and it's as if I can still feel it." He pressed a stethoscope to her chest. "But I'd do it again, if it meant I could stay with the people I love."

Yoke Soo's lips twitched as if she fought a smile. She nodded.

"Now, no more questions until I say." He glanced at Elizabeth and lowered his voice. "I've been spoiled, lecturing at the medical college this past year. It's been a while since I've done an exam."

"I appreciate it, Gerald." Elizabeth stroked Yoke Soo's leg. "Ruby said it wasn't safe for her to come."

"We don't want to take any chances. She probably had measles as a child, but she couldn't remember for certain. She's going to telephone your mother to check."

Elizabeth rubbed her arms to chase off the chilly thought. "Ruby was in here last night."

"That's why she's checking." A crooked smile spread across his lips. "After everything I went through last year—diphtheria, the heart complications, the cancer surgery—I never dreamed we'd have a child of our own. This baby is a miracle."

"I'm so happy for you two, I could burst."

"He'll be treasured—more aunts and uncles than he can handle."

Elizabeth placed a hand on her hip. "You mean *she*. And I'm the fun aunt. All the King nephews and nieces say so." Her heart sank. "Or, I was. Now I'm the disgraced aunt."

"You'll always have a place with us. You know that."

"How is Abby taking the news about the baby?"

"She appeared excited to me, but I'm not the best judge of women's feelings. You'd best ask your sister."

Elizabeth laughed. "To tell you the truth, we can't even judge our own emotions. How is a man supposed to do better?"

Yoke Soo mumbled, the thermometer bouncing between her lips.

Gerald jerked. "Oh, sorry." He pulled the device out of her mouth and squinted at the tiny numbers. "Not too bad." He patted the girl on the shoulder. "I want the three of you to stay in bed and get lots of sleep, drink plenty of fluids, and take your medicine."

"Yes, sir." Yoke Soo snuggled into the pillow.

"Their rashes will develop over the next day or two. I'll have Robert stop in tomorrow." The doctor stood, gathering his implements. "Remember, the house is under quarantine. I don't want any children going in or out, and keep the sick isolated. Adults may pass, if they've had the illness."

"I understand."

"And, I'd like to check on Miss Cameron."

"Please." Elizabeth tucked the covers back around Yoke Soo's shoulders before leading the way to Donaldina's room.

Fifteen minutes later, he emerged with a darkened expression. "I'm afraid her situation is worse than the girls. It looks like pneumonia, probably brought on by exhaustion. I'm prescribing complete bed rest. It might even be best if she went elsewhere to convalesce. She's unlikely to get the recuperation she needs with all the children underfoot."

Elizabeth's knees weakened. "We can't do without her. You heard what happened yesterday. As soon as the board meets, I'll be out. Kum Yong and Mrs. Lee can't run the Mission alone."

"I'm afraid they'll have to." He shrugged. "Or the board will need to make other arrangements. She can't continue like she has. If she doesn't get some time away, the Mission will be running without her permanently."

❧

The brick building draped Charles in its shadow. He needed Donaldina's signature on the newest set of guardianship papers, but the idea of facing Elizabeth sent a tremor through his gut. Over the past two days, his trust waxed and waned like the moon. Last night he'd convinced himself of Elizabeth's innocence, but with morning light, his doubts surged back. Did he really want to know the truth?

He pushed himself up the steps. A white notice board hung on the door, warning visitors about the quarantine. Thankfully, he'd had measles years ago. Charles rang the bell. After he finished here, he needed to drag himself to the haberdashery in search of evening clothes.

The door creaked open a notch, Kum Yong's dark eyes peeking through the gap. A moment later, she beckoned him inside. "Charles, so glad to see you."

"I need to see Miss Cameron." He stepped over the threshold. "I have papers she needs to look over."

She closed the door behind him. "I'm afraid Miss Cameron is ill." Kum Yong pushed a lock of dark hair away from her face.

"I'm sorry to hear that. How is the little girl?"

"Ah Cheng? She was just the first. We have three girls down with measles, now. And Miss Cameron is fighting pneumonia."

His chest tightened. "Pneumonia? She seemed fine two days ago."

Kum Yong shook her head. "She'd not felt well for a while, but Lo Mo is very good at hiding it."

"Everyone else is well?" He couldn't bring himself to say Elizabeth's name.

The young woman tightened her lips and gazed at him. "Yes. Tired and worried, but yes."

Her meaning struck him squarely in the chest. "Do you think she'll see me?"

"Miss Cameron?"

"Elizabeth." He might as well get this over with, though his instincts wanted nothing more than to back out the door and hop a ferry across the bay. Holding on to a thread of hope seemed preferable to facing the truth.

"I'll tell her you're here. Why don't you wait in Donaldina's office?"

The office seemed dark and cold without its usual occupant, the fragrance of tea still lingering in the air. *Please, Lord.* His mind remained too scattered to pull together a decent prayer. "Please" would have to do. He set his briefcase by the door and walked to the window, pulling back the curtains.

"I sewed those." Elizabeth's voice floated in from the doorway.

He turned, his heart seizing at the sight. Studying the dark circles around her eyes and the wisps of honey-blonde hair trailing about her ears, he had to fight not to jump forward and embrace her.

Elizabeth walked over to the corner and clicked on a floor lamp. "I'm surprised to see you."

The words cut through him. "Did you really think I'd just walk away?"

"You should." The guarded look in her eyes reminded him of his sister on the day of her sentencing.

"I'd like to know the truth." He gestured to the tiny sitting area.

Elizabeth crushed both arms to her chest, shoulders rounding. "I'm not sure you do, but I'll answer any questions you have." She crossed the floor and took a seat in the chair nearest the door.

Sucking in a deep breath, he pulled Donaldina's usual chair back a few inches and sat. "I heard what that woman said—Mrs. Carver. She claimed..." He couldn't bring himself to say it.

"She claimed I enticed her husband into an affair. That I wasn't worthy to be a teacher because I'm morally incompetent."

"Yes." He leaned forward. "Tell me it's untrue."

"Which part?"

His stomach dropped. "You're not on the witness stand, Elizabeth. Talk to me. Tell me what I want to hear."

"You want me to say she lied? None of it is true?" Her gaze flickered.

"I want you to tell me the truth."

"I told you the truth months ago. You wouldn't hear it." Her eyes glistened, as if tears threatened to spill over her lower lids. "I told you I wasn't the woman for you."

"Elizabeth…" He sat back in the chair, propping his elbow against the armrest.

"Yes, I had an affair with him. Is that what you wish to know?"

The truth gouged a mortal wound. All will and purpose emptied out of him, like sand falling to the bottom of an hourglass. "Why?"

"Does it matter?" Her voice strained. "I'm guilty. The board casts me out tomorrow. You can go do your good deeds, earn your political accolades, and never have to face me again. But know this…" Elizabeth stood, her hands shaking. "I didn't seduce him. Not that it excuses my behavior in any way."

His throat felt thick. "Were there others?"

She swayed on her feet, eyes widening. "How can you even ask me such a question?"

"I'm struggling to accept what you've already confessed to me. How do I know what you're capable of?"

Her complexion faded until her skin resembled dusty porcelain. "There were no others." The words barely crossed the space between them. Tears spilled down her cheeks, but she didn't bother to wipe them away. "I came here to escape what I'd become, to redeem myself in God's eyes and in my own. I've failed at both. And adding your disappointment on top is more than I can bear. I'm sorry, but I will not beg your forgiveness. I'm not worthy of it." She turned like a spool and dashed out the door, the breeze sending several papers fluttering from the top of Donaldina's desk.

Charles fell back in the chair, the truth clawing at his throat.

Guilty.

29

The pungent aromas of George's shop carried Elizabeth back to her first visit to Chinatown several months earlier. To think, she'd been worried to walk the streets, imagining every person as a potential threat. The scents of licorice root and ginger brought a calm she hadn't experienced in days. The board would meet tomorrow and Elizabeth had already moved most of her things to her trunk in anticipation. Though Donaldina insisted, even in her feverish state, that Elizabeth be offered grace—the board was responsible for the final decision. The girls needed a teacher they could look up to, not one who'd fallen headlong into sin.

George popped out from the back room. "Miss King. So happy you come to my shop. I'm still celebrating my little Yoke Soo's success. Such a little firecracker, that one."

Elizabeth's throat tightened. How she'd miss her students. "She performed beautifully. You must be so proud."

"Like a papa." He shrugged. "I've got little hope of children in my life. I hope it's not wrong to imagine she is my own."

"You rescued her. I think you're right to claim her as a daughter." Elizabeth swallowed, wishing she didn't need to deliver bad news. "George, I came to ask for some of your marvelous remedies."

His brow furrowed. "Ah Cheng is still sick?"

"Not just Ah Cheng, I'm afraid. Yoke Soo and Ah Lon, also."

He grasped the edge of the counter. "How bad is it?"

"The girls will be fine. My brother-in-law, Dr. Larkspur, saw them yesterday. He didn't think any of their cases were severe. But Miss Cameron has come down with pneumonia."

"My mother always said, 'Misfortune does not walk alone.'" George rubbed his chin. "I suppose the doctor left medicine?"

"Yes, and the girls are improving. But Donaldina prefers your herbs. She thought you might have something to help with the cough."

"I have just the thing." George walked down a row of boxes near the counter until he found the ones he wanted. He measured the dried roots into two paper bags. "Astragalus and pleurisy root. Mrs. Lee will know how to prepare them."

Elizabeth took the packets from his hand. "Thank you. And I'll let you know if things worsen with Yoke Soo, but I think she'll be up and around in a few weeks."

He bowed his head. "Let me know if there's anything else I can do."

Elizabeth turned to leave, but George's voice stopped her before she reached the door. He came out from behind the counter. "How are the other teachers? Is everyone else well?" A tiny crease formed between his brows.

"Yes, indeed." Elizabeth leaned close and touched his sleeve. "Kum Yong will be happy you asked."

Hurrying down the busy street, Elizabeth pressed the parcels to her chest. Robert had telephoned earlier saying he'd come by today to check on the patients. She'd survived the awkward moment, the conversation bringing a measure of peace as well. Everyone knew her secret. There would be no more hiding. She'd lost Charles, and likely her job, but life would continue in some form.

She paused before crossing the narrow street, a large wagon pulled by draft horses rattling past. A Chinese man stood on the opposite sidewalk, his dark eyes riveted on Elizabeth. A prickle crept across her arms. She turned and continued on the same path instead of crossing.

He followed, a black derby pulled low over his forehead and a shirtlike jacket hanging loose over his thin frame.

Elizabeth ducked into a florist shop, her pulse racing. *This is ridiculous.* Just because a man looks at you, doesn't mean he wishes you ill. She handed a few coins to the old woman at the counter and chose a dripping bouquet from one of the pails. The girls had enjoyed receiving Charles's flowers at the concert. Maybe another bunch would cheer those who were sick.

Pushing her way outside, she added the blossoms to her basket and turned toward home. Three steps later, the dour-faced man stepped out of the alley to her left, jostling her elbow. "You Mission girl?"

Elizabeth took a step back, her breath catching in her chest. "Yes."

"Need help. Come."

"If you could accompany me back to the—"

"No time. You must come now." Grooves formed in his forehead, his eyes earnest.

Her heart softened. "What's wrong?"

"*Mui Tsai.*" The man's voice quavered.

A child slave. Elizabeth chewed her lip. Donaldina forbid them from going on rescues alone, though she'd been known to do it herself. But now, with Donaldina sick and Kum Yong busy caring for everyone—who would be able to go but her? And it wasn't as if she was raiding a brothel. "I don't know. Maybe I should go get help."

"No time—dying."

The image of Yoke Soo, Ah Cheng, and the other little ones swam before her eyes. Elizabeth gripped her basket and nodded. "All right. Show me."

⁂

The busy office provided the hum of activity Charles needed to relax. *Put her out of your mind.* He adjusted the lamp on his desk, trying to throw more light on the stack of files. Spencer went to court tomorrow, and Charles was determined to provide a little extra content for the case. His pen scratched along the notepad, the ink blotting as fast as he could write.

He rubbed stained fingers against his weary jaw. Every time his thoughts went astray—back to Elizabeth—his teeth clenched. How could she give herself to a man like Carver, but act like Charles was a cad for simply touching her hand? He'd never have dreamed of asking for such favors. Well, perhaps he'd dreamed...but certainly not more than that.

His chest ached, as if his heart had forgotten how to keep rhythm without her.

Her confession changed everything. She wasn't the woman she claimed to be. The Elizabeth King he'd fallen in love with didn't actually exist. A woman of great compassion, intelligence, beauty, strength—and interested in him? He should have known.

It didn't matter if she hadn't enticed the man. She hadn't turned Carver away, either. Charles lifted his arm, splotches of ink soaking through his sleeve.

Yanking open the drawer, Charles dug for an extra sheet of blotting paper. Illegible notes would be useless, and he had no desire to write them out again. His hand bumped into something jammed in the rear of the drawer. Bending down, he peered into the dark recesses. He slid the manila envelope out and lifted it into the circle of light. Another one?

A message was clipped to the top—*take another look.* He tore it off, glancing at the names written underneath.

McKinley/King '06.

Charles lifted his gaze and scanned the busy office. No one paid him any attention.

He emptied the papers onto the desk and thumbed through the pages. He'd seen this all before. Why bother going over it again? And who wanted him to?

Near the back of the stack, he stumbled over a series of dog-eared sales receipts. Skimming down the lines, he frowned. More building investments Uncle Silas had dumped days before the quake? Sold to—he sucked in a breath—the estate of William King. Sweat dampened his palms.

If these forms were correct, it appeared Uncle Silas transferred the bulk of his investments to the King family mere days before disaster. He'd pocketed the cash, leaving Dr. King's heirs responsible for the doomed buildings.

It made no sense. He couldn't have foretold the earthquake, especially the scope of the disaster. Had he needed to secure a cash flow for another activity? Under normal circumstances, he'd find another buyer, not place it all in the estate's name.

A throbbing ache settled behind Charles's eyes. He glanced across the room to where Henry sat beside a leaning tower of law books. Charles walked over to the coffeepot and filled a tall mug. Tucking the records under one arm, he carried the cup over to his friend's desk and placed it in front of him.

Henry swiped the back of his hand across his lower lip. "Attorneys don't get coffee for clerks, it's supposed to be the other way around. I'd think you'd have figured that out by now."

Perching on the edge of the desk, Charles spread the documents on the blotter. "Explain these to me."

Henry adjusted his spectacles and scanned the forms. "This isn't right."

Charles lowered his voice. "Why would my uncle dump so many investments just days before the earthquake? He's not a prophet. No one saw this coming."

Henry ran his finger down the rows of numbers. "And he took a huge loss. From the looks of these figures, the King estate didn't have the necessary funds to cover all of this. Look here—" He took a pencil and lightly marked one of the figures. "In this case, he transferred the King's portion of an investment to himself. See the address?"

"Outside the fire zone."

"Right."

Charles's stomach churned. "No one could be that lucky. What happened? Did he get a divine message or something?"

Henry pulled off his glasses, the muscle over his jaw twitching. "Maybe that's exactly what he wants you to think."

❧

Elizabeth trembled as she followed the stranger through the shadowy hall, keeping an eye on the braided queue hanging down the center of his spine. The cloying scent of opium drifted through the silent house. She slowed, letting him get further ahead. "I think...I think I should go back."

He turned and gazed at her with dark eyes before disappearing into a room on the right.

What was she thinking? Elizabeth edged back. Robert would be arriving at the Mission any minute. She could run back and get him. "I'll—I'll return with help." The words echoed around the empty apartment.

An elderly woman appeared behind her, dressed in emerald-colored silk. She poked a finger into the small of Elizabeth's back. "Keep going. Almost there." She smiled, several teeth missing from her upper jaw.

"I made a mistake. I should—"

Before she could finish her statement, her escort reappeared. He grabbed her arm, yanking her off-balance. "Come." He dragged her into the dark room and shut the door.

Elizabeth stumbled, dropping to one knee on the wooden floor. "What are you doing?"

Two more men grasped her from either side, lifting her off her feet and forcing her into a chair. One stooped behind her and bound her wrists.

"Jesus woman." A familiar man hissed in her face, his hot breath filling her nostrils. He held a small gun in his shaking hand.

Elizabeth's stomach wrenched. Tien Gum's captor—the one from the rooftop.

"You will pay for my property."

30

*C*harles stood before the cheval glass and tugged at the tuxedo's lapels. "Is it supposed to be so tight?"

The Hasting's tailor sighed for the third time. "Evening wear is not worn for comfort. I've already adjusted the seams twice." He swiped a small brush across Charles's back. "This is not a sack suit, Mr. McKinley. It is designed to give you an air of sophistication, as if personal comfort is the furthest thing from your mind." He adjusted the long mirror on its hinge for a better angle. "And frankly, if you think this is uncomfortable, you should see what the ladies will be wearing."

The image of Elizabeth in her midnight blue gown flooded his thoughts. The idea of a political future without her at his side had lost its appeal. "I suppose you're right. It's only one evening." The first of many, if his uncle had any say in it. After spending the morning poring over his uncle's financial records, the idea made him ill. "I'm told a top hat would be the only appropriate head wear."

"I've taken the liberty of having three set out for your perusal." He gestured to a nearby counter, a row of smart-looking hats beckoning.

"I'm not on the ranch anymore, am I?"

"Certainly not." The tailor scoffed. "We don't sell cowboy duds in here. Only the finest in men's fashions."

A frustrating itch had developed between Charles's shoulders. "You choose. I've never worn one. How would I know the difference?"

The man made a guttural sound in his throat and reached for the nearest hat. He placed it on Charles's head, standing on his toes to reach. With a few adjustments, he made a face and pulled it off. "Seems your head is as large as the rest of you. I'll have to retrieve another size. Just a moment."

Charles tried to cross his arms, but the fabric tugged across his back. He'd chosen the tuxedo yesterday, but he'd hoped the tailor could make it wearable. He felt like a child trying to fit into last year's school clothes.

"Mr. McKinley?"

A young saleslady motioned to him. "There's a telephone call for you, sir."

"For me?" Charles lifted his shoulders and tried to settle the jacket more comfortably before following her to a corner office. He took the receiver from the hook. "This is Charles McKinley."

"Charles, it's Robert King. Your office told me where to reach you."

Charles ran a finger under the stiff collar, suddenly unable to draw a decent breath. *Robert?* "How can I help you?"

"I need to know if you've seen Elizabeth."

"We spoke yesterday." The memory of the heartrending conversation still dragged at his heels.

"You haven't seen her today?"

The uncertainty in Robert's voice made him pause. "No. Why do you ask?"

"I'm at the Mission. Kum Yong says Elizabeth went on an errand to Chinatown hours ago and hasn't returned."

"Perhaps she stopped for lunch."

"By herself?"

His stomach turned. "No." Charles pressed fingers against his temples. He was due at the banquet in two hours. "I'll be right there."

He lowered the receiver, his mind jumping from one dark thought to another. Elizabeth, living under the shadow of disgrace—she had every reason to disappear. But to abandon Donaldina, Yoke Soo, Kum Yong? To leave her family without a word? It didn't make sense.

The alternative sent an icy chill through his chest.

Elizabeth bit her lip, willing away the tears. The show of emotion would only give her captors confidence in their fear-mongering tactics. She pulled at the bonds on her wrists, the twine cutting into her skin.

Two of the men argued in the next room, their voices carrying through the wall as if it were paper. She could make out a word or two, but regretted not spending more time learning the language.

The third man sat in a rocker nearby, a Chinese newspaper open on his lap. His gaze darted toward her every few minutes, as if he half-expected her to leap from the chair and jump out the shuttered window.

"Why are you doing this?" She studied his threadbare clothes, quite different from the other troublemakers. "What do you want with me?"

He lifted the paper and hid behind it.

She kept her voice low so as not to attract attention. "You know the police will tear this place apart."

"They don't know where you are." The paper didn't move, but he hadn't turned the page since she'd arrived, either. At least she knew he spoke English. Better English than he'd used on the street.

Elizabeth yanked against the rope, her shoulder protesting at being bent behind her. "There are no secrets in Chinatown. I've lived here long enough to know that. Someone saw me follow you."

"People know better than to challenge the tongs."

She swallowed hard, trying to push away the fear threatening to consume her. Robert had warned her about the dangers, and she'd cast his wisdom aside like meaningless chatter. How maddening to prove him right.

The argument grew louder, punctuated by a loud clatter, as if someone had thrown something against the wall. Had she told anyone where she was going? *Lord, what do I do?* She strained to listen to the discussion next door, but other than some choice phrases, she couldn't make sense of the conversation.

She closed her eyes. Everything she'd worked for had crumbled like a castle made of sand. Elizabeth remembered Donaldina's words at the musicale. She'd praised Elizabeth's teaching, her musical skills, and her love of the children. But when Tobias arrived on the doorstep, all her laurels had vaporized under the light of truth, like the fog on a sunny day.

Lord, I gave up everything for You, but it's never going to be enough. I'll never be able to make up for what I've done.

She couldn't free herself from the chains of the past any more than she could loosen the ropes now binding her hands.

⚘

Charles burst into George's shop, his pulse hammering in his ears.

The apothecary's wooden tongs clattered across the floor. "Mr. McKinley? What's wrong? Is it Yoke Soo?"

Taking a moment to catch his breath, Charles shook his head. "Elizabeth. Has she been here?"

"She came by earlier." He checked a clock on the wall. "Maybe two and a half hours ago?"

"Did she say where she planned to go afterward?"

George stepped out from behind the counter. "She said she had to get back to the Mission. I gave her herbs for Miss Cameron."

Charles's windpipe threatened to close. "She never made it."

"We'll find her." The shopkeeper untied his apron and tossed it toward the back room.

Moments after locking the shop door, the two men hurried down Stockton, tracing Elizabeth's mostly likely path. George stopped and spoke to a few storekeepers, but everyone shook their heads.

Charles pressed a palm against the back of his neck. "I don't care for the way people are looking at us. Do you think they know more than they're saying?"

"Tensions have increased between rival tongs. Highbinders are everywhere. No one wants to answer questions that might get them noticed." The merchant glanced sideways at Charles. "Your unusual attire is not helping matters."

In his haste, Charles hadn't bothered to change out of the tuxedo. "Do you think she was abducted?"

"It is likely. The man who took Tien Gum has been increasingly violent. He lost others' respect because Miss King and Miss Cameron deceived him."

His chest tightened. "Might this be revenge, then? What would he do to her?"

"I'm not certain. They usually deal in fear and posturing, not true violence—except with rival tongs."

"Killing her wouldn't gain him anything, right? Perhaps their motivation is to frighten Donaldina and her supporters."

"Perhaps."

Charles lungs ached as if he'd been submerged into an icy pool. What horrors could Elizabeth be experiencing right now? Would he ever see her again? He balled his fists, glancing around at the ramshackle buildings lining the street. "This can't be happening. I'll break down every door if I have to."

George grasped Charles's forearm. "It would only drive them further underground. We need to get information first." His face darkened. "The only way people will trust me is if I'm discreet. You should go back to the Mission. Notify the police and have them ready."

"I can't just sit around and wait."

"Not sit. Pray. Wait on Him."

Charles glared at the passing crowds, their curious stares tearing at his self-restraint. George's request made sense, as much as it rankled. "All right. I'll wait for your call."

George nodded. "We will find her."

"I hope so." He swallowed. "Because I can't live without her."

31

$\mathscr{T}$he neighboring room grew eerily silent. Elizabeth leaned her head against the framework of the chair, staring up at the water-stained ceiling. Her guard refused to speak and her wrists could take no more struggling. How long had she been here?

"*Not every Chinese man is evil.*" Kum Yong's admonishment filtered into her thoughts. Elizabeth closed her eyes, focusing on George and the many good souls she'd met during her visits to Chinatown. Would any of them help her now?

She opened her eyes and turned her head to study the guard. He'd finally dropped the newspaper and now held a small book in his hands, a delicate pair of eyeglasses perched on his nose. He certainly didn't resemble the other highbinders. "Who are you? You're not one of them."

His gaze flickered up to meet hers, but he grunted and returned to his reading material.

"Of course, I'm not like the other women at the Mission, either." She returned her focus to the ceiling. At least she could converse with herself to pass the time. "They were going to kick me out tomorrow, anyway."

"You're a Jesus woman. All alike." He flipped another page.

"My brother used to say the Chinese were all alike."

He grunted.

Well, that was something, anyway. "I've learned differently since working at the Mission. I've discovered that many Chinese care deeply for their fellow men and women. That's probably why

I extended grace, trusting you when you told me someone needed help."

The man's lips pulled downward.

Grace. Donaldina's favorite word. She tossed it around as easily as *hello* and *good-bye.* Elizabeth's heart ached for her friend. How would she react when she discovered Elizabeth's predicament? Donaldina could have judged her harshly when she heard Elizabeth's secrets unfurled the evening of the musicale; instead she'd responded with love. With grace.

Amazing grace, how sweet the sound. Elizabeth returned to staring at the wall, humming the tune she'd played so often as a child. Why had her father adored it so? *'Twas grace that taught my heart to fear and grace my fears relieved.* She closed her eyes. If only it would relieve her fears now. But how could grace do such a thing? As she understood the song, the word meant God loved her even though she didn't deserve it.

A prickle clambered across her skin. She turned to her captor. "I trusted you, even though you did nothing to earn it." Elizabeth bit her lip. She had done everything she could to earn God's love. The thought stabbed through her. *None of it mattered. Nothing was good enough.*

The guard snorted. "You talk too much."

She glared at the man. "You don't talk at all."

"Maybe your Jesus wants you to close your mouth and listen."

Elizabeth set her jaw, wrenching her arm against the ropes. A searing pain shot through her wrist. How did one listen to a silent God? The occasional turn of a page provided the only sound in the room.

The quiet reminded her of the precious moment that followed every performance. In the stillness, everyone held their breath and listened. But for what?

Father, I'm listening.

After a few moments of concentration, her mind strayed back to the night of the musicale—Charles's face, the whispers spreading through the room. Unworthy.

Donaldina's words echoed in her memory. *"That's why Christ went to the cross. To pay for our mistakes, so we could be wiped clean. It's grace, nothing less."*

Nothing less.

A lump formed in Elizabeth's throat. What if true faith wasn't about the good things she did for God?

What if it was about what Christ had already done?

꧁

Robert paced around the hall. "We should be searching. I can't stay here and do nothing when my sister is in danger."

Charles slid his fingers over the piano's chipped keys. "George Wu knows Chinatown inside and out."

"So does the Chinatown Squad. Officer Kelley said they were ready to go."

"There's no point until we have a location. We can't just tear into every building in the neighborhood, hoping to find her." Not that he didn't want to do the same.

Robert sank down at one of the long tables, lowering his forehead into his hands. "I told her this was too dangerous."

Charles crossed the room and pulled up the next chair. "You can't expect her to be someone she's not. Reaching out to the hurting is part of her character—one of the best parts, if you ask me."

"I'm surprised to hear you, of all people, defending her."

The jab hit home. "I didn't see you leaping to her defense that evening."

Robert sighed. "I spent too much of my childhood defending her against neighborhood bullies."

"I'm sure she appreciated it."

"Not a bit. She wanted to fight her own battles—little tomboy." His face fell. "If only I could have protected her from Carver."

A hollow opened in Charles's chest. "My sister was eight years older than me. I couldn't shield her, either."

The doctor lifted his gaze. "Abby tells me things had grown serious between you and my sister. What will you do now—if Elizabeth comes home safely?"

Charles scrubbed a fist across his face. "I don't know. My head says one thing, my heart says another."

"What does God say?"

"I haven't asked Him."

"And there's your problem. Afraid of what He might ask of you?"

Charles fell silent, the truth of Robert's words sinking into his soul. He sensed God's answer before he even asked. Could he love a woman who'd been with another man—a married man? If he succeeded in politics, Elizabeth's secrets could haunt them. Carver had already displayed an arrogant, possessive nature. What if he showed up at a campaign rally or a state dinner?

He dragged fingers through his hair. When had he begun thinking like his uncle?

His sister had been ruined by the actions of a violent man and the decisions of an unmerciful court. The women at the Mission lived under the specter of their pasts. Elizabeth endured the shame of her choices. If God washed them clean of sin—who was Charles to condemn?

He still loved Elizabeth. Her past didn't change that. A surge of energy flooded his system at the realization. *Lord, please give me a chance to tell her.*

The jarring doorbell broke Charles from his thoughts. Both men jumped from their seats and hurried out to the main hall.

Kum Yong was already unbolting the door.

⚬

Elizabeth jerked alert at the distant sound of slamming doors. "What's going on?"

Her guard stood and hurried to the hall, querying someone in a low voice.

Tien Gum's captor shoved past him and strode to Elizabeth's side. "Get up. We're moving."

"Why?" Elizabeth winced as he yanked at the cords holding her to the chair.

The highbinder didn't answer, just hauled her upright and shoved her across the room toward the woman she'd seen earlier.

The guard hurried over, placing a supportive hand under her elbow.

The old woman spoke in sharp tones, gesturing for them to follow. She led the way through a dim passage and down a rickety staircase.

Elizabeth's escort maintained a steady grip on her arm, as if to ensure she made it the bottom in one piece. "Almost there." He kept his voice low. They passed through several dank rooms, before coming to a small cavernlike space, reed mats covering the cement floor.

"In there." The highbinder pointed.

Elizabeth stumbled forward, lowering herself to the floor. "How long are you keeping me here?" She received no answer, not that she'd expected one.

After a brief conversation with the two strangers, the guard shrugged and took a seat on the floor, leaning his back against the wall. The others vanished back the way they'd come.

"Why did they move us? What's happening?" Elizabeth shifted, trying to get comfortable on the thin mat.

The man lit an oil lamp and set it on low shelf. "People asking questions. They're jumpy."

"People? What people?"

He leveled his gaze at her. "Your people."

She dug her heels into the floor and scooted back against the wall, her hands still bound behind her. "Do you think you could loosen these?"

He didn't respond, burying his nose back in the book.

"What are you reading?" She couldn't handle another hour of tense silence.

He grunted.

She leaned against the damp surface and sighed. It must be getting late. At least it had given her plenty of time to consider her situation. Both Donaldina and Ruby had struggled to explain the concept of grace to her, but she'd never grasped it until now. Even after years of playing her father's favorite hymn—it was as if she'd never heard the words.

Elizabeth closed her eyes. *God, I beg Your forgiveness—for all my mistakes and for all the time I've spent trying to fix things by myself. I am the wretch of whom the song speaks. I was so blind.*

A shiver raced though her, from her chest outward to the tips of her fingers and toes. Tears welled in her eyes. *Thank You, Father.*

The guard made a guttural sound in his throat. Getting up and stretching, he paced around the room.

Elizabeth wiped her face on her shoulder. "Will you stay all night?"

"If I must."

"I can't undo these bonds, but you could."

He paused, gazing at her. "Why would I do such a thing?"

"Because I don't think you're a highbinder. Am I right?"

"I'm a scholar."

"A scholar?" She frowned. "Then why are you doing this?"

"I came from China to learn more of the world." He shrugged, folding both arms across his chest. "Now, I hardly leave Chinatown. I'm not welcome anywhere else. I teach English to help men get better jobs. Your captor was a fast learner. He offered me better-paying work." The man shook his head. "I didn't know what he asked." He sighed, rubbing fingers across his chin. "Now, I live in disgust of what I've become. You say I'm not like them, but you're wrong. I am them."

An odd tingling raced across Elizabeth's skin. "As am I."

He tipped his head. "What?"

"I'm guilty, too. I—I took another woman's husband." She closed her eyes for a moment, sucking in a deep breath. Even with her new-found understanding, the words still hurt. "Even though I walked away, my sins followed. My guilt. I couldn't get free—just like I cannot now."

The guard nodded. "I'll never be free, either."

"But I realize now, God has forgiven me. I no longer have to live under the shame because He already paid my debt."

The man frowned, tiny creases forming in his brow. "Why would He do so?"

"Because that's how much He loves me. And He loves you just as much. It's a free gift to all who believe."

He shook his head and strode to the chair. Picking up the book, he held it in front of Elizabeth. Emblazoned across the front, in gold letters, "HOLY BIBLE."

She gasped. "That's what you've been reading all this time?"

"One of your people gave me this. I sense much truth in it, but I don't understand why He would love me as you say. I'm not worthy of anyone's forgiveness."

A jolt of energy shot through Elizabeth's limbs. She scooted forward, pushing up to her knees. "None of us are. My Papa was a doctor. He used to tell me a Bible story of when Christ sat to eat with tax collectors and prostitutes, the worst of the sinners. The scholars—men like you—asked Jesus why He would do such things. He said people who were well didn't need a doctor, only the sick needed healing. Christ said he came to bring sinners—like us—to repentance."

The man nodded. "I am one of the sick. So were you."

"Yes, but I didn't understand that until now." She shifted on the hard floor. "I have some friends who could do a better job of explaining it."

His eyes gleamed. "George?"

Elizabeth's breath caught in her chest. "You know him?"

The guard drew the Bible to his chest. "He gave me the book." He sat back in the chair, his face crumpling. "I don't know why the highbinders want you, but it can't be for good." He pushed up to his feet and drew a knife. "Hold still."

Elizabeth froze as the guard slid a knife between her wrist and the cords, sawing them loose. Her shoulders drew forward as her hands fell free. "Thank you." She rubbed her wrists. "Thank you so much."

A noise from upstairs caught their attention. The guard's eyes widened. "They're coming back. Quick—" He gestured to the corner.

She scooted back against the wall as he stepped in front of her, legs splayed. Elizabeth's heart hammered as footsteps sounded down the hall—more than just the two men this time. Angry shouts rang through the small space. No longer caring about appearances, she dropped to a crouch and covered her head.

When firm hands gripped her arms, Elizabeth screamed.

"Elizabeth, it's me." Fingers squeezed against her skin.

She jerked her head upward, the sight of Charles's face bringing a rush of air to her lungs. Officer Kelley and George stood behind him.

His face swam in front of her eyes. "Are you all right?"

"Y-yes." Her voice quavered, as if her body just now realized she should be frightened. "Yes, I'm fine. I can't believe you're here."

"Where else would I be?" Charles pulled her into a crushing embrace. "Elizabeth, I'm sorry. Please forgive me."

"Forgive you?" A tremor raced through her body, his words not making sense.

Robert appeared over Charles's shoulders, his brown eyes wide. "Elizabeth, I've never been so glad to see you. Are you hurt?"

"No. They didn't harm me." She lifted her wrists, seeing the red welts for the first time. She jerked around, searching for her guard. "Officer Kelley—be good to him. He's not one of the highbinders."

The policeman stepped back, examining the round-shouldered man. "Are you certain, Miss?"

The scholar gave Elizabeth a tight-lipped smile, clutching the Bible to his chest. "It's all right. I will answer for my sins, but I'd like to hear more about this God of yours." He dipped his head.

"We will find a way to visit you." She blinked back tears.

Officer Kelley led him down the hall toward the stairway.

Charles squeezed Elizabeth's shoulders. "Can you walk?"

"I think so."

"Then let's get you home. Donaldina is worried sick."

She leaned on his arm, her legs still trying to unfold from her position on the icy floor. "Why are you dressed like this?"

"I'm supposed to be dining with the mayor." He slipped a hand behind her waist. "But I'd rather be here with you."

32

*E*lizabeth rubbed her arms to banish the shivers plaguing her since last night. The Mission's front hall was still decorated with festive banners. *How I will miss this place.* Lifting her chin, she strode into the dining room, the smell of coffee lingering in the morning air.

The board sat around one of the long tables—four men and six women, all dressed in their Sunday best, except for the severe expressions on their faces. Donaldina sat at the end, wrapped in a wool blanket.

Elizabeth hurried to her friend's side. "You shouldn't be out of bed."

The missionary coughed into a crumpled handkerchief. "I wouldn't let you face this alone, Elizabeth. You're one of my best teachers and a dear friend."

Elizabeth's spirits lifted. It was unlikely Donaldina could change the board's decision, but her friend's presence was welcome, all the same.

Mrs. Byrd gestured for Elizabeth to take the seat at the far end of the table. "Miss King, I have been going over your class notes for the past few months. Your work is impressive." She opened a large folder, spilling over with scraps of stationery. "Many of the girls have written letters on your behalf, as well." She leveled her gaze at Elizabeth. "I want you to know, we've taken these items into consideration. But no accolades can blot away the serious nature of these accusations."

"The decision is made then?" Elizabeth leaned forward. Just as well. Another few days of waiting would only delay the inevitable.

"Not completely." Mrs. Byrd's gaze shifted to Donaldina. "I'm inclined to grant you an opportunity to speak on your own behalf. Perhaps you can shed light on your behavior in a way that might affect our deliberation."

Elizabeth's limbs grew heavy. "I don't know what good it will do. I make no excuses for my past. What Mrs. Carver told you…" She swallowed, determined not to let emotion chase away her words. "She spoke the truth. I had an inappropriate relationship, I cannot deny that." She lowered her eyes. "One could argue I was young, and Tobias Carver was my teacher—but I will not. I take full accounting of my actions."

A coughing spasm gripped Donaldina, cutting through the quiet room. When she'd finished, Donaldina cleared her throat. "Continue. Please."

Continue? Was there more to say? Elizabeth folded her hands in her lap to keep from fidgeting. "I understand it is the board's duty to protect the girls and women of the Presbyterian Mission Home from influences with the potential to lead them astray. I do not ask for mercy." She closed her eyes for a moment, praying for a calm heart to face what lay ahead. Opening them, she studied the group. "God's mercy is sufficient for me, and He's already granted it. When I arrived, I didn't understand grace. I thought, if I could be good enough…work hard enough…I might earn back His love, and He might give me a second chance. I didn't realize God was already waiting, eager to grant this new life just for the asking—fresh, clean, and washed by His blood. It took the events of the past three days to show me the truth. Donaldina has assured me that nothing I have done, or will do, separates me from His love. And forgiveness comes from Him alone, not by any works of my own hand."

She focused on each board member in turn. "I want to thank you, with all my heart, for allowing me the opportunity of working here. Had I not done so, I never would have understood the depth of God's love for me. So, whatever you decide, I am content."

A smile crossed Donaldina's face. "I am pleased, Elizabeth." She glanced around the room. "The function of 920 is to rescue girls and women from sin and suffering. I don't believe our duty is to the

Chinese people, alone, but to all of God's children. And who can better understand than one who has walked through the shadows of sin and been redeemed?" She wrapped the covering around her narrow shoulders and stood. "We will leave you to make your decision."

Elizabeth waited until Donaldina reached her side. She wove an arm around the missionary's waist as they left the room.

Donaldina leaned close and whispered in her ear. "I couldn't be more proud of you."

Elizabeth squeezed her friend's fingers. "I meant every word. God brought me here for a reason, it just wasn't what I originally believed."

☙

Charles stood in his uncle's office, the weight of the man's wrath hanging in the air. His uncle hadn't even asked him to sit.

"Never have I seen a young man so ungrateful, so unworthy to carry the McKinley name. I had dozens of powerful figures waiting to meet you—men who could launch your career and see you not just as a city councilman, but as a state congressman, perhaps even governor one day. And what do you do? You don't even show up." Red splotches dotted his uncle's cheeks. "It will take months for us to recover from this blow. I spent weeks currying favors and pulling strings—all for naught. My opponents are laughing in their coffee this morning, I tell you."

He rounded on Charles. "Where were you? What do you have to say for yourself?"

Charles kept his tone steady. "There was a problem at the Mission, sir. One of the teachers had been abducted by highbinders."

Uncle Silas slammed his palm on the desk. "They are not your problem. You were there to impress the Byrds and to make a name for yourself, not to act like a two-bit policeman. I told you to keep your hands clean."

Charles's throat clenched. "The teacher was Elizabeth King."

His uncle lapsed into temporary silence, his mouth open a crack.

Interesting how the King name always made him stumble. "You needn't worry. With the help of a local merchant, we were able to recover her with no injury."

Uncle Silas's eyes narrowed. "Who said I was worried?" His Adam's apple bobbed. "Still, you had engagements elsewhere. Your duty was to this firm and to your family, not gallivanting around the likes of Chinatown. You can forget the council seat, you practically delivered it into Joseph Miller's lap—all the good he'll do with it."

"I'm sorry to have disappointed you, but I feel my time was well spent. I'm not certain I'm ready for a council position, anyway. I've only lived in the city a few months."

Uncle Silas snarled. "I told you, I'd dealt with that issue."

A wave of heat rushed through Charles's chest. "Like you dealt with the King family's investments?"

His uncle stepped back, nostrils flaring. "What do you mean by that?"

There was no point in groveling anymore. Charles folded his arms. "I understand now why you wanted the King case buried. You sold your portion of the investments to the family's trust. You took their money and pocketed it."

Uncle Silas's brows lowered over his eyes like an executioner's hood. "I'd caution you against making unsubstantiated allegations. Remember who holds your future, not to mention your debts."

"I have the investment records."

His uncle curled his fingers into a ball. "Spencer gave them to you, did he? I knew the man wanted to derail me. You can't believe a word he says, you know that."

Spencer? A lead weight sunk into Charles's stomach. Spencer aspired to be a partner—what better way to achieve it? "The documents show you transferred money from the King's account on April 16, 1906."

"And if you remember your dates, that's two days prior to the quake. I made a calculated decision regarding the value of those properties, and I took a huge loss in doing so."

"You'd have seen a bigger loss if you'd waited a few days."

"I didn't know that."

Charles leaned forward, bracing himself on the back of the chair. "That's what it looked like. The problem is, all of the paperwork was destroyed when the Hall of Records burned."

"I had my own copies. We hired wagons to haul boxes of our company records across the Bay. I told you that."

"Not these documents."

His face darkened. "What are you saying, Charles?"

"You forged these contracts knowing the records department wouldn't dare question the illustrious Silas McKinley. You changed the dates so it appeared the sale had been made days before the quake, and you left the King family to pick up the pieces."

"You forget yourself, Charles." Uncle Silas sank into his swivel chair, eyes cold. "These allegations are ludicrous. Even if they were true, you cross me and you'll doom yourself in the process. Drag the McKinley name through the muck, and you'll never recover from the shame."

"You're the one who has brought shame on the McKinley name. If I follow in your footsteps, I'll share in your guilt."

His uncle tented his hands and pressed them to his chin. "I had to think of the firm. Our future. The future of this whole city." He slapped the desk. "You want it rebuilt like a bunch of soda crackers, just waiting for the next big cataclysm to wipe it from the map? Someone had to take control."

"And the 'someone' had to be you." Charles's stomach twisted.

Uncle Silas jumped from his chair, sending it spinning. "Us, boy. Us. That's what I've been trying to tell you all along. To achieve power, you must make sacrifices."

Charles turned to the door. "There's no us. There never will be."

Silas scowled. "Pursue this and I'll ruin you."

"I know."

⟨⟩

Elizabeth placed her fingers over the well-worn keys and tapped out the simple melody line without all the frills. If only she could express to her father the love she'd discovered in the age-old hymn.

He'd be so pleased. And thanks to the board's shocking decision, she'd be able to teach many more children about God's gift of grace.

"The tune sounds familiar." Charles's voice called from the doorway.

She spun on the stool to face him, breath catching in her chest. "I didn't know you were coming today."

"I needed to see you again." He strode to her side, a smile teasing. "To restore my hope in humanity and faith in the future."

"Oh, dear." She stood. "Sounds serious."

He glanced around the empty room before capturing her hands. "Kiss me and I'll tell you."

His charms were difficult to resist. She slid her arms around his waist, underneath his jacket. "Mr. McKinley, there are children about."

He scanned the room. "Not right now." A crooked smile crossed his face.

She stretched up on her tiptoes, brushing her lips to his. "Like this?"

He lowered his head, capturing her mouth with a hunger that stole the breath from her lungs and forced her to lean against him for support. He nuzzled her hair, his breath teasing her earlobe. "I love you, Elizabeth."

The words rippled through her heart. After all they'd been through, the declaration carried more significance than three words were meant to bear. "I love you, too, but..." Her throat tightened, squeezing off her reply. *But I still can't burden you with my disgrace.*

"I think it's time for you to hear about my day."

She fought to retrieve her thoughts. "Tell me."

"Let's see. Where should I begin?" He held his palm under her chin, his gaze roaming her face. "I quit my job, sacrificed my future, and ruined my family's name—pretty normal day at the office. Oh, yes, and I restored your father's estate."

"What?" His statement made no sense. She stepped out of his grasp. "Slow down. I have no idea what you're talking about."

Charles lowered his eyes for a moment, as if gathering his thoughts. He grasped her wrist. "Come, sit with me."

She followed him over to the table and sat down.

Charles claimed the chair beside her. "For the past three months, I've been going over your family's accounts and investments. I knew the numbers didn't add up, but I couldn't make heads nor tails of it until recently."

"You found something new?"

He traced a distracting finger along her knuckles. "I'd been suspicious my uncle was involved, but I didn't want to believe it." After a moment's hesitation, Charles launched into a detailed explanation of what he'd found and his confrontation with his uncle.

Elizabeth sat back, her mind reeling. "I'm stunned. I never imagined…" She shook her head, pushing away her own concerns for the moment. "But you can't sacrifice your future for my sake."

"How can I hold myself up as an idealist, knowing my success came at your family's expense—at anyone's expense?" He squeezed her hand. "I went into law to protect those with no voice. All this time my uncle's been trying to convince me I need to sacrifice my ideals to get myself into a position of power." He shook his head. "But if I do, I'll be no better than the men I'm seeking to replace."

"So, what then?"

"I spent all morning in the district attorney's office. They're seeking an indictment against him for fraud. There will likely be other charges as well, by the time all is said and done."

Elizabeth covered her mouth. "Oh, Charles. You must be devastated."

"I'm sad for him. He is my uncle, after all, and he defended my sister when no one else would." He sighed. "But he's also controlled every step I've taken since before I entered law school. I'm eager to walk on my own for once."

"What about your political future?"

"I'll have to earn it on my own merit, I suppose. That's not a bad thing. And if it's in God's will, I'm confident He can make it happen."

She touched the base of her throat. "Then I'm pleased for you. And I'm relieved for my mother. I wasn't sure what she would do." Her breath caught in her chest. "We need to tell Robert and Ruby."

He leaned forward and placed another kiss on her lips, trailing fingers down the edge of her jaw. "I've just come from Robert's office."

She scooted back. "You went to Robert before me? Why would you do such a thing?"

Charles stood, his face grim. "Because your father's no longer alive."

"I know Robert's in charge of the estate, but I—"

"Elizabeth." He lifted his palm to stop her flow of words. "Don't misunderstand me. I didn't go to see him about the money."

The objection died in her throat. "Then why?"

He pulled her to her feet. "I wanted to ask his permission."

Every hair on Elizabeth's head stood to attention. "His—his permission?"

"I was going to wait and take you back to Union Square or Golden Gate Park, but I don't want to delay another moment." He dropped to his knee on the wood floor.

Elizabeth's legs wobbled. "Charles... no. You don't want someone like me—you don't."

A wide grin claimed his face. "Elizabeth King, I know exactly what I want. I want you beside me every day of my life. I want you to argue with me and keep me on my toes. I want you to spur me to greater actions on behalf of God's kingdom. And I want to be able to kiss you whenever and wherever I want."

The sound of giggling drew Elizabeth's gaze to the kitchen door where Kum Yong and Tien Gum stood, peeking around the corner. Their laughter knocked a crack in Elizabeth's reserve. Tears gathered in her eyes.

He squeezed her hand. "When you first met me, I was an ambitious up-and-comer. Now I'm a penniless, ruined man with no future and little to offer. My only hope is in God and His promises. Perhaps it's you who shouldn't be saddled with the likes of me." His brown eyes locked on hers. "I'm the one begging here. I want to marry you. Will you have me?"

Elizabeth nodded, clutching his arm. "Yes." She managed to choke out the single word.

He jumped to his feet and folded her in his arms.

Elizabeth closed her eyes, content to be crushed in his embrace, aware only of the sound of his heartbeat against her ear. "I cannot take it all in."

He kissed the top of her head. "I feel like I've won my first election."

"Perhaps your last, as well, if you're adding me to the ticket." She lifted her face to meet his lips, pushing closer to him with every breath. "I can't wait to tell everyone."

Charles rubbed his cheek against her brow before answering. "I don't think you'll have to. Kum Yong and some of the girls are in the kitchen. Robert and Abby are in the other room."

"What?" She wriggled from his grasp.

"They promised to wait, but Abby has peeked in a few times. Ruby wished to come, but Gerald talked her out of it, what with the quarantine." He grinned. "Kiss me once more before we go greet them. I'm not ready to share this joy quite yet. I want you all to myself."

She stepped close, brushing her lips against his cheek and then his mouth. "I can't tell you how good it is to hear you say those words."

"Not as good as it was to hear you say yes. You had me worried for a moment."

"You must have been confident if you brought my family. What would you have done if I'd said no?"

"The press will find immense gratification with my uncle's trial— don't you think I can handle one more humiliation?"

She wove her hand through his. "Trust me, I know a few things about humiliation. I'll stand by you every step of the trial."

"And when it's done, we'll live out our shameful lives together. Shall we?"

"No." She traced a finger over his lips. "We'll live our grace-filled lives together."

33

October 15, 1909

The fall sunshine poured through the high windows of the Conservatory of Flowers, glinting off the gold designs on Elizabeth's dress. She ran a trembling fingertip across the embroidered phoenix. "I can't believe they did this for me." The words caught in her throat. "It must have taken them months."

"Your students adore you. This is their way of showing their devotion." Ruby fastened the delicate braided loops. "It's quite an unusual color for a wedding dress, though."

Abby slipped an arm around Elizabeth's waist. "Kum Yong insisted red is lucky for brides."

"Then we'll need to make one for her soon." Elizabeth slid her feet into the matching slippers. "George waited long enough to court her. I don't think he'll waste much time before proposing."

The sounds from the gathering crowd filtered into the room. Abby peeked outside. "So many people."

A quiver traveled through Elizabeth's stomach. "We wanted a simple family wedding, but with all of my students, the Chinese community, and Charles's campaign supporters—the invitation list got a bit out of hand. Thankfully, it's a big lawn."

"Charles has done well for himself." Ruby reached for the bouquet of white roses. "Considering how the trial was splashed through the newspapers, his political success is quite a testimony to his character."

Abby nodded. "After everything the city has endured, people are ready for leaders they can trust. He's demonstrated great integrity."

Ruby sighed as she passed Elizabeth the flowers. "You couldn't be any more beautiful today, little sister. He's a fortunate man."

Elizabeth blinked back tears. She didn't want her eyes to match the gown. "I'm the fortunate one. I never thought this could happen after he learned the truth."

Her sister squeezed her hand. "The truth is you're a blessed child of God. So is he. Don't ever forget that."

The sound of a fussy baby caught their attention. A quick knock followed.

Abby smiled. "Speaking of blessed children…"

"Is everyone dressed?" Gerald's voice carried through the closed door. "Someone says Papa just won't do right now."

Ruby pulled it open. "Then Mama will come to the rescue."

Gerald stepped inside, passing little Mildred Mae to Ruby. His eyes rounded at the sight of Elizabeth. "You're lovely, Elizabeth. Will you be ready soon? Your groom is looking a bit green about the gills."

"As did you, on our big day." Ruby tucked a hand under his elbow as she rocked the baby.

"True." He squeezed her against his side. "Charles told me to warn everyone, there is a society reporter here from *The Call*."

Abby pursed her lips. "I hope they focus on the wedding. They've wasted enough newsprint on the trial already."

Elizabeth pressed the roses to her chest. "I'm just relieved the sentencing phase is complete. Now we can move on."

"Five years in San Quentin doesn't seem like enough, considering all Silas McKinley took from you." Abby fingered her gold locket.

"He took nothing of lasting value. God gave us so much in exchange. If it weren't for my father's estate, would Charles and I ever have met?"

Gerald nodded. "Like it says in the Book of Romans, 'And we know that all things work together for good to them that love God, to them who are the called according to his purpose.'"

Ruby nuzzled Mildred's pink cheeks. "Look at all of us. It's humbling to think what we've been through—earthquake, fires, sickness, and now trials. It's time we put those things behind us and enjoy these precious blessings He's provided."

Elizabeth moved toward the door. "He's brought me through the shadows and into the light. I'll be forever grateful." She turned and faced her family. "I'm ready."

The green grass was soft under her feet as she walked to the large white tent. Her gaze swept past the seated guests until it settled on the man waiting near the front.

His smile set her heart ablaze. *Thank You, Lord. I didn't deserve this, but You made it happen anyway.* She stepped forward, eager to stand at his side and to begin their new life together.

THE SAN FRANCISCO CALL
OCTOBER 1909

McKinley-King Society Wedding
San Francisco, October 15

The long-awaited wedding of Charles L. McKinley and Miss Elizabeth King took place Friday at the Conservatory of Flowers in Golden Gate Park. Mr. McKinley is an attorney with the San Francisco firm of McClintock and Spencer, located on Market Street.

Readers may recall the young couple as the subject of a variety of stories in *The Call* during the past several months. Mr. McKinley recently testified in the prosecution of his uncle, prominent San Francisco attorney, Silas McKinley. The younger McKinley is considered a strong candidate for next month's city council elections, despite his unfortunate family connections.

The blushing bride, Miss Elizabeth King, teaches sewing and music at the Presbyterian Mission Home for Girls, located at 920 Sacramento. According to the home's director, Miss Donaldina Cameron, the soon-to-be Mrs. McKinley plans to continue teaching for the foreseeable future.

Reporter Lydia Harrell informs us that the bride was resplendent in an unusual, but breathtaking, red Oriental silk gown designed and sewed by her Chinese students.

The happy couple will make their home, at least temporarily, at a luxurious residence previously owned by an unnamed member of the groom's family and located on Van Ness Avenue.

Historical Note

Most of the characters mentioned in *Through the Shadows* are fictional, with a few brief references to some well-known San Francisco historical figures: Mayor Eugene Schmitz, attorney Abe Ruef, and Governor James Gillett.

The missionary Donaldina Cameron was also a real person. Miss Cameron dedicated her life to serving at the Presbyterian Mission, rescuing as many as three thousand Chinese and Japanese women and girls. Now called Cameron House in her honor, the building located at 920 Sacramento Street still serves the local community. I simplified the workings of the Mission for the sake of story, so I encourage you to spend time reading more about this wonderful woman and those who worked alongside her.

You can learn more at www.cameronhouse.org/aboutus/history .html.

Group Discussion Questions

1. The hymn "Amazing Grace" helped open Elizabeth's eyes to the meaning of grace. Which hymns or worship songs have caused you to view God in a new light?

2. When Elizabeth first hears missionary Donaldina Cameron speak, she senses God calling her into ministry. Have you ever felt like God was calling you to do something? How did you respond?

3. Elizabeth takes great comfort in the love of her family, especially her sister Ruby. Who do you turn to when you need a listening ear?

4. Donaldina says, "The deeper you involve yourself in His work, the more you're aware of the actions of His hands." Have you seen signs of God's fingerprints on your life? In what ways?

5. Both main characters in *Through the Shadows* receive gifts they think they don't deserve. Elizabeth learns about grace, and Charles is given preferential treatment because of his family connections. Have you ever received something you didn't believe you deserved (good or bad)? How did it make you feel?

6. As Christians, we frequently talk about God's gift of grace, but we often cling to a long list of activities that make us appear "good." Do you ever find yourself still trying to work your way into God's good *graces* instead of feeling secure in His grace?

7. Robert King's bias against the Chinese in San Francisco was very commonplace among the people of his time. Unfortunately, prejudice and intolerance are still issues today. What can we do as Christians to battle this in ourselves and in our culture? How did Abby persuade Robert to reconsider his position?

8. Charles and Elizabeth are drawn together by a common interest in politics and helping the disadvantaged. If you are

married or in a relationship, what interests do you hold in common? If you are single, what interests do you hope a potential mate might share?

9. It is estimated that Donaldina Cameron and her predecessor, Margaret Culbertson, rescued over three thousand Chinese and Japanese girls and women from lives of slavery and prostitution. According to the U.S. Department of Justice, as many as three hundred thousand children are at risk for sexual exploitation in the United States each year. How has sex trafficking changed in today's world? What has stayed the same?

10. Political corruption was rampant in 1908 San Francisco, and it's still common today. Do you think it's possible to gain political power without compromising one's beliefs? If you were counseling Charles on his future, how would you recommend he stay on the straight and narrow?

Want to learn more about Karen Barnett
and check out other great fiction from
Abingdon Press?

Check out our website at
www.AbingdonFiction.com
to read interviews with your favorite authors,
find tips for starting a reading group,
and stay posted on what new titles are on the horizon.

Be sure to visit Karen online!

http://www.karenbarnettbooks.com/

We hope you've enjoyed this third book in Karen Barnett's Golden Gate Chronicles. If you missed the first book in the series, *Out of the Ruins*, please enjoy this sample.

1

San Jose, California
August 16, 1905

"The doctor could be wrong." Abby's words cut through the suffocating silence in the bedroom. She placed her fingers on the sun-warmed windowsill, but it did little to thaw the chill gripping her heart.

Cecelia's voice barely stirred the air. "He's not."

Abby glanced down at the novel she'd been reading, her thumb holding a place between the pages. If only she could stick her thumb on this day and prevent life from moving forward. When had time become the enemy?

She rose from the window seat and paced back to the wooden chair pulled close to her sister's bedside. The faded rosebud quilt covered Cecelia's body like a shroud. Abby kept her voice crisp and no-nonsense. "Papa telephoned Cousin Gerald last night. Gerald thinks there might be doctors in San Francisco who could actually do something, despite what Dr. Greene says."

Cecelia opened her eyes, the flash of blue seeming out of place in her otherwise colorless face. Her unbound hair—once like so many strands of golden silk—now covered the white pillowcase, tangled and matted.

Abby fingered her own brown braid. She hadn't even bothered to pin it up this morning. "I'm not giving up, and neither should you."

Cecelia's eyes closed again, dark circles framing their sunken depths. "I'm too tired. If God's calling, I'm ready to go home."

Abby thumped the novel down on the bedside table. "Stop saying that. I'm not going to let you die and leave me here alone."

Her sister shifted under the covers, as if the very weight of the quilt caused her pain. "You're—" she stopped for a breath, "not alone."

The deluge of fear returned, sweeping over Abby like waves across the shore. Who would she be without Cecelia?

She returned to the window, staring at the summer sky strewn with a few lacelike clouds. Back when they were children, Papa always called Cecelia his "sky-girl" because of her blue eyes and her grace. And a sky-girl she remained, even as they aged. Until this illness, Cecelia had moved with charm and style, bringing light to a room simply by entering. Young men flocked to her side, anxious to spend a moment captivated by her beauty and her gift for conversation.

Abby, a year younger—nineteen to Cecelia's twenty—had none of her sister's poise. Instead, she took turns stumbling over her tongue and her feet. And with her brown hair and eyes, and those incessant freckles, the only thing she ever attracted were mosquitoes on a warm summer evening. If Cecelia was the sky, Abby was the earth.

So while Cecelia danced at the parties, Abby strolled in the family orchard, content to talk to the peach trees. There she could speak her mind without worrying about social graces.

But if Cecelia left her . . .

"Abby—" Cecelia broke off with a weak cough.

Abby crossed the room in a heartbeat. "What is it? What do you need?"

Her sister lay silent for a long moment, staring up at her. Finally, after a labored breath she pushed the words out. "Have you prayed?"

"What?" Abby sank down into the high-backed chair where she had spent so many hours. "Cecelia . . ." Her voice faltered.

Cecelia sighed, her eyelids closing. "I thought maybe you would make an exception . . . for me."

Abby's heart sank down into her stomach. Her sister never did play fair.

"Just talk to Him. It's all I ask."

Fidgeting, Abby twisted the hem of her apron. Her sister's ragged breathing snatched at her heart. Abby squeezed the fabric into a ball. "Fine. I will."

The corners of Cecelia's mouth turned upward with a meager hint of a smile. "God will answer." She stirred under the covers once more. "You'll see."

When her sister's breathing finally evened into sleep, Abby reached over and smoothed the quilt. As she gazed at Cecelia's chalk-white face, Abby's throat clenched. The doctor's words chanted in her mind like a group of bullies in a schoolyard.

She tiptoed to the doorway. Catching a quick glimpse in the looking glass, Abby frowned at her unkempt hair and wrinkled dress. Turning away, she continued down the hall, pausing to glance into the nursery where her brother napped. The sight of his flushed cheeks brought a different kind of ache to her heart. No one but four-year-old Davy slept well these days.

She stole down the stairs and out through the kitchen, hearing her parents' hushed voices in the family room. They must be discussing the doctor's announcement, even though he'd left no room for debate.

Pushing open the back door, Abby escaped into the fresh air, untainted by sickness and the decaying scent of fading hope. She trudged through the pasture and up the hillside toward the orchard, dragging the weight of her family's problems with her. By the time she reached the edge of the trees, beyond sight of the house, the heaviness lessened and she picked up her skirts and fled.

As she charged into the orchard, Abby's throat ached with words held captive. *First Dr. Greene discounts Cecelia's symptoms, now he has the audacity to say we should prepare for the worst?*

Abby curled her fingers around the branch of a large cherry tree, placed a foot against the trunk, and hoisted herself upward into its leafy heights. Seeking to lose herself in the greenery, she climbed until her rust-colored skirt wedged between two branches. Holding on with one hand, Abby yanked the fabric loose with the other. Several years had passed since she had climbed one of these trees, and her arms and legs trembled with the effort. *My skirts were shorter* back then, and I never cared about soiling them. *A grown woman doesn't climb trees.*

Unless her sister is dying.

When a bough bent under her shoes, she halted. Wrapping one arm around the trunk, Abby laid her head against the tree. She slapped the palm of her hand against the bark until her skin stung.

Cecelia's request echoed. *"Just talk to Him. It's all I ask."*

Abby sighed, brushing a loose strand of hair from her face. Maybe prayer came easily to some people, but to her, God seemed too far away and indifferent. She took a deep breath and closed her eyes. "God, save her. I'll do anything—anything you want."

The words sounded foolish, like a child wishing on a star. Abby forced herself to continue. "She believes You love us. If it's true, then it makes sense You should heal her whether or not I ask. You know Mama and Papa couldn't bear to live without her. And Davy—" her breath caught in her throat as she thought about her baby brother.

Straddling a branch, Abby rested her back against the tree's strength and let her legs dangle. "The doctor says there's nothing more he can do." Abby paused, letting the thought soak in. "So, I guess it's up to You to take the cancer away."

Her stomach twisted at the word. Mama didn't like it spoken aloud, as if naming the disease would make the nightmare real.

The doctor had no such reservations. With today's visit, he added an even more formidable word: leukemia. "Some cancers you can cut out, but leukemia is in the blood." He raised his hands in surrender. "You can't fight it."

Abby tightened her fist and pressed it against her thigh. *Maybe you won't fight it, but I will. Somehow.*

She continued her prayer, speaking as much to herself as to any higher power. "I—I don't want to live here without her." She picked at a piece of lace dangling loose from its stitching along the hem of her dress. "I don't want to be alone."

Abby gazed up through the tree limbs. When her eyes blurred, the branches looked like jagged cracks in the sky. Was God even listening? Why should He care about her wishes? She'd never wanted anything beyond her family and the orchard she loved. The peach and cherry trees were better friends than any schoolmate, standing forever faithful in their well-ordered rows. She'd tended them by her father's side since she was old enough to hold the pruning shears. Papa promised someday they would belong to her. What more could she need?

The sound of footsteps crunching through the leaves stole the thought from her mind. She pulled her feet up to the limb and gripped the branch above her head to steady herself.

A man strolled through the orchard, his hands thrust deep into the pockets of his gray twill pants, a dark jacket slung casually over one shoulder.

Abby bit her lip and leaned to the side for a better view. As she shifted her weight, the limb cracked, the sound echoing through the orchard. Abby grabbed the branch above her just as her perch gave way. Swinging awkwardly, she wrapped her ankles around the tree trunk.

"I'm okay," she whispered, under her breath.

"Are you sure about that?" An amused voice floated up.

The man had removed his derby and looked up at her with eyes as brown as Aunt Mae's irresistible chocolate fudge.

From her clumsy vantage point, Abby examined his strong jaw and pleasing smile. *Of course—he's handsome, and I'm hanging from a tree like a monkey.*

"There's a sturdy-looking branch just below you and to the left."

Stretching out a foot, she groped for the limb with her toe. Locating it, Abby tucked her skirts tight around her legs before scurrying down.

The stranger reached up his hand to assist her on the last step to the earth. "I suppose I should apologize for frightening you."

Abby plucked a twig from her apron. "You surprised me." She regretted not taking time to fix her hair before leaving the house. Or put on a hat. What must he think?

A crooked smile crossed the man's face. "Well, then we're even, because no one ever told me girls grew on trees here in California. If I'd known, I might have gone into farming instead of medicine."

He slid his hands back into his pockets. "I certainly didn't expect a beautiful woman to fall out of one."

A wave of heat climbed Abby's neck. "I didn't fall out." She straightened her skirt, annoyed to find this smooth-talking stranger waltzing through her family's orchard. Beautiful, indeed. She narrowed her eyes at him. "Who are you, anyway?"

As he nodded, the light glinted off of his dark hair. "My name is Robert King—Dr. King. I'm Dr. Larkspur's new assistant. Are you Miss Fischer?"

The breath caught in Abby's throat. "Dr. Larkspur—you mean Gerald? He's here?"

"Yes, we drove all night—"

"I'm sorry—I've got to go." Abby grabbed up her skirts and raced back through the meadow toward the house, her braid bouncing against her back. Halfway across the field she realized her rudeness at leaving their guest in the orchard, but she pushed onward. Manners could wait.

Spotting an automobile in front of the house, surprise slowed her steps. Automobiles belonged to rich men. She'd never thought of her mother's cousin in those terms.

With a fresh burst of speed, Abby pounded up the stairs onto the back porch, finishing her prayer in a rush. "God, I'll do anything. I'll be anything. Whatever You want—name it. Just make her better."

As she grasped the doorknob, Abby paused to catch her breath. "And You'd better be listening God, because I'm going to make one last promise. If You dare take her away…"

She pulled the door open, casting one last glance toward the stranger in the orchard.

"…I'll never speak to You again."

CPSIA information can be obtained at www.ICGtesting.com
Printed in the USA
BVOW02*1728070516

447101BV00001B/1/P